AMERICA WAR

MARVEL UNIVERSE AVENGERS
ASSEMBLE SEASON 2 #4
BASED ON "GHOSTS OF THE PAST"
WRITTEN BY TODD CASEY
DIRECTED BY PHIL PIGNOTTI
ART BY MARVEL ANIMATION
ADAPTED BY JOE CARAMAGNA

MARVEL UNIVERSE AVENGERS
ASSEMBLE SEASON 2 #6
BASED ON "THE AGE OF TONY STARK"
WRITTEN BY KEVIN BURKE & CHRIS "DOC" WYATT
DIRECTED BY TIM ELDRED
ART BY MARVEL ANIMATION
ADAPTED BY JOE CARAMAGNA

AVENGERS: EARTH'S
MIGHTIEST HEROES #1
WRITER: CHRISTOPHER YOST
ARTIST: PATRICK SCHERBERGER
COLORIST: JEAN-FRANCOIS BEAULIEU
LETTERER: DAVE SHARPE

MARVEL UNIVERSE AVENGERS:
EARTH'S MIGHTIEST HEROES #8
WRITER: ELLIOTT KALAN
PENCILER: CHRISTOPHER JONES
INKER: POND SCUMM
COLORIST: SOTOCOLOR
LETTERER: VC'S CLAYTON COWLES

MARVEL UNIVERSE
AVENGERS ASSEMBLE #3
BASED ON "GHOST OF A CHANCE"
WRITTEN BY MAN OF ACTION &
PAUL GIACOPPO
DIRECTED BY JEFF ALLEN
ART BY MARVEL ANIMATION
ADAPTED BY JOE CARAMAGNA

MARVEL UNIVERSE
AVENGERS ASSEMBLE #11
BASED ON "HULKED OUT HEROES"
WRITTEN BY MAN OF ACTION
& JACOB SEMAHN
DIRECTED BY JEFF ALLEN
ART BY MARVEL ANIMATION
ADAPTED BY JOE CARAMAGNA

MARVEL UNIVERSE
AVENGERS ASSEMBLE #13
BASED ON "IN DEEP"
WRITTEN BY MAN OF ACTION & JACOB SEMAHN
DIRECTED BY JEFF ALLEN
ART BY MARVEL ANIMATION
ADAPTED BY JOE CARAMAGNA

IN 2016, MANY OF EARTH'S MIGHTIEST HEROES ARE ON A CINEMATIC COLLISION COURSE IN MARVEL'S *CAPTAIN AMERICA: CIVIL WAR* — with Cap and Iron Man leading the charge! But before the battle lines are drawn, join the movie's biggest stars in this collection of some of their most exciting adventures. A new partnership is forged as an old one comes to haunt Steve Rogers—but what does the Winter Soldier want with the Red Skull? The Time Gem wreaks havoc as the Armored Avenger gets younger and younger—from teen Tony to the Invincible Iron Kid! Black Widow must handle her Hulked-out teammates, Black Panther faces the mayhem of the Madbomb, and a little ghost-busting makes Falcon feel good! But you won't believe Steve and Tony's disguises when they go undercover in Hydra's super-villain army! Any chance Hawkeye can get in on the dress-up action? They're titanic tales of team-ups and takedowns that can be enjoyed time and again. It's all action for all comers, and now it's all yours!

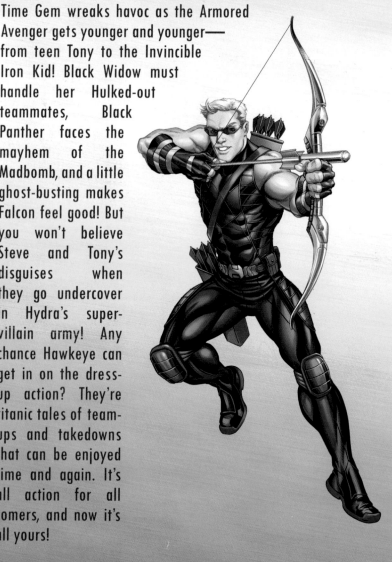

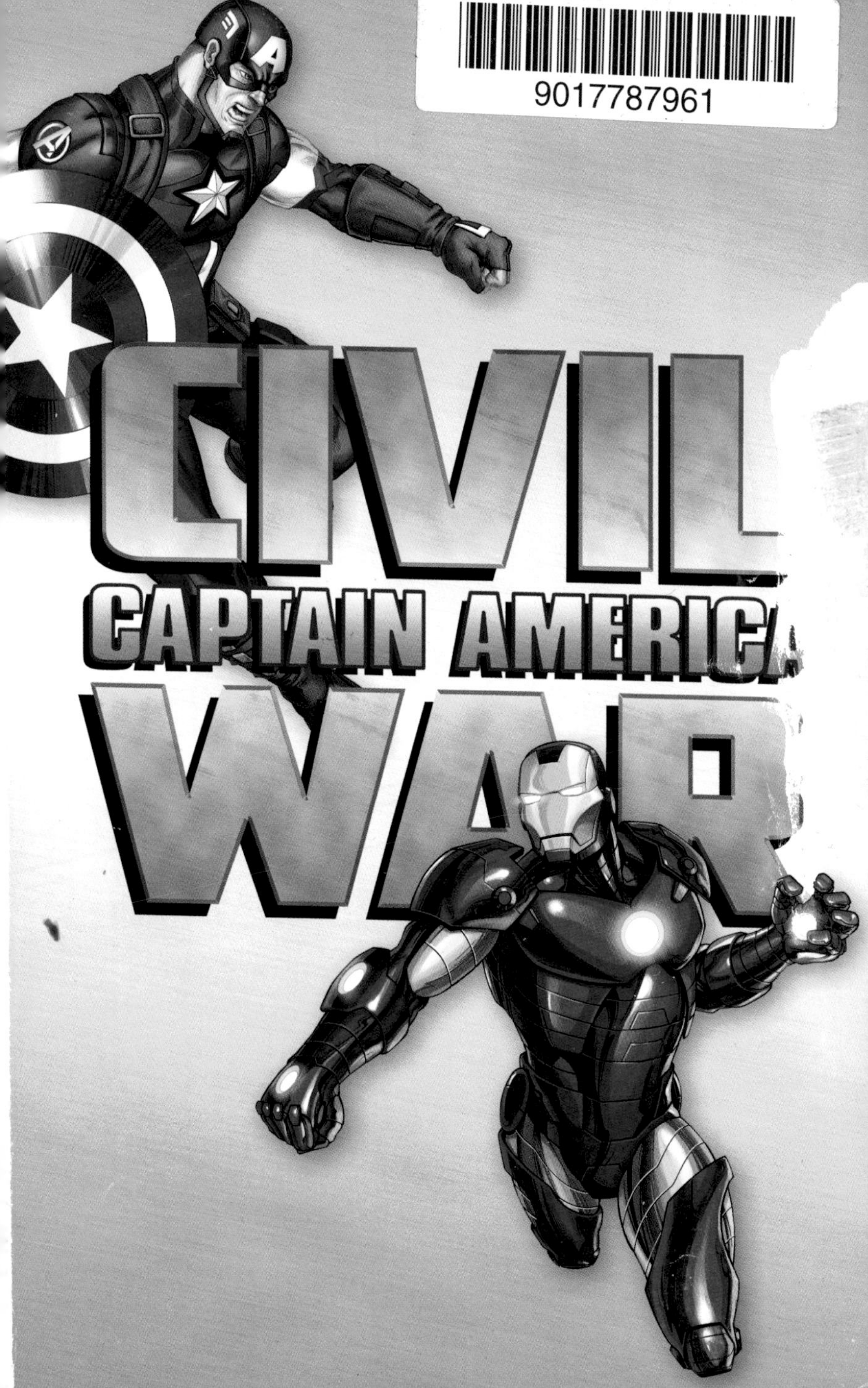
CAPTAIN AMERICA
CIVIL WAR

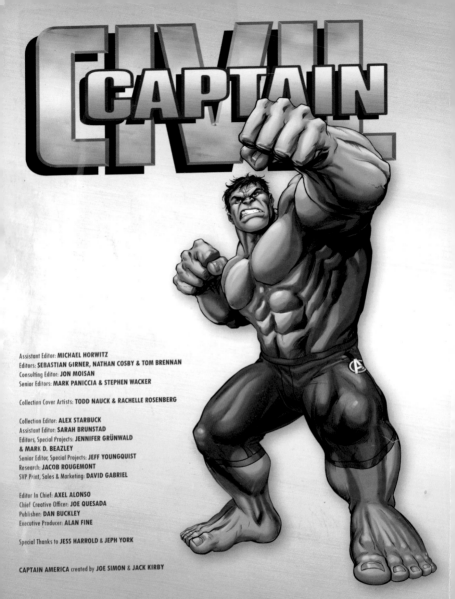

CAPTAIN

Assistant Editor: **MICHAEL HORWITZ**
Editors: **SEBASTIAN GIRNER, NATHAN COSBY & TOM BRENNAN**
Consulting Editor: **JON MOISAN**
Senior Editors: **MARK PANICCIA & STEPHEN WACKER**

Collection Cover Artists: **TODD NAUCK & RACHELLE ROSENBERG**

Collection Editor: **ALEX STARBUCK**
Assistant Editor: **SARAH BRUNSTAD**
Editors, Special Projects: **JENNIFER GRÜNWALD
& MARK D. BEAZLEY**
Senior Editor, Special Projects: **JEFF YOUNGQUIST**
Research: **JACOB ROUGEMONT**
SVP Print, Sales & Marketing: **DAVID GABRIEL**

Editor In Chief: **AXEL ALONSO**
Chief Creative Officer: **JOE QUESADA**
Publisher: **DAN BUCKLEY**
Executive Producer: **ALAN FINE**

Special Thanks to **JESS HARROLD & JEPH YORK**

CAPTAIN AMERICA created by **JOE SIMON** & **JACK KIRBY**

MARVEL UNIVERSE CAPTAIN AMERICA: CIVIL WAR. Contains material originally published in magazine form as MARVEL UNIVERSE AVENGERS ASSEMBLE #3, #11 and #13; MARVEL UNIVERSE AVENGERS ASSEMBLE SEASON 2 #4 and #6; AVENGERS: EARTH'S MIGHTIEST HEROES #1; and MARVEL UNIVERSE AVENGERS: EARTH'S MIGHTIEST HEROES #8. First printing 2016. ISBN# 978-0-7851-9584-9. Published by MARVEL WORLDWIDE, INC., a subsidiary of MARVEL ENTERTAINMENT, LLC. OFFICE OF PUBLICATION: 135 West 50th Street, New York, NY 10020. Copyright © 2016 MARVEL No similarity between any of the names, characters, persons, and/or institutions in this magazine with those of any living or dead person or institution is intended, and any such similarity which may exist is purely coincidental. **Printed in the U.S.A.** ALAN FINE, President, Marvel Entertainment; DAN BUCKLEY, President, TV, Publishing and Brand Management; JOE QUESADA, Chief Creative Officer; TOM BREVOORT, SVP of Publishing; DAVID BOGART, SVP of Operations & Procurement, Publishing; C.B. CEBULSKI, VP of International Development & Brand Management; DAVID GABRIEL, SVP Print, Sales & Marketing; JIM O'KEEFE, VP of Operations & Logistics; DAN CARR, Executive Director of Publishing Technology; SUSAN CRESPI, Editorial Operations Manager; ALEX MORALES, Publishing Operations Manager; STAN LEE, Chairman Emeritus. For information regarding advertising in Marvel Comics or on Marvel.com, please contact Jonathan Rheingold, VP of Custom Solutions & Ad Sales, at jrheingold@marvel.com. For Marvel subscription inquiries, please call 800-217-9158. **Manufactured between** 12/18/2015 and 1/25/2016 by SHERIDAN BOOKS, INC., CHELSEA, MI, USA.

10 9 8 7 6 5 4 3 2 1

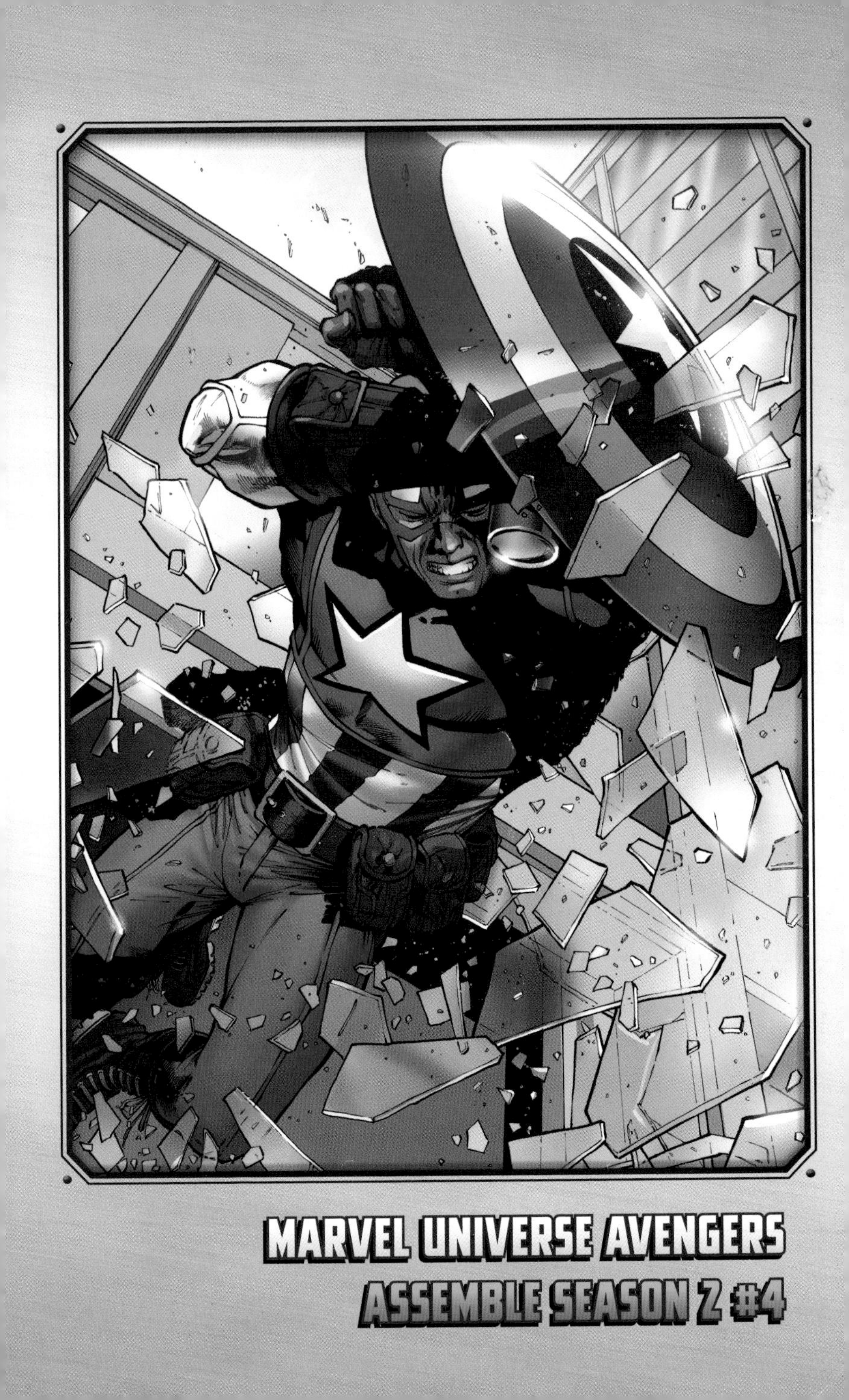

MARVEL UNIVERSE AVENGERS ASSEMBLE SEASON 2 #4

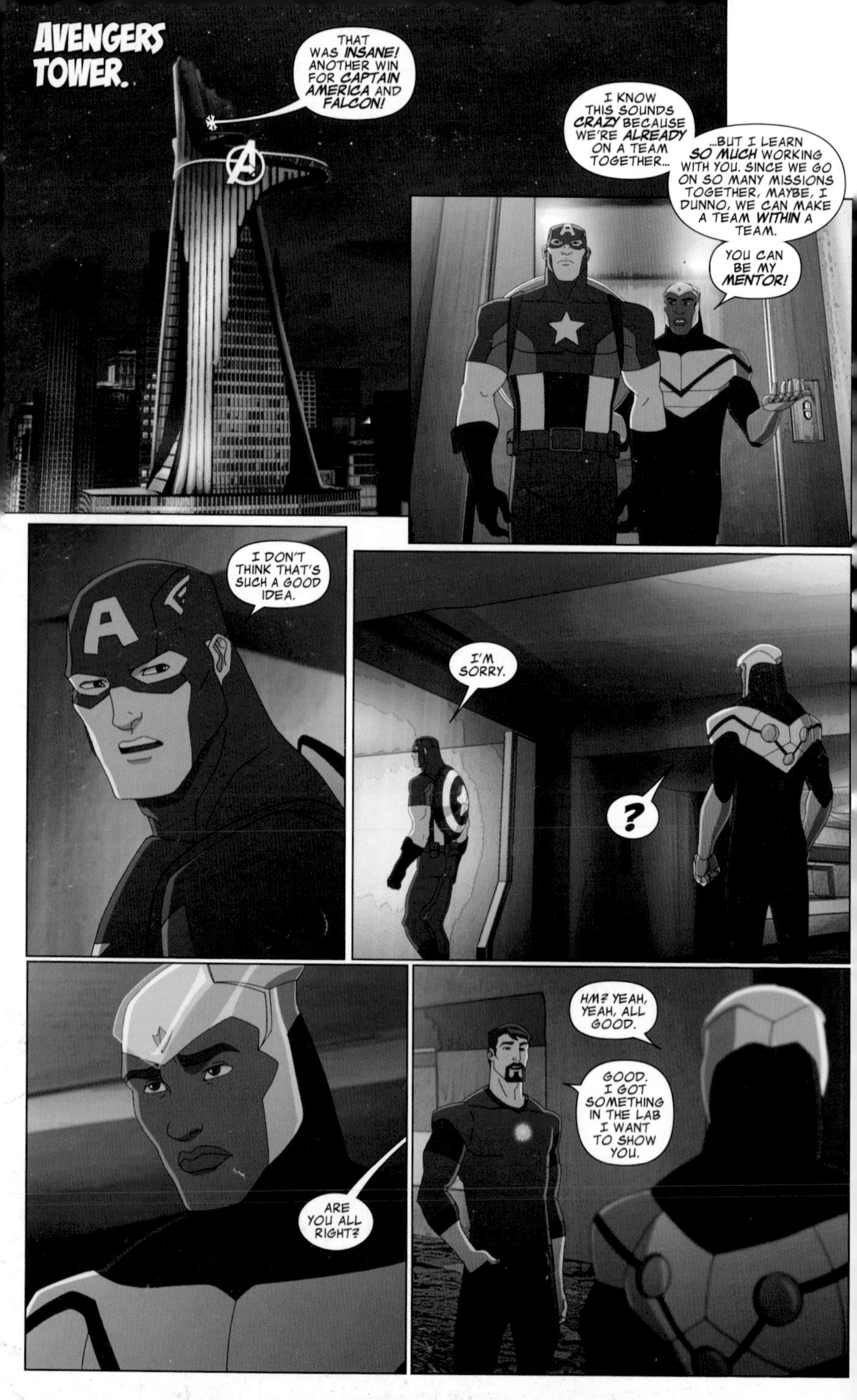
AVENGERS TOWER.
THAT WAS INSANE! ANOTHER WIN FOR CAPTAIN AMERICA AND FALCON!
I KNOW THIS SOUNDS CRAZY BECAUSE WE'RE ALREADY ON A TEAM TOGETHER...
...BUT I LEARN SO MUCH WORKING WITH YOU. SINCE WE GO ON SO MANY MISSIONS TOGETHER, MAYBE, I DUNNO, WE CAN MAKE A TEAM WITHIN A TEAM.
YOU CAN BE MY MENTOR!
I DON'T THINK THAT'S SUCH A GOOD IDEA.
I'M SORRY.
?
ARE YOU ALL RIGHT?
HM? YEAH, YEAH, ALL GOOD.
GOOD. I GOT SOMETHING IN THE LAB I WANT TO SHOW YOU.

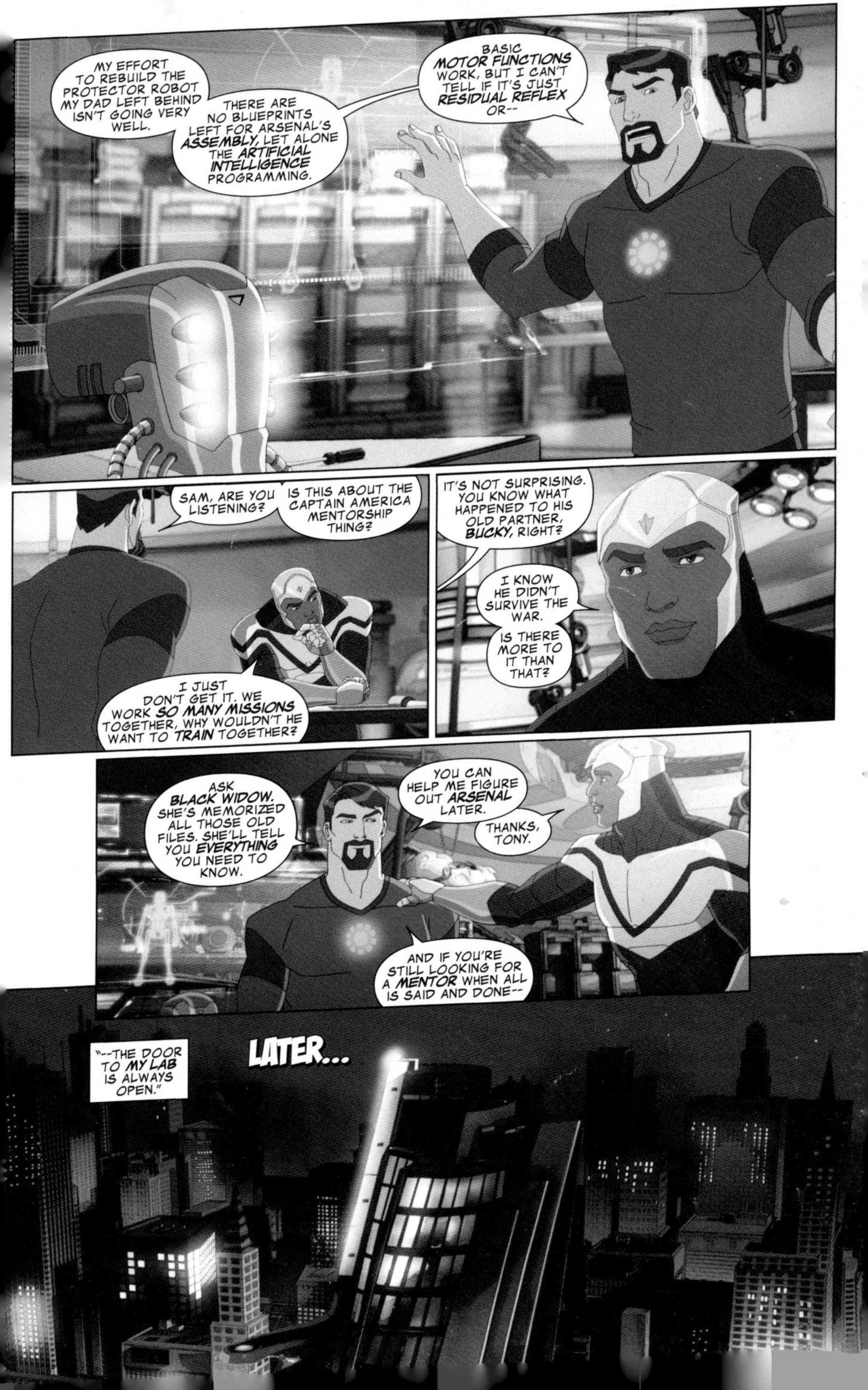

MY EFFORT TO REBUILD THE PROTECTOR ROBOT MY DAD LEFT BEHIND ISN'T GOING VERY WELL.
THERE ARE NO BLUEPRINTS LEFT FOR ARSENAL'S ASSEMBLY, LET ALONE THE ARTIFICIAL INTELLIGENCE PROGRAMMING.
BASIC MOTOR FUNCTIONS WORK, BUT I CAN'T TELL IF IT'S JUST RESIDUAL REFLEX OR--
SAM, ARE YOU LISTENING?
IS THIS ABOUT THE CAPTAIN AMERICA MENTORSHIP THING?
I JUST DON'T GET IT. WE WORK SO MANY MISSIONS TOGETHER, WHY WOULDN'T HE WANT TO TRAIN TOGETHER?
IT'S NOT SURPRISING. YOU KNOW WHAT HAPPENED TO HIS OLD PARTNER, BUCKY, RIGHT?
I KNOW HE DIDN'T SURVIVE THE WAR.
IS THERE MORE TO IT THAN THAT?
ASK BLACK WIDOW. SHE'S MEMORIZED ALL THOSE OLD FILES. SHE'LL TELL YOU EVERYTHING YOU NEED TO KNOW.
YOU CAN HELP ME FIGURE OUT ARSENAL LATER.
THANKS, TONY.
AND IF YOU'RE STILL LOOKING FOR A MENTOR WHEN ALL IS SAID AND DONE--
"--THE DOOR TO MY LAB IS ALWAYS OPEN."
LATER...

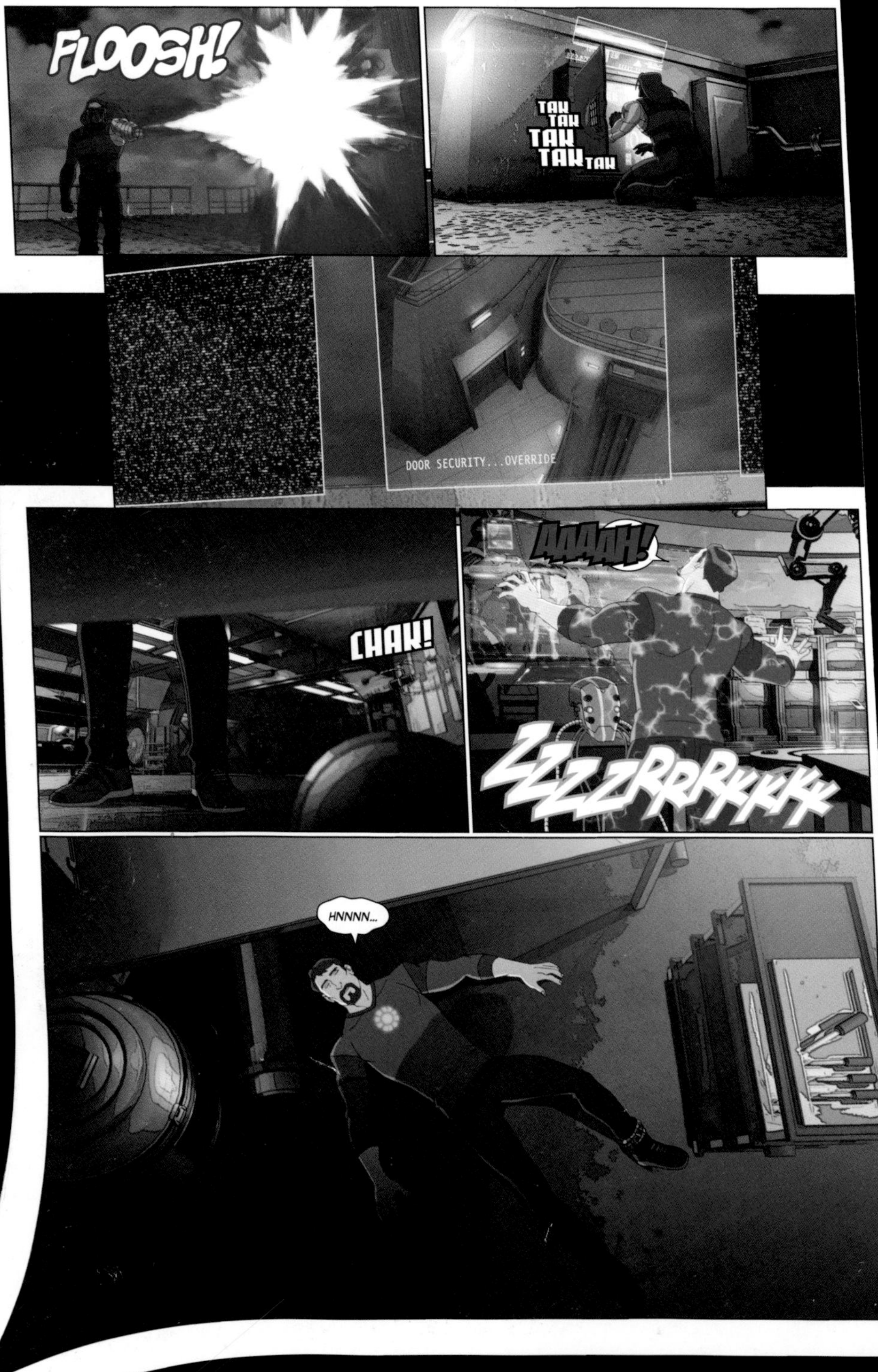
FLOOSH!
TAK TAK TAK TAK TAK
DOOR SECURITY...OVERRIDE
CHAK!
AAAAH!
ZZZZZRRRKKKK
HNNNN...

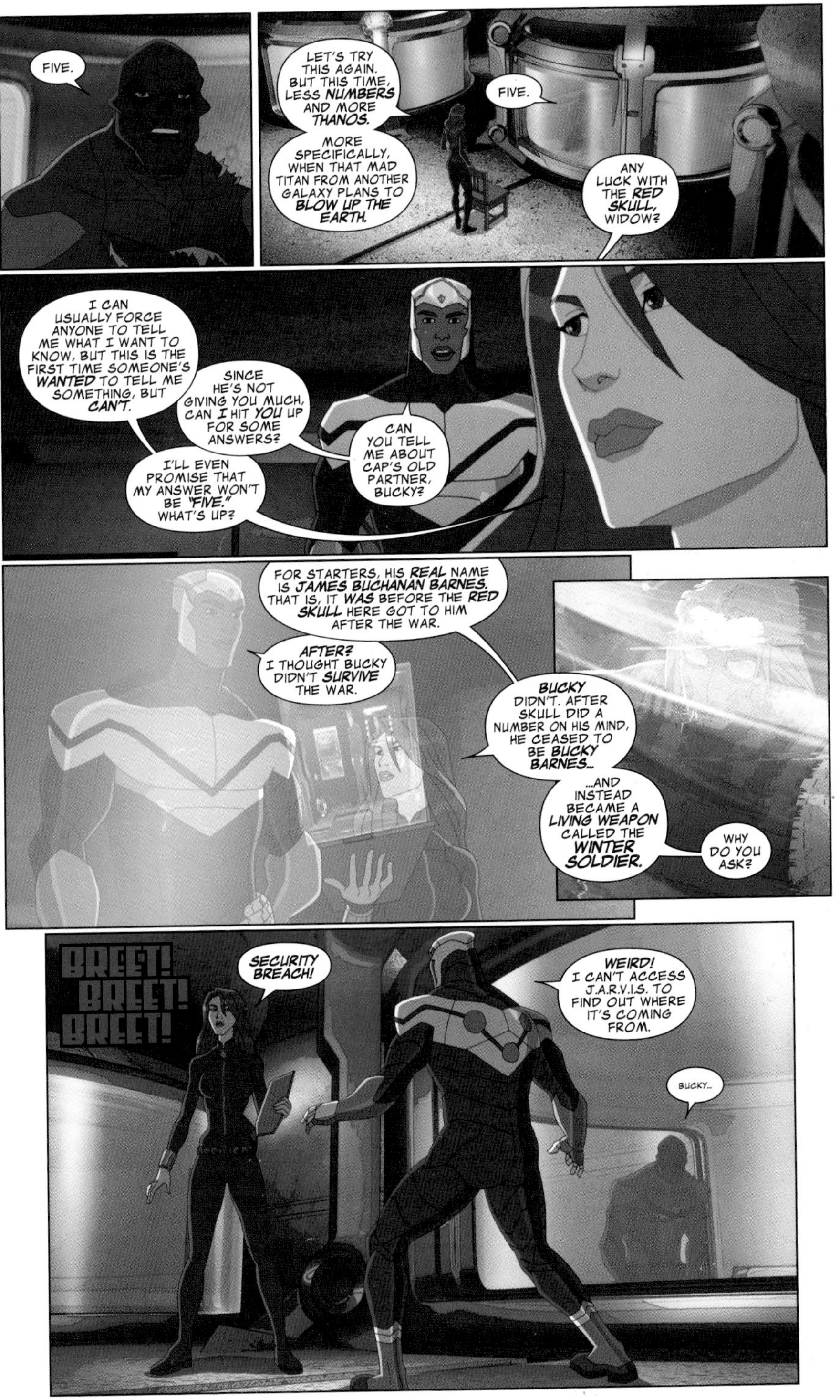

FIVE.
LET'S TRY THIS AGAIN. BUT THIS TIME, LESS NUMBERS AND MORE THANOS.
MORE SPECIFICALLY, WHEN THAT MAD TITAN FROM ANOTHER GALAXY PLANS TO BLOW UP THE EARTH.
FIVE.
ANY LUCK WITH THE RED SKULL, WIDOW?
I CAN USUALLY FORCE ANYONE TO TELL ME WHAT I WANT TO KNOW, BUT THIS IS THE FIRST TIME SOMEONE'S WANTED TO TELL ME SOMETHING, BUT CAN'T.
SINCE HE'S NOT GIVING YOU MUCH, CAN I HIT YOU UP FOR SOME ANSWERS?
I'LL EVEN PROMISE THAT MY ANSWER WON'T BE "FIVE." WHAT'S UP?
CAN YOU TELL ME ABOUT CAP'S OLD PARTNER, BUCKY?
FOR STARTERS, HIS REAL NAME IS JAMES BUCHANAN BARNES. THAT IS, IT WAS BEFORE THE RED SKULL HERE GOT TO HIM AFTER THE WAR.
AFTER? I THOUGHT BUCKY DIDN'T SURVIVE THE WAR.
BUCKY DIDN'T. AFTER SKULL DID A NUMBER ON HIS MIND, HE CEASED TO BE BUCKY BARNES...
...AND INSTEAD BECAME A LIVING WEAPON CALLED THE WINTER SOLDIER.
WHY DO YOU ASK?
BREET! BREET! BREET!
SECURITY BREACH!
WEIRD! I CAN'T ACCESS J.A.R.V.I.S. TO FIND OUT WHERE IT'S COMING FROM.
BUCKY...

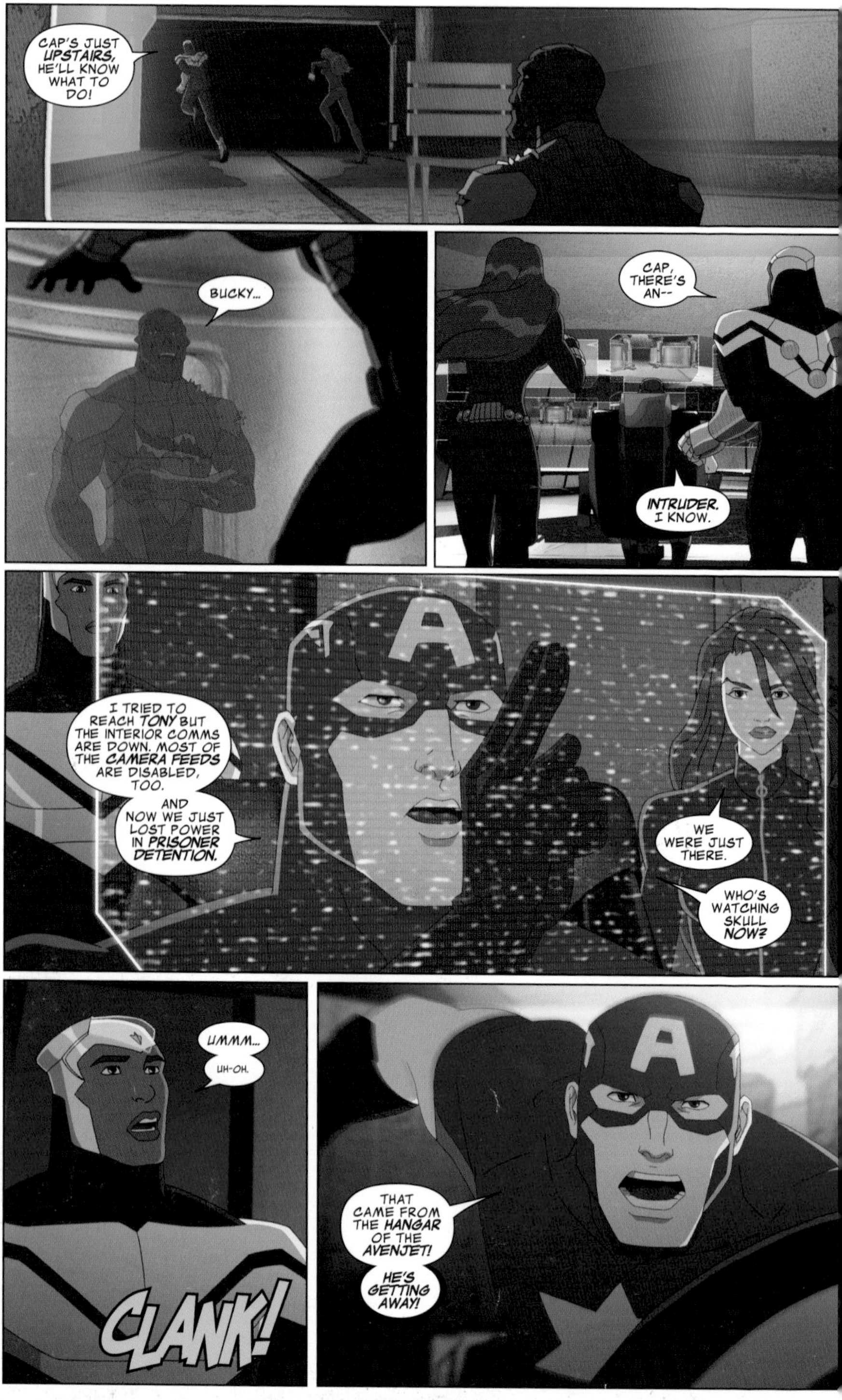

CAP'S JUST UPSTAIRS, HE'LL KNOW WHAT TO DO!
BUCKY...
CAP, THERE'S AN--
INTRUDER. I KNOW.
I TRIED TO REACH TONY BUT THE INTERIOR COMMS ARE DOWN. MOST OF THE CAMERA FEEDS ARE DISABLED, TOO.
AND NOW WE JUST LOST POWER IN PRISONER DETENTION.
WE WERE JUST THERE.
WHO'S WATCHING SKULL NOW?
UMMM...
UH-OH.
CLANK!
THAT CAME FROM THE HANGAR OF THE AVENJET!
HE'S GETTING AWAY!

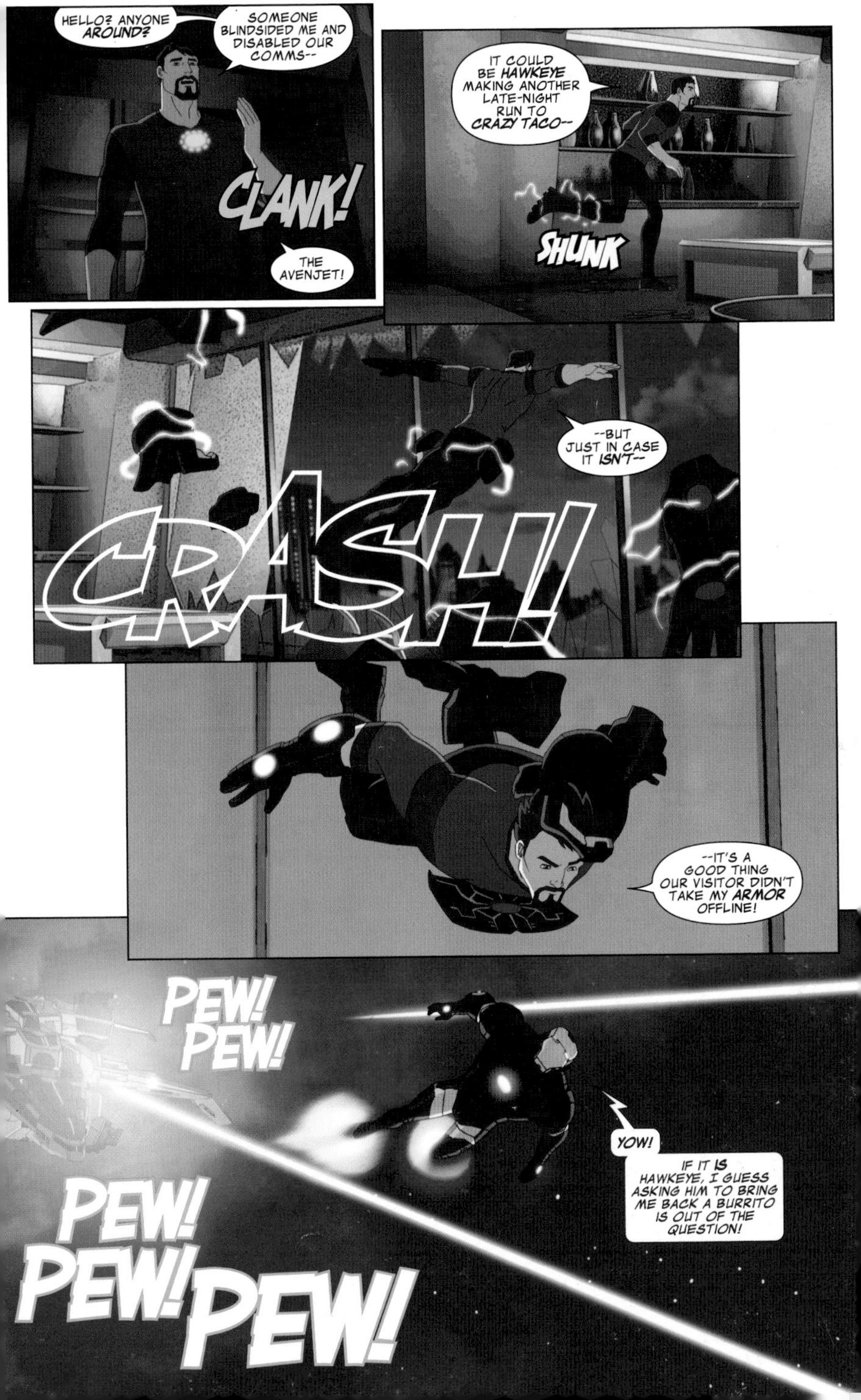
HELLO? ANYONE AROUND?
SOMEONE BLINDSIDED ME AND DISABLED OUR COMMS--
CLANK!
THE AVENJET!
IT COULD BE HAWKEYE MAKING ANOTHER LATE-NIGHT RUN TO CRAZY TACO--
SHUNK
--BUT JUST IN CASE IT ISN'T--
CRASH!
--IT'S A GOOD THING OUR VISITOR DIDN'T TAKE MY ARMOR OFFLINE!
PEW! PEW!
YOW!
IF IT IS HAWKEYE, I GUESS ASKING HIM TO BRING ME BACK A BURRITO IS OUT OF THE QUESTION!
PEW! PEW! PEW!

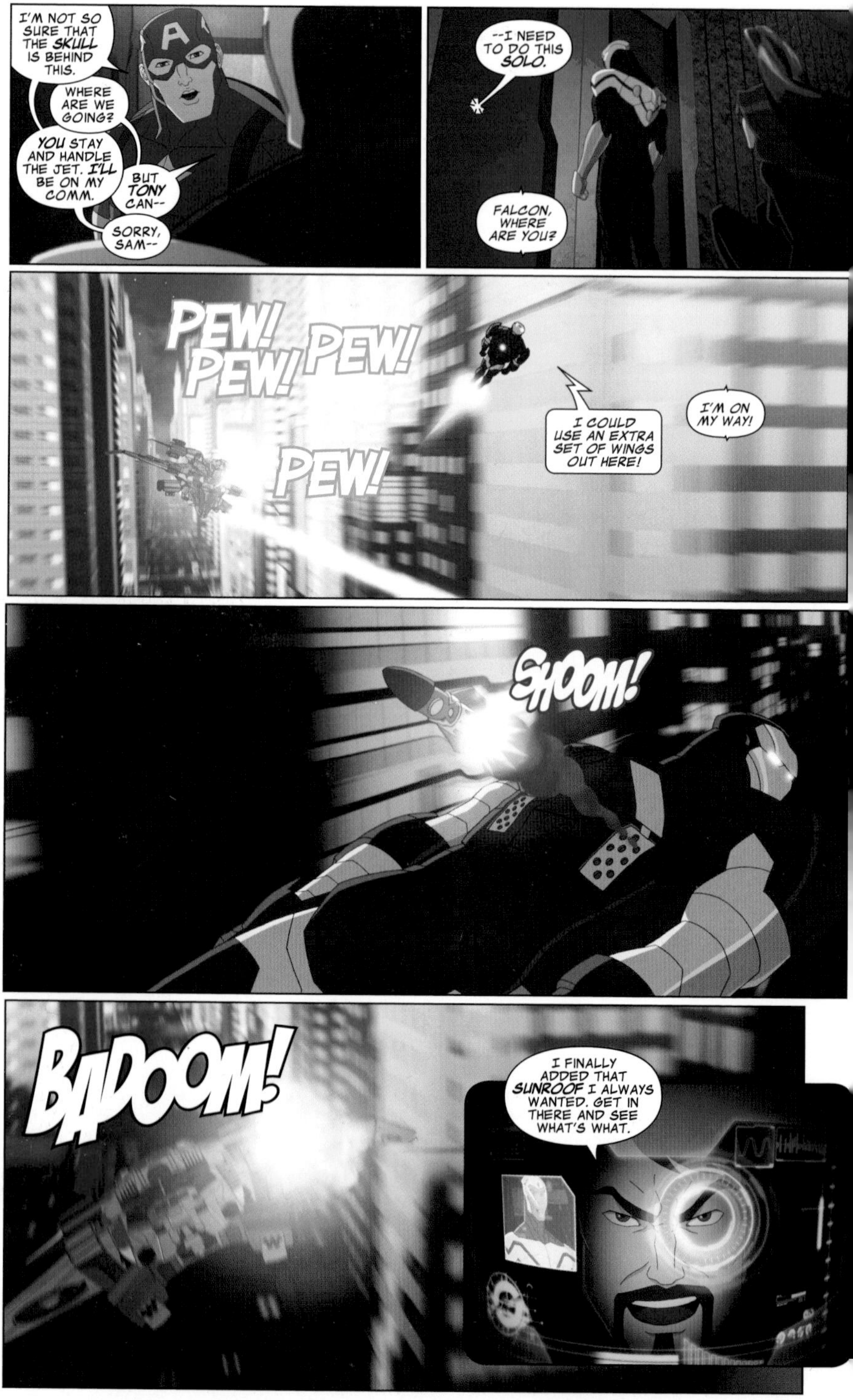

I'M NOT SO SURE THAT THE SKULL IS BEHIND THIS.
WHERE ARE WE GOING?
YOU STAY AND HANDLE THE JET. I'LL BE ON MY COMM.
BUT TONY CAN--
SORRY, SAM--
--I NEED TO DO THIS SOLO.
FALCON, WHERE ARE YOU?
PEW! PEW! PEW!
PEW!
I COULD USE AN EXTRA SET OF WINGS OUT HERE!
I'M ON MY WAY!
SHOOM!
BADOOM!
I FINALLY ADDED THAT SUNROOF I ALWAYS WANTED. GET IN THERE AND SEE WHAT'S WHAT.

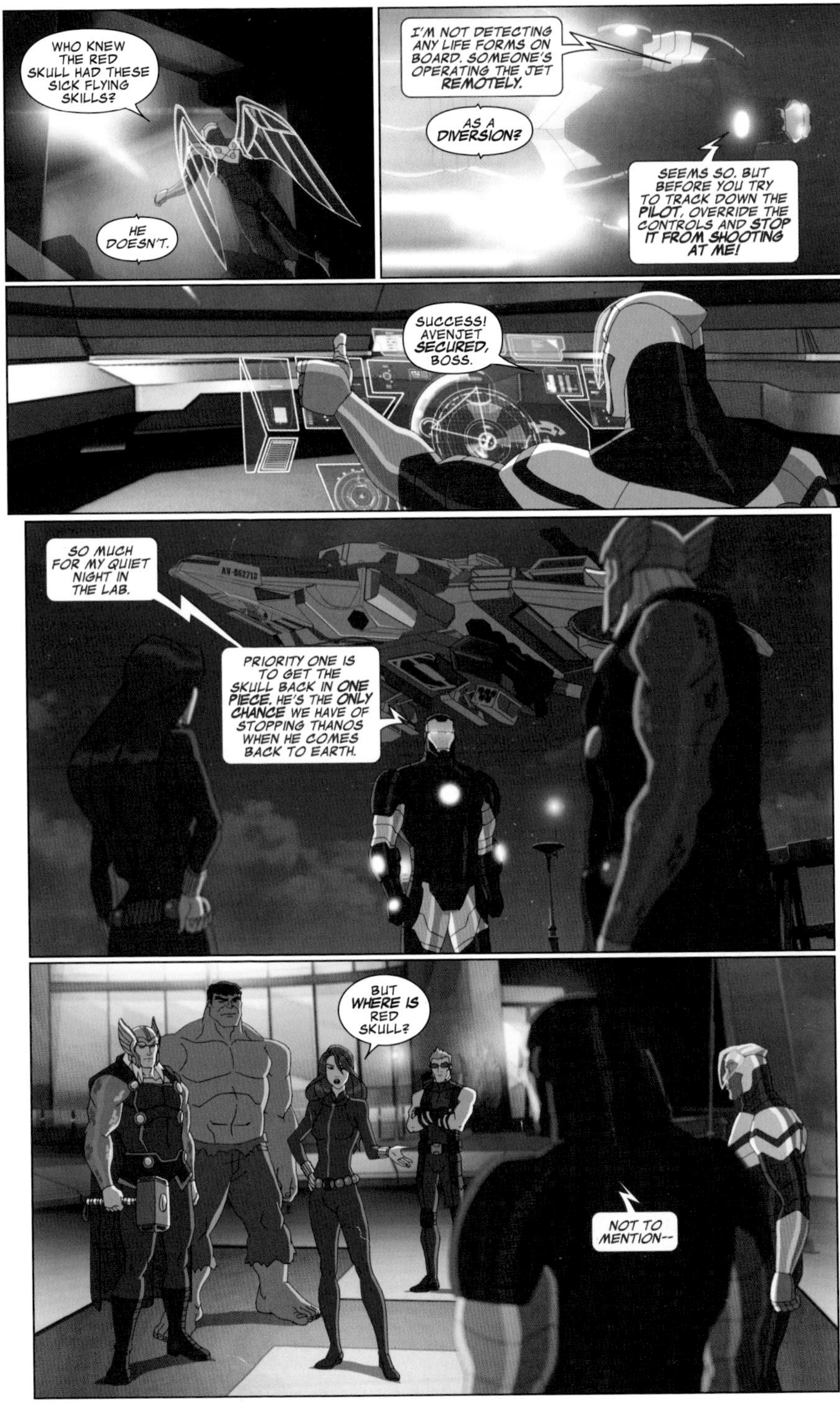
WHO KNEW THE RED SKULL HAD THESE SICK FLYING SKILLS?
HE DOESN'T.
I'M NOT DETECTING ANY LIFE FORMS ON BOARD. SOMEONE'S OPERATING THE JET **REMOTELY.**
AS A **DIVERSION?**
SEEMS SO. BUT BEFORE YOU TRY TO TRACK DOWN THE **PILOT**, OVERRIDE THE CONTROLS AND **STOP IT FROM SHOOTING AT ME!**
SUCCESS! AVENJET **SECURED,** BOSS.
SO MUCH FOR MY QUIET NIGHT IN THE LAB.
AV-862712
PRIORITY ONE IS TO GET THE SKULL BACK IN **ONE PIECE.** HE'S THE **ONLY CHANCE** WE HAVE OF STOPPING THANOS WHEN HE COMES BACK TO EARTH.
BUT **WHERE IS** RED SKULL?
NOT TO MENTION--

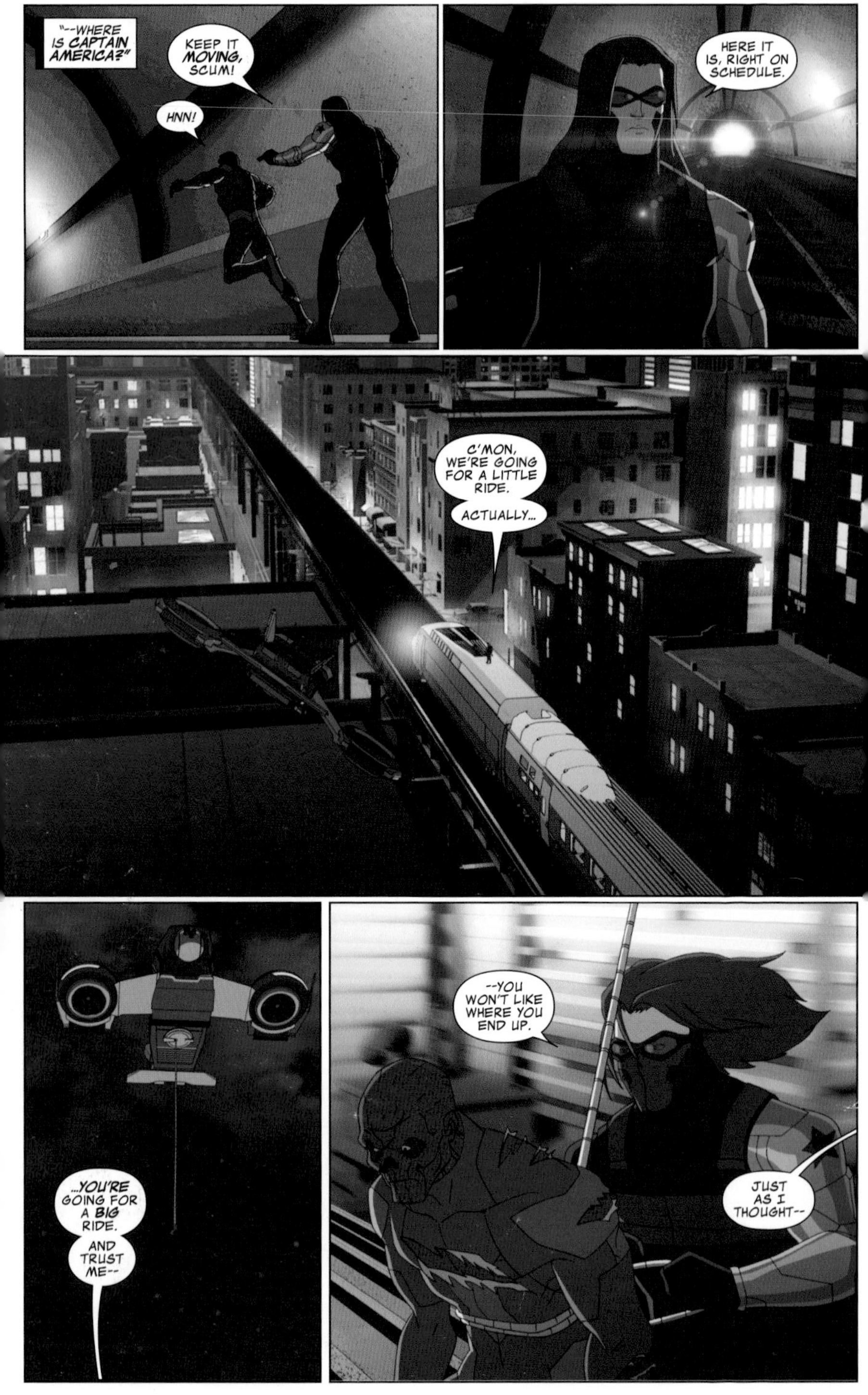
"--WHERE IS CAPTAIN AMERICA?"
KEEP IT MOVING, SCUM!
HNN!
HERE IT IS, RIGHT ON SCHEDULE.
C'MON, WE'RE GOING FOR A LITTLE RIDE.
ACTUALLY...
...YOU'RE GOING FOR A BIG RIDE.
AND TRUST ME--
--YOU WON'T LIKE WHERE YOU END UP.
JUST AS I THOUGHT--

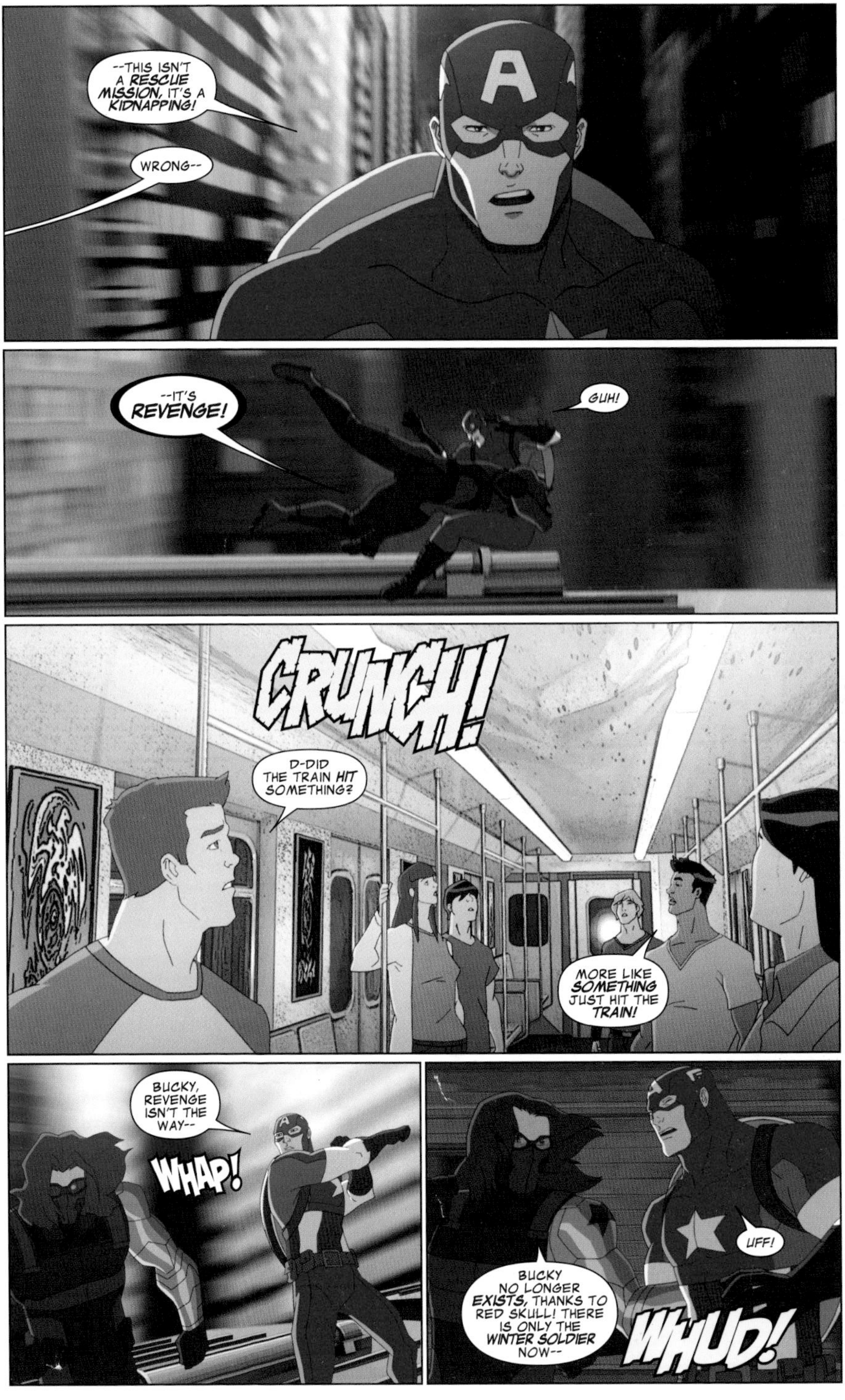

--THIS ISN'T A RESCUE MISSION, IT'S A KIDNAPPING!
WRONG--
--IT'S REVENGE!
GUH!
CRUNCH!
D-DID THE TRAIN HIT SOMETHING?
MORE LIKE SOMETHING JUST HIT THE TRAIN!
BUCKY, REVENGE ISN'T THE WAY--
WHAP!
UFF!
BUCKY NO LONGER EXISTS, THANKS TO RED SKULL! THERE IS ONLY THE WINTER SOLDIER NOW--
WHUD!

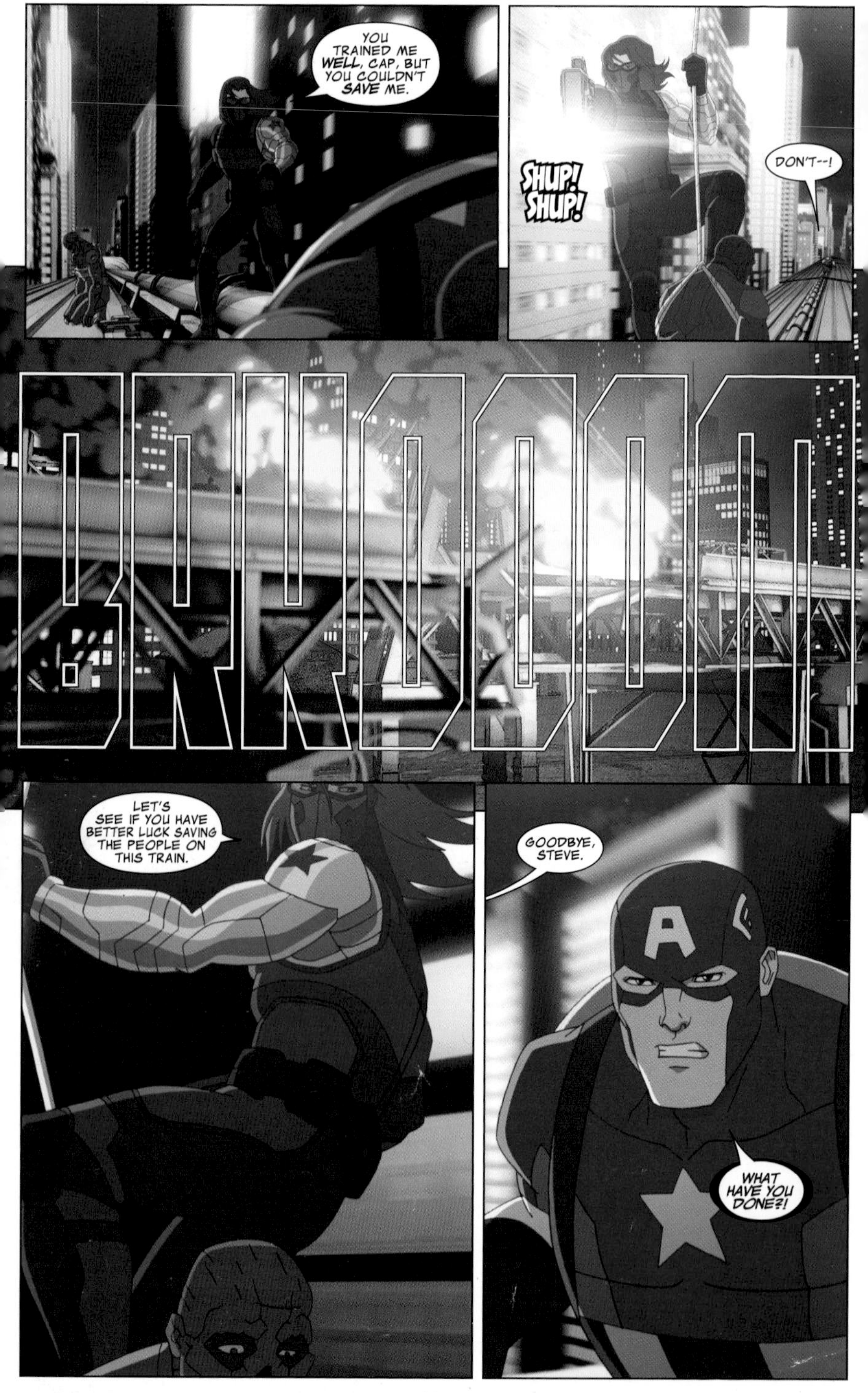

YOU TRAINED ME WELL, CAP, BUT YOU COULDN'T SAVE ME.
SHUP! SHUP!
DON'T--!
LET'S SEE IF YOU HAVE BETTER LUCK SAVING THE PEOPLE ON THIS TRAIN.
GOODBYE, STEVE.
WHAT HAVE YOU DONE?!

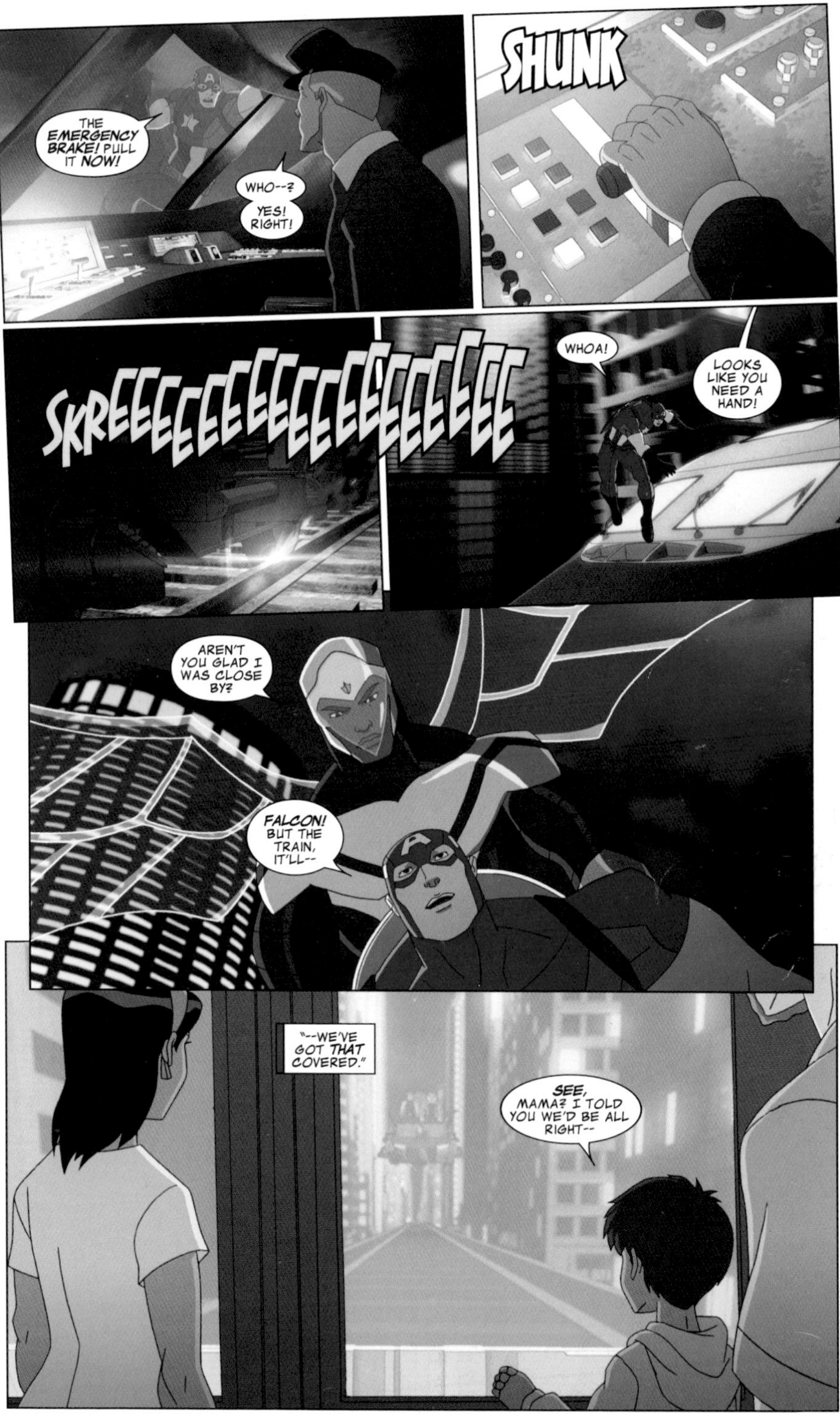
THE EMERGENCY BRAKE! PULL IT NOW!
WHO--?
YES! RIGHT!
SHUNK
SKREEEEEEEEEEEEEEEEEEEE
WHOA!
LOOKS LIKE YOU NEED A HAND!
AREN'T YOU GLAD I WAS CLOSE BY?
FALCON! BUT THE TRAIN, IT'LL--
"--WE'VE GOT THAT COVERED."
SEE, MAMA? I TOLD YOU WE'D BE ALL RIGHT--

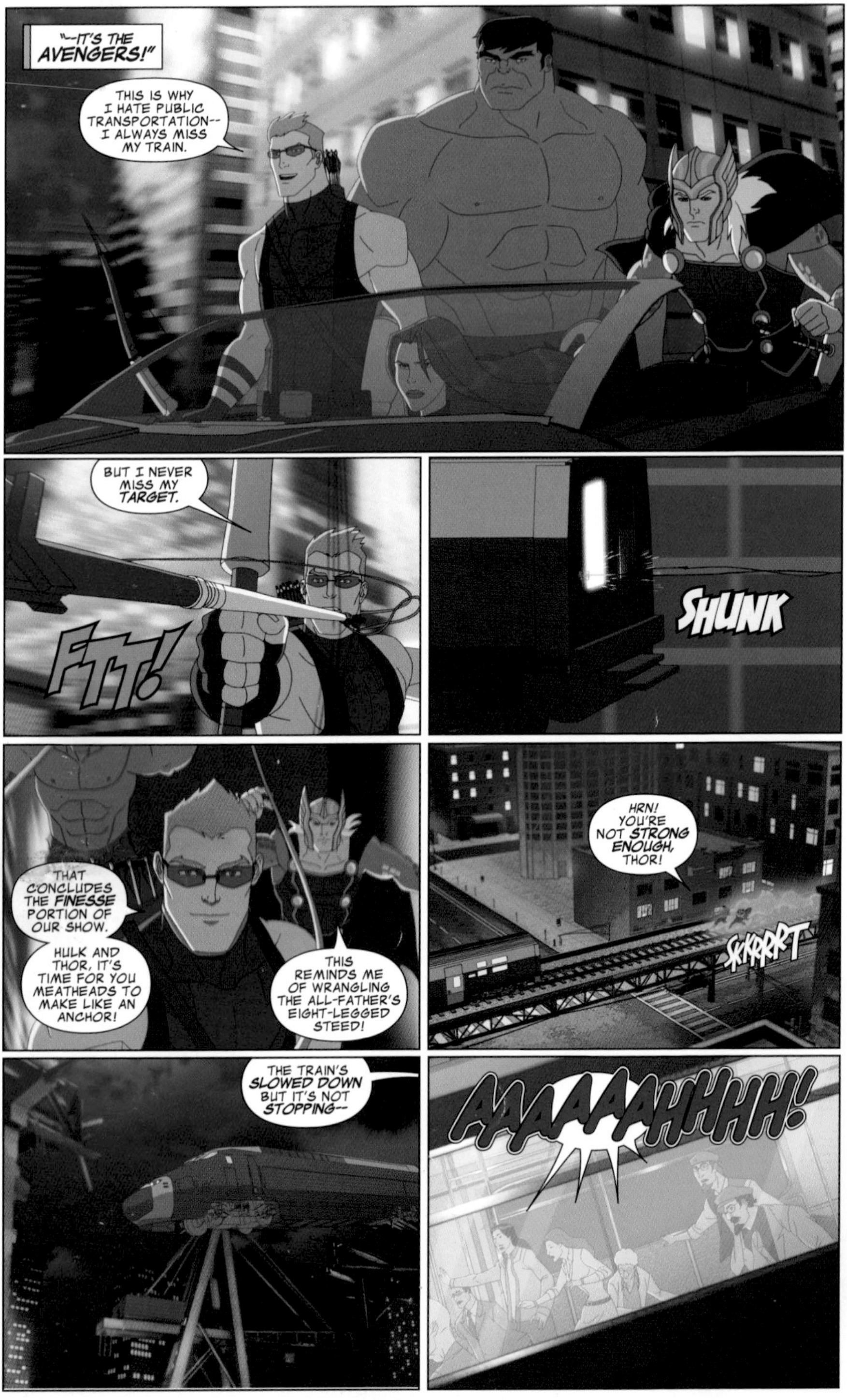
"--IT'S THE AVENGERS!"
THIS IS WHY I HATE PUBLIC TRANSPORTATION-- I ALWAYS MISS MY TRAIN.
BUT I NEVER MISS MY TARGET.
FTT!
SHUNK
THAT CONCLUDES THE FINESSE PORTION OF OUR SHOW.
HULK AND THOR, IT'S TIME FOR YOU MEATHEADS TO MAKE LIKE AN ANCHOR!
THIS REMINDS ME OF WRANGLING THE ALL-FATHER'S EIGHT-LEGGED STEED!
HRN! YOU'RE NOT STRONG ENOUGH, THOR!
SKKRRRT
THE TRAIN'S SLOWED DOWN BUT IT'S NOT STOPPING--
AAAAAAHHHH!

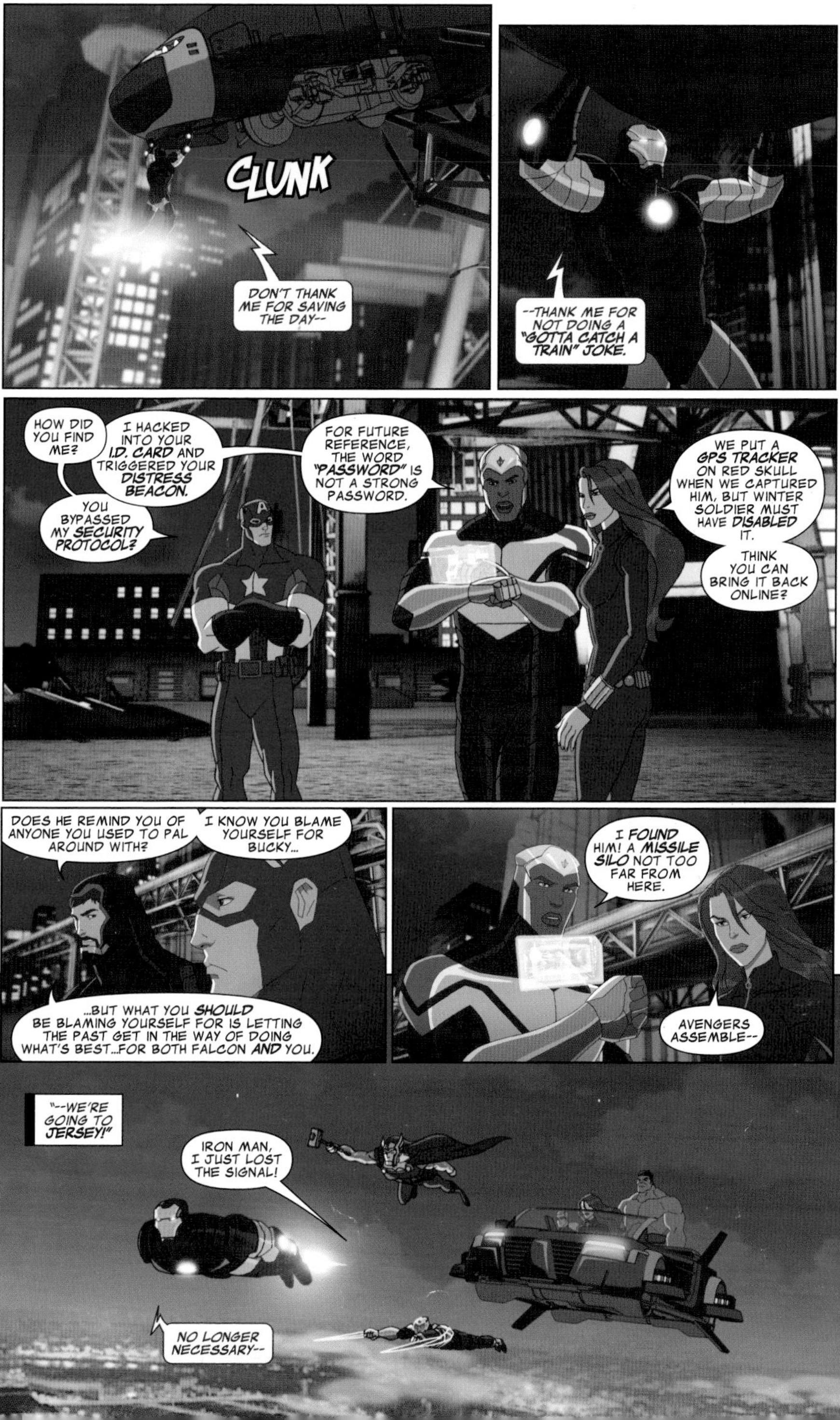
CLUNK
DON'T THANK ME FOR SAVING THE DAY--
--THANK ME FOR NOT DOING A "GOTTA CATCH A TRAIN" JOKE.
HOW DID YOU FIND ME?
I HACKED INTO YOUR I.D. CARD AND TRIGGERED YOUR DISTRESS BEACON.
YOU BYPASSED MY SECURITY PROTOCOL?
FOR FUTURE REFERENCE, THE WORD "PASSWORD" IS NOT A STRONG PASSWORD.
WE PUT A GPS TRACKER ON RED SKULL WHEN WE CAPTURED HIM, BUT WINTER SOLDIER MUST HAVE DISABLED IT.
THINK YOU CAN BRING IT BACK ONLINE?
DOES HE REMIND YOU OF ANYONE YOU USED TO PAL AROUND WITH?
I KNOW YOU BLAME YOURSELF FOR BUCKY...
...BUT WHAT YOU SHOULD BE BLAMING YOURSELF FOR IS LETTING THE PAST GET IN THE WAY OF DOING WHAT'S BEST...FOR BOTH FALCON AND YOU.
I FOUND HIM! A MISSILE SILO NOT TOO FAR FROM HERE.
AVENGERS ASSEMBLE--
"--WE'RE GOING TO JERSEY!"
IRON MAN, I JUST LOST THE SIGNAL!
NO LONGER NECESSARY--

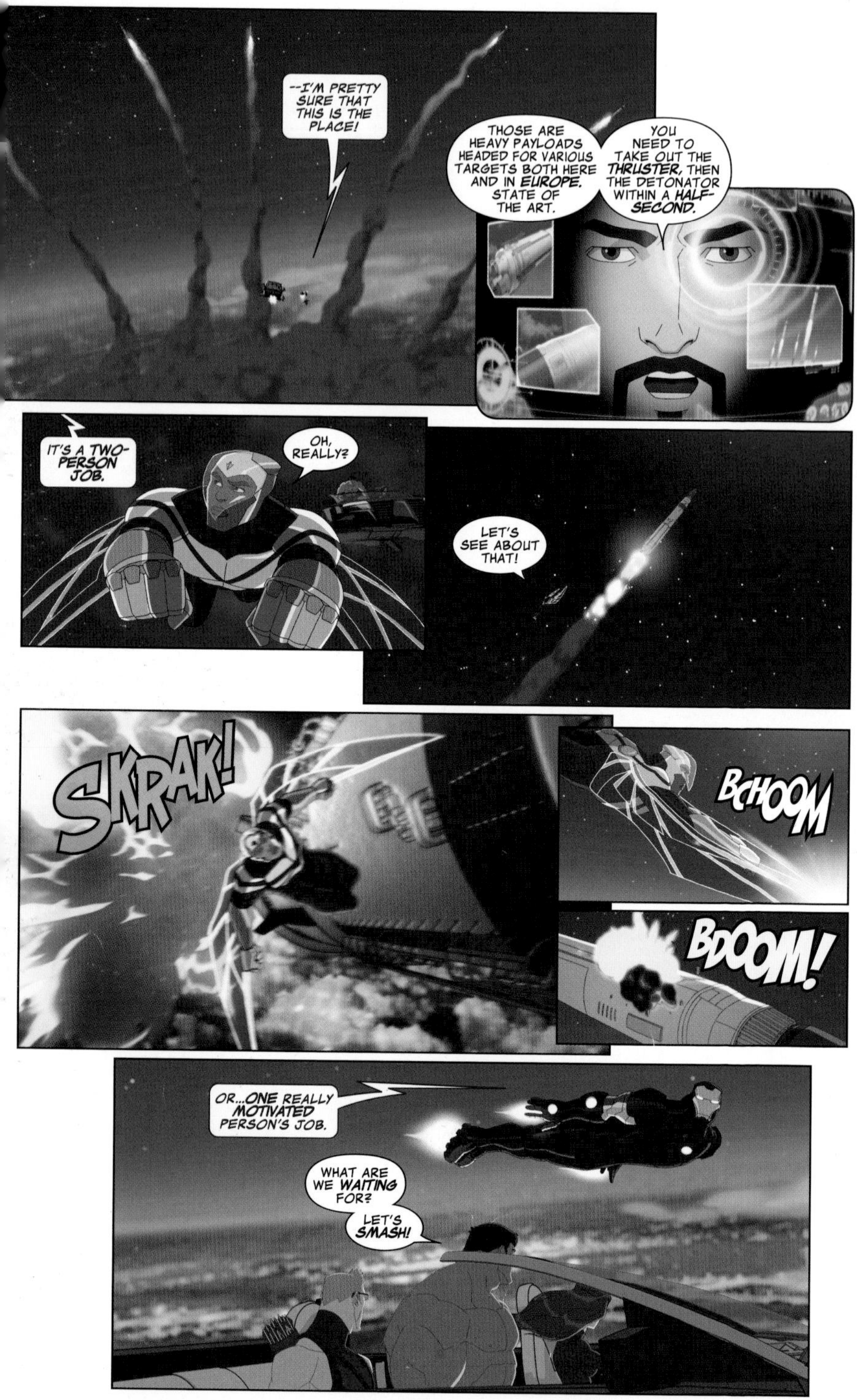

--I'M PRETTY SURE THAT THIS IS THE PLACE!
THOSE ARE HEAVY PAYLOADS HEADED FOR VARIOUS TARGETS BOTH HERE AND IN EUROPE. STATE OF THE ART.
YOU NEED TO TAKE OUT THE THRUSTER, THEN THE DETONATOR WITHIN A HALF-SECOND.
IT'S A TWO-PERSON JOB.
OH, REALLY?
LET'S SEE ABOUT THAT!
SKRAK!
BCHOOM
BDOOM!
OR...ONE REALLY MOTIVATED PERSON'S JOB.
WHAT ARE WE WAITING FOR?
LET'S SMASH!

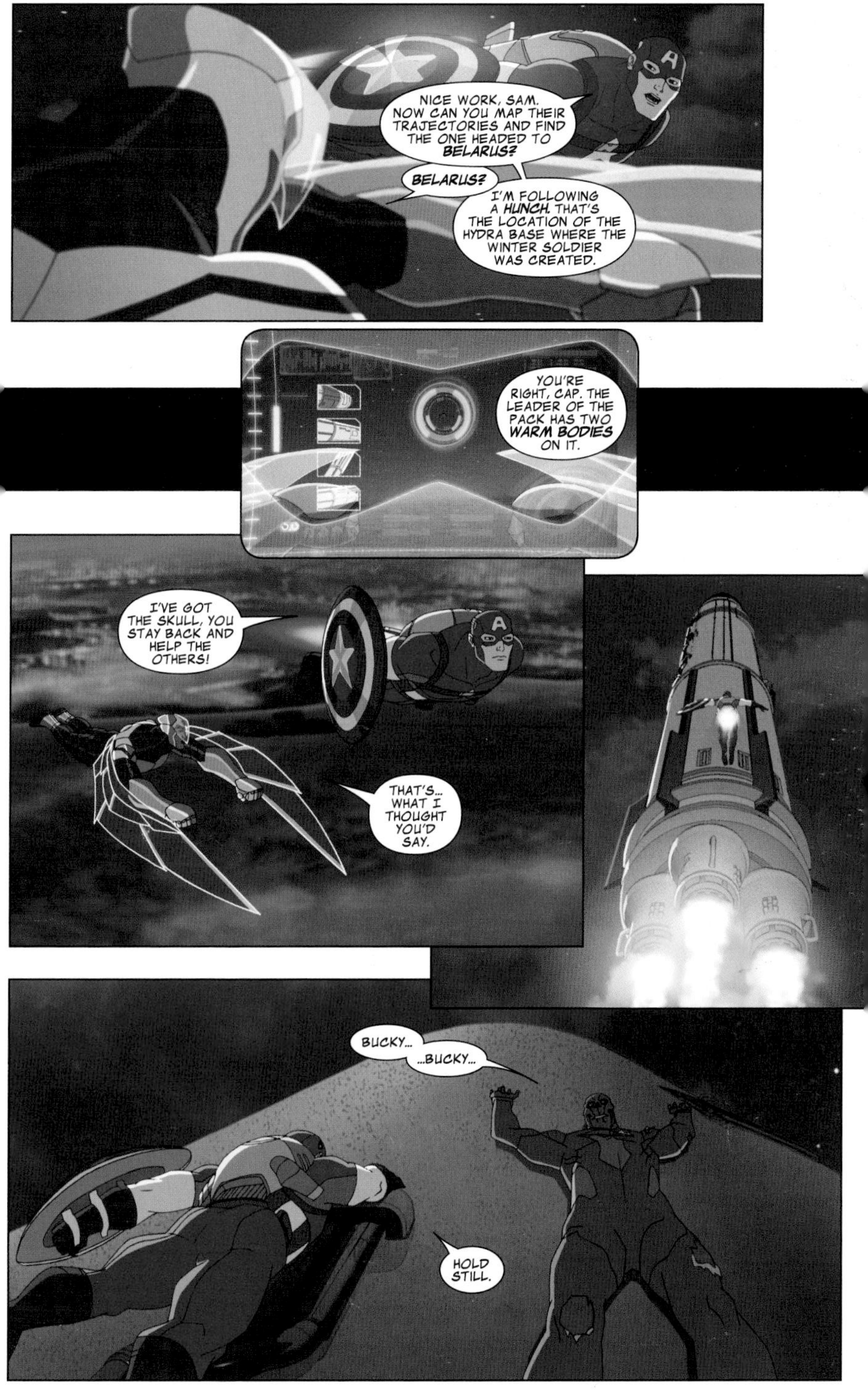
NICE WORK, SAM. NOW CAN YOU MAP THEIR TRAJECTORIES AND FIND THE ONE HEADED TO **BELARUS?**
BELARUS?
I'M FOLLOWING A **HUNCH.** THAT'S THE LOCATION OF THE HYDRA BASE WHERE THE WINTER SOLDIER WAS CREATED.
YOU'RE RIGHT, CAP. THE LEADER OF THE PACK HAS TWO **WARM BODIES** ON IT.
I'VE GOT THE SKULL, YOU STAY BACK AND HELP THE OTHERS!
THAT'S... WHAT I THOUGHT YOU'D SAY.
BUCKY...
...BUCKY...
HOLD STILL.

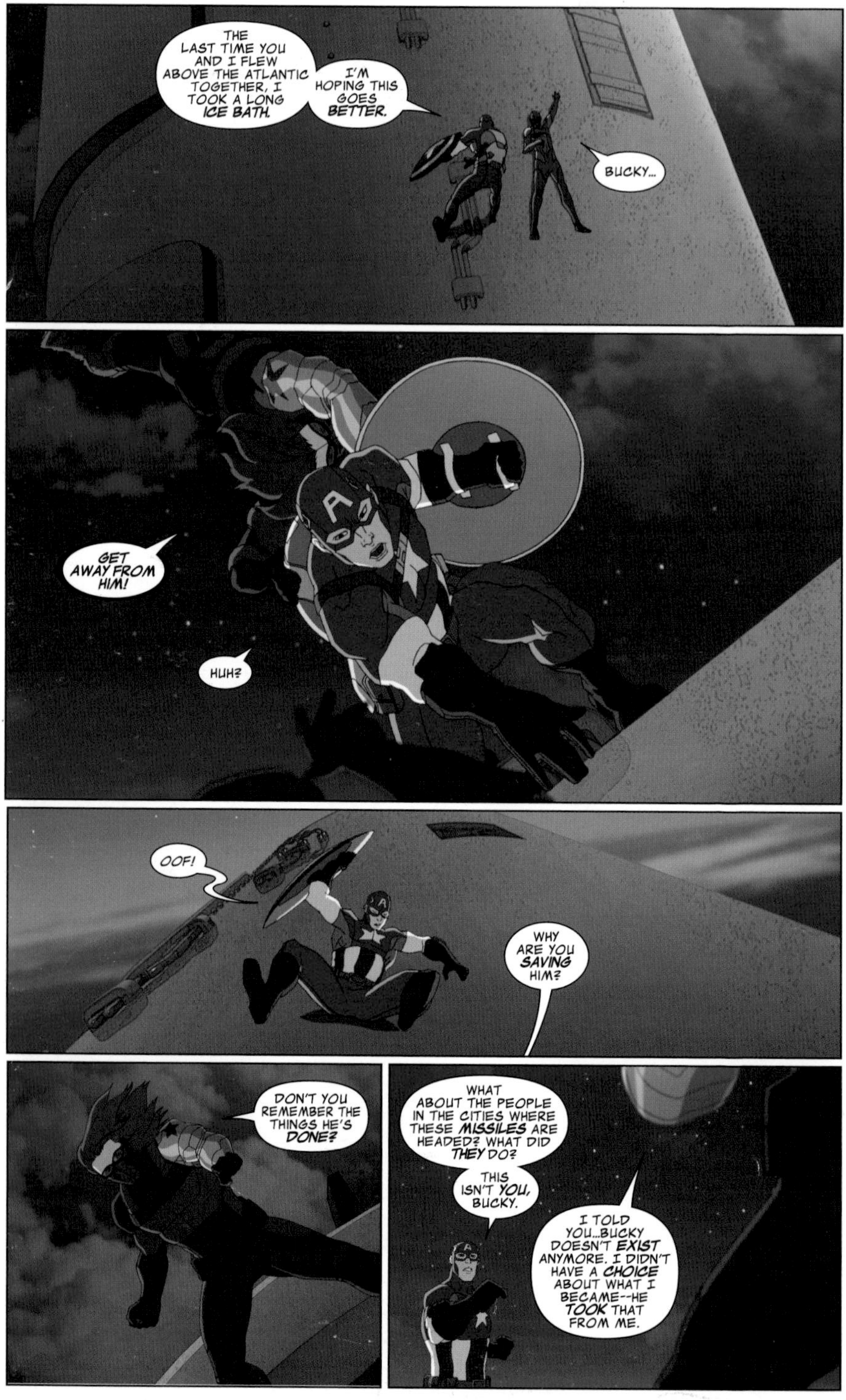
THE LAST TIME YOU AND I FLEW ABOVE THE ATLANTIC TOGETHER, I TOOK A LONG ICE BATH.
I'M HOPING THIS GOES BETTER.
BUCKY...
GET AWAY FROM HIM!
HUH?
OOF!
WHY ARE YOU SAVING HIM?
DON'T YOU REMEMBER THE THINGS HE'S DONE?
WHAT ABOUT THE PEOPLE IN THE CITIES WHERE THESE MISSILES ARE HEADED? WHAT DID THEY DO?
THIS ISN'T YOU, BUCKY.
I TOLD YOU...BUCKY DOESN'T EXIST ANYMORE. I DIDN'T HAVE A CHOICE ABOUT WHAT I BECAME--HE TOOK THAT FROM ME.

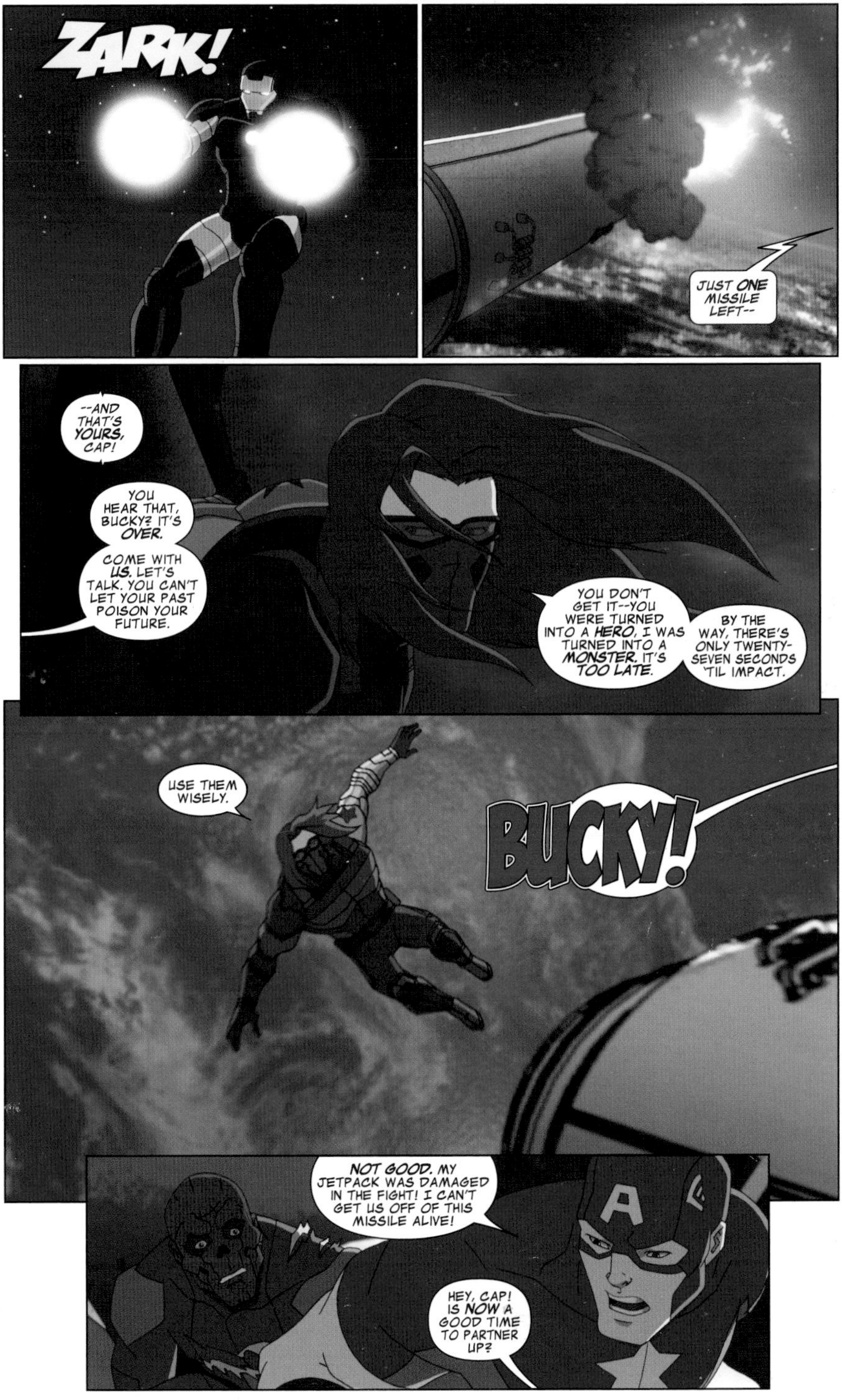
ZARK!
JUST ONE MISSILE LEFT--
--AND THAT'S YOURS, CAP!
YOU HEAR THAT, BUCKY? IT'S OVER.
COME WITH US. LET'S TALK. YOU CAN'T LET YOUR PAST POISON YOUR FUTURE.
YOU DON'T GET IT--YOU WERE TURNED INTO A HERO, I WAS TURNED INTO A MONSTER. IT'S TOO LATE.
BY THE WAY, THERE'S ONLY TWENTY-SEVEN SECONDS 'TIL IMPACT.
USE THEM WISELY.
BUCKY!
NOT GOOD. MY JETPACK WAS DAMAGED IN THE FIGHT! I CAN'T GET US OFF OF THIS MISSILE ALIVE!
HEY, CAP! IS NOW A GOOD TIME TO PARTNER UP?

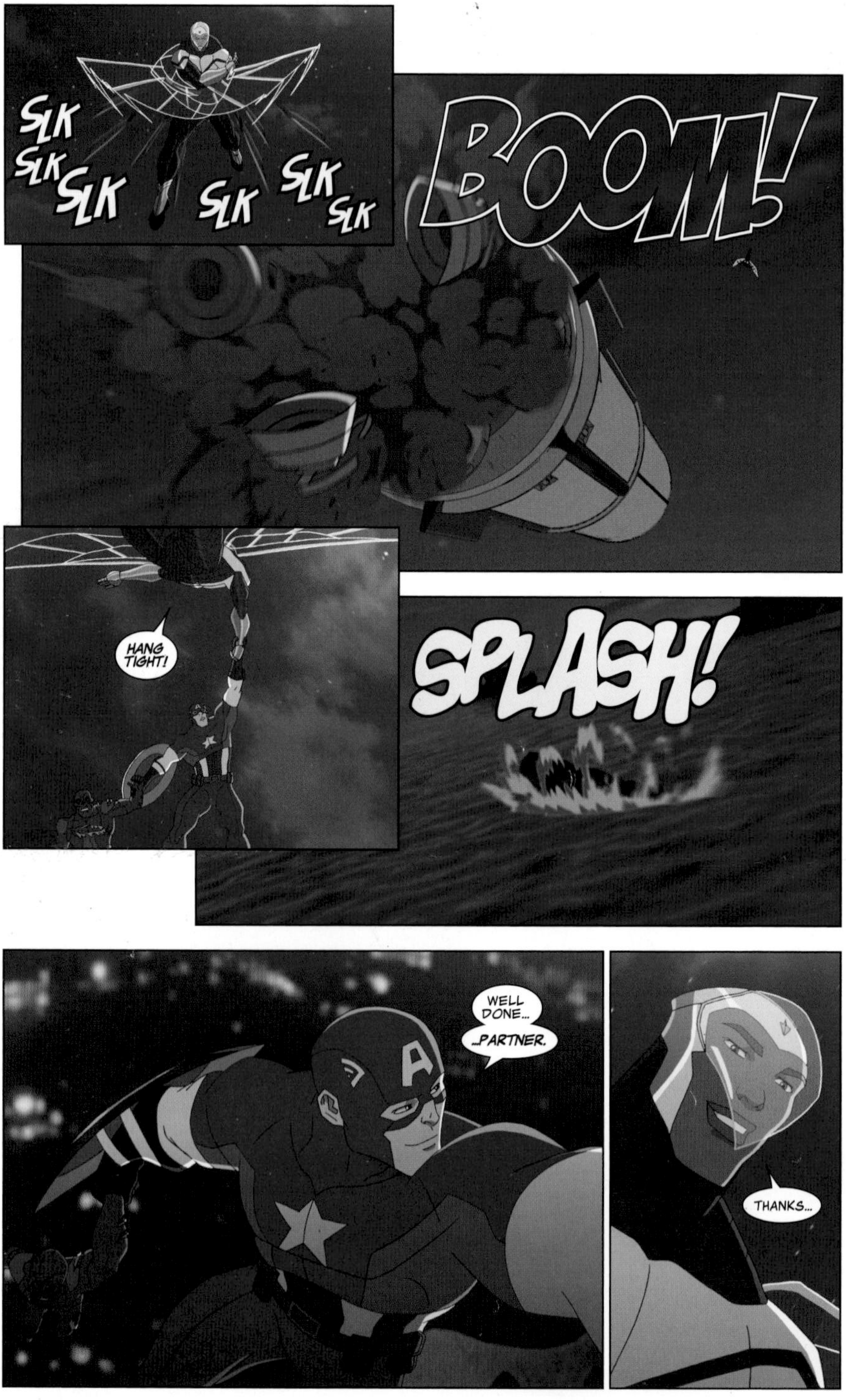
SLK SLK SLK
SLK SLK SLK
BOOM!
HANG TIGHT!
SPLASH!
WELL DONE...
...PARTNER.
THANKS...

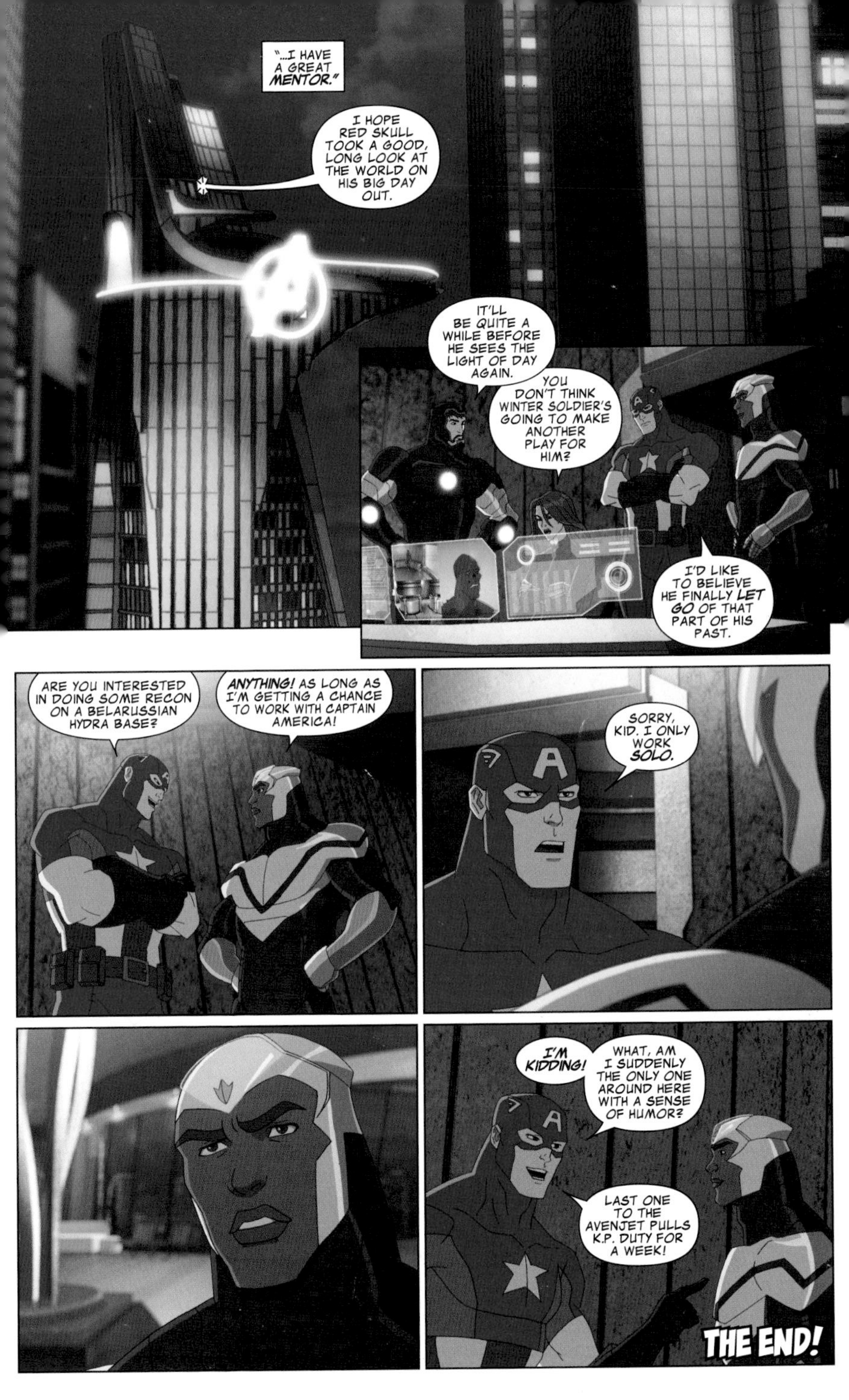
"...I HAVE A GREAT MENTOR."
I HOPE RED SKULL TOOK A GOOD, LONG LOOK AT THE WORLD ON HIS BIG DAY OUT.
IT'LL BE QUITE A WHILE BEFORE HE SEES THE LIGHT OF DAY AGAIN.
YOU DON'T THINK WINTER SOLDIER'S GOING TO MAKE ANOTHER PLAY FOR HIM?
I'D LIKE TO BELIEVE HE FINALLY LET GO OF THAT PART OF HIS PAST.
ARE YOU INTERESTED IN DOING SOME RECON ON A BELARUSSIAN HYDRA BASE?
ANYTHING! AS LONG AS I'M GETTING A CHANCE TO WORK WITH CAPTAIN AMERICA!
SORRY, KID. I ONLY WORK SOLO.
I'M KIDDING!
WHAT, AM I SUDDENLY THE ONLY ONE AROUND HERE WITH A SENSE OF HUMOR?
LAST ONE TO THE AVENJET PULLS K.P. DUTY FOR A WEEK!
THE END!

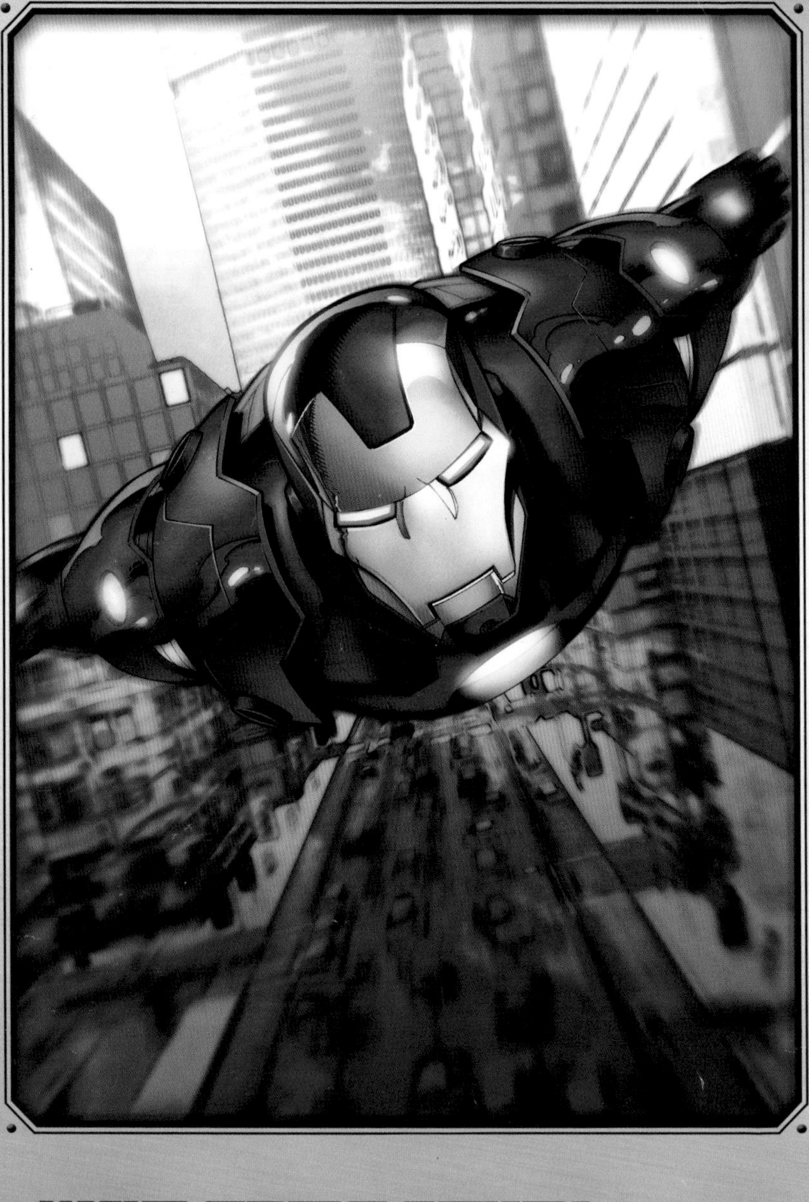

MARVEL UNIVERSE AVENGERS ASSEMBLE SEASON 2 #6

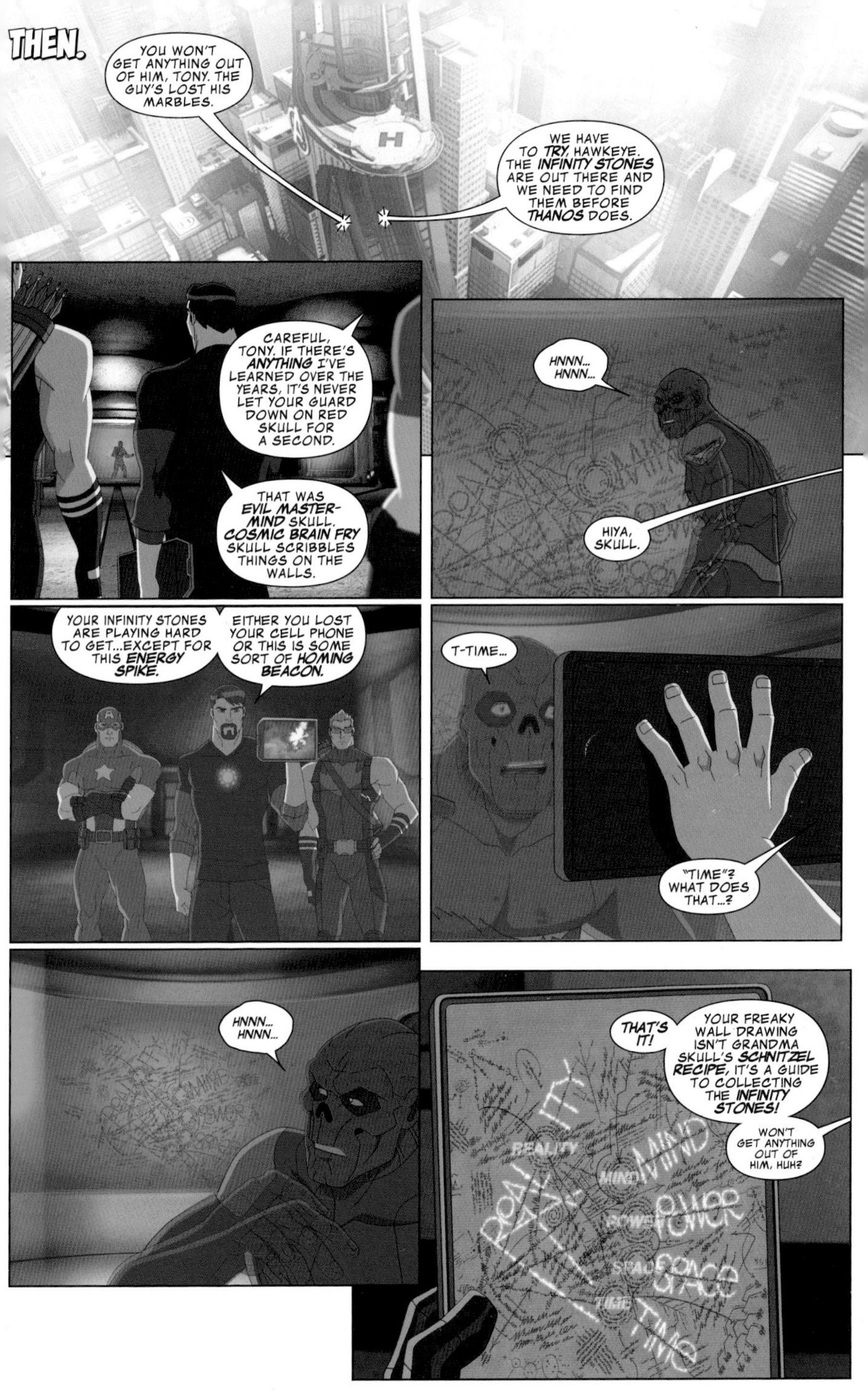
THEN.
YOU WON'T GET ANYTHING OUT OF HIM, TONY. THE GUY'S LOST HIS MARBLES.
WE HAVE TO TRY, HAWKEYE. THE INFINITY STONES ARE OUT THERE AND WE NEED TO FIND THEM BEFORE THANOS DOES.
CAREFUL, TONY. IF THERE'S ANYTHING I'VE LEARNED OVER THE YEARS, IT'S NEVER LET YOUR GUARD DOWN ON RED SKULL FOR A SECOND.
THAT WAS EVIL MASTER-MIND SKULL. COSMIC BRAIN FRY SKULL SCRIBBLES THINGS ON THE WALLS.
HNNN... HNNN...
HIYA, SKULL.
YOUR INFINITY STONES ARE PLAYING HARD TO GET...EXCEPT FOR THIS ENERGY SPIKE.
EITHER YOU LOST YOUR CELL PHONE OR THIS IS SOME SORT OF HOMING BEACON.
T-TIME...
"TIME"? WHAT DOES THAT...?
HNNN... HNNN...
THAT'S IT!
YOUR FREAKY WALL DRAWING ISN'T GRANDMA SKULL'S SCHNITZEL RECIPE, IT'S A GUIDE TO COLLECTING THE INFINITY STONES!
WON'T GET ANYTHING OUT OF HIM, HUH?
REALITY
MIND
POWER
SPACE
TIME

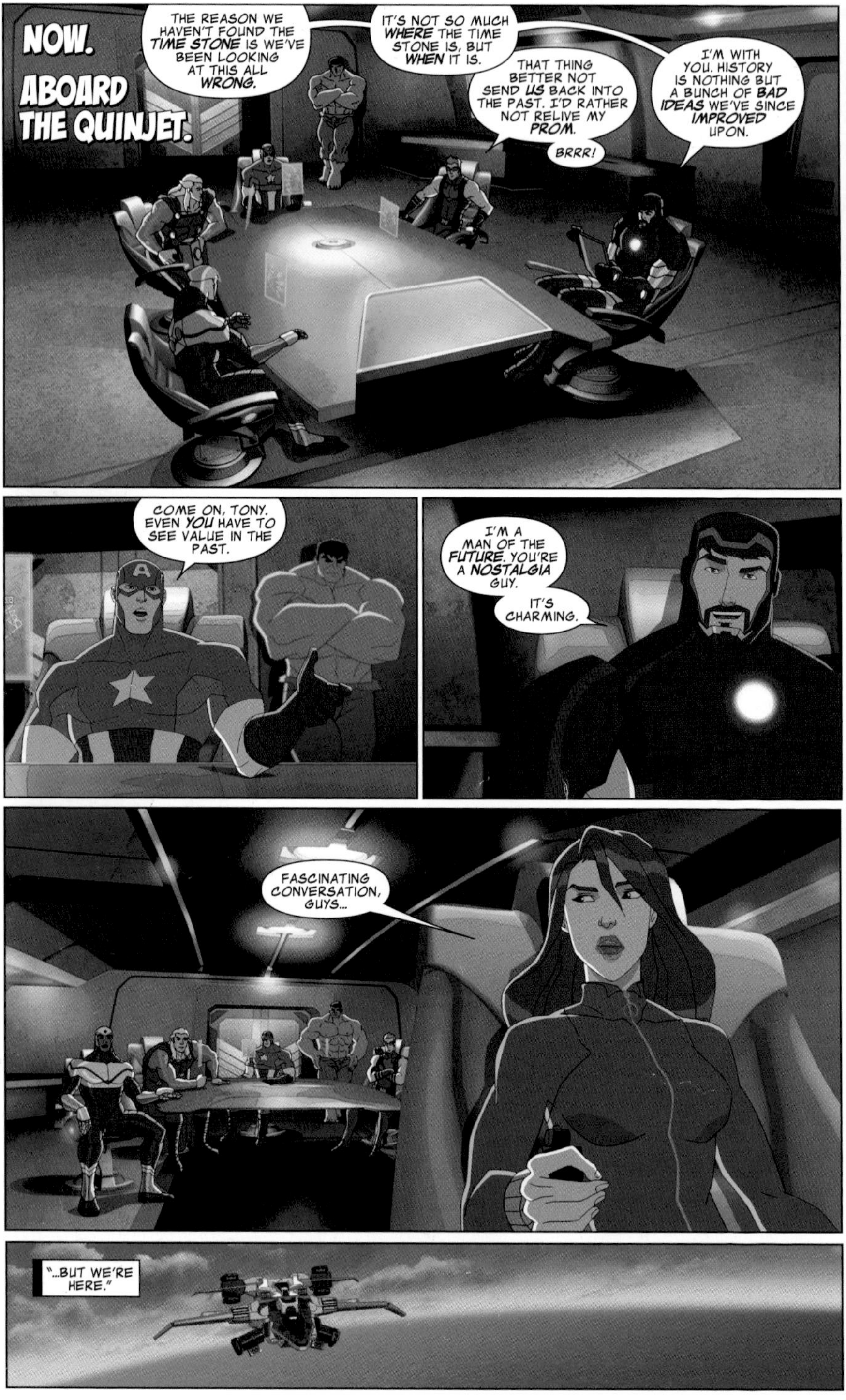

NOW.
ABOARD THE QUINJET.
THE REASON WE HAVEN'T FOUND THE TIME STONE IS WE'VE BEEN LOOKING AT THIS ALL WRONG.
IT'S NOT SO MUCH WHERE THE TIME STONE IS, BUT WHEN IT IS.
THAT THING BETTER NOT SEND US BACK INTO THE PAST. I'D RATHER NOT RELIVE MY PROM.
BRRR!
I'M WITH YOU. HISTORY IS NOTHING BUT A BUNCH OF BAD IDEAS WE'VE SINCE IMPROVED UPON.
COME ON, TONY. EVEN YOU HAVE TO SEE VALUE IN THE PAST.
I'M A MAN OF THE FUTURE. YOU'RE A NOSTALGIA GUY.
IT'S CHARMING.
FASCINATING CONVERSATION, GUYS...
"...BUT WE'RE HERE."

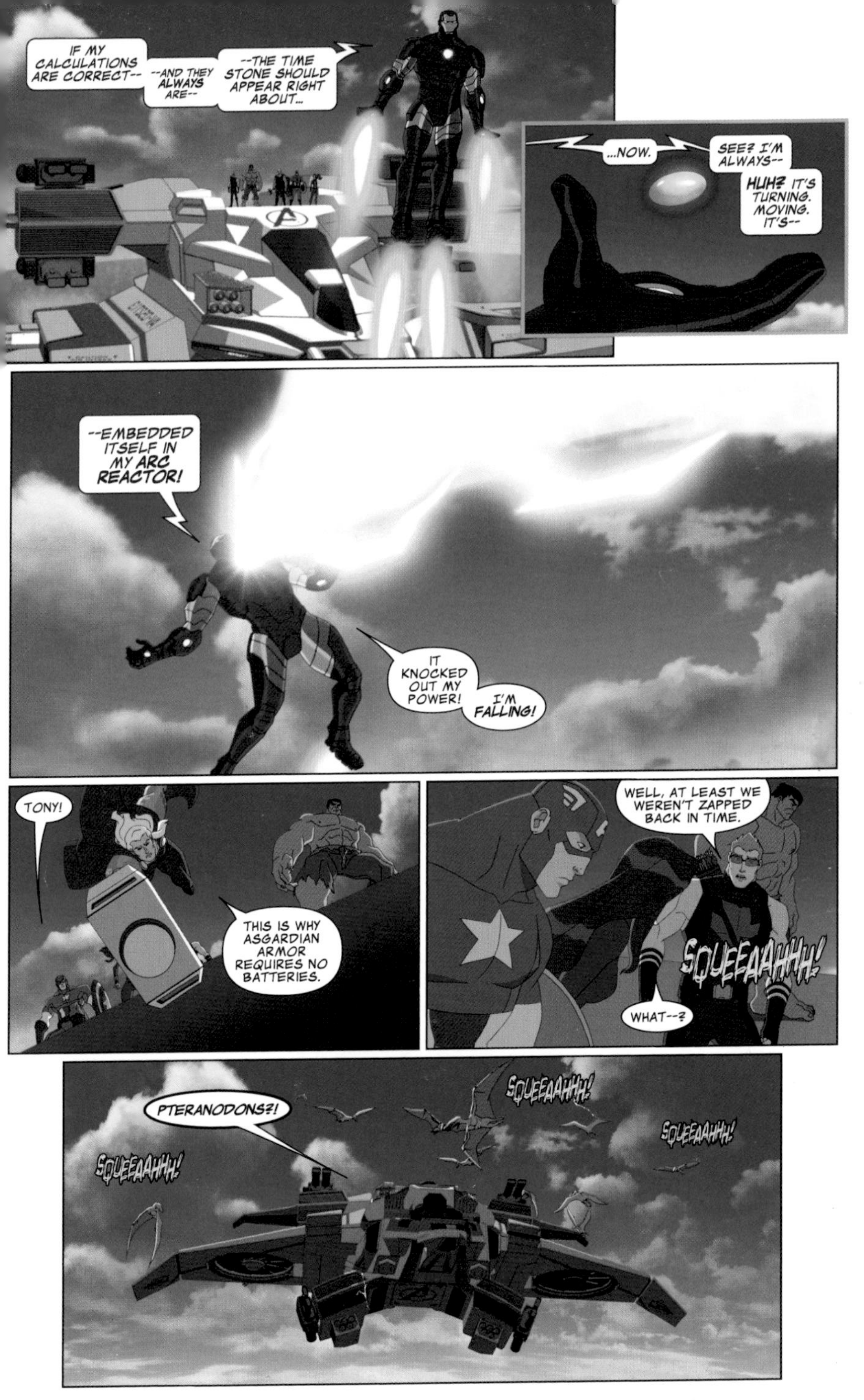
IF MY CALCULATIONS ARE CORRECT--
--AND THEY ALWAYS ARE--
--THE TIME STONE SHOULD APPEAR RIGHT ABOUT...
...NOW.
SEE? I'M ALWAYS--
HUH? IT'S TURNING. MOVING. IT'S--
--EMBEDDED ITSELF IN MY ARC REACTOR!
IT KNOCKED OUT MY POWER!
I'M FALLING!
TONY!
THIS IS WHY ASGARDIAN ARMOR REQUIRES NO BATTERIES.
WELL, AT LEAST WE WEREN'T ZAPPED BACK IN TIME.
SQUEEAAHHH!
WHAT--?
SQUEEAAHHH!
PTERANODONS?!
SQUEEAAHHH!
SQUEEAAHHH!

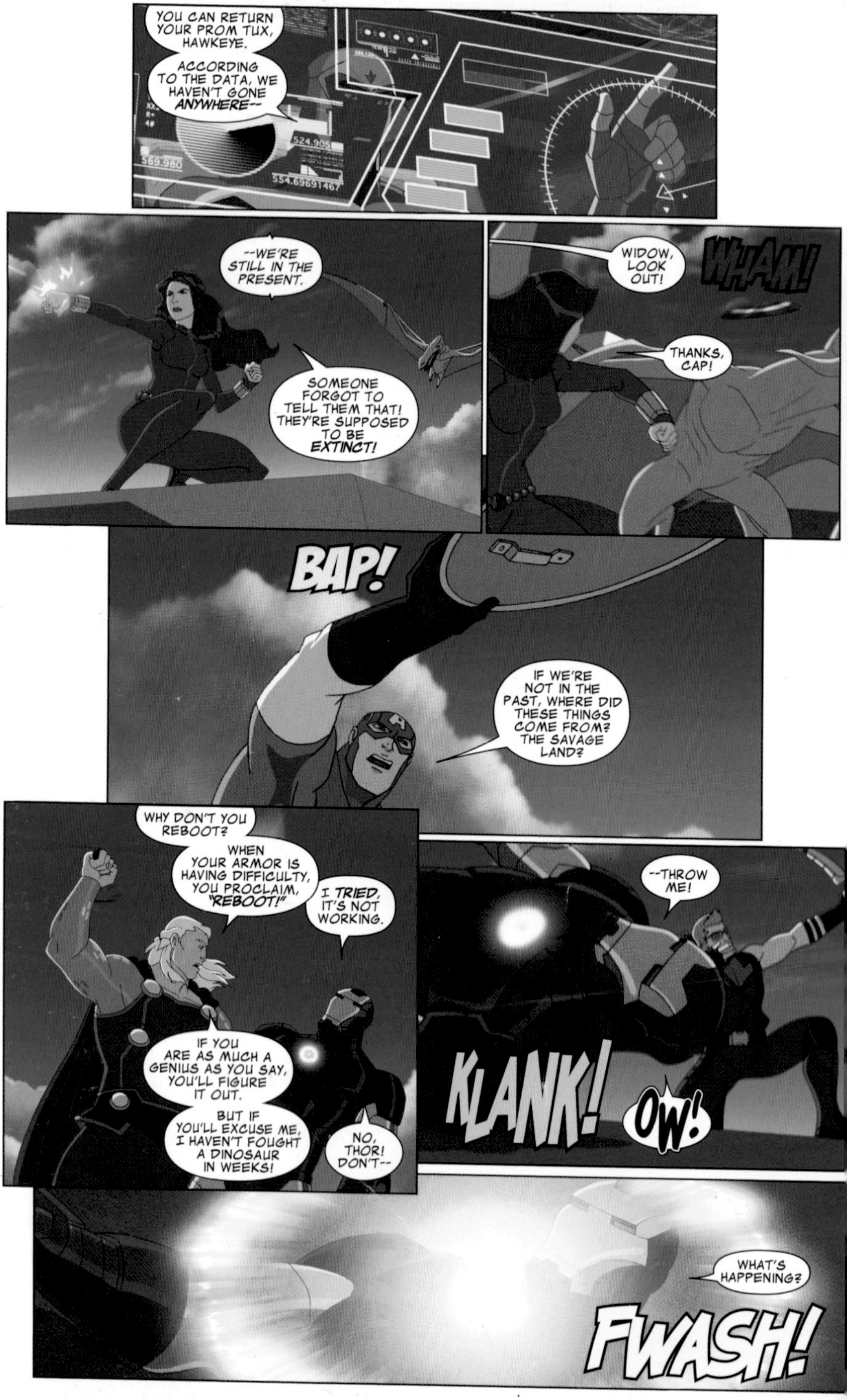

YOU CAN RETURN YOUR PROM TUX, HAWKEYE.
ACCORDING TO THE DATA, WE HAVEN'T GONE ANYWHERE--
--WE'RE STILL IN THE PRESENT.
SOMEONE FORGOT TO TELL THEM THAT! THEY'RE SUPPOSED TO BE EXTINCT!
WIDOW, LOOK OUT!
WHAM!
THANKS, CAP!
BAP!
IF WE'RE NOT IN THE PAST, WHERE DID THESE THINGS COME FROM? THE SAVAGE LAND?
WHY DON'T YOU REBOOT?
WHEN YOUR ARMOR IS HAVING DIFFICULTY, YOU PROCLAIM, "REBOOT!"
I TRIED, IT'S NOT WORKING.
IF YOU ARE AS MUCH A GENIUS AS YOU SAY, YOU'LL FIGURE IT OUT.
BUT IF YOU'LL EXCUSE ME, I HAVEN'T FOUGHT A DINOSAUR IN WEEKS!
NO, THOR! DON'T--
--THROW ME!
KLANK!
OW!
WHAT'S HAPPENING?
FWASH!

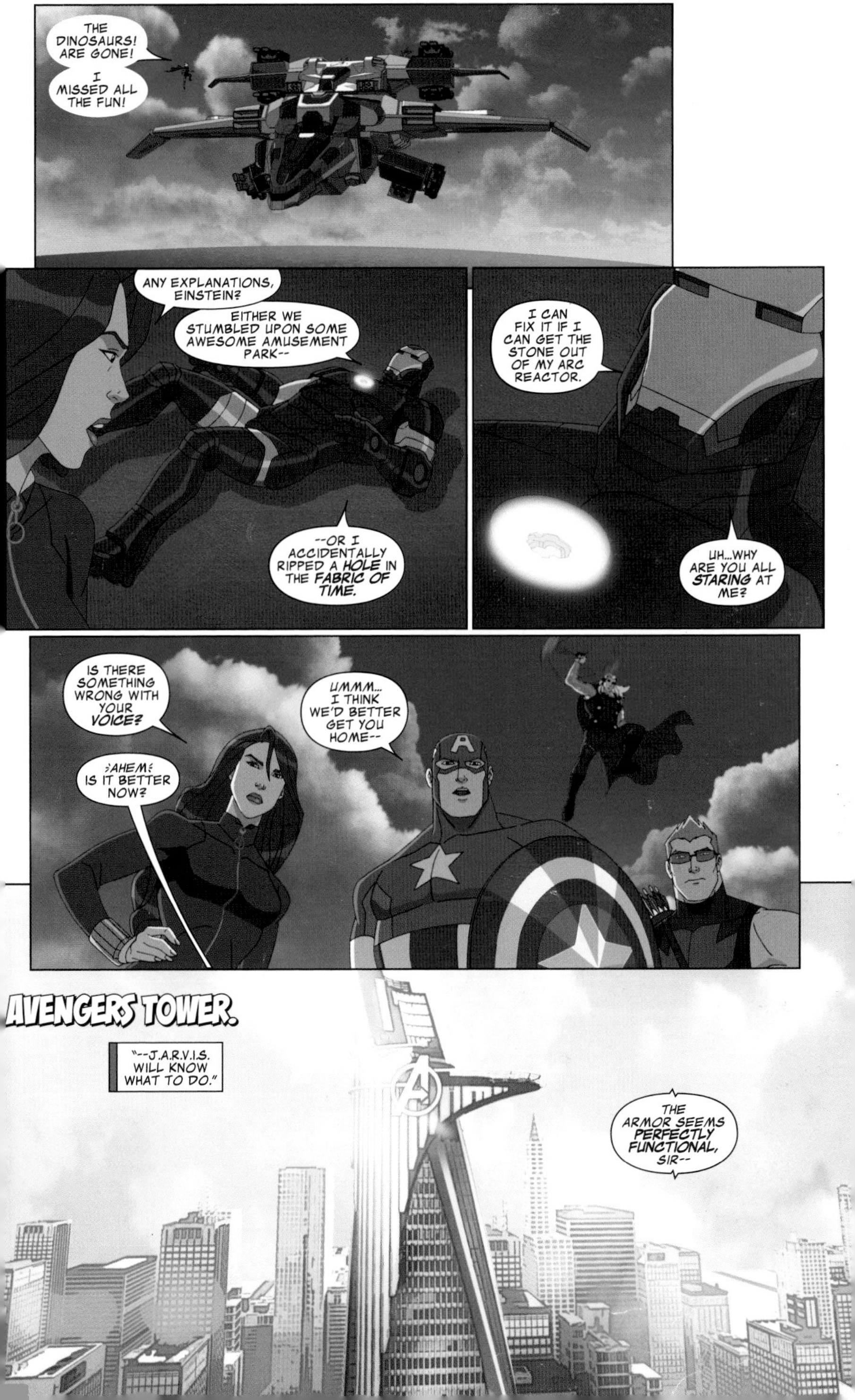
THE DINOSAURS! ARE GONE!
I MISSED ALL THE FUN!
ANY EXPLANATIONS, EINSTEIN?
EITHER WE STUMBLED UPON SOME AWESOME AMUSEMENT PARK--
--OR I ACCIDENTALLY RIPPED A HOLE IN THE FABRIC OF TIME.
I CAN FIX IT IF I CAN GET THE STONE OUT OF MY ARC REACTOR.
UH...WHY ARE YOU ALL STARING AT ME?
IS THERE SOMETHING WRONG WITH YOUR VOICE?
UMMM... I THINK WE'D BETTER GET YOU HOME--
AHEM IS IT BETTER NOW?
AVENGERS TOWER.
"--J.A.R.V.I.S. WILL KNOW WHAT TO DO."
THE ARMOR SEEMS PERFECTLY FUNCTIONAL, SIR--

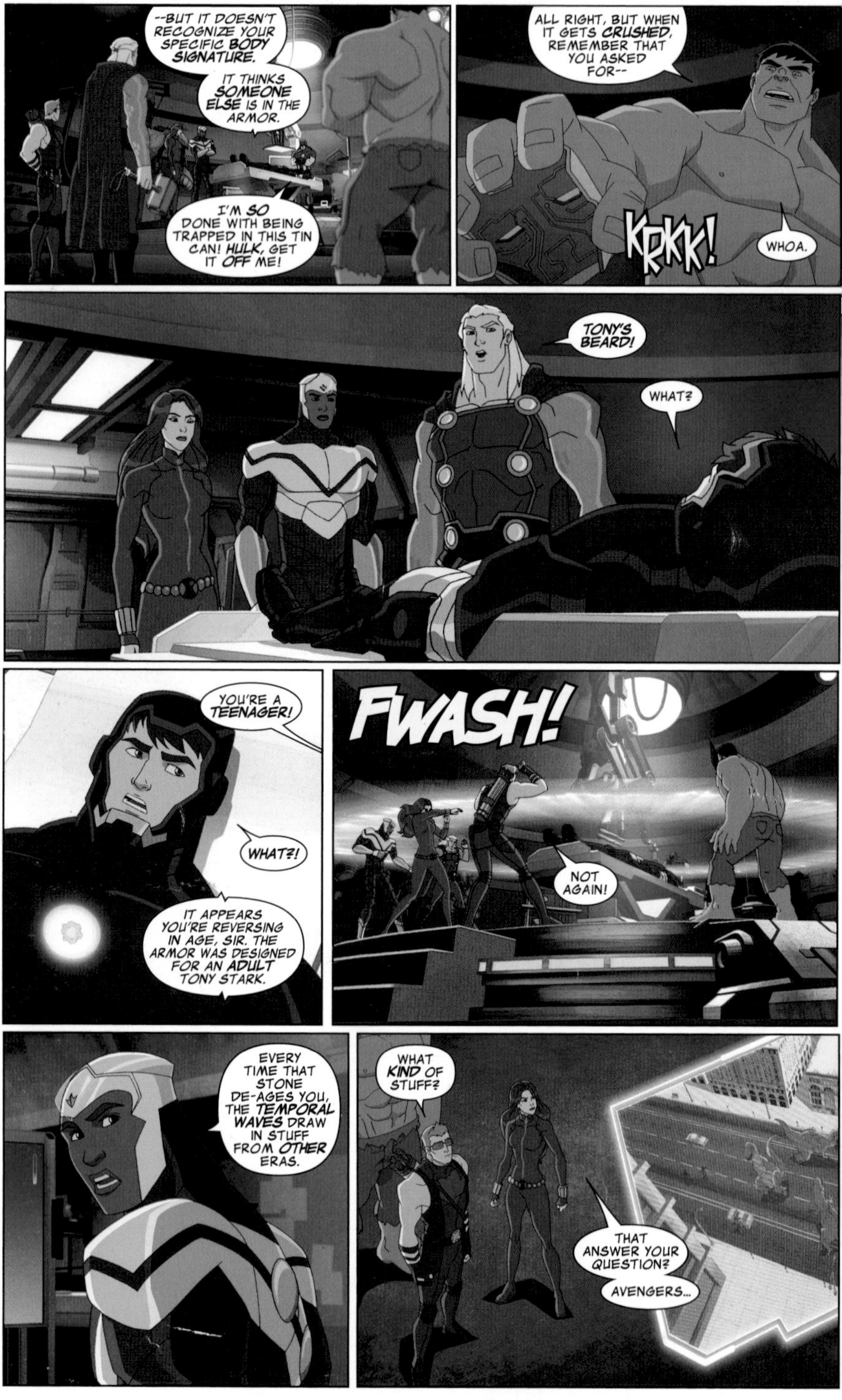
--BUT IT DOESN'T RECOGNIZE YOUR SPECIFIC BODY SIGNATURE.
IT THINKS SOMEONE ELSE IS IN THE ARMOR.
I'M SO DONE WITH BEING TRAPPED IN THIS TIN CAN! HULK, GET IT OFF ME!
ALL RIGHT, BUT WHEN IT GETS CRUSHED, REMEMBER THAT YOU ASKED FOR--
KRKK!
WHOA.
TONY'S BEARD!
WHAT?
YOU'RE A TEENAGER!
WHAT?!
IT APPEARS YOU'RE REVERSING IN AGE, SIR. THE ARMOR WAS DESIGNED FOR AN ADULT TONY STARK.
FWASH!
NOT AGAIN!
EVERY TIME THAT STONE DE-AGES YOU, THE TEMPORAL WAVES DRAW IN STUFF FROM OTHER ERAS.
WHAT KIND OF STUFF?
THAT ANSWER YOUR QUESTION?
AVENGERS...

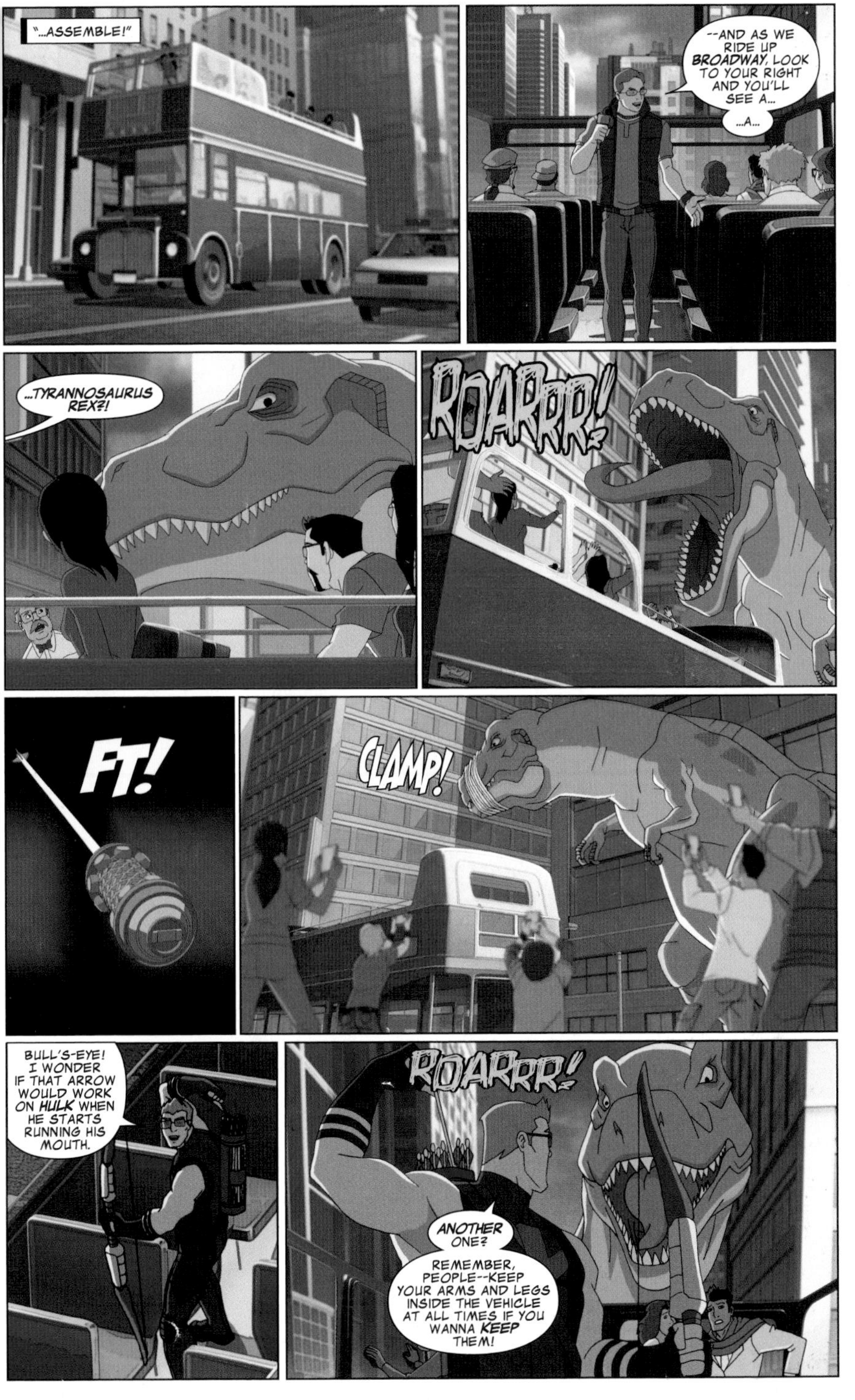

"...ASSEMBLE!"
--AND AS WE RIDE UP BROADWAY, LOOK TO YOUR RIGHT AND YOU'LL SEE A...
...A...
...TYRANNOSAURUS REX?!
ROARRR!
FT!
CLAMP!
BULL'S-EYE! I WONDER IF THAT ARROW WOULD WORK ON HULK WHEN HE STARTS RUNNING HIS MOUTH.
ROARRR!
ANOTHER ONE?
REMEMBER, PEOPLE--KEEP YOUR ARMS AND LEGS INSIDE THE VEHICLE AT ALL TIMES IF YOU WANNA KEEP THEM!

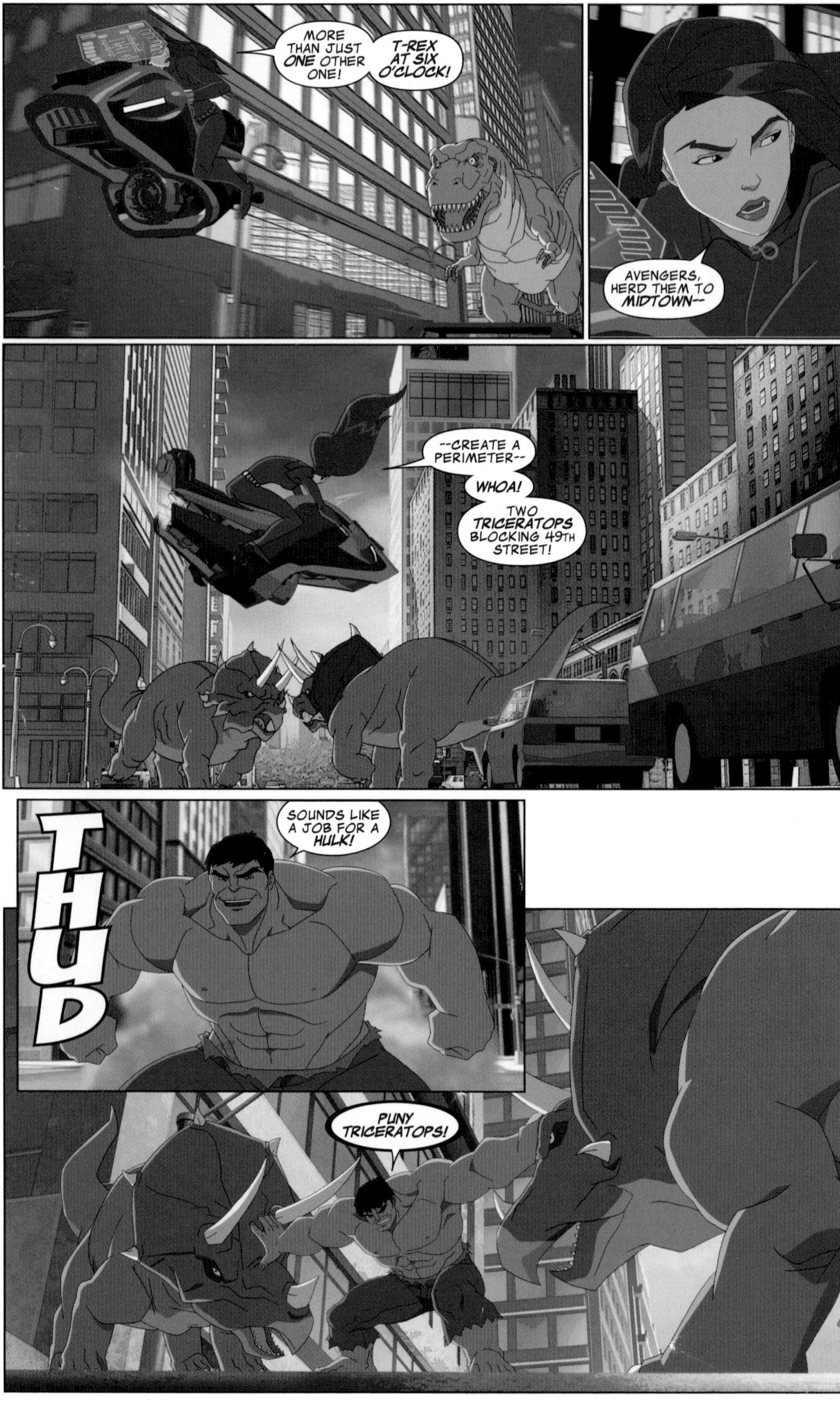

MORE THAN JUST ONE OTHER ONE!
T-REX AT SIX O'CLOCK!
AVENGERS, HERD THEM TO MIDTOWN--
--CREATE A PERIMETER--
WHOA!
TWO TRICERATOPS BLOCKING 49TH STREET!
THUD
SOUNDS LIKE A JOB FOR A HULK!
PUNY TRICERATOPS!

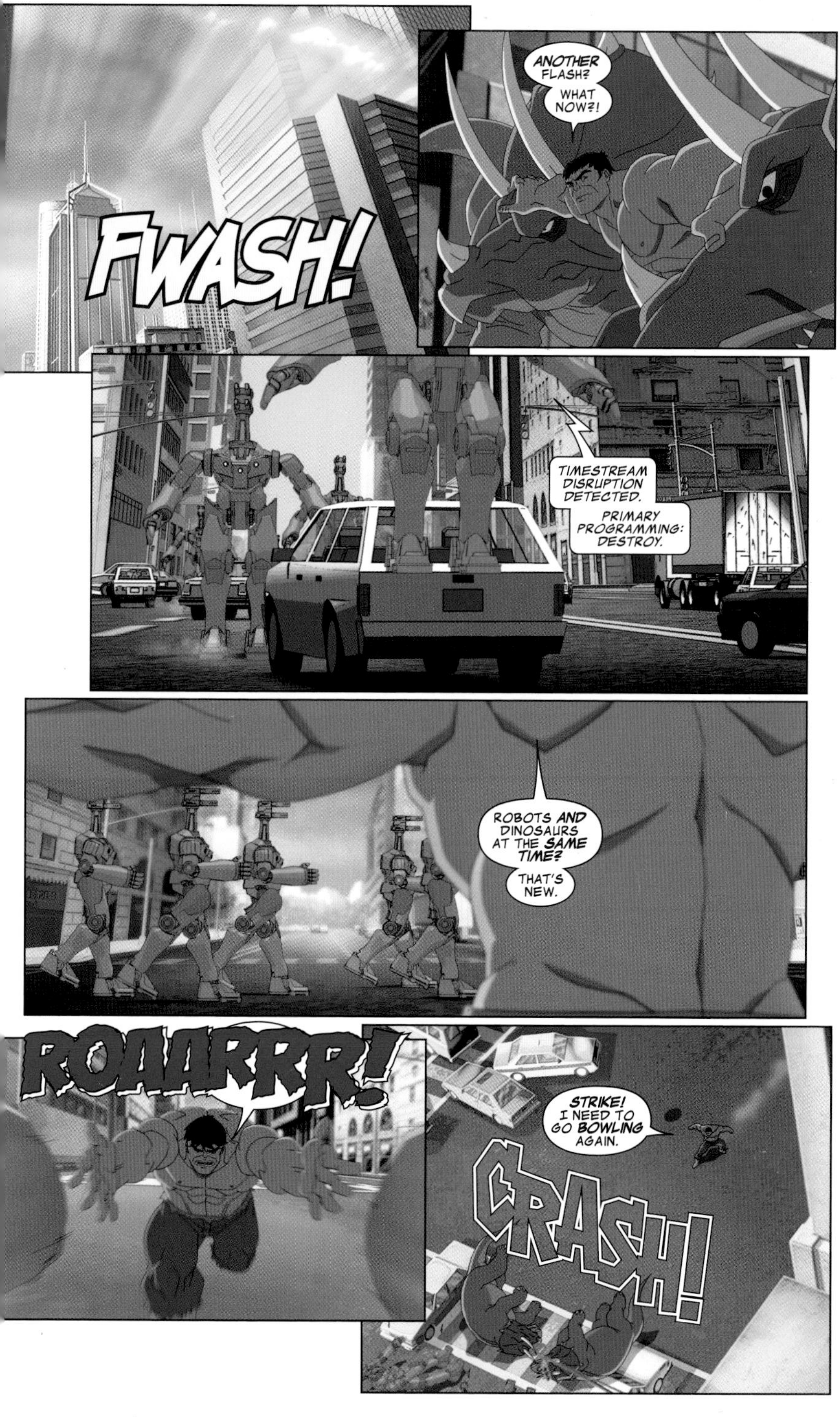
FWASH!
ANOTHER FLASH?
WHAT NOW?!
TIMESTREAM DISRUPTION DETECTED.
PRIMARY PROGRAMMING: DESTROY.
ROBOTS AND DINOSAURS AT THE SAME TIME?
THAT'S NEW.
ROAARRR!
STRIKE! I NEED TO GO BOWLING AGAIN.
CRASH!

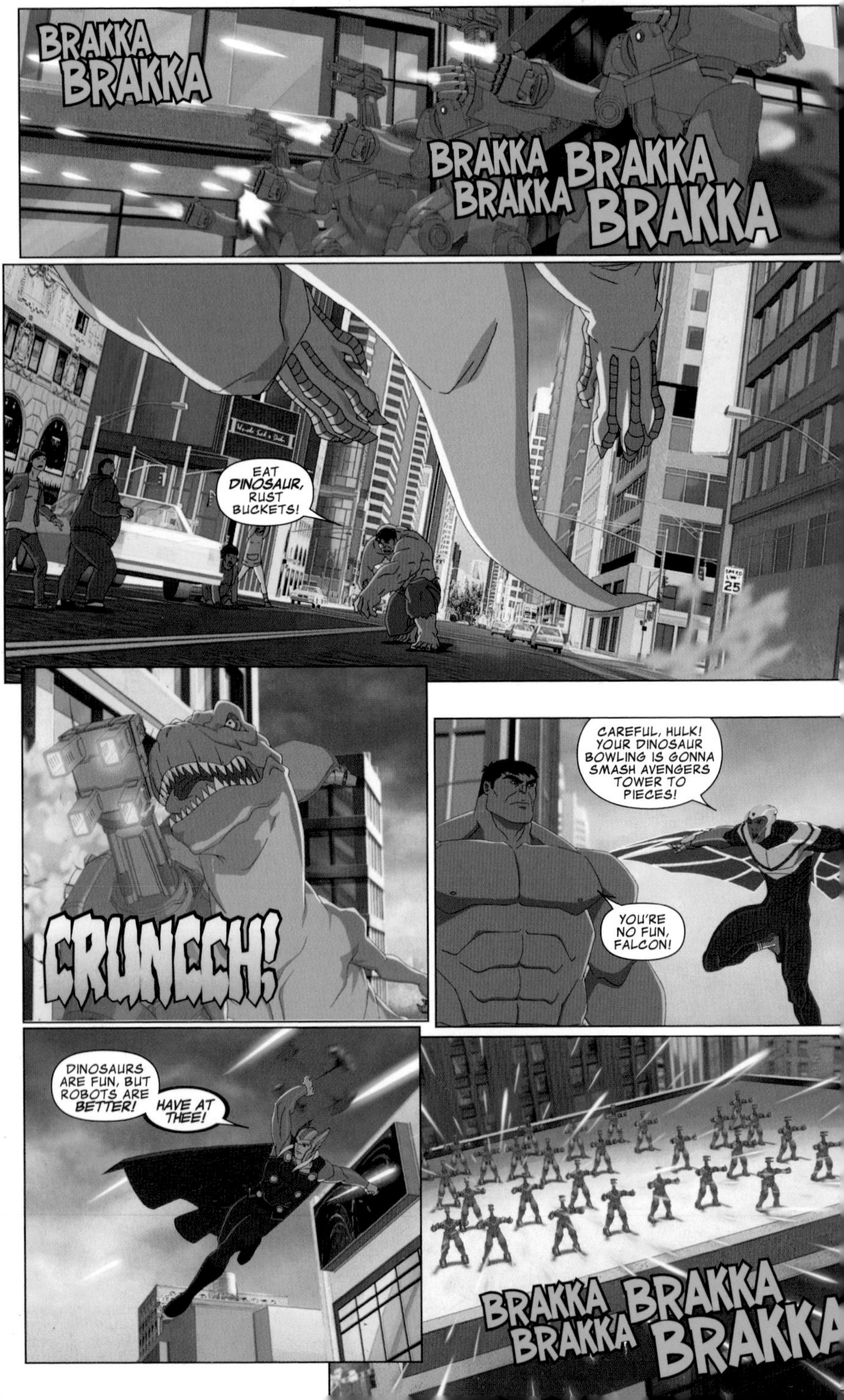
BRAKKA BRAKKA
BRAKKA BRAKKA BRAKKA BRAKKA
EAT DINOSAUR, RUST BUCKETS!
CRUNCCH!
CAREFUL, HULK! YOUR DINOSAUR BOWLING IS GONNA SMASH AVENGERS TOWER TO PIECES!
YOU'RE NO FUN, FALCON!
DINOSAURS ARE FUN, BUT ROBOTS ARE BETTER!
HAVE AT THEE!
BRAKKA BRAKKA BRAKKA BRAKKA

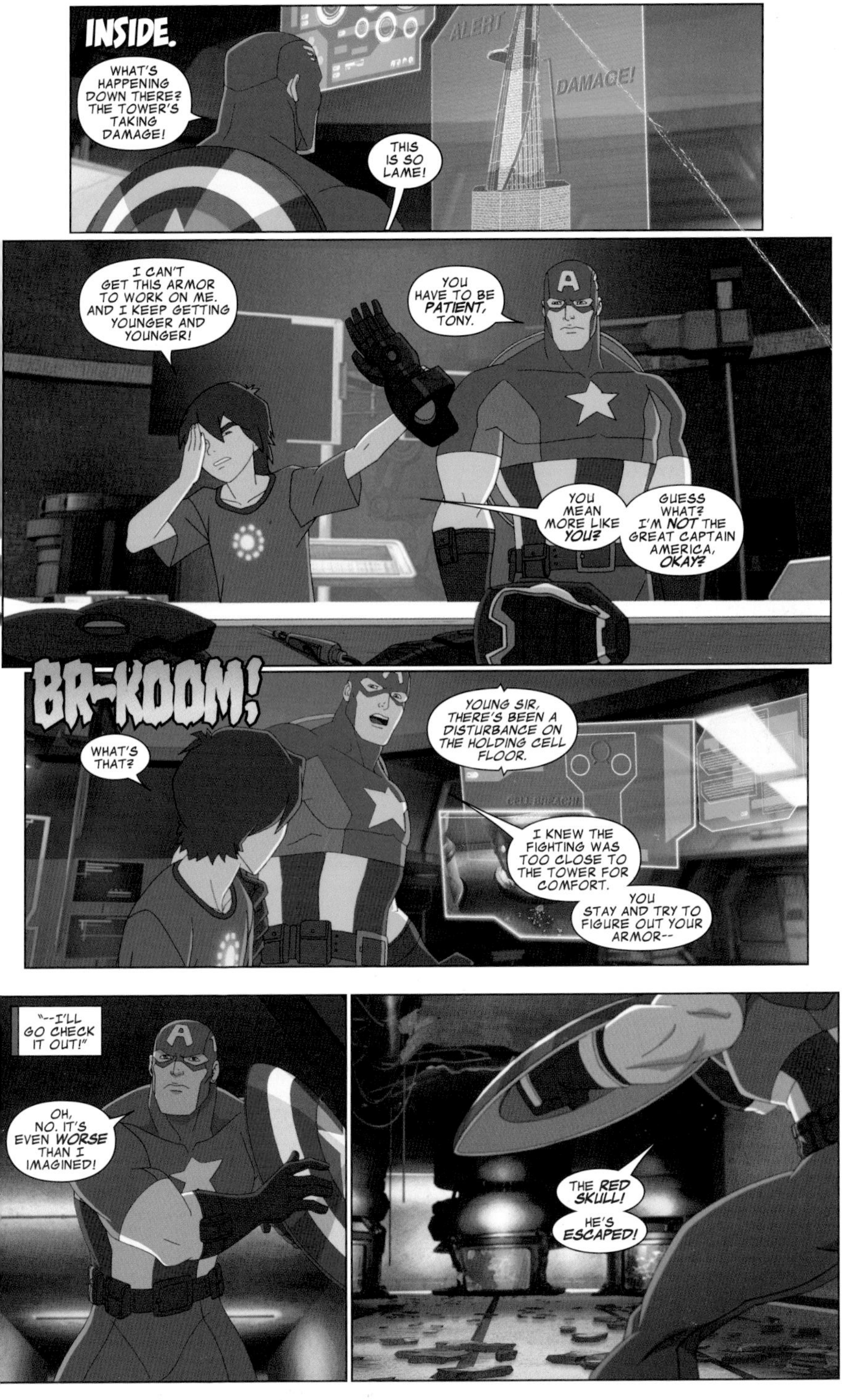
INSIDE.
WHAT'S HAPPENING DOWN THERE? THE TOWER'S TAKING DAMAGE!
THIS IS SO LAME!
ALERT
DAMAGE!
I CAN'T GET THIS ARMOR TO WORK ON ME. AND I KEEP GETTING YOUNGER AND YOUNGER!
YOU HAVE TO BE PATIENT, TONY.
YOU MEAN MORE LIKE YOU?
GUESS WHAT? I'M NOT THE GREAT CAPTAIN AMERICA, OKAY?
BR-KOOM!
WHAT'S THAT?
YOUNG SIR, THERE'S BEEN A DISTURBANCE ON THE HOLDING CELL FLOOR.
I KNEW THE FIGHTING WAS TOO CLOSE TO THE TOWER FOR COMFORT.
YOU STAY AND TRY TO FIGURE OUT YOUR ARMOR--
"--I'LL GO CHECK IT OUT!"
OH, NO. IT'S EVEN WORSE THAN I IMAGINED!
THE RED SKULL!
HE'S ESCAPED!

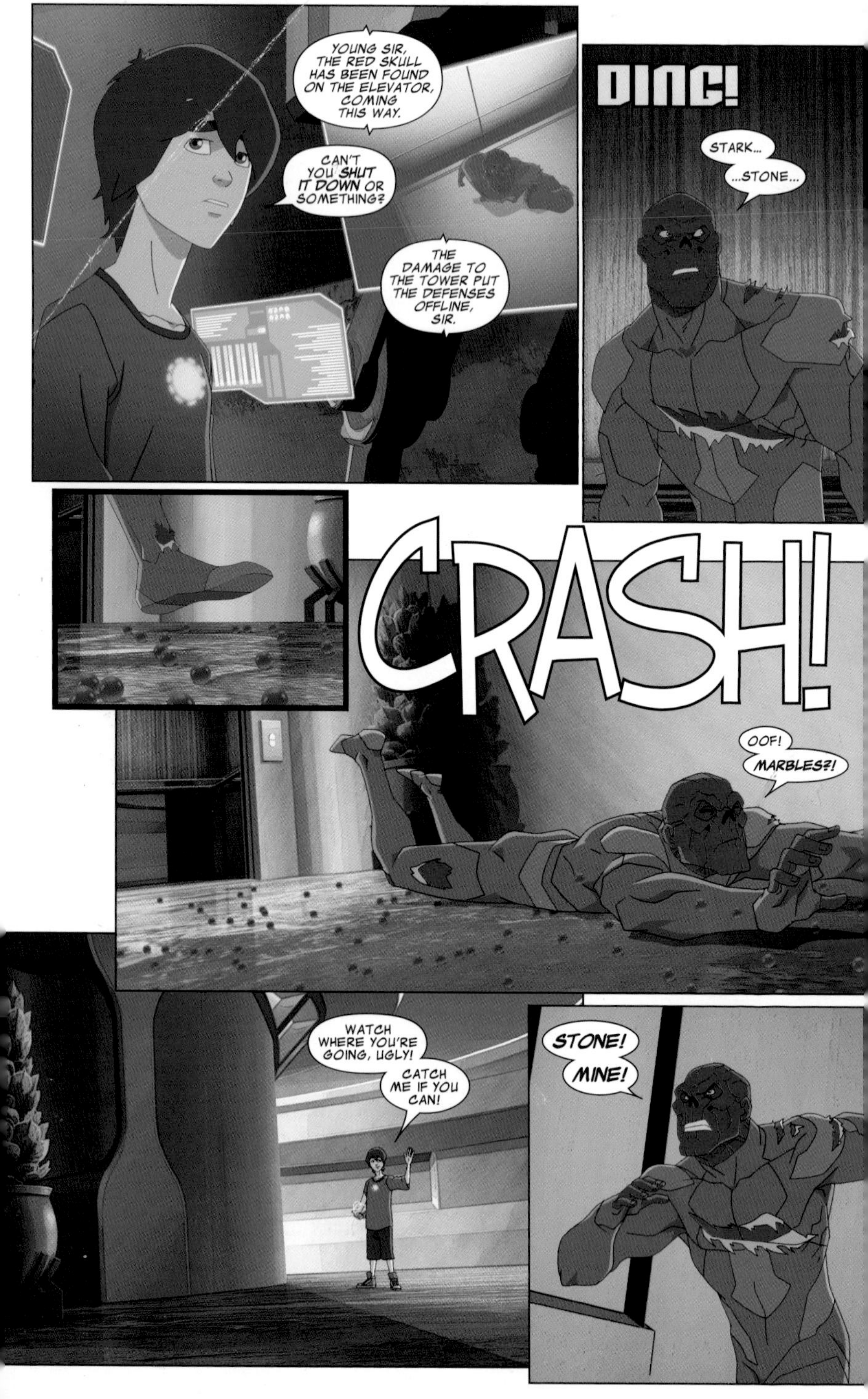
YOUNG SIR, THE RED SKULL HAS BEEN FOUND ON THE ELEVATOR, COMING THIS WAY.
CAN'T YOU SHUT IT DOWN OR SOMETHING?
THE DAMAGE TO THE TOWER PUT THE DEFENSES OFFLINE, SIR.
DING!
STARK...
...STONE...
CRASH!
OOF! MARBLES?!
WATCH WHERE YOU'RE GOING, UGLY!
CATCH ME IF YOU CAN!
STONE!
MINE!

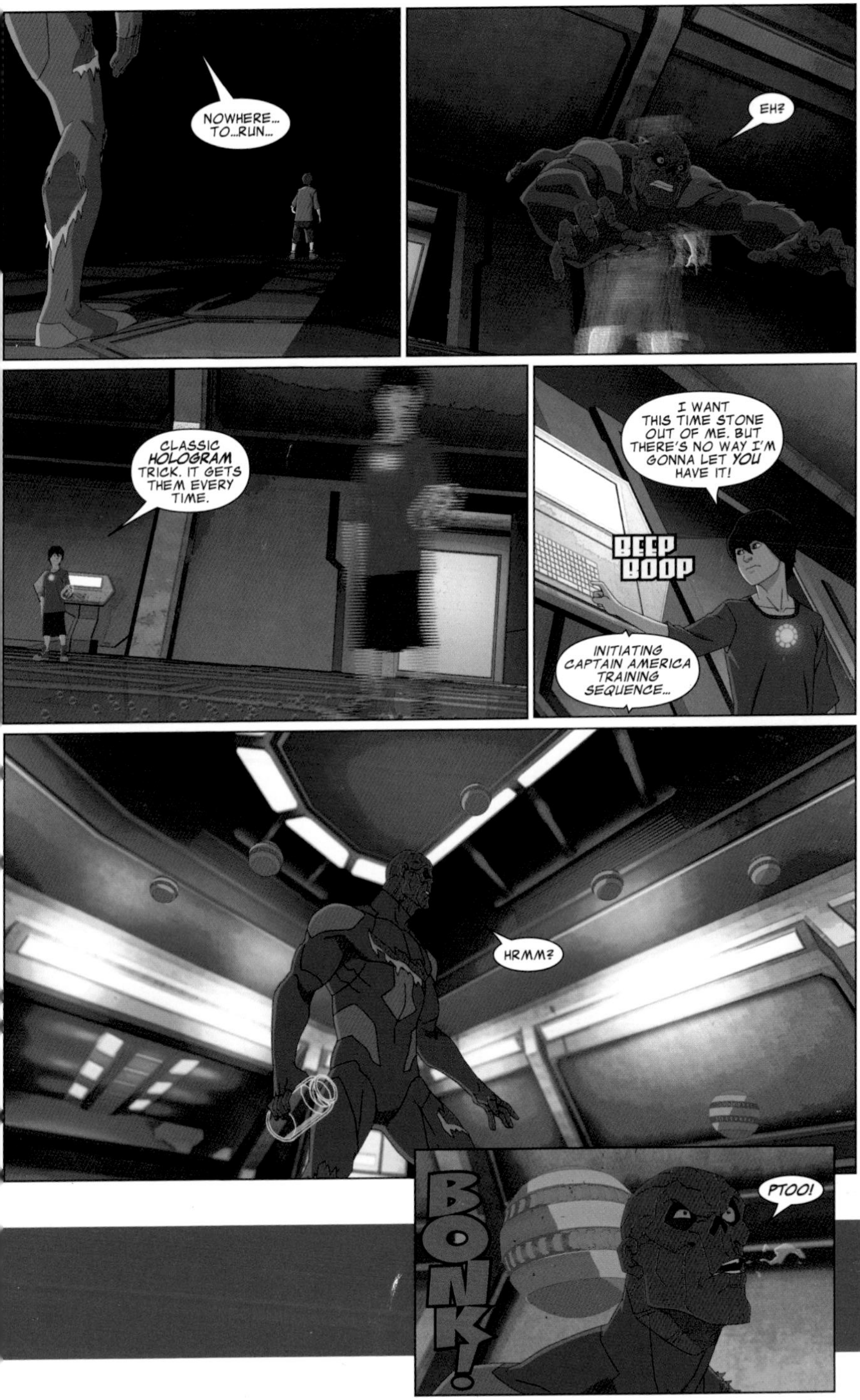
NOWHERE... TO...RUN...
EH?
CLASSIC HOLOGRAM TRICK. IT GETS THEM EVERY TIME.
I WANT THIS TIME STONE OUT OF ME. BUT THERE'S NO WAY I'M GONNA LET YOU HAVE IT!
BEEP BOOP
INITIATING CAPTAIN AMERICA TRAINING SEQUENCE...
HRMM?
BONK!
PTOO!

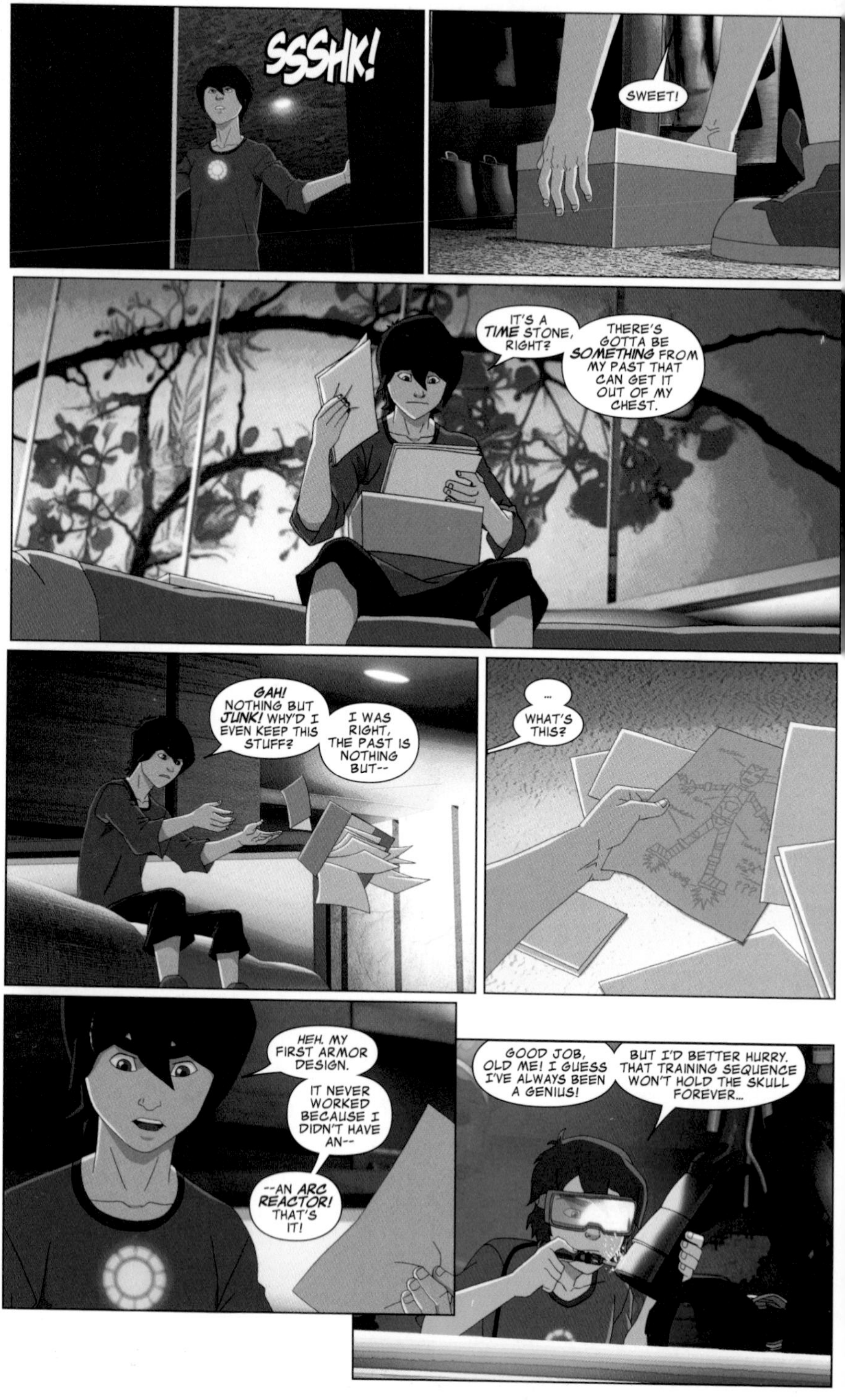
SSSHK!
SWEET!
IT'S A TIME STONE, RIGHT?
THERE'S GOTTA BE SOMETHING FROM MY PAST THAT CAN GET IT OUT OF MY CHEST.
GAH! NOTHING BUT JUNK! WHY'D I EVEN KEEP THIS STUFF?
I WAS RIGHT, THE PAST IS NOTHING BUT--
... WHAT'S THIS?
HEH. MY FIRST ARMOR DESIGN.
IT NEVER WORKED BECAUSE I DIDN'T HAVE AN--
--AN ARC REACTOR! THAT'S IT!
GOOD JOB, OLD ME! I GUESS I'VE ALWAYS BEEN A GENIUS!
BUT I'D BETTER HURRY. THAT TRAINING SEQUENCE WON'T HOLD THE SKULL FOREVER...

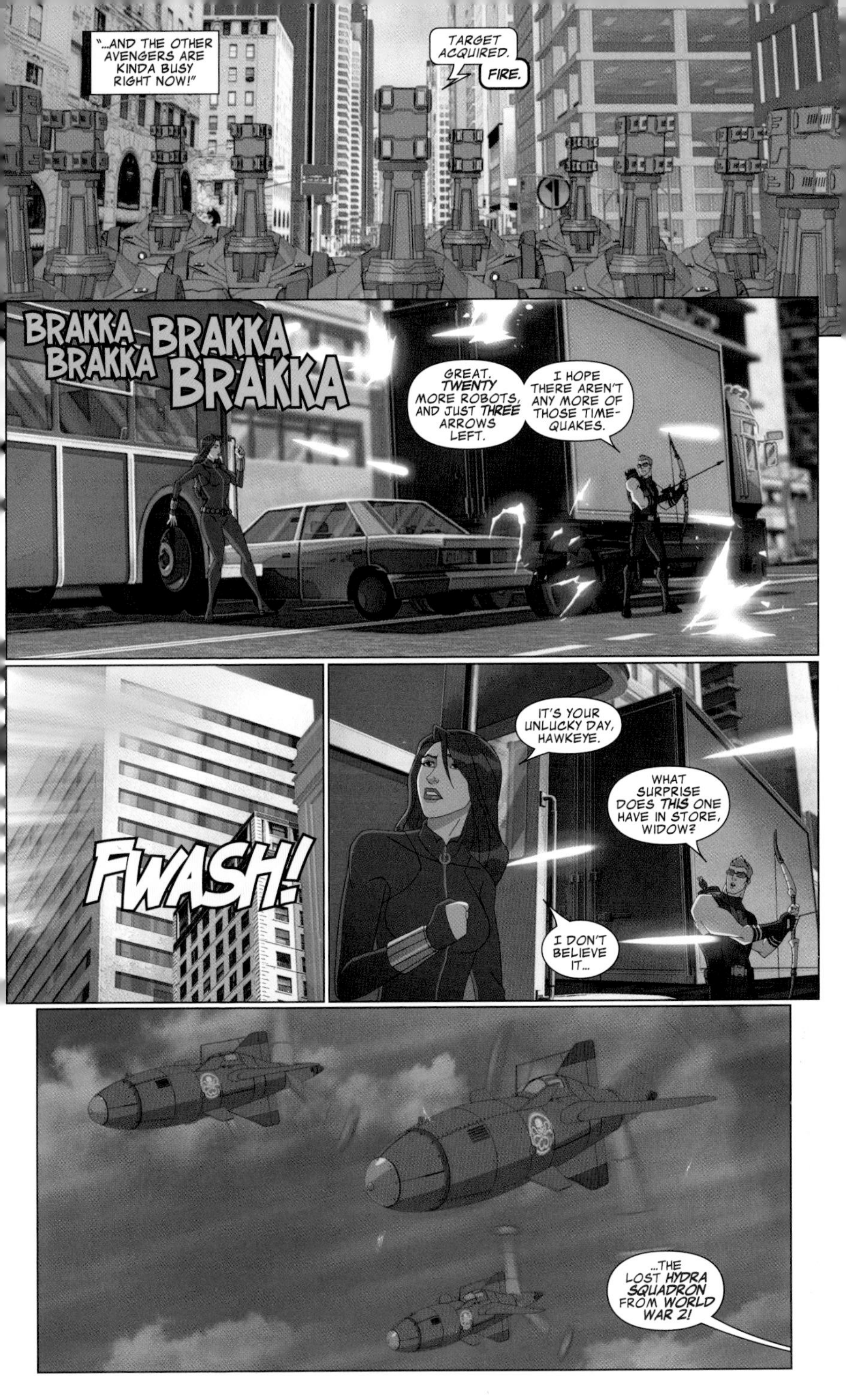
"...AND THE OTHER AVENGERS ARE KINDA BUSY RIGHT NOW!"
TARGET ACQUIRED.
FIRE.
BRAKKA BRAKKA BRAKKA BRAKKA
GREAT. TWENTY MORE ROBOTS, AND JUST THREE ARROWS LEFT.
I HOPE THERE AREN'T ANY MORE OF THOSE TIME-QUAKES.
FWASH!
IT'S YOUR UNLUCKY DAY, HAWKEYE.
WHAT SURPRISE DOES THIS ONE HAVE IN STORE, WIDOW?
I DON'T BELIEVE IT...
...THE LOST HYDRA SQUADRON FROM WORLD WAR 2!

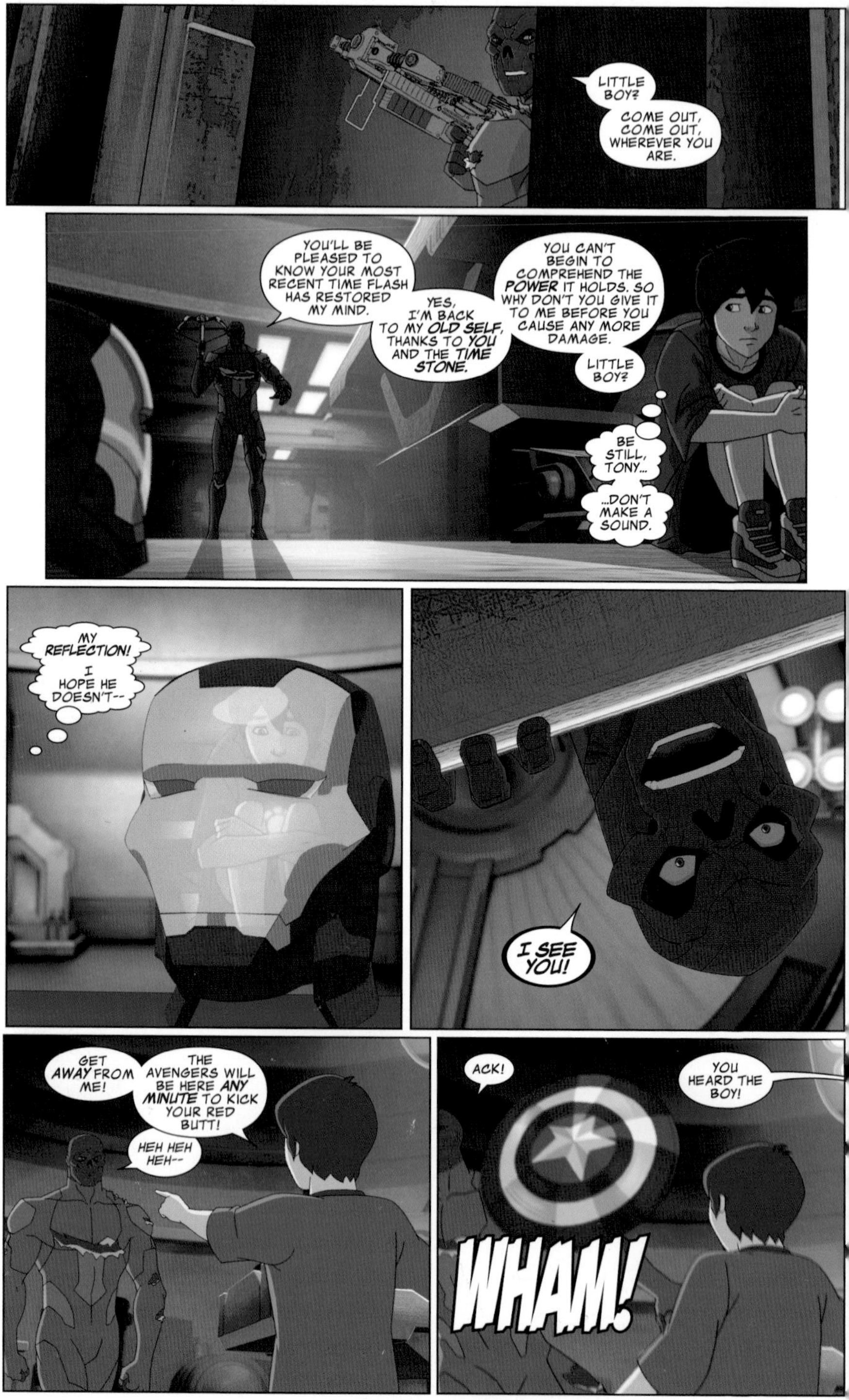
LITTLE BOY?
COME OUT, COME OUT, WHEREVER YOU ARE.
YOU'LL BE PLEASED TO KNOW YOUR MOST RECENT TIME FLASH HAS RESTORED MY MIND.
YES, I'M BACK TO MY OLD SELF, THANKS TO YOU AND THE TIME STONE.
YOU CAN'T BEGIN TO COMPREHEND THE POWER IT HOLDS. SO WHY DON'T YOU GIVE IT TO ME BEFORE YOU CAUSE ANY MORE DAMAGE.
LITTLE BOY?
BE STILL, TONY...
...DON'T MAKE A SOUND.
MY REFLECTION!
I HOPE HE DOESN'T--
I SEE YOU!
GET AWAY FROM ME!
THE AVENGERS WILL BE HERE ANY MINUTE TO KICK YOUR RED BUTT!
HEH HEH HEH--
ACK!
YOU HEARD THE BOY!
WHAM!

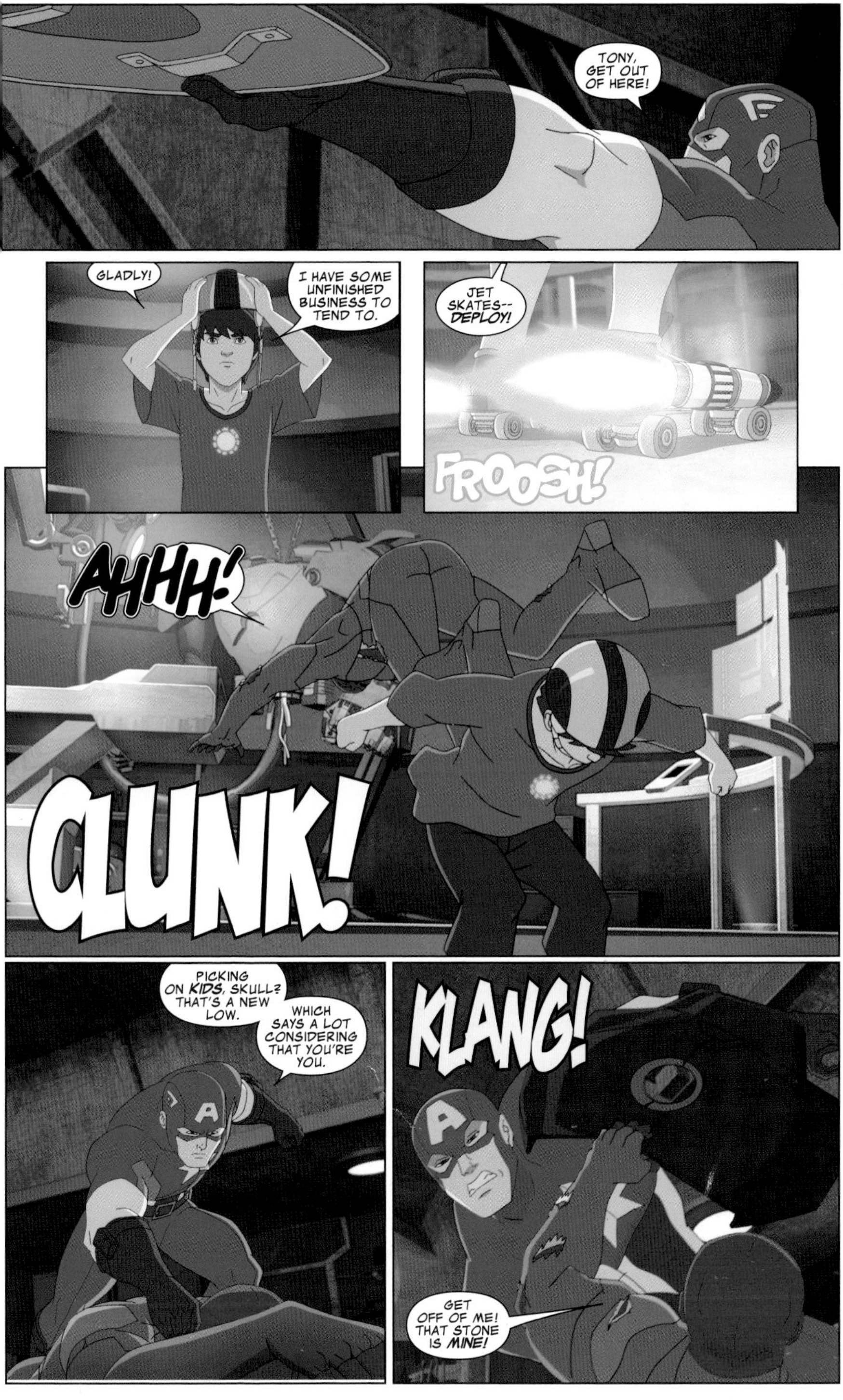
TONY, GET OUT OF HERE!
GLADLY!
I HAVE SOME UNFINISHED BUSINESS TO TEND TO.
JET SKATES-- DEPLOY!
FROOSH!
AHHH!
CLUNK!
PICKING ON KIDS, SKULL? THAT'S A NEW LOW.
WHICH SAYS A LOT CONSIDERING THAT YOU'RE YOU.
KLANG!
GET OFF OF ME! THAT STONE IS MINE!

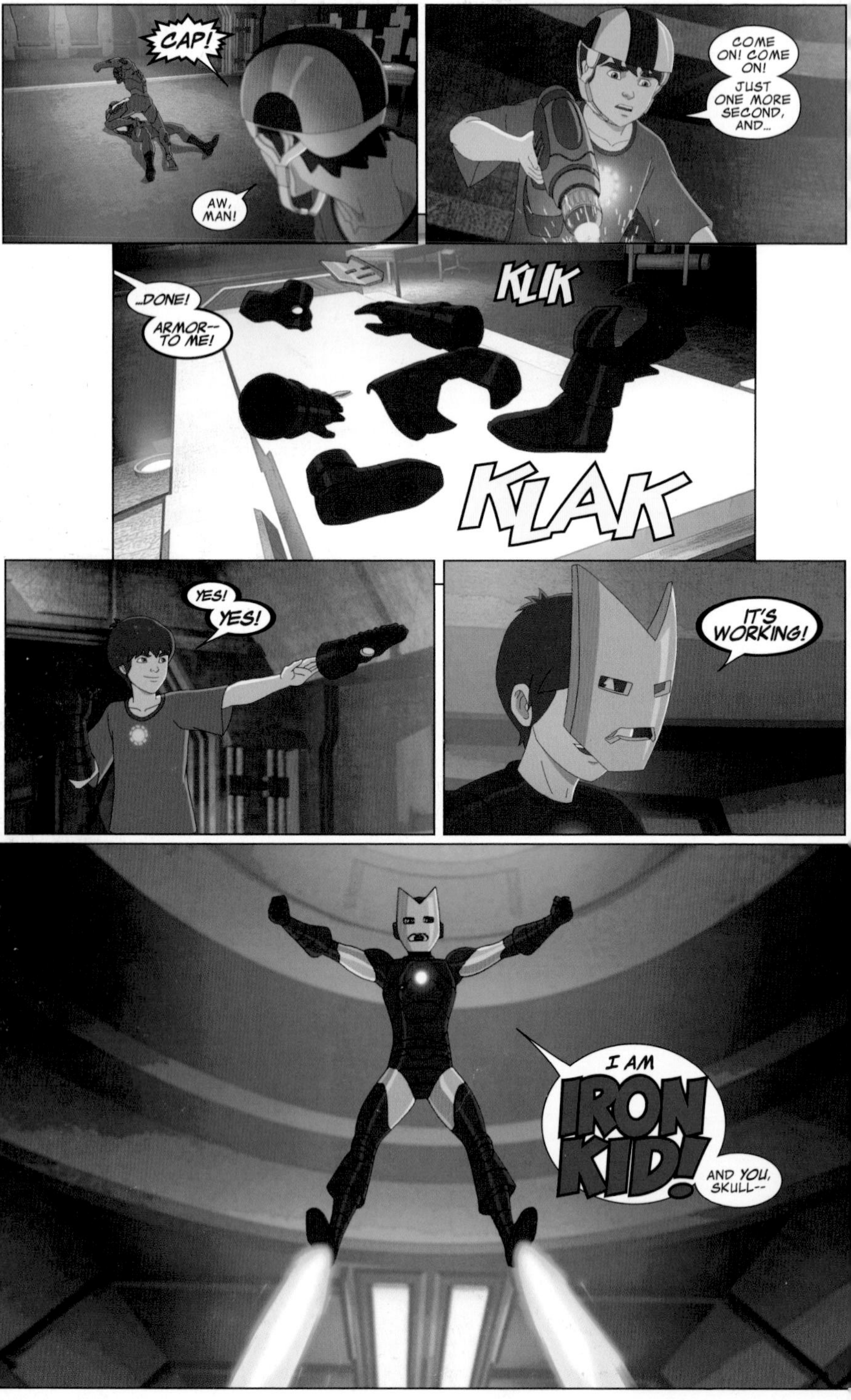
CAP!
AW, MAN!
COME ON! COME ON!
JUST ONE MORE SECOND, AND...
...DONE!
ARMOR-- TO ME!
KLIK
KLAK
YES! YES!
IT'S WORKING!
I AM IRON KID!
AND YOU, SKULL--

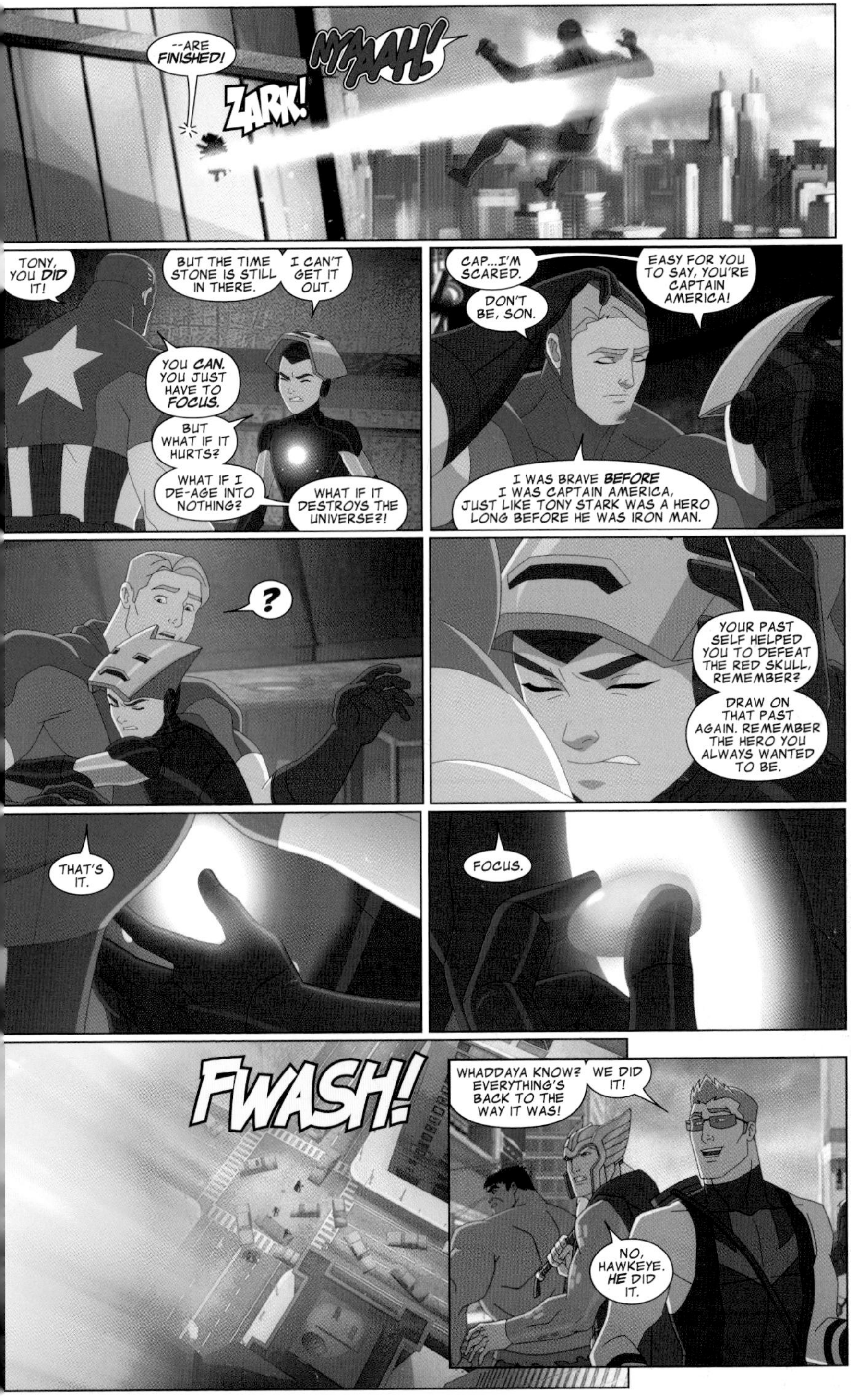
--ARE FINISHED!
NYAAAH!
ZARK!
TONY, YOU DID IT!
BUT THE TIME STONE IS STILL IN THERE.
I CAN'T GET IT OUT.
YOU CAN. YOU JUST HAVE TO FOCUS.
BUT WHAT IF IT HURTS?
WHAT IF I DE-AGE INTO NOTHING?
WHAT IF IT DESTROYS THE UNIVERSE?!
CAP...I'M SCARED.
DON'T BE, SON.
EASY FOR YOU TO SAY, YOU'RE CAPTAIN AMERICA!
I WAS BRAVE BEFORE I WAS CAPTAIN AMERICA, JUST LIKE TONY STARK WAS A HERO LONG BEFORE HE WAS IRON MAN.
?
YOUR PAST SELF HELPED YOU TO DEFEAT THE RED SKULL, REMEMBER?
DRAW ON THAT PAST AGAIN. REMEMBER THE HERO YOU ALWAYS WANTED TO BE.
THAT'S IT.
FOCUS.
FWASH!
WHADDAYA KNOW? EVERYTHING'S BACK TO THE WAY IT WAS!
WE DID IT!
NO, HAWKEYE. HE DID IT.

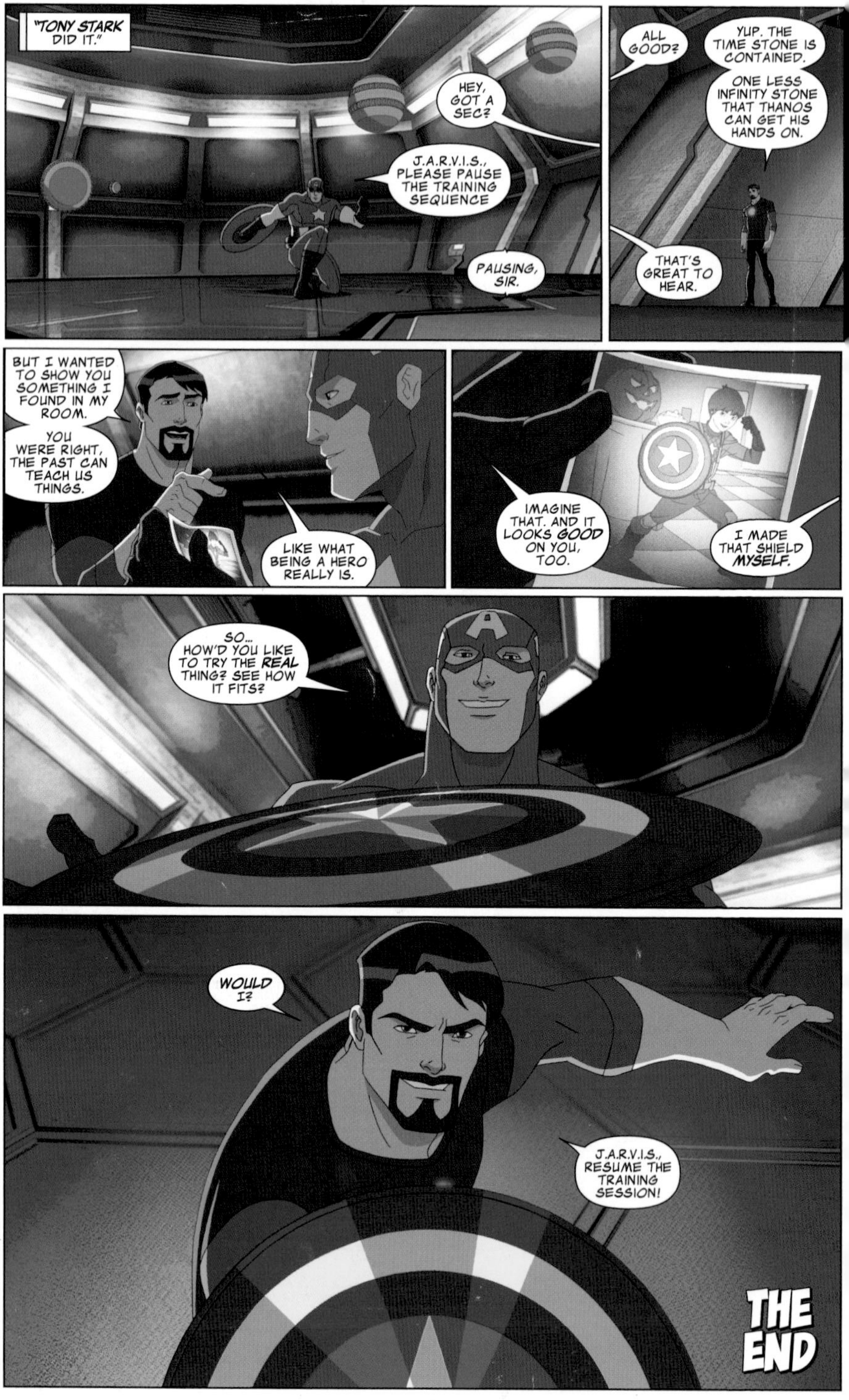

"TONY STARK DID IT."
HEY, GOT A SEC?
J.A.R.V.I.S., PLEASE PAUSE THE TRAINING SEQUENCE
PAUSING, SIR.
ALL GOOD?
YUP. THE TIME STONE IS CONTAINED.
ONE LESS INFINITY STONE THAT THANOS CAN GET HIS HANDS ON.
THAT'S GREAT TO HEAR.
BUT I WANTED TO SHOW YOU SOMETHING I FOUND IN MY ROOM.
YOU WERE RIGHT, THE PAST CAN TEACH US THINGS.
LIKE WHAT BEING A HERO REALLY IS.
IMAGINE THAT. AND IT LOOKS GOOD ON YOU, TOO.
I MADE THAT SHIELD MYSELF.
SO... HOW'D YOU LIKE TO TRY THE REAL THING? SEE HOW IT FITS?
WOULD I?
J.A.R.V.I.S., RESUME THE TRAINING SESSION!
THE END

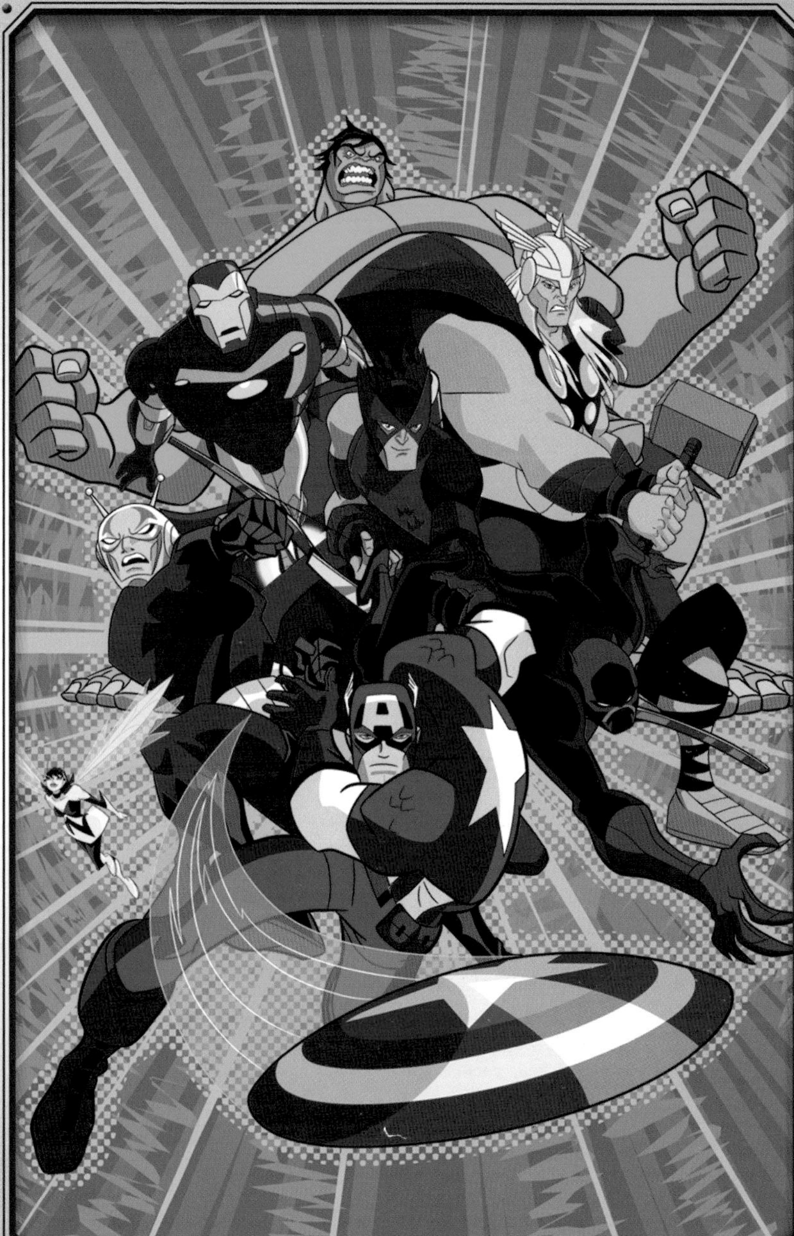

AVENGERS: EARTH'S MIGHTIEST HEROES #1

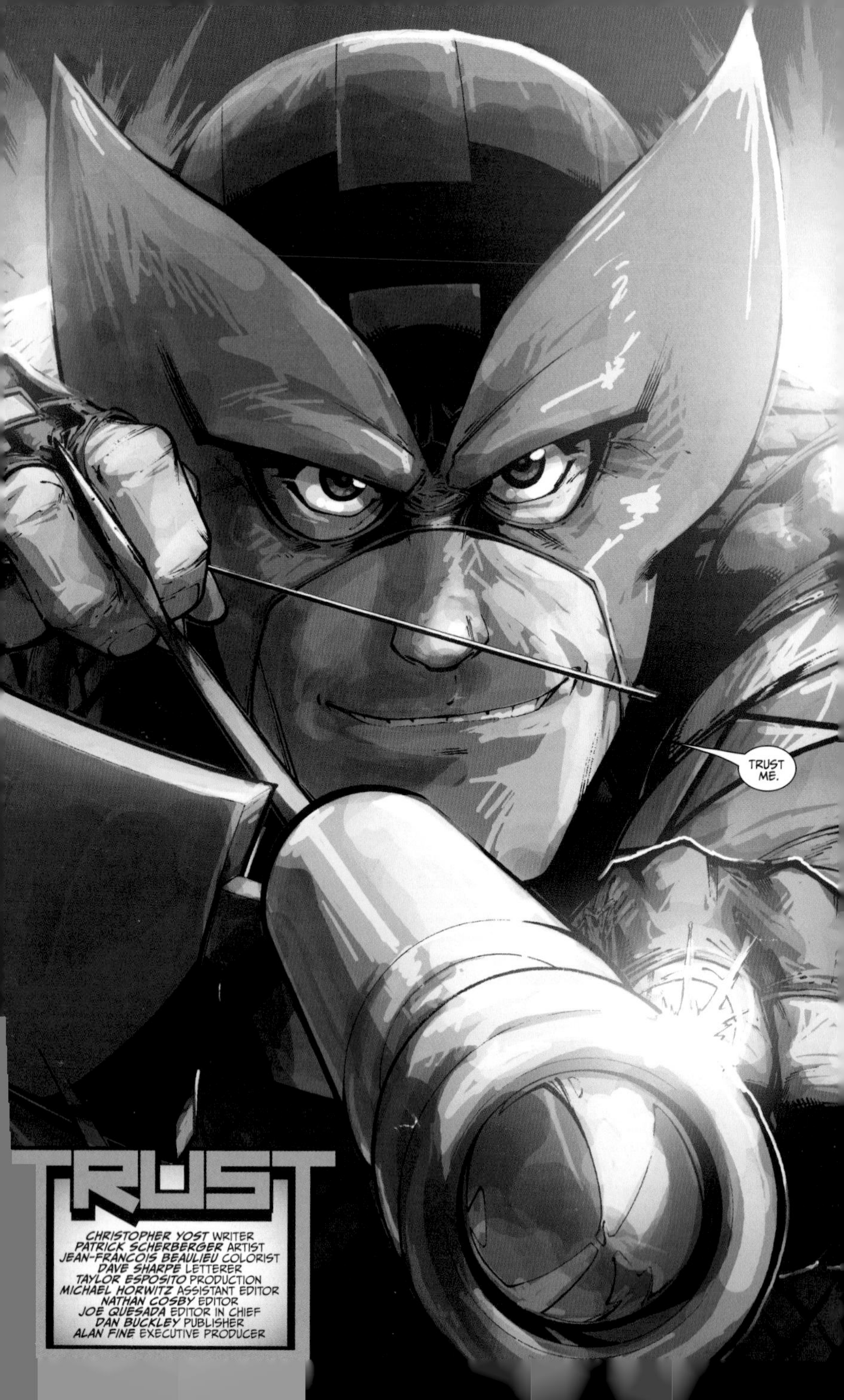

TRUST ME.
TRUST
CHRISTOPHER YOST WRITER
PATRICK SCHERBERGER ARTIST
JEAN-FRANCOIS BEAULIEU COLORIST
DAVE SHARPE LETTERER
TAYLOR ESPOSITO PRODUCTION
MICHAEL HORWITZ ASSISTANT EDITOR
NATHAN COSBY EDITOR
JOE QUESADA EDITOR IN CHIEF
DAN BUCKLEY PUBLISHER
ALAN FINE EXECUTIVE PRODUCER

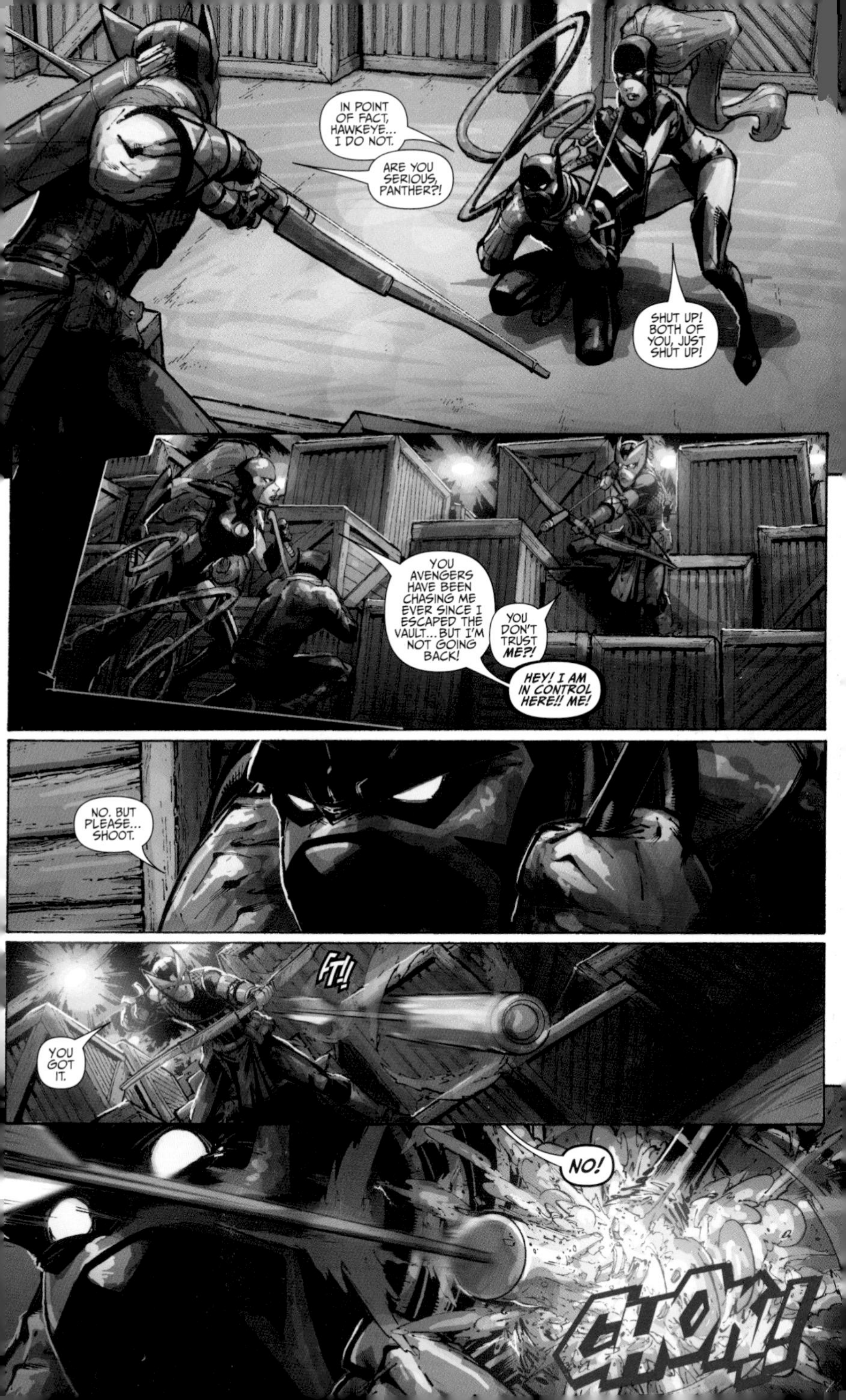

IN POINT OF FACT, HAWKEYE... I DO NOT.
ARE YOU SERIOUS, PANTHER?!
SHUT UP! BOTH OF YOU, JUST SHUT UP!
YOU AVENGERS HAVE BEEN CHASING ME EVER SINCE I ESCAPED THE VAULT...BUT I'M NOT GOING BACK!
YOU DON'T TRUST ME?!
HEY! I AM IN CONTROL HERE!! ME!
NO. BUT PLEASE... SHOOT.
FT!!
YOU GOT IT.
NO!

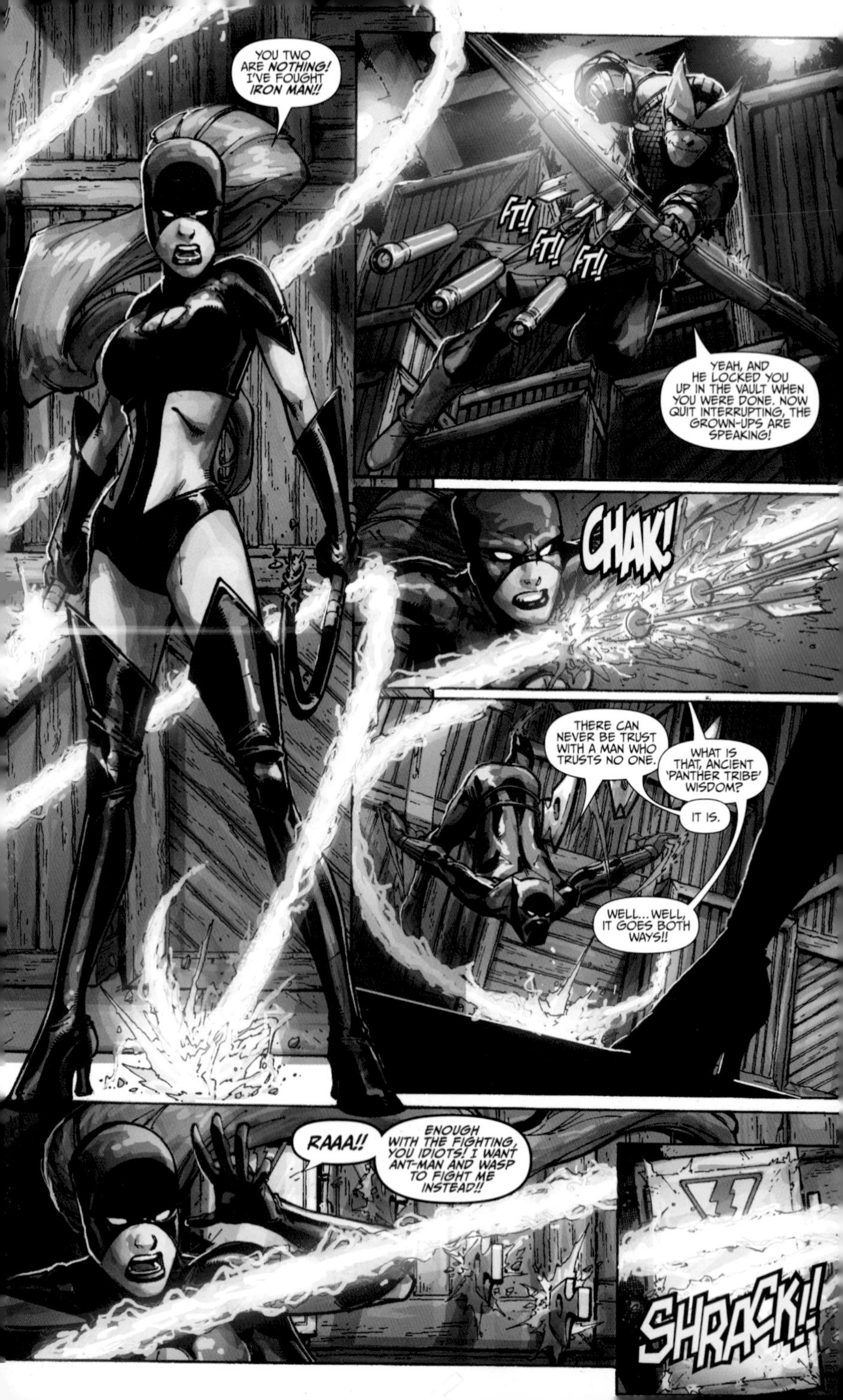
YOU TWO ARE NOTHING! I'VE FOUGHT IRON MAN!!
FT!!
FT!!
FT!!
YEAH, AND HE LOCKED YOU UP IN THE VAULT WHEN YOU WERE DONE. NOW QUIT INTERRUPTING, THE GROWN-UPS ARE SPEAKING!
CHAK!
THERE CAN NEVER BE TRUST WITH A MAN WHO TRUSTS NO ONE.
WHAT IS THAT, ANCIENT 'PANTHER TRIBE' WISDOM?
IT IS.
WELL...WELL, IT GOES BOTH WAYS!!
RAAA!!
ENOUGH WITH THE FIGHTING, YOU IDIOTS! I WANT ANT-MAN AND WASP TO FIGHT ME INSTEAD!!
SHRACK!!

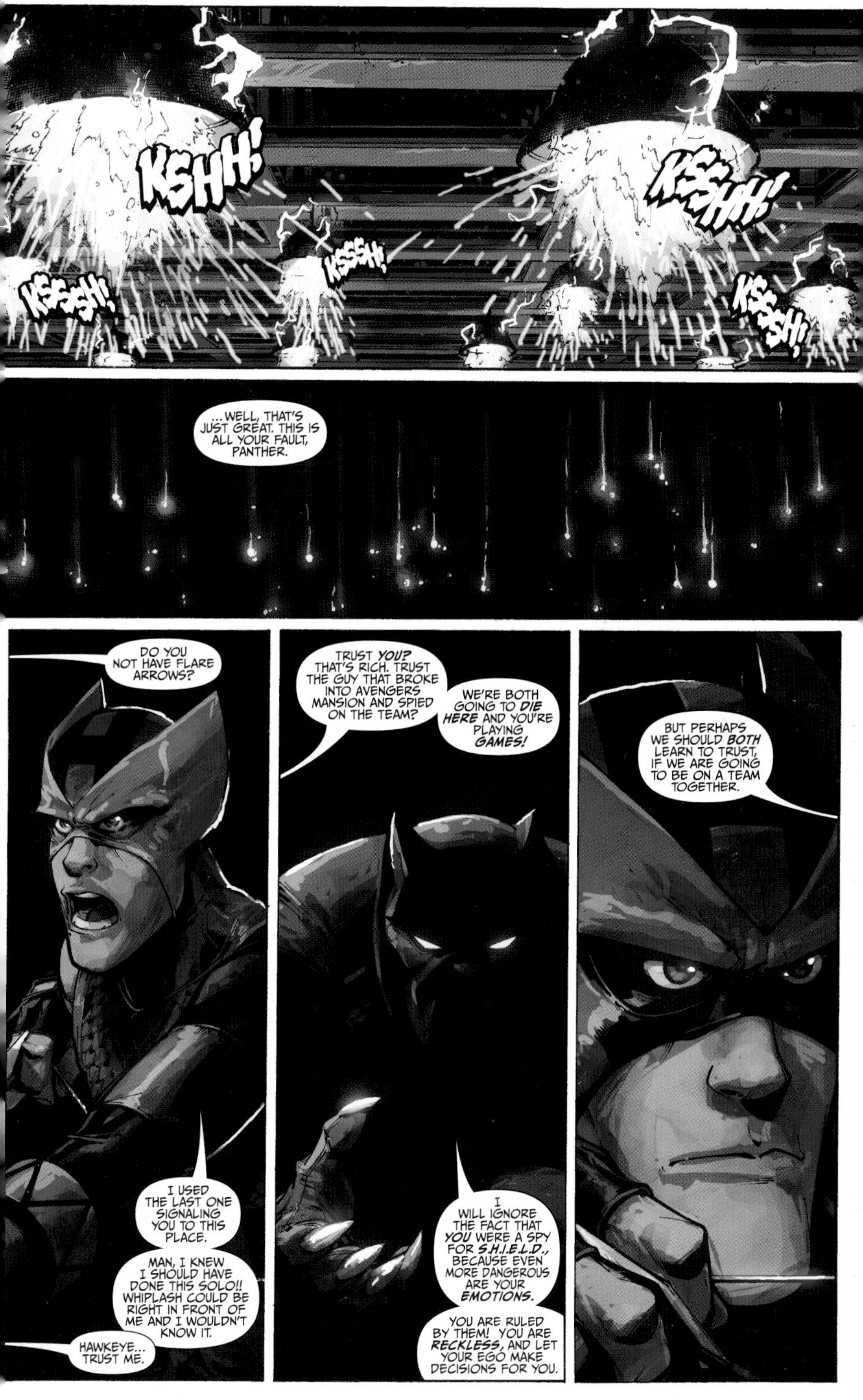
KSHH!
KSSSH!
KSSSH!
KSSHH!
KSSSH!
...WELL, THAT'S JUST GREAT. THIS IS ALL YOUR FAULT, PANTHER.
DO YOU NOT HAVE FLARE ARROWS?
I USED THE LAST ONE SIGNALING YOU TO THIS PLACE.
MAN, I KNEW I SHOULD HAVE DONE THIS SOLO!! WHIPLASH COULD BE RIGHT IN FRONT OF ME AND I WOULDN'T KNOW IT.
HAWKEYE... TRUST ME.
TRUST YOU? THAT'S RICH. TRUST THE GUY THAT BROKE INTO AVENGERS MANSION AND SPIED ON THE TEAM?
WE'RE BOTH GOING TO DIE HERE AND YOU'RE PLAYING GAMES!
I WILL IGNORE THE FACT THAT YOU WERE A SPY FOR S.H.I.E.L.D., BECAUSE EVEN MORE DANGEROUS ARE YOUR EMOTIONS.
YOU ARE RULED BY THEM! YOU ARE RECKLESS, AND LET YOUR EGO MAKE DECISIONS FOR YOU.
BUT PERHAPS WE SHOULD BOTH LEARN TO TRUST, IF WE ARE GOING TO BE ON A TEAM TOGETHER.

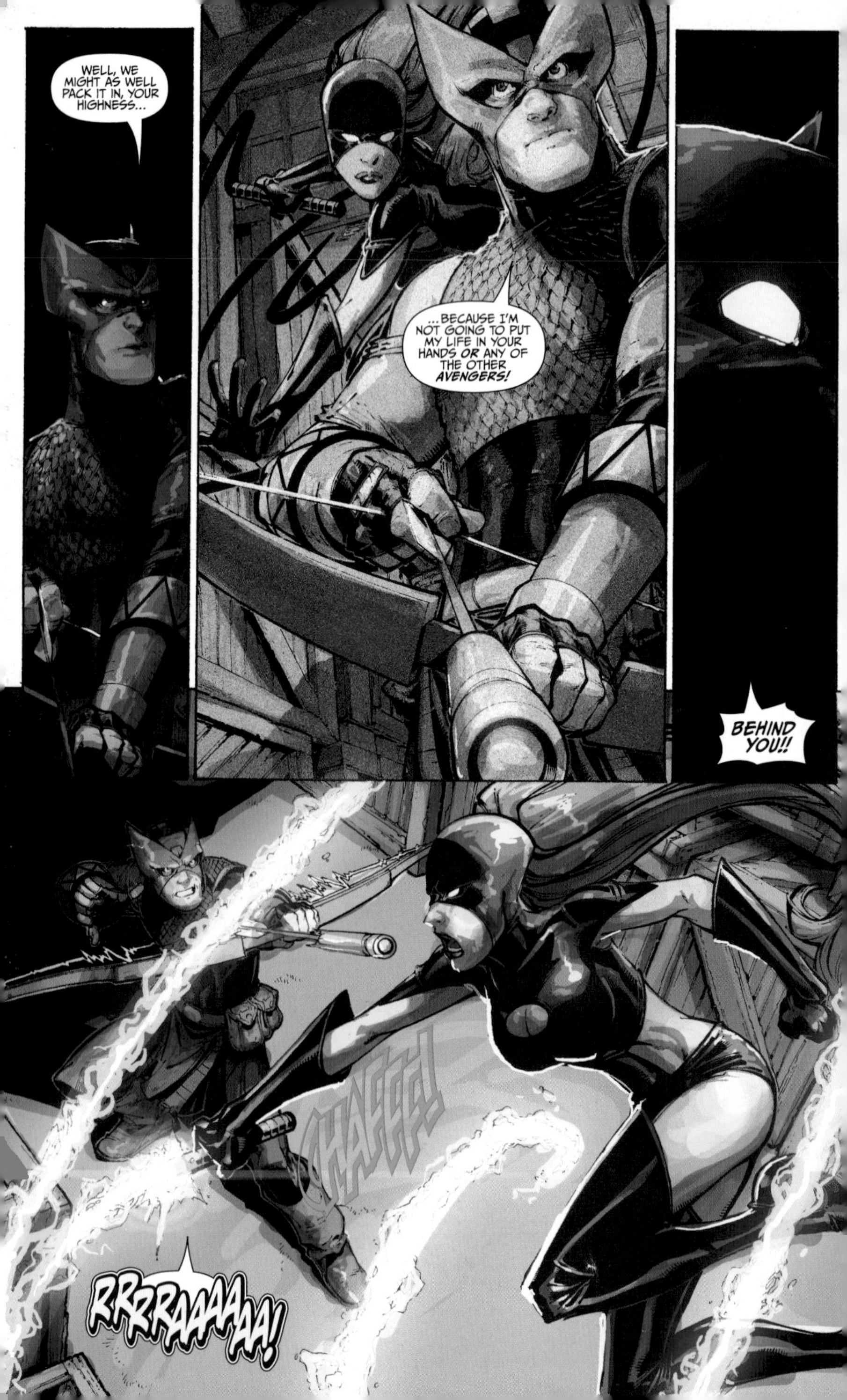
WELL, WE MIGHT AS WELL PACK IT IN, YOUR HIGHNESS...
...BECAUSE I'M NOT GOING TO PUT MY LIFE IN YOUR HANDS OR ANY OF THE OTHER AVENGERS!
BEHIND YOU!!
RRRRAAAAAAA!

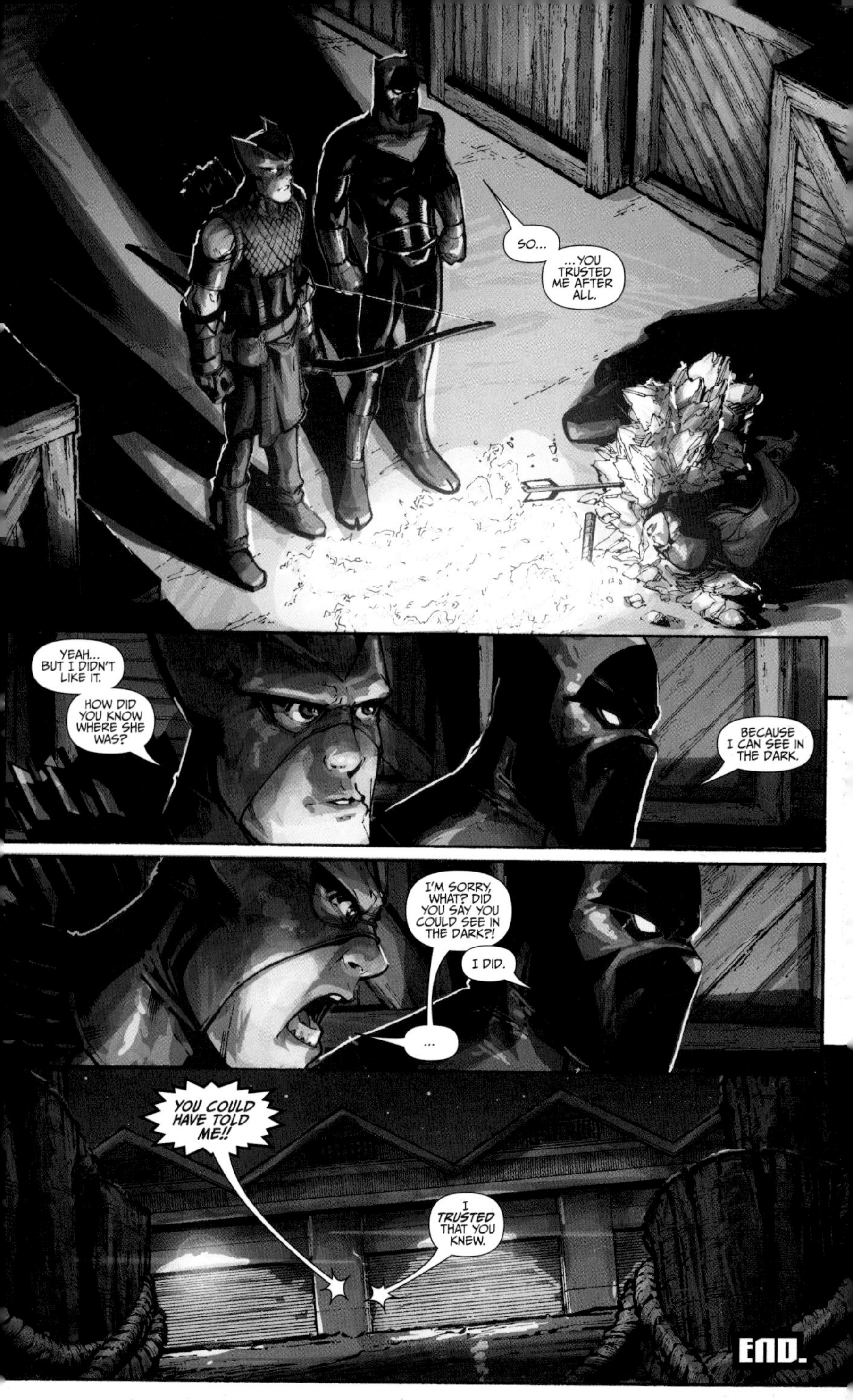
SO...
...YOU TRUSTED ME AFTER ALL.
YEAH... BUT I DIDN'T LIKE IT.
HOW DID YOU KNOW WHERE SHE WAS?
BECAUSE I CAN SEE IN THE DARK.
I'M SORRY, WHAT? DID YOU SAY YOU COULD SEE IN THE DARK?!
I DID.
...
YOU COULD HAVE TOLD ME!!
I TRUSTED THAT YOU KNEW.
END.

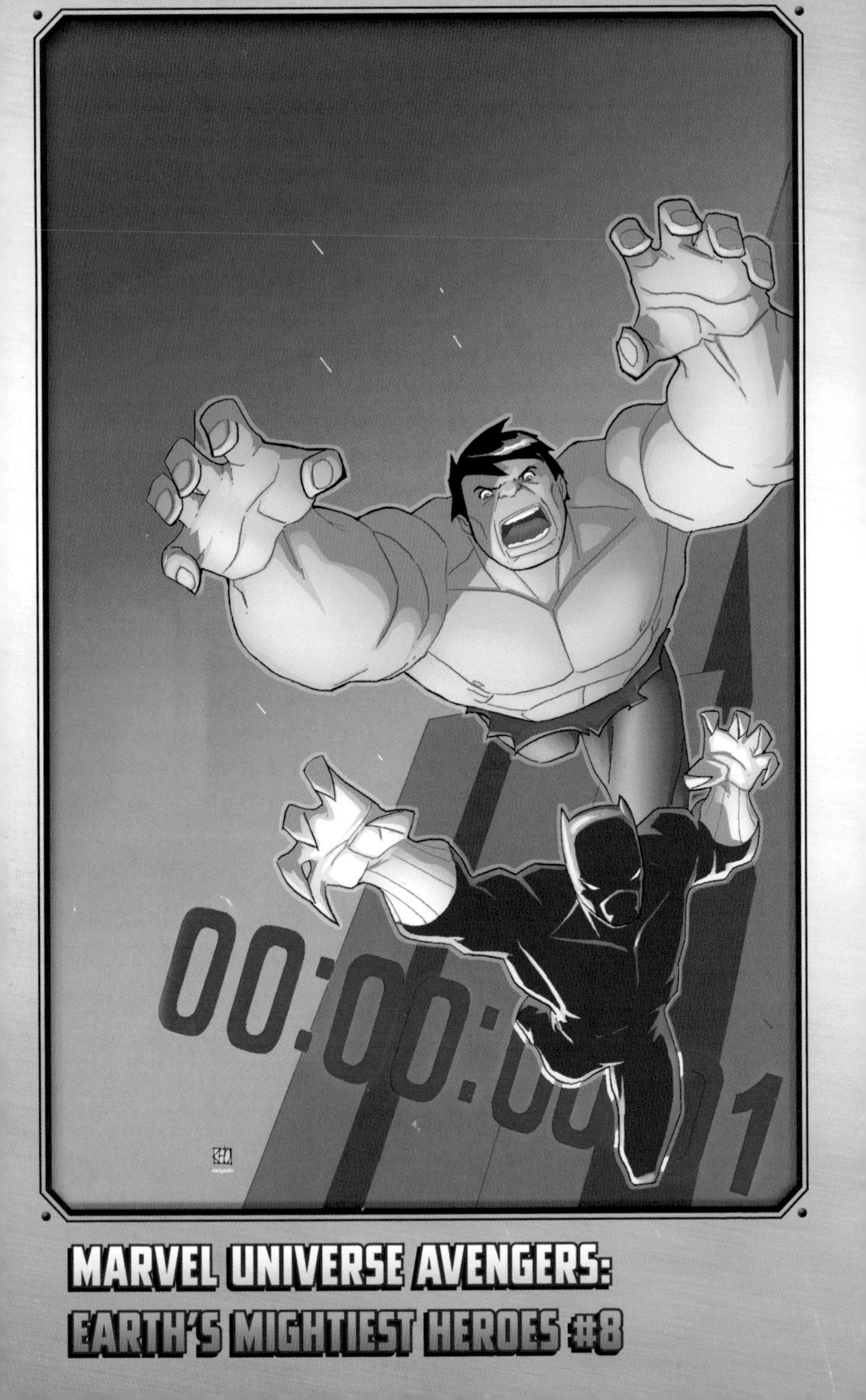

MARVEL UNIVERSE AVENGERS: EARTH'S MIGHTIEST HEROES #8

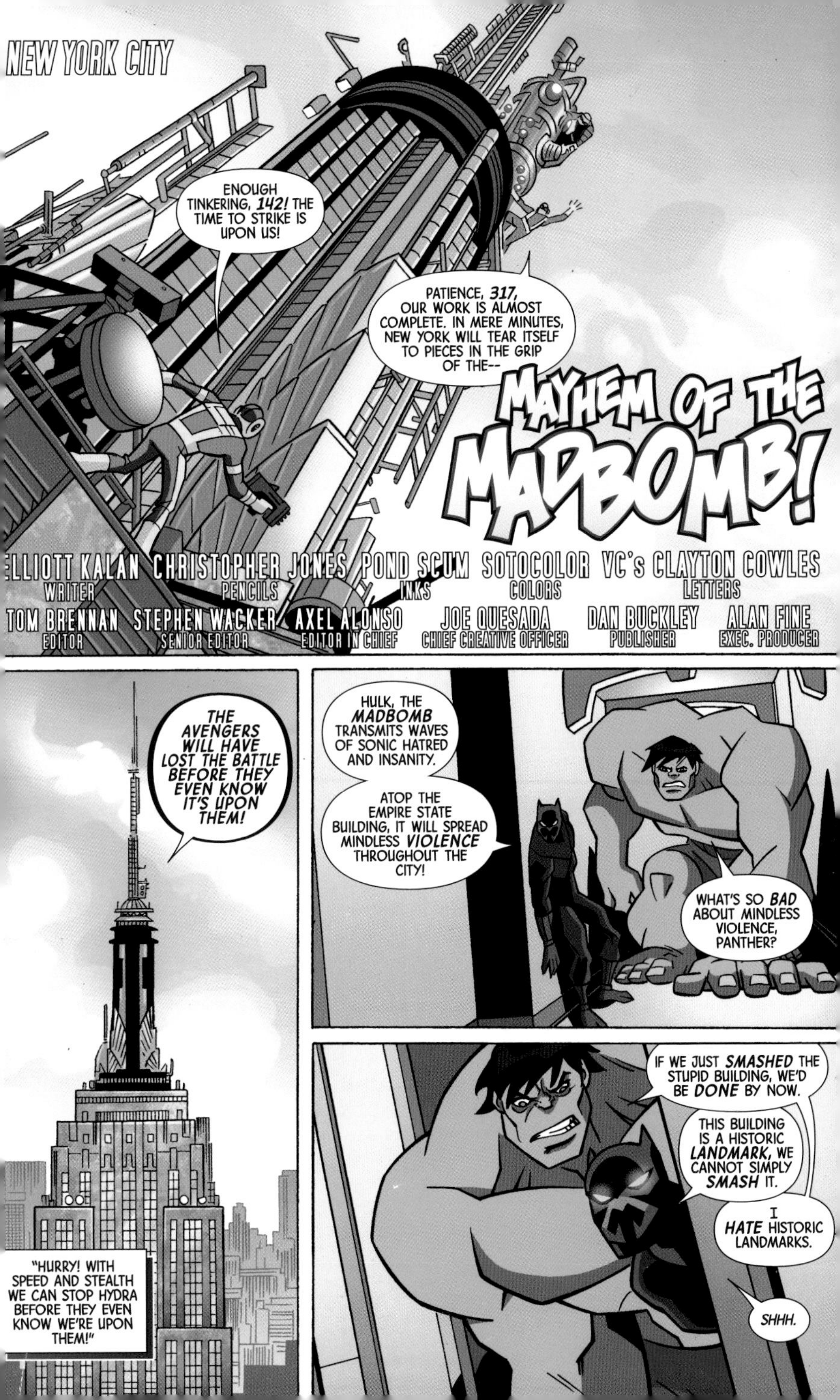
NEW YORK CITY
ENOUGH TINKERING, 142! THE TIME TO STRIKE IS UPON US!
PATIENCE, 317, OUR WORK IS ALMOST COMPLETE. IN MERE MINUTES, NEW YORK WILL TEAR ITSELF TO PIECES IN THE GRIP OF THE--
MAYHEM OF THE MADBOMB!
ELLIOTT KALAN WRITER
CHRISTOPHER JONES PENCILS
POND SCUM INKS
SOTOCOLOR COLORS
VC's CLAYTON COWLES LETTERS
TOM BRENNAN EDITOR
STEPHEN WACKER SENIOR EDITOR
AXEL ALONSO EDITOR IN CHIEF
JOE QUESADA CHIEF CREATIVE OFFICER
DAN BUCKLEY PUBLISHER
ALAN FINE EXEC. PRODUCER
THE AVENGERS WILL HAVE LOST THE BATTLE BEFORE THEY EVEN KNOW IT'S UPON THEM!
"HURRY! WITH SPEED AND STEALTH WE CAN STOP HYDRA BEFORE THEY EVEN KNOW WE'RE UPON THEM!"
HULK, THE MADBOMB TRANSMITS WAVES OF SONIC HATRED AND INSANITY.
ATOP THE EMPIRE STATE BUILDING, IT WILL SPREAD MINDLESS VIOLENCE THROUGHOUT THE CITY!
WHAT'S SO BAD ABOUT MINDLESS VIOLENCE, PANTHER?
IF WE JUST SMASHED THE STUPID BUILDING, WE'D BE DONE BY NOW.
THIS BUILDING IS A HISTORIC LANDMARK, WE CANNOT SIMPLY SMASH IT.
I HATE HISTORIC LANDMARKS.
SHHH.

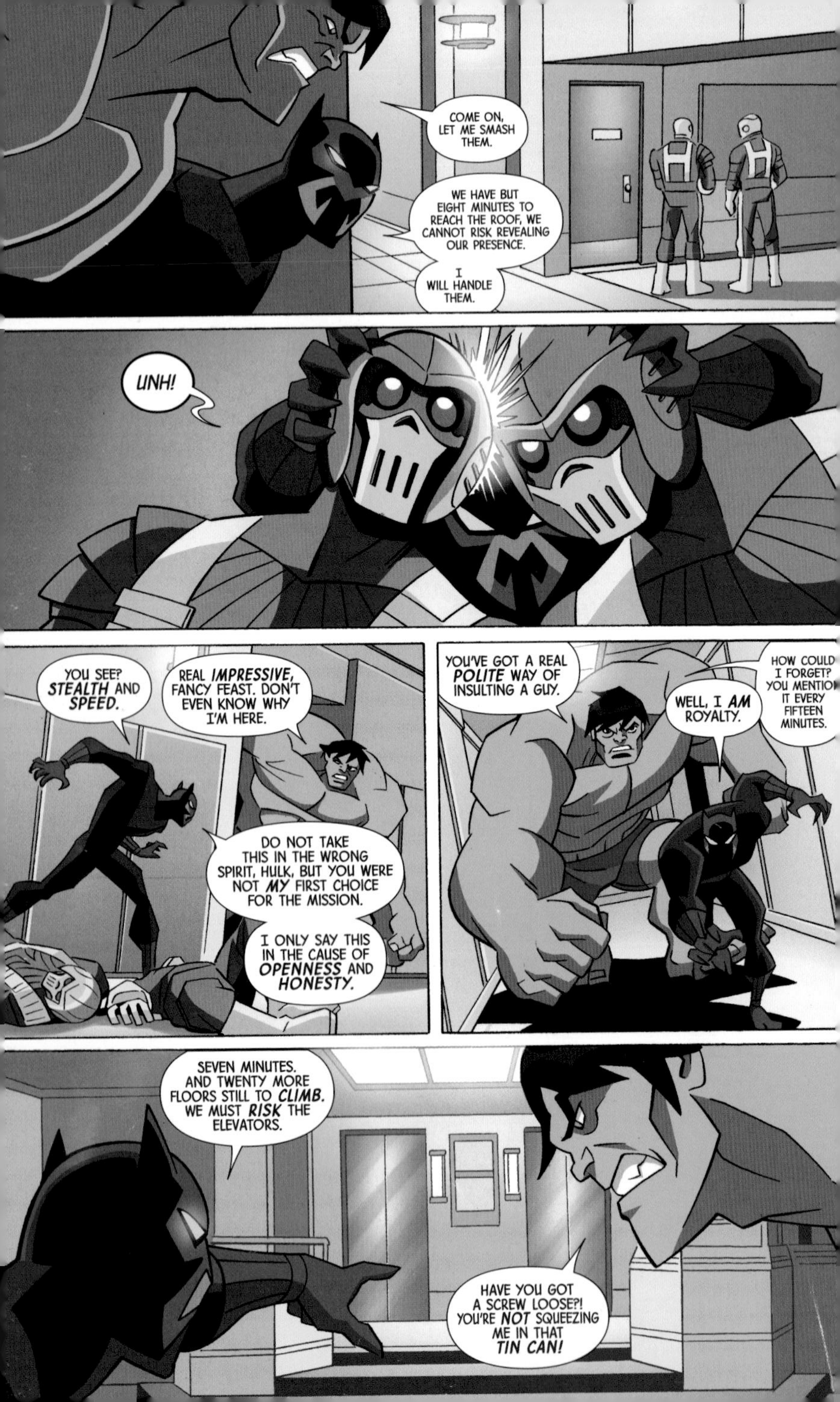

COME ON, LET ME SMASH THEM.
WE HAVE BUT EIGHT MINUTES TO REACH THE ROOF, WE CANNOT RISK REVEALING OUR PRESENCE.
I WILL HANDLE THEM.
UNH!
YOU SEE? STEALTH AND SPEED.
REAL IMPRESSIVE, FANCY FEAST. DON'T EVEN KNOW WHY I'M HERE.
DO NOT TAKE THIS IN THE WRONG SPIRIT, HULK, BUT YOU WERE NOT MY FIRST CHOICE FOR THE MISSION.
I ONLY SAY THIS IN THE CAUSE OF OPENNESS AND HONESTY.
YOU'VE GOT A REAL POLITE WAY OF INSULTING A GUY.
WELL, I AM ROYALTY.
HOW COULD I FORGET? YOU MENTIO IT EVERY FIFTEEN MINUTES.
SEVEN MINUTES. AND TWENTY MORE FLOORS STILL TO CLIMB. WE MUST RISK THE ELEVATORS.
HAVE YOU GOT A SCREW LOOSE?! YOU'RE NOT SQUEEZING ME IN THAT TIN CAN!

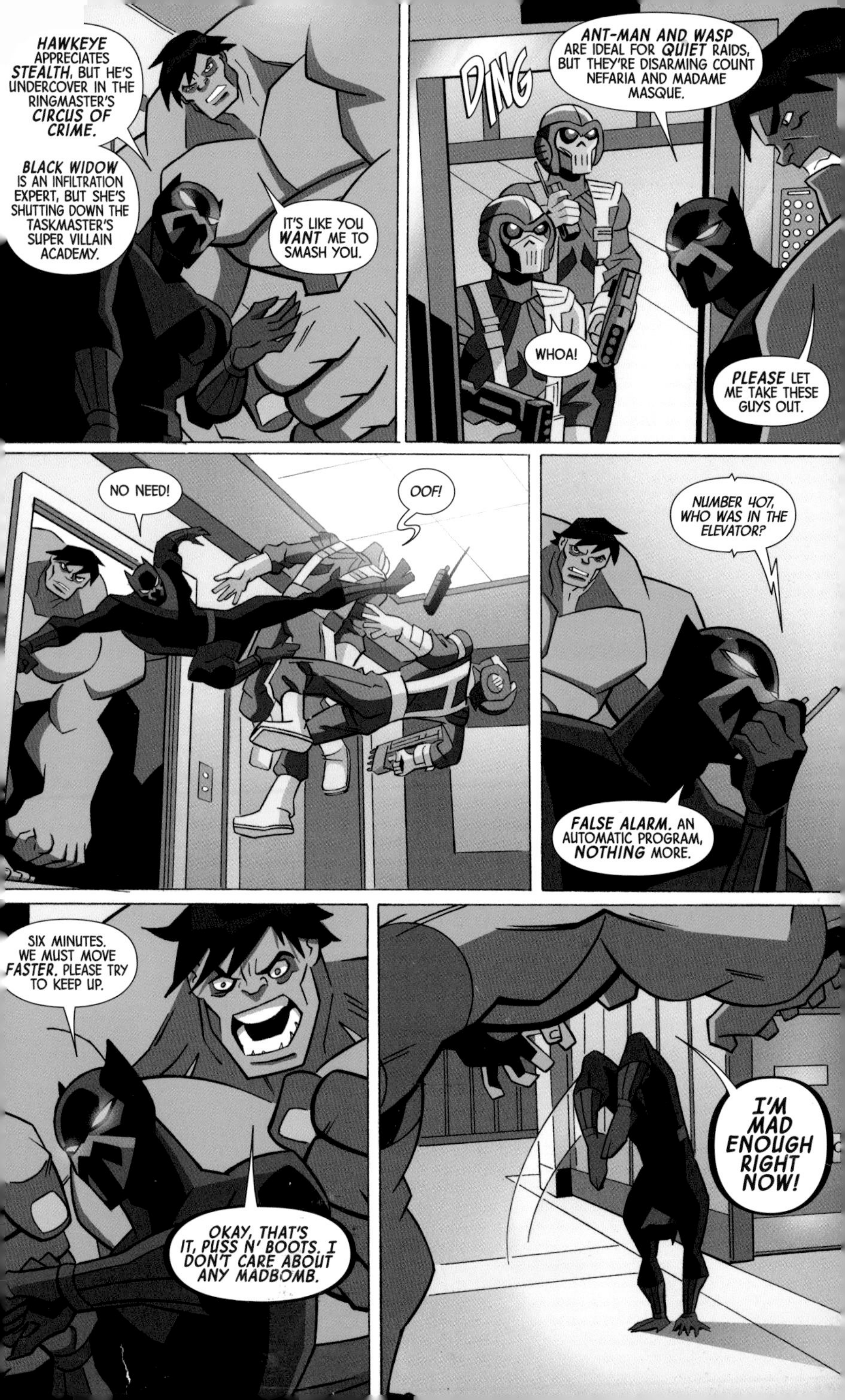
HAWKEYE APPRECIATES STEALTH, BUT HE'S UNDERCOVER IN THE RINGMASTER'S CIRCUS OF CRIME.
BLACK WIDOW IS AN INFILTRATION EXPERT, BUT SHE'S SHUTTING DOWN THE TASKMASTER'S SUPER VILLAIN ACADEMY.
IT'S LIKE YOU WANT ME TO SMASH YOU.
DING
ANT-MAN AND WASP ARE IDEAL FOR QUIET RAIDS, BUT THEY'RE DISARMING COUNT NEFARIA AND MADAME MASQUE.
WHOA!
PLEASE LET ME TAKE THESE GUYS OUT.
NO NEED!
OOF!
NUMBER 407, WHO WAS IN THE ELEVATOR?
FALSE ALARM. AN AUTOMATIC PROGRAM, NOTHING MORE.
SIX MINUTES. WE MUST MOVE FASTER. PLEASE TRY TO KEEP UP.
OKAY, THAT'S IT, PUSS N' BOOTS. I DON'T CARE ABOUT ANY MADBOMB.
I'M MAD ENOUGH RIGHT NOW!

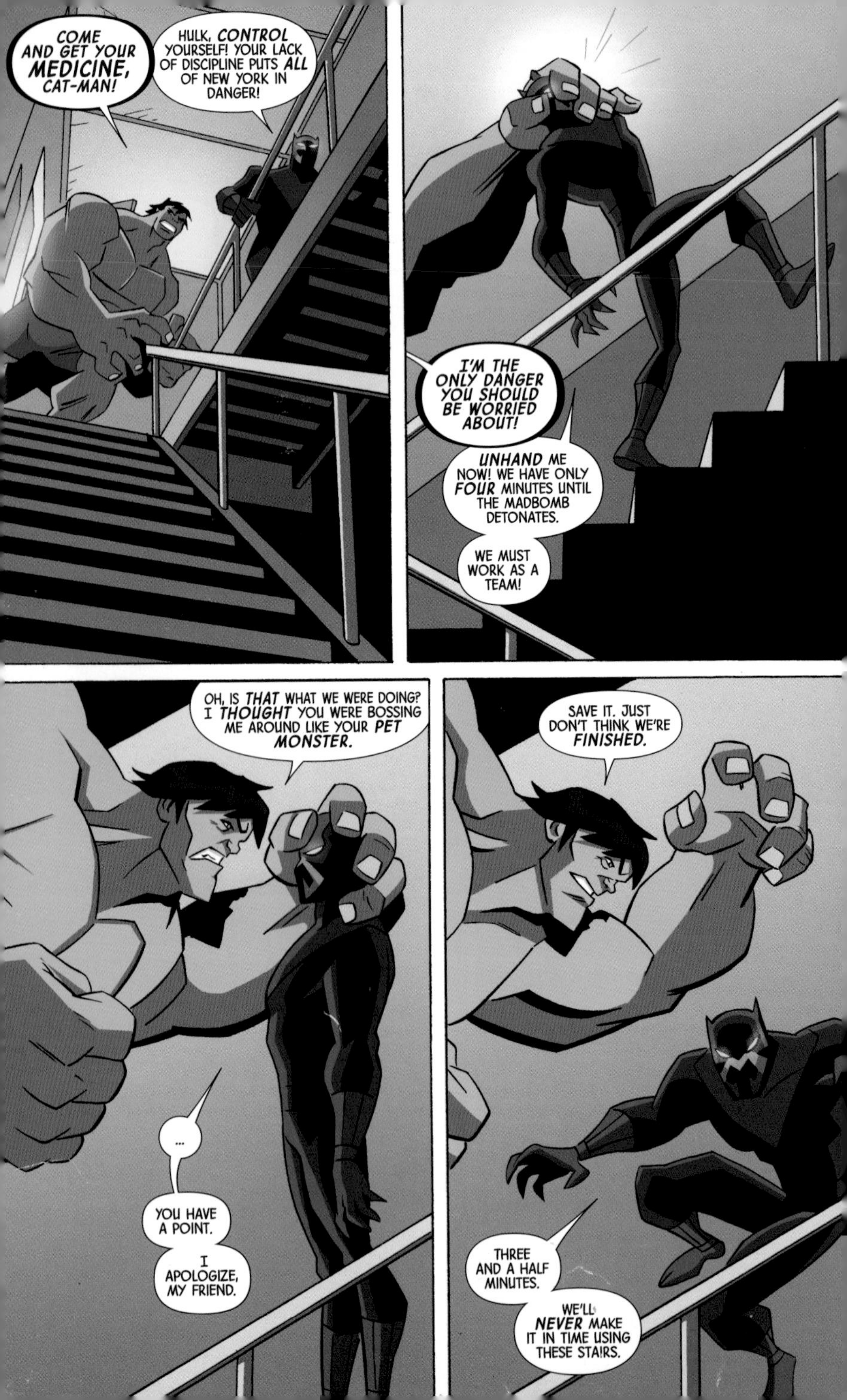
COME AND GET YOUR MEDICINE, CAT-MAN!
HULK, CONTROL YOURSELF! YOUR LACK OF DISCIPLINE PUTS ALL OF NEW YORK IN DANGER!
I'M THE ONLY DANGER YOU SHOULD BE WORRIED ABOUT!
UNHAND ME NOW! WE HAVE ONLY FOUR MINUTES UNTIL THE MADBOMB DETONATES.
WE MUST WORK AS A TEAM!
OH, IS THAT WHAT WE WERE DOING? I THOUGHT YOU WERE BOSSING ME AROUND LIKE YOUR PET MONSTER.
...
YOU HAVE A POINT.
I APOLOGIZE, MY FRIEND.
SAVE IT. JUST DON'T THINK WE'RE FINISHED.
THREE AND A HALF MINUTES.
WE'LL NEVER MAKE IT IN TIME USING THESE STAIRS.

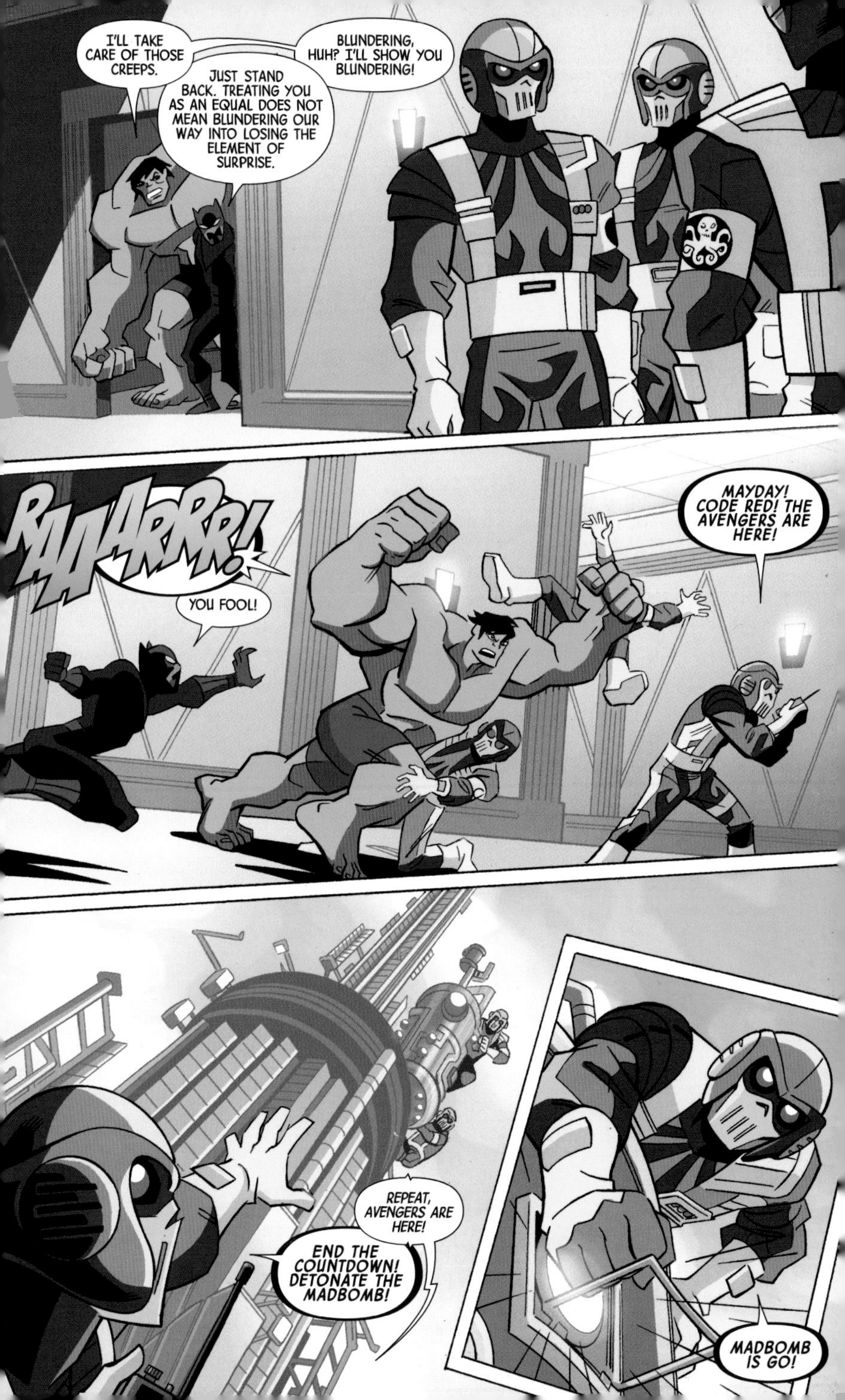

I'LL TAKE CARE OF THOSE CREEPS.
JUST STAND BACK. TREATING YOU AS AN EQUAL DOES NOT MEAN BLUNDERING OUR WAY INTO LOSING THE ELEMENT OF SURPRISE.
BLUNDERING, HUH? I'LL SHOW YOU BLUNDERING!
RAAARRR!
YOU FOOL!
MAYDAY! CODE RED! THE AVENGERS ARE HERE!
REPEAT, AVENGERS ARE HERE!
END THE COUNTDOWN! DETONATE THE MADBOMB!
MADBOMB IS GO!

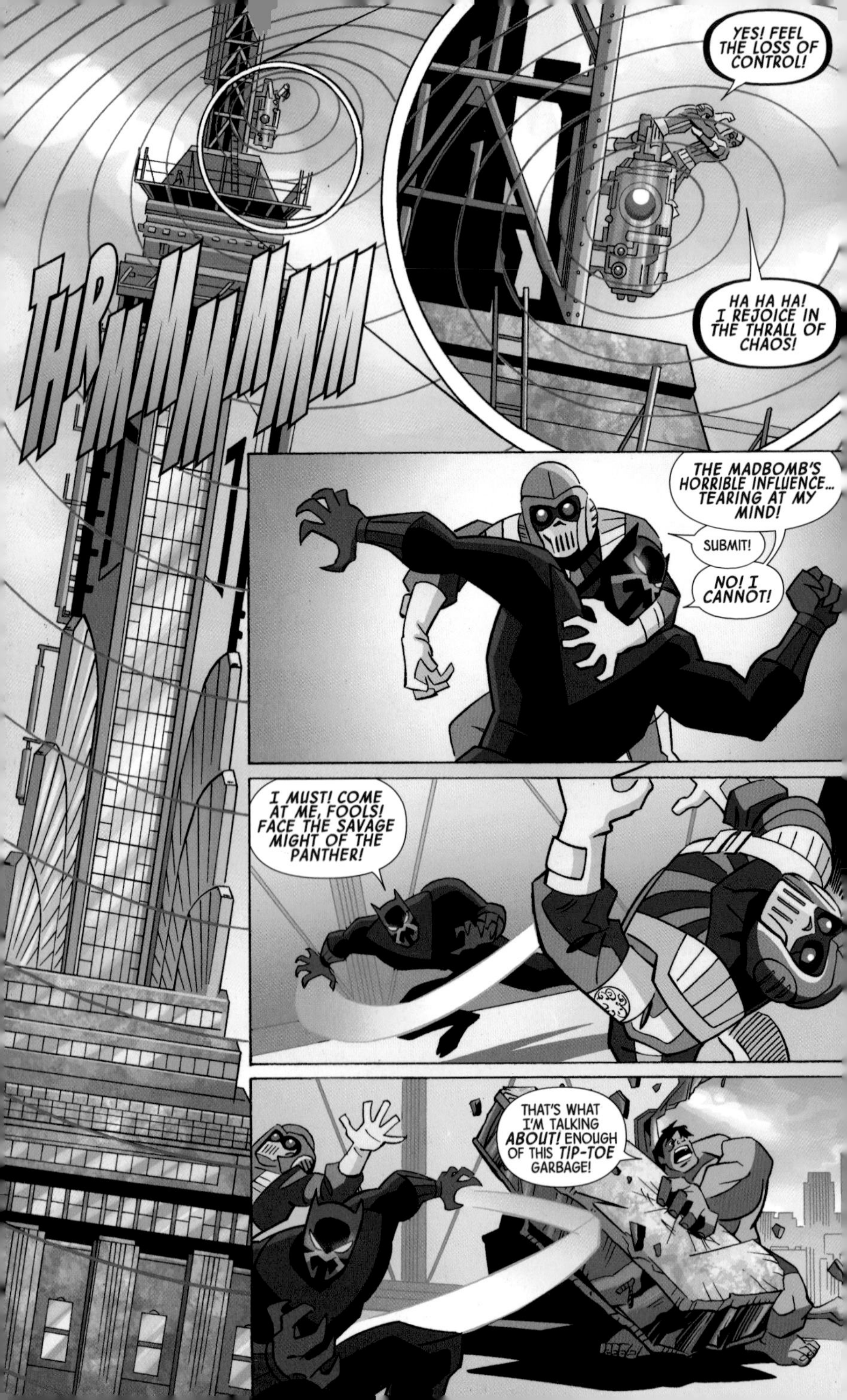
THRMMMMMMMM
YES! FEEL THE LOSS OF CONTROL!
HA HA HA! I REJOICE IN THE THRALL OF CHAOS!
THE MADBOMB'S HORRIBLE INFLUENCE... TEARING AT MY MIND!
SUBMIT!
NO! I CANNOT!
I MUST! COME AT ME, FOOLS! FACE THE SAVAGE MIGHT OF THE PANTHER!
THAT'S WHAT I'M TALKING ABOUT! ENOUGH OF THIS TIP-TOE GARBAGE!

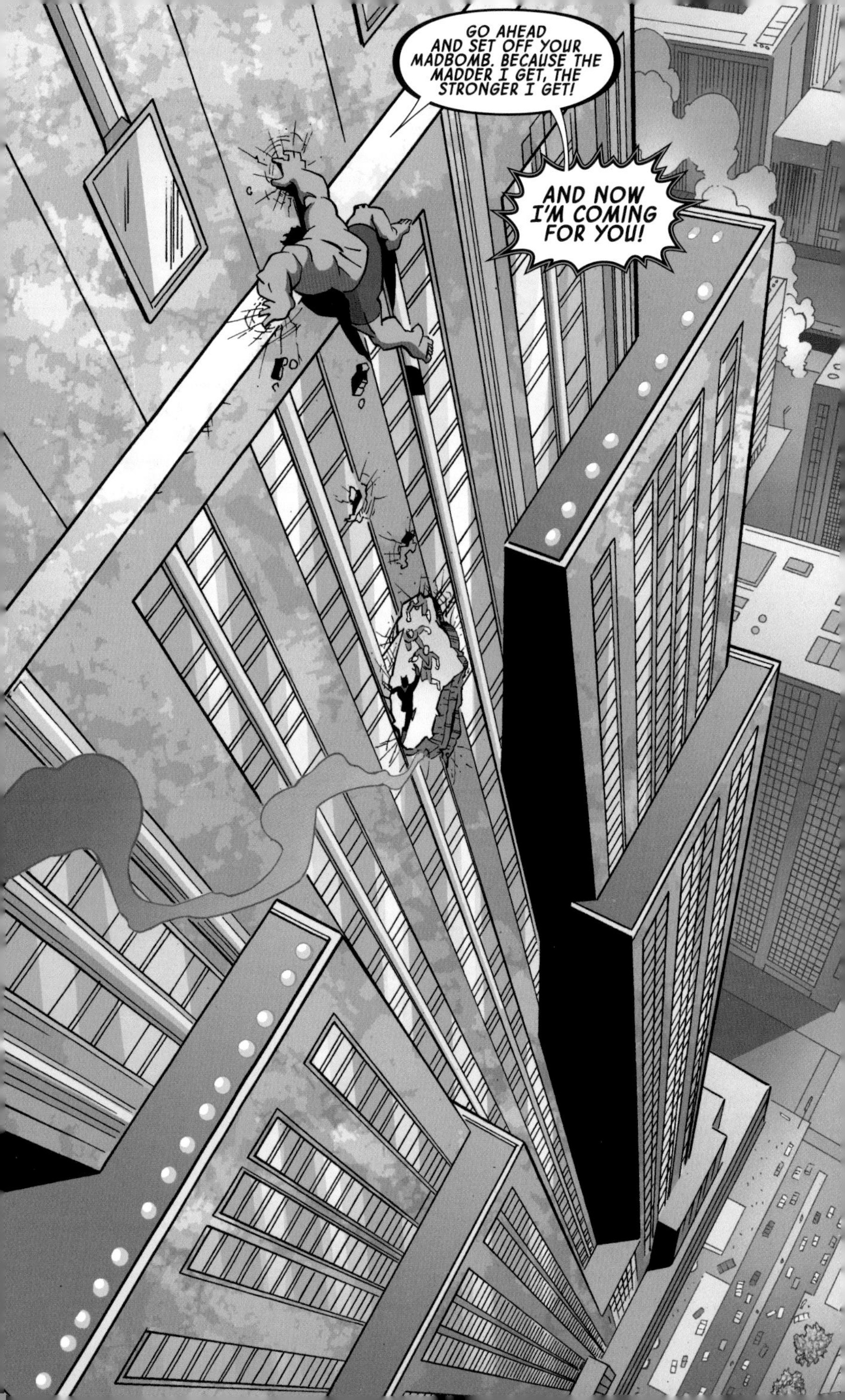
GO AHEAD AND SET OFF YOUR MADBOMB. BECAUSE THE MADDER I GET, THE STRONGER I GET!
AND NOW I'M COMING FOR YOU!

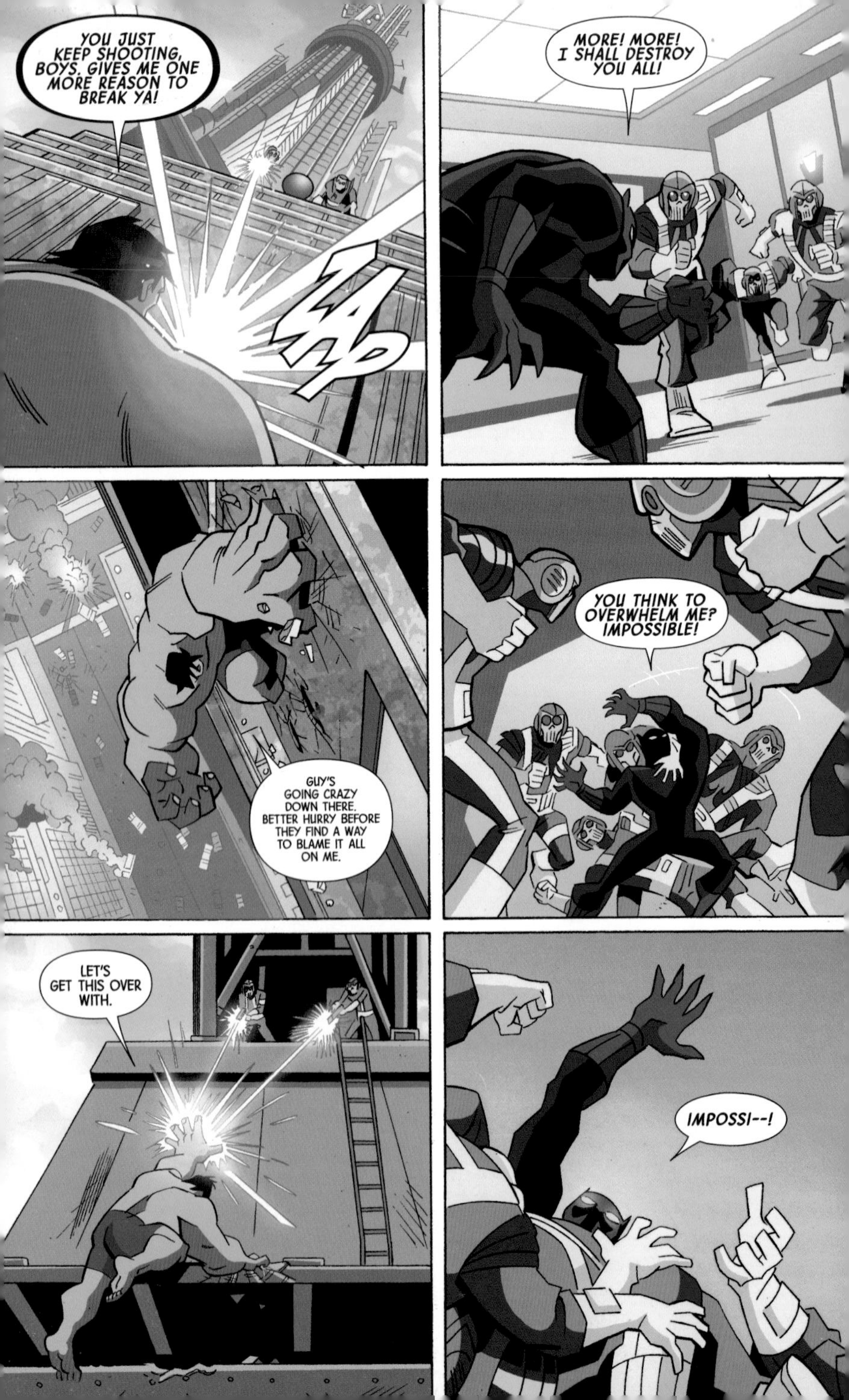
YOU JUST KEEP SHOOTING, BOYS. GIVES ME ONE MORE REASON TO BREAK YA!
ZAP
MORE! MORE! I SHALL DESTROY YOU ALL!
GUY'S GOING CRAZY DOWN THERE. BETTER HURRY BEFORE THEY FIND A WAY TO BLAME IT ALL ON ME.
YOU THINK TO OVERWHELM ME? IMPOSSIBLE!
LET'S GET THIS OVER WITH.
IMPOSSI--!

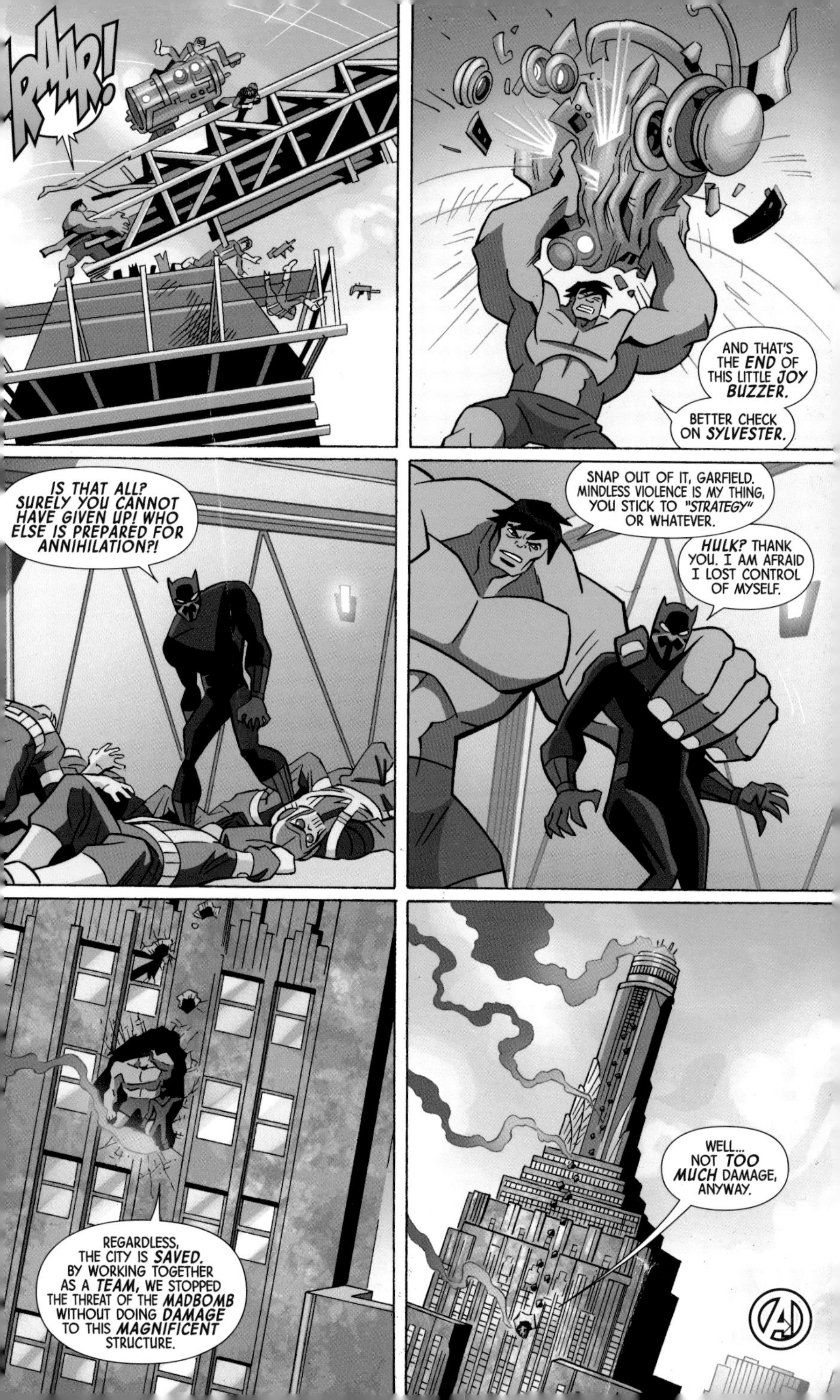
RAAR!
AND THAT'S THE END OF THIS LITTLE JOY BUZZER.
BETTER CHECK ON SYLVESTER.
IS THAT ALL? SURELY YOU CANNOT HAVE GIVEN UP! WHO ELSE IS PREPARED FOR ANNIHILATION?!
SNAP OUT OF IT, GARFIELD. MINDLESS VIOLENCE IS MY THING, YOU STICK TO "STRATEGY" OR WHATEVER.
HULK? THANK YOU. I AM AFRAID I LOST CONTROL OF MYSELF.
REGARDLESS, THE CITY IS SAVED. BY WORKING TOGETHER AS A TEAM, WE STOPPED THE THREAT OF THE MADBOMB WITHOUT DOING DAMAGE TO THIS MAGNIFICENT STRUCTURE.
WELL... NOT TOO MUCH DAMAGE, ANYWAY.

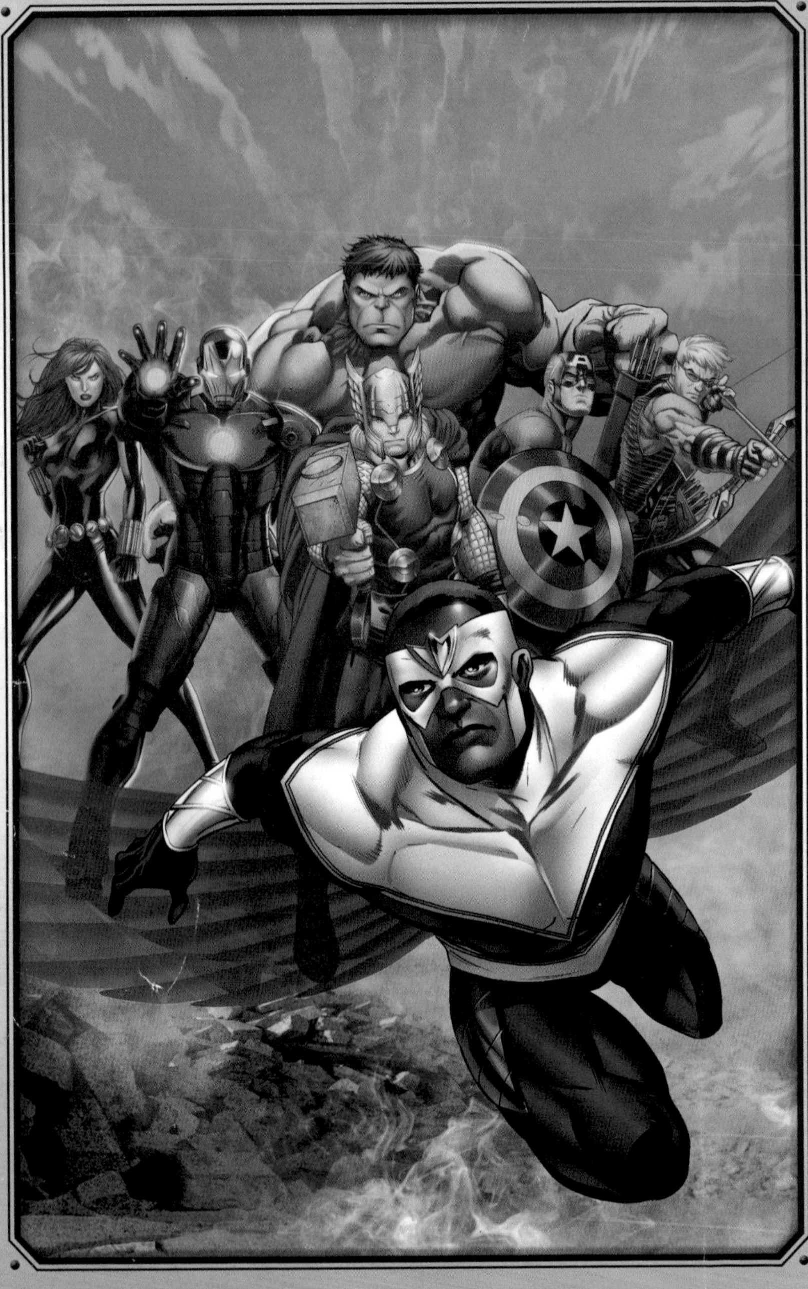

MARVEL UNIVERSE
AVENGERS ASSEMBLE #3

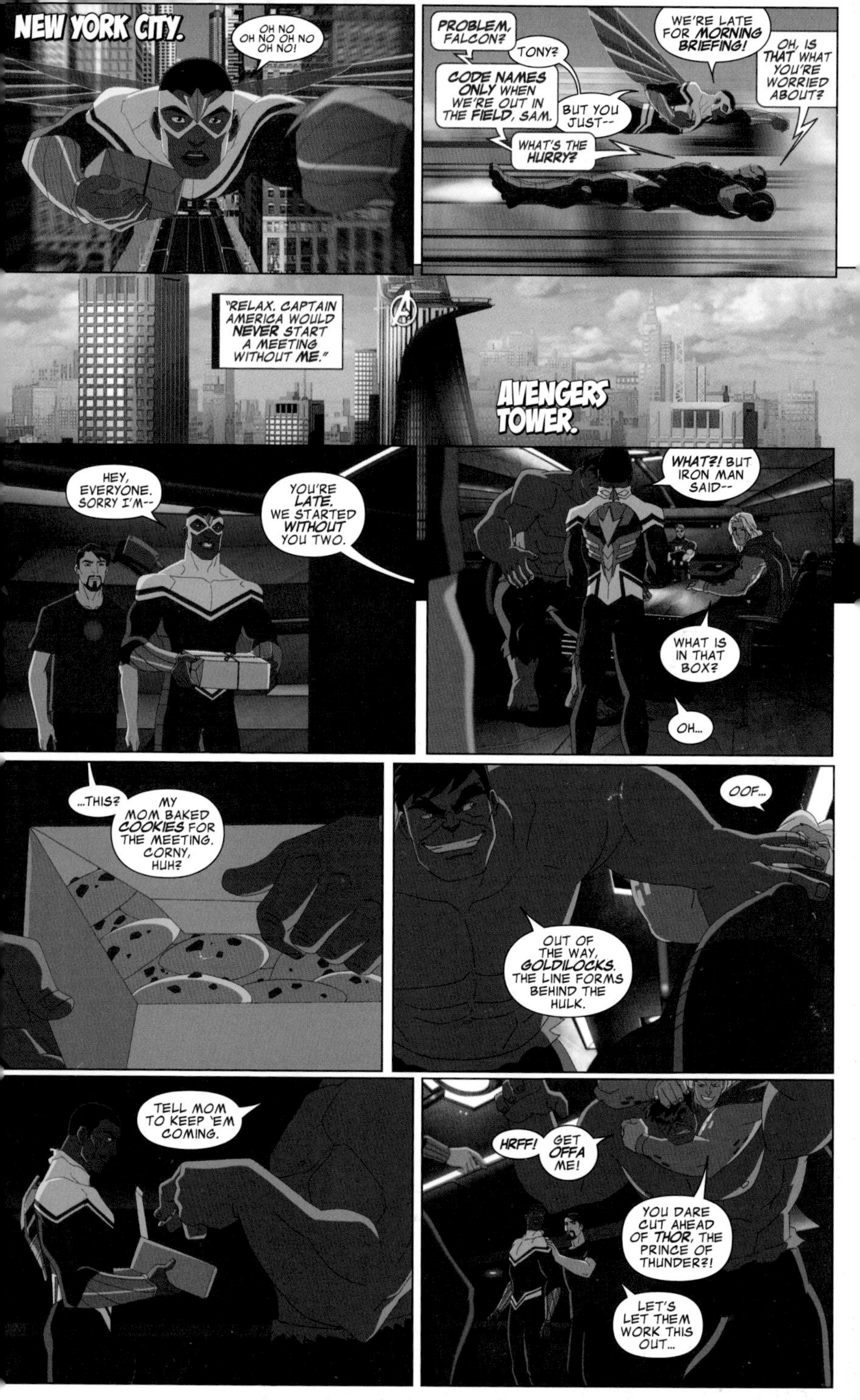
NEW YORK CITY.
OH NO OH NO OH NO OH NO!
PROBLEM, FALCON?
TONY?
CODE NAMES ONLY WHEN WE'RE OUT IN THE FIELD, SAM.
BUT YOU JUST--
WHAT'S THE HURRY?
WE'RE LATE FOR MORNING BRIEFING!
OH, IS THAT WHAT YOU'RE WORRIED ABOUT?
"RELAX. CAPTAIN AMERICA WOULD NEVER START A MEETING WITHOUT ME."
AVENGERS TOWER.
HEY, EVERYONE. SORRY I'M--
YOU'RE LATE. WE STARTED WITHOUT YOU TWO.
WHAT?! BUT IRON MAN SAID--
WHAT IS IN THAT BOX?
OH...
...THIS?
MY MOM BAKED COOKIES FOR THE MEETING. CORNY, HUH?
OOF...
OUT OF THE WAY, GOLDILOCKS. THE LINE FORMS BEHIND THE HULK.
TELL MOM TO KEEP 'EM COMING.
HRFF!
GET OFFA ME!
YOU DARE CUT AHEAD OF THOR, THE PRINCE OF THUNDER?!
LET'S LET THEM WORK THIS OUT...

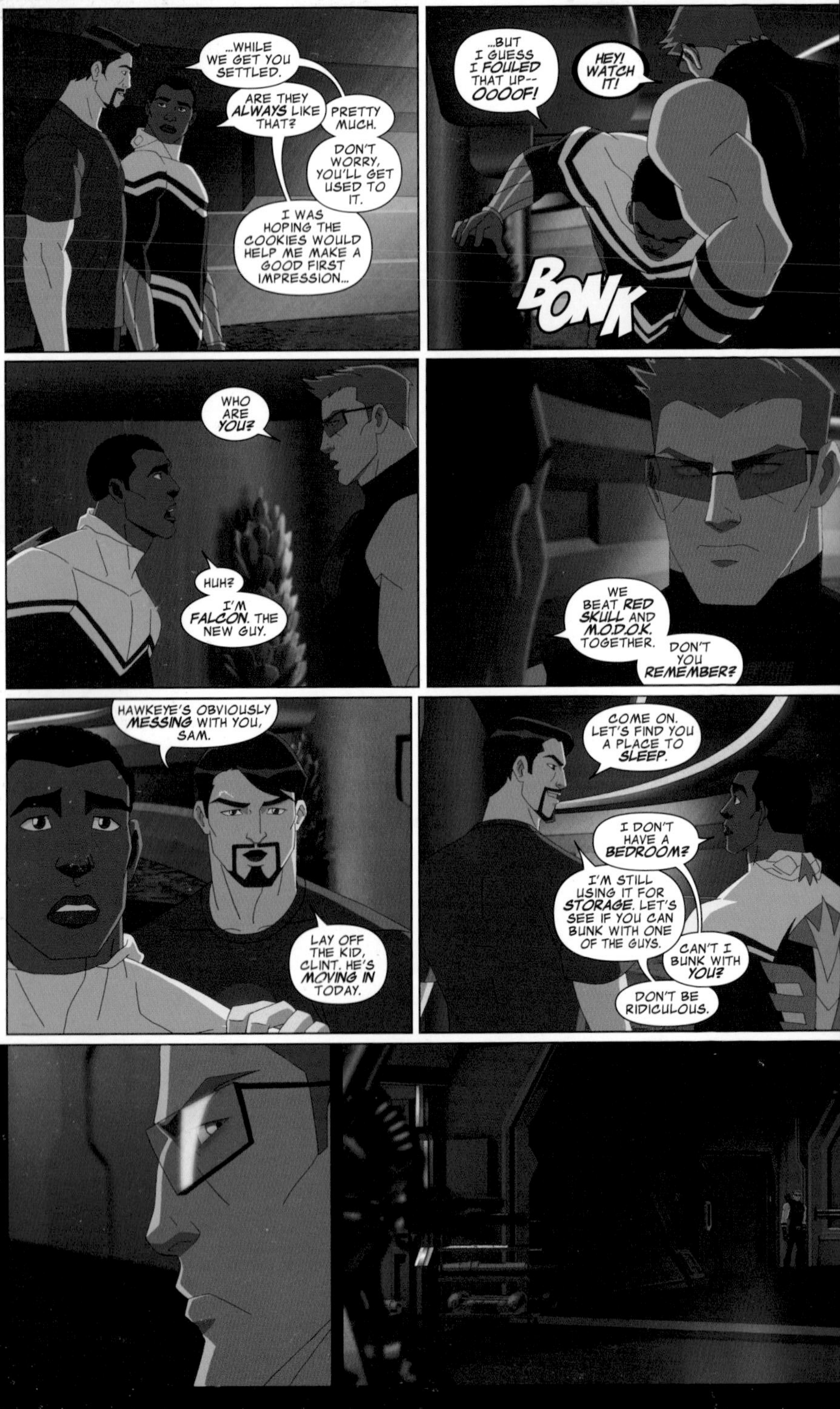
...WHILE WE GET YOU SETTLED.
ARE THEY ALWAYS LIKE THAT?
PRETTY MUCH.
DON'T WORRY, YOU'LL GET USED TO IT.
I WAS HOPING THE COOKIES WOULD HELP ME MAKE A GOOD FIRST IMPRESSION...
...BUT I GUESS I FOULED THAT UP-- OOOOF!
HEY! WATCH IT!
BONK
WHO ARE YOU?
HUH?
I'M FALCON. THE NEW GUY.
WE BEAT RED SKULL AND M.O.D.O.K. TOGETHER.
DON'T YOU REMEMBER?
HAWKEYE'S OBVIOUSLY MESSING WITH YOU, SAM.
LAY OFF THE KID, CLINT. HE'S MOVING IN TODAY.
COME ON. LET'S FIND YOU A PLACE TO SLEEP.
I DON'T HAVE A BEDROOM?
I'M STILL USING IT FOR STORAGE. LET'S SEE IF YOU CAN BUNK WITH ONE OF THE GUYS.
CAN'T I BUNK WITH YOU?
DON'T BE RIDICULOUS.

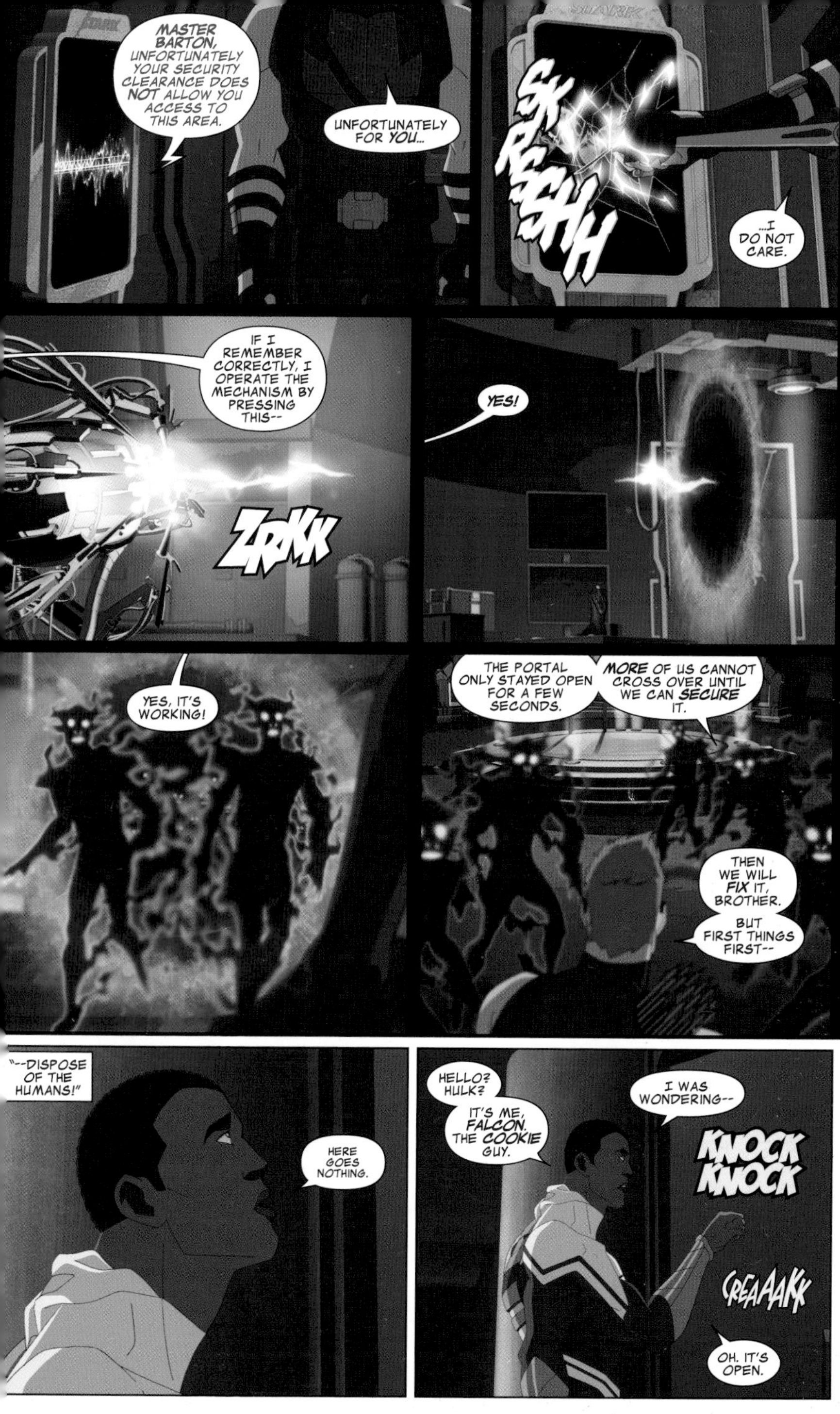
MASTER BARTON, UNFORTUNATELY YOUR SECURITY CLEARANCE DOES NOT ALLOW YOU ACCESS TO THIS AREA.
UNFORTUNATELY FOR YOU...
SKRRSSHH
...I DO NOT CARE.
IF I REMEMBER CORRECTLY, I OPERATE THE MECHANISM BY PRESSING THIS--
ZRAKK
YES!
YES, IT'S WORKING!
THE PORTAL ONLY STAYED OPEN FOR A FEW SECONDS.
MORE OF US CANNOT CROSS OVER UNTIL WE CAN SECURE IT.
THEN WE WILL FIX IT, BROTHER.
BUT FIRST THINGS FIRST--
"--DISPOSE OF THE HUMANS!"
HERE GOES NOTHING.
HELLO? HULK?
IT'S ME, FALCON. THE COOKIE GUY.
I WAS WONDERING--
KNOCK KNOCK
CREAAAKK
OH. IT'S OPEN.

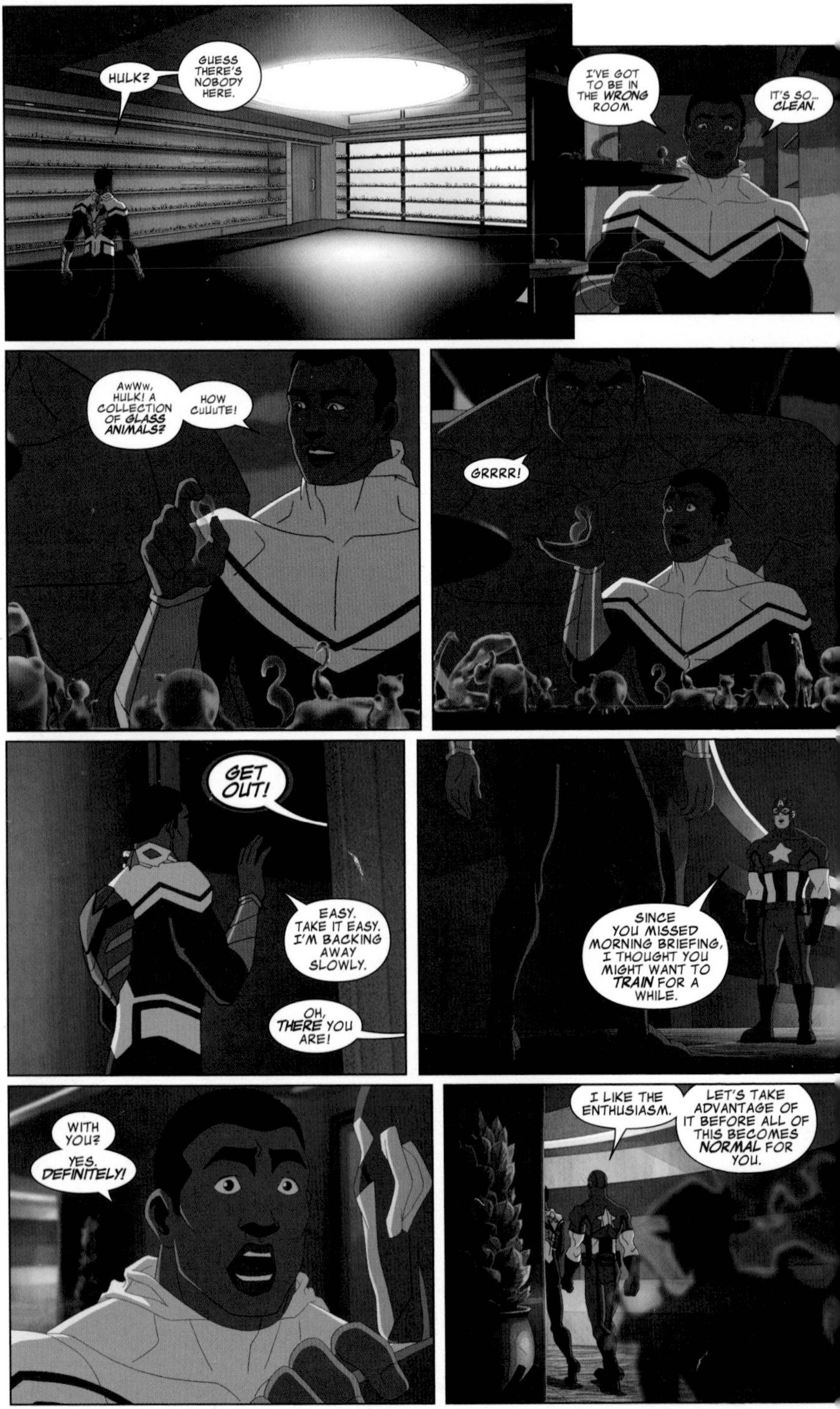
HULK?
GUESS THERE'S NOBODY HERE.
I'VE GOT TO BE IN THE WRONG ROOM.
IT'S SO... CLEAN.
AWWW, HULK! A COLLECTION OF GLASS ANIMALS?
HOW CUUUTE!
GRRRR!
GET OUT!
EASY. TAKE IT EASY. I'M BACKING AWAY SLOWLY.
OH, THERE YOU ARE!
SINCE YOU MISSED MORNING BRIEFING, I THOUGHT YOU MIGHT WANT TO TRAIN FOR A WHILE.
WITH YOU?
YES. DEFINITELY!
I LIKE THE ENTHUSIASM.
LET'S TAKE ADVANTAGE OF IT BEFORE ALL OF THIS BECOMES NORMAL FOR YOU.

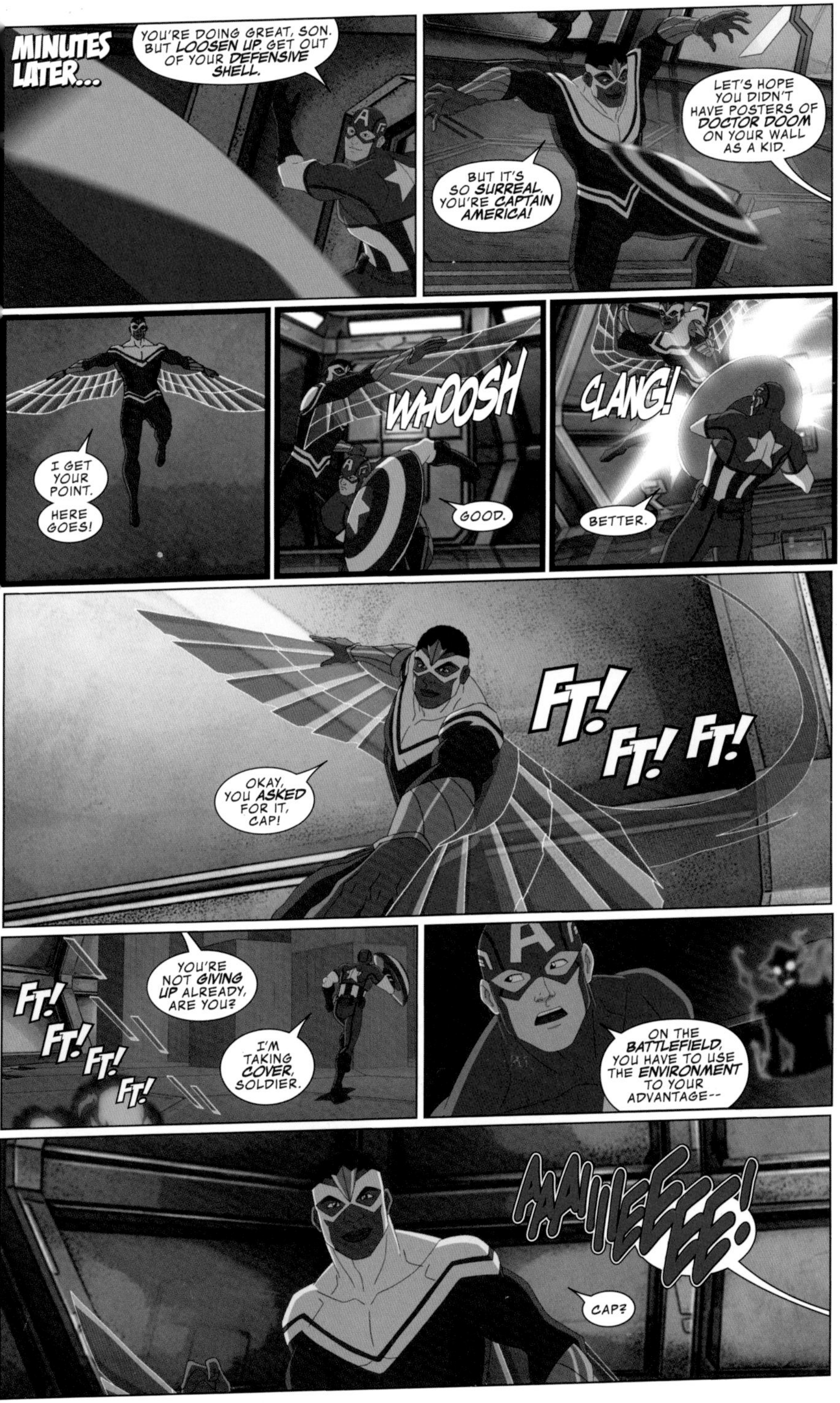
MINUTES LATER...
YOU'RE DOING GREAT, SON. BUT LOOSEN UP. GET OUT OF YOUR DEFENSIVE SHELL.
BUT IT'S SO SURREAL. YOU'RE CAPTAIN AMERICA!
LET'S HOPE YOU DIDN'T HAVE POSTERS OF DOCTOR DOOM ON YOUR WALL AS A KID.
I GET YOUR POINT.
HERE GOES!
WHOOSH
GOOD.
CLANG!
BETTER.
FT!
FT! FT!
OKAY, YOU ASKED FOR IT, CAP!
FT!
FT!
FT!
FT!
YOU'RE NOT GIVING UP ALREADY, ARE YOU?
I'M TAKING COVER, SOLDIER.
ON THE BATTLEFIELD, YOU HAVE TO USE THE ENVIRONMENT TO YOUR ADVANTAGE--
AAAIIIEEEEE!
CAP?

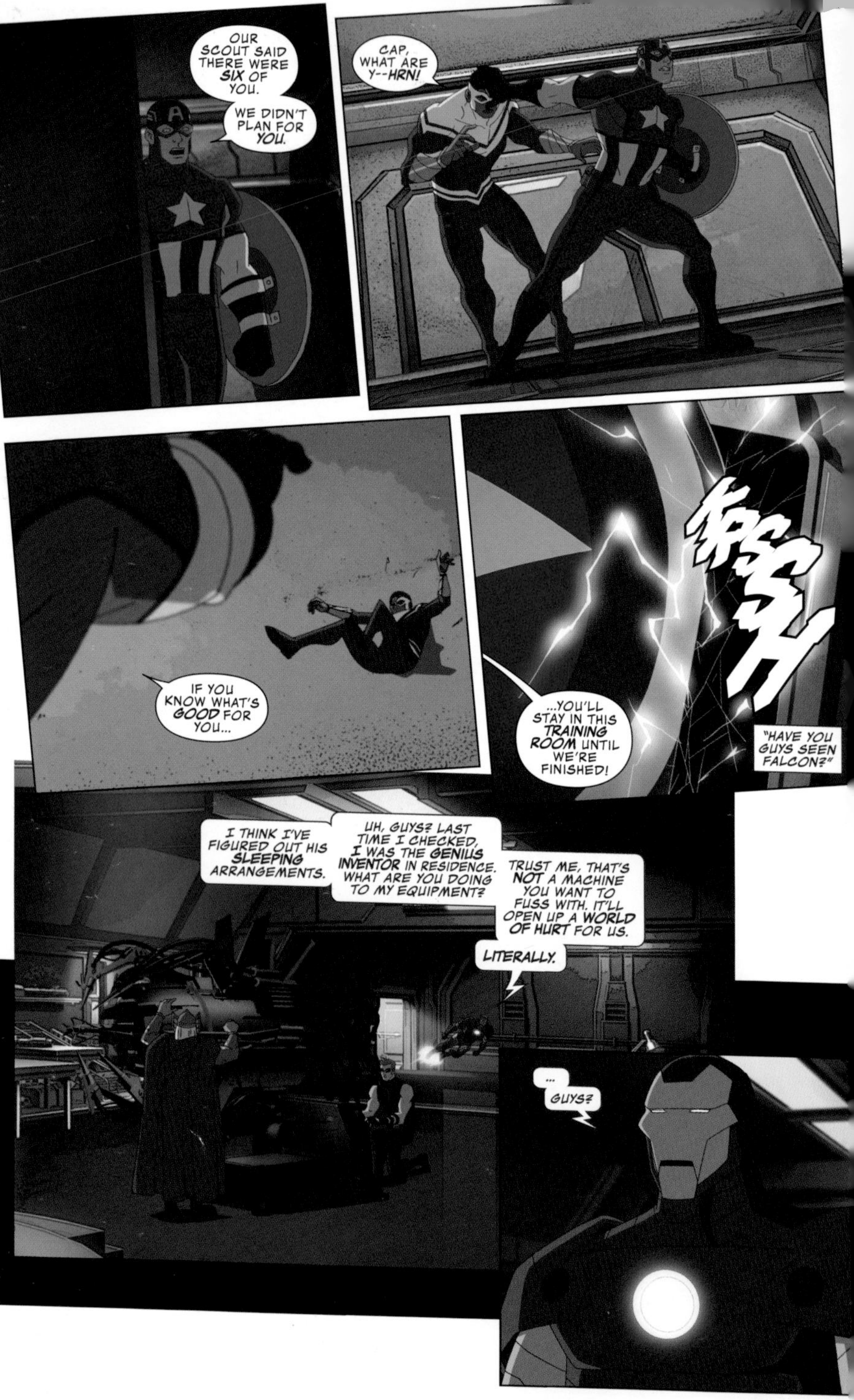
OUR SCOUT SAID THERE WERE SIX OF YOU.
WE DIDN'T PLAN FOR YOU.
CAP, WHAT ARE Y--HRN!
IF YOU KNOW WHAT'S GOOD FOR YOU...
...YOU'LL STAY IN THIS TRAINING ROOM UNTIL WE'RE FINISHED!
KRSSH
"HAVE YOU GUYS SEEN FALCON?"
I THINK I'VE FIGURED OUT HIS SLEEPING ARRANGEMENTS.
UH, GUYS? LAST TIME I CHECKED, I WAS THE GENIUS INVENTOR IN RESIDENCE. WHAT ARE YOU DOING TO MY EQUIPMENT?
TRUST ME, THAT'S NOT A MACHINE YOU WANT TO FUSS WITH. IT'LL OPEN UP A WORLD OF HURT FOR US.
LITERALLY.
...
GUYS?

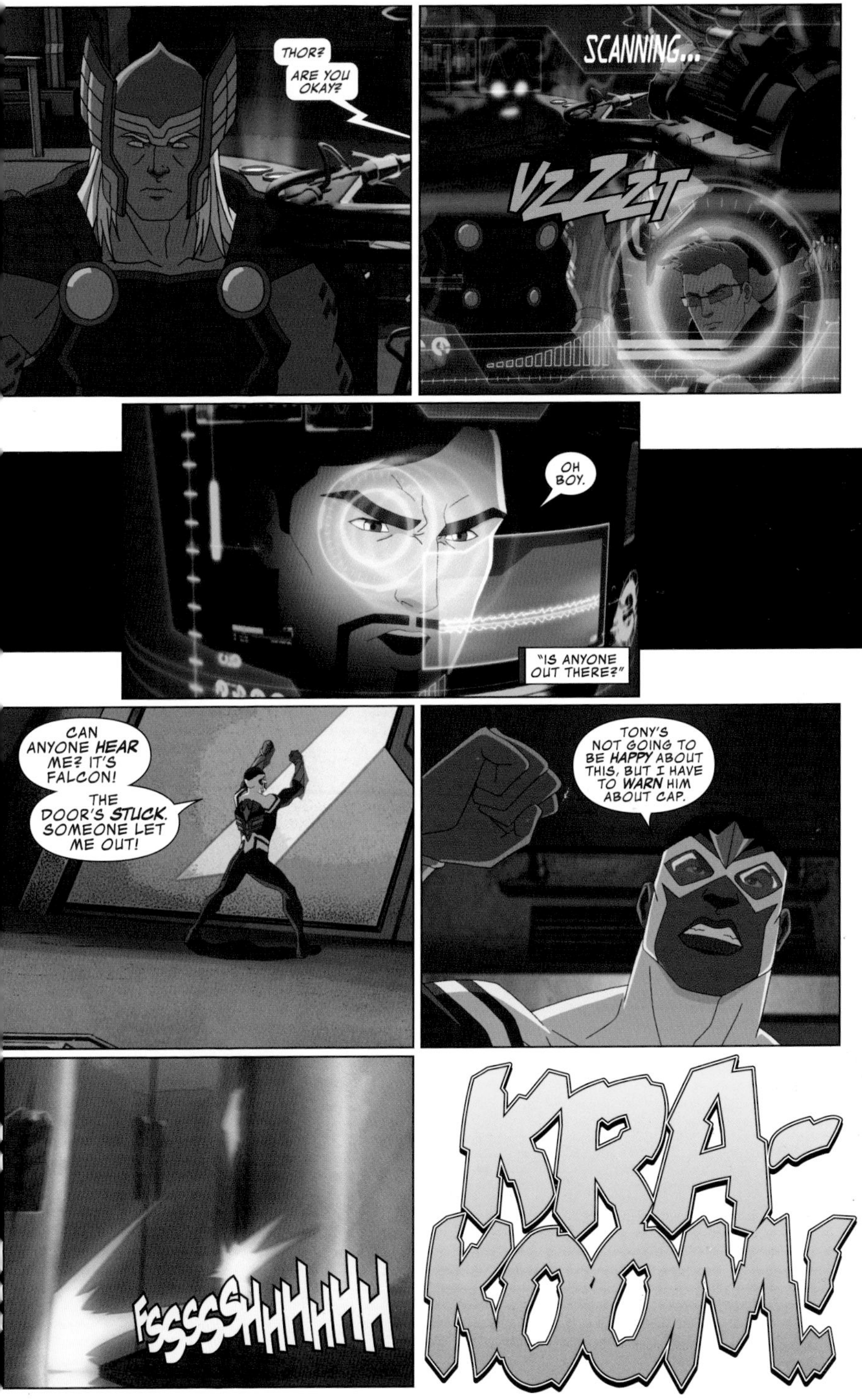
THOR? ARE YOU OKAY?
SCANNING...
VZZZT
OH BOY.
"IS ANYONE OUT THERE?"
CAN ANYONE HEAR ME? IT'S FALCON!
THE DOOR'S STUCK. SOMEONE LET ME OUT!
TONY'S NOT GOING TO BE HAPPY ABOUT THIS, BUT I HAVE TO WARN HIM ABOUT CAP.
FSSSSSHHHHHHH
KRA-KOOM!

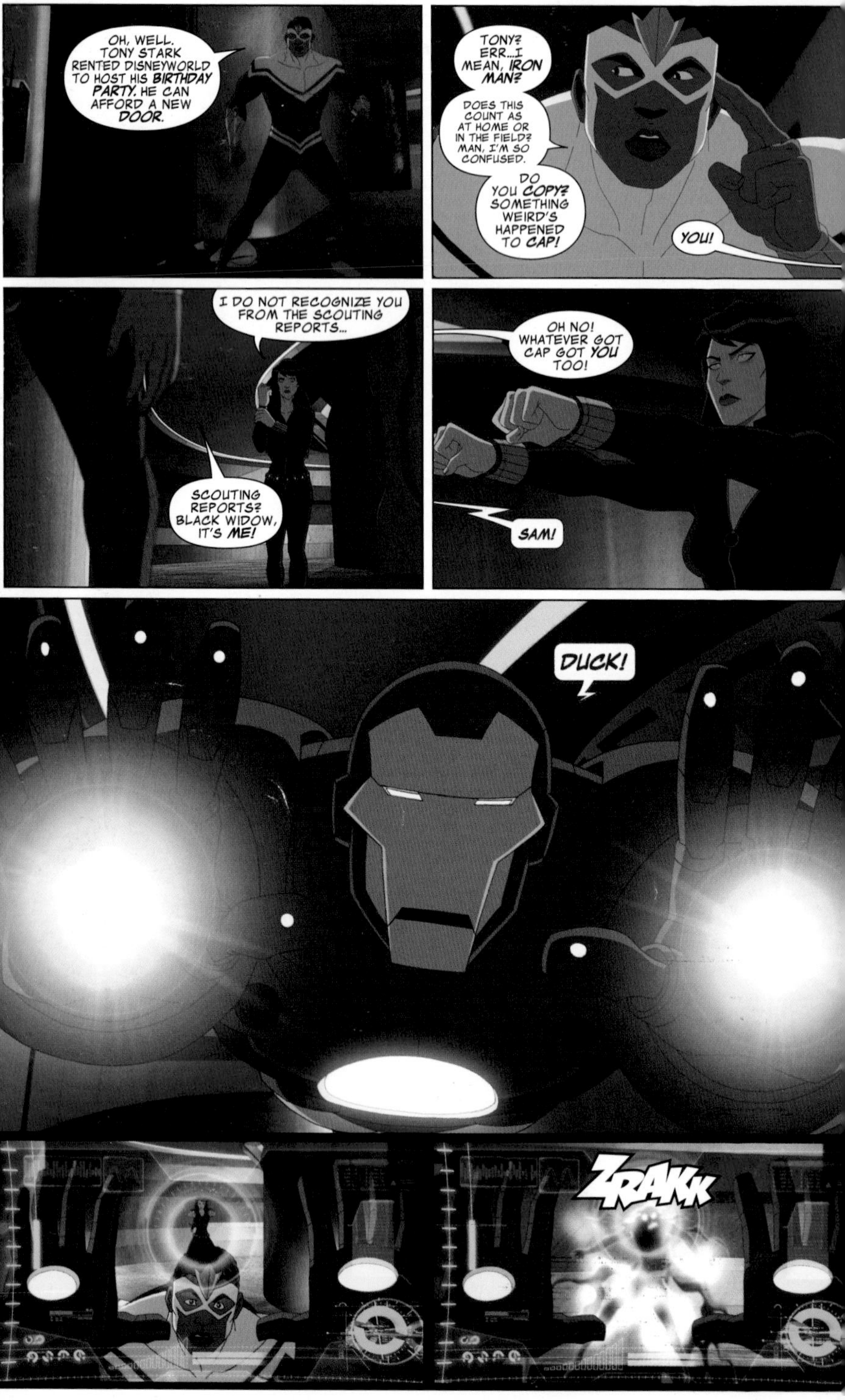
OH, WELL. TONY STARK RENTED DISNEYWORLD TO HOST HIS BIRTHDAY PARTY. HE CAN AFFORD A NEW DOOR.
TONY? ERR...I MEAN, IRON MAN?
DOES THIS COUNT AS AT HOME OR IN THE FIELD? MAN, I'M SO CONFUSED.
DO YOU COPY? SOMETHING WEIRD'S HAPPENED TO CAP!
YOU!
I DO NOT RECOGNIZE YOU FROM THE SCOUTING REPORTS...
SCOUTING REPORTS? BLACK WIDOW, IT'S ME!
OH NO! WHATEVER GOT CAP GOT YOU TOO!
SAM!
DUCK!
ZRAKK

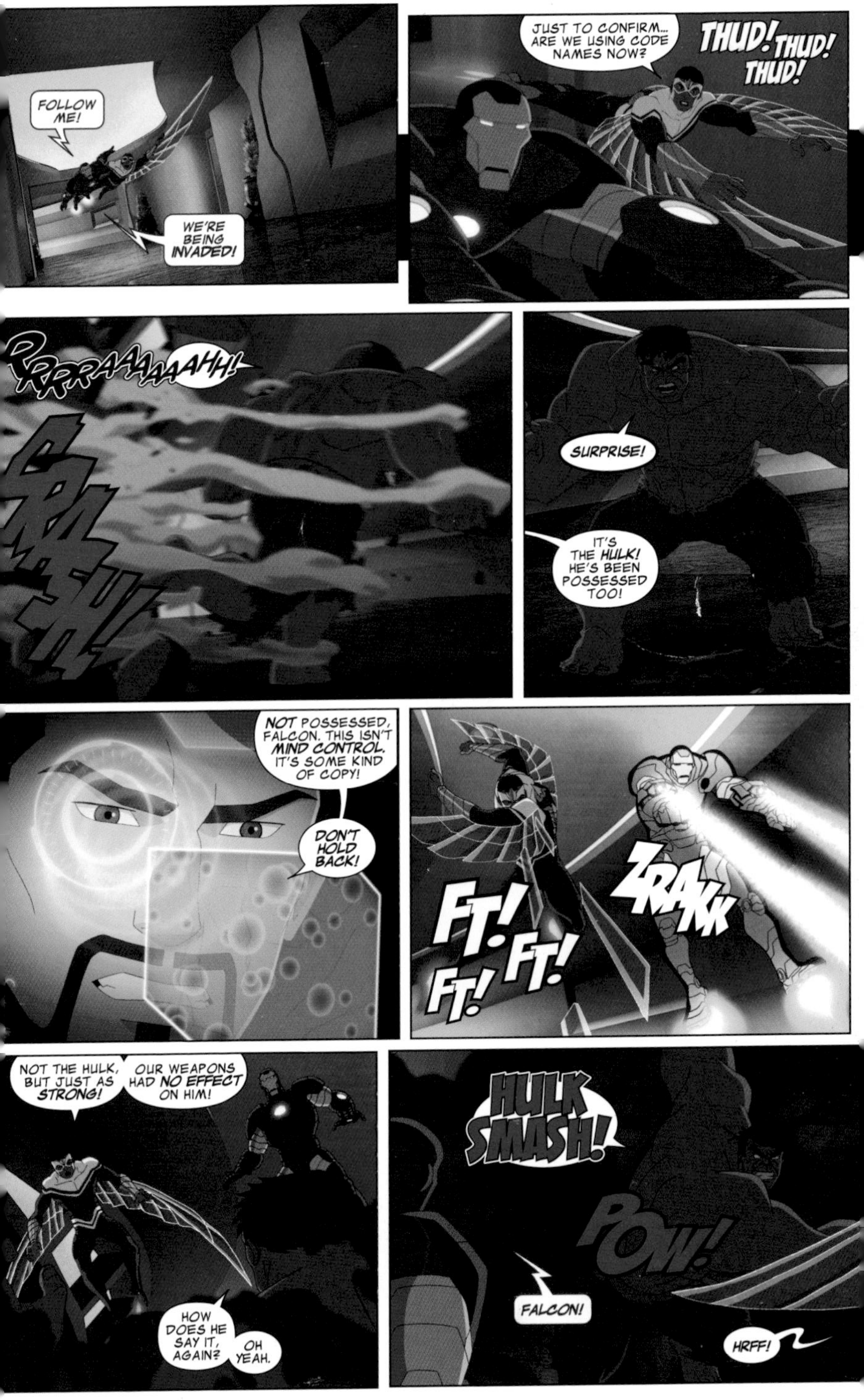
FOLLOW ME!
WE'RE BEING INVADED!
JUST TO CONFIRM... ARE WE USING CODE NAMES NOW?
THUD! THUD! THUD!
RRRRAAAAAAHH!
CRASHH!
SURPRISE!
IT'S THE HULK! HE'S BEEN POSSESSED TOO!
NOT POSSESSED, FALCON. THIS ISN'T MIND CONTROL. IT'S SOME KIND OF COPY!
DON'T HOLD BACK!
ZRAKK
FT! FT! FT!
NOT THE HULK, BUT JUST AS STRONG!
OUR WEAPONS HAD NO EFFECT ON HIM!
HOW DOES HE SAY IT, AGAIN?
OH YEAH.
HULK SMASH!
POW!
FALCON!
HRFF!

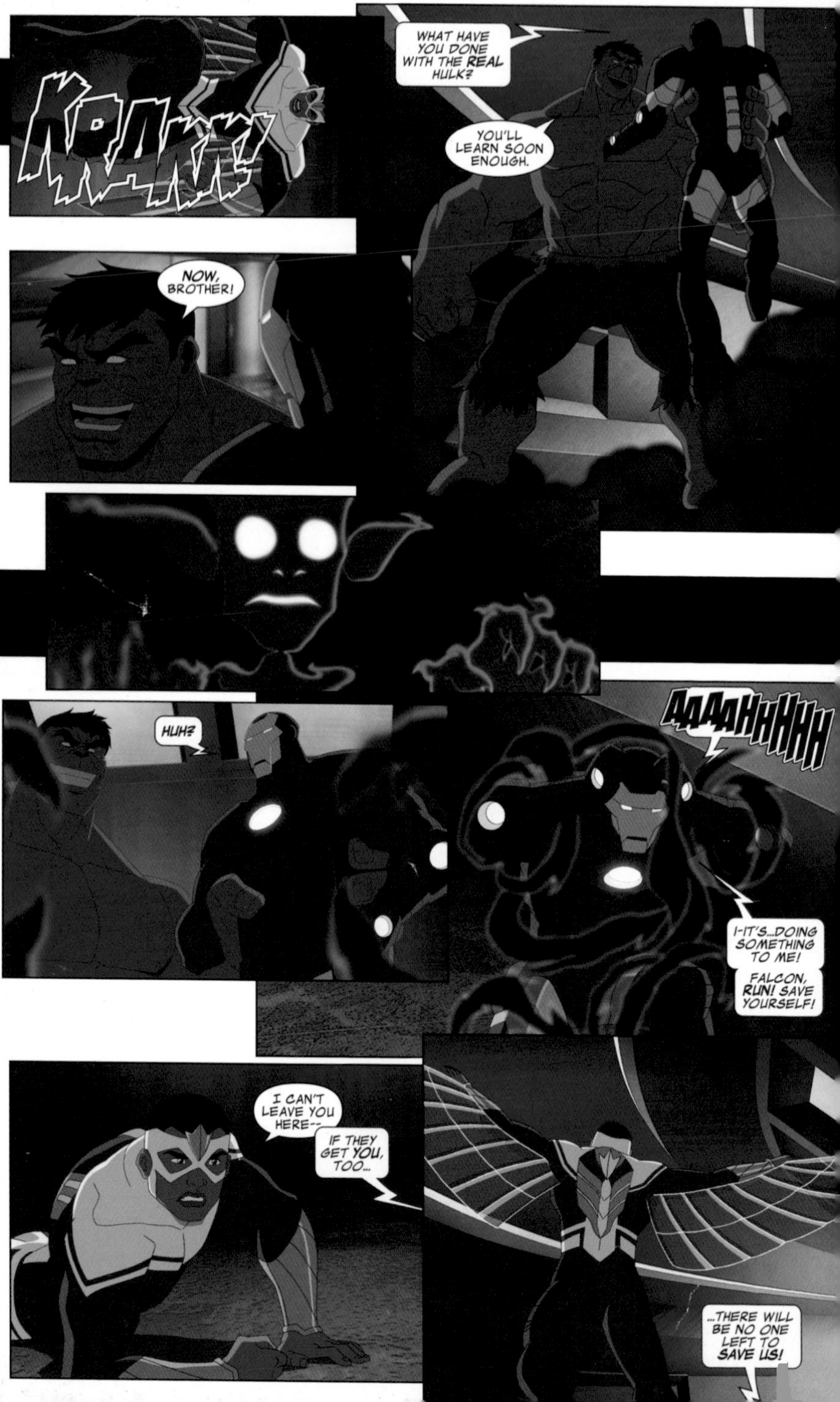

KRAKK!
WHAT HAVE YOU DONE WITH THE REAL HULK?
YOU'LL LEARN SOON ENOUGH.
NOW, BROTHER!
HUH?
AAAAHHHHH
I-IT'S...DOING SOMETHING TO ME!
FALCON, RUN! SAVE YOURSELF!
I CAN'T LEAVE YOU HERE--
IF THEY GET YOU, TOO...
...THERE WILL BE NO ONE LEFT TO SAVE US!

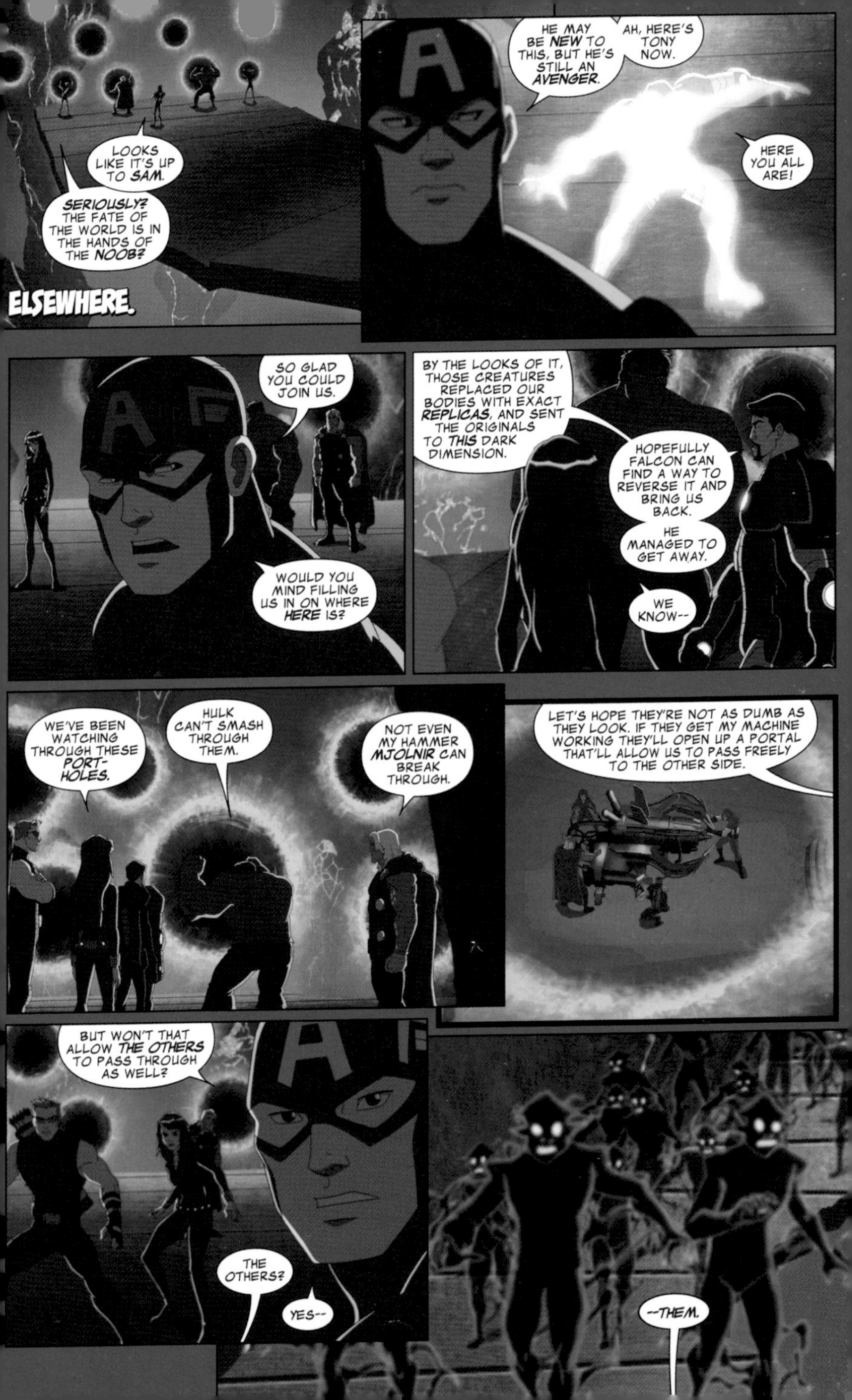
LOOKS LIKE IT'S UP TO SAM.
SERIOUSLY? THE FATE OF THE WORLD IS IN THE HANDS OF THE NOOB?
ELSEWHERE.
HE MAY BE NEW TO THIS, BUT HE'S STILL AN AVENGER.
AH, HERE'S TONY NOW.
HERE YOU ALL ARE!
SO GLAD YOU COULD JOIN US.
WOULD YOU MIND FILLING US IN ON WHERE HERE IS?
BY THE LOOKS OF IT, THOSE CREATURES REPLACED OUR BODIES WITH EXACT REPLICAS, AND SENT THE ORIGINALS TO THIS DARK DIMENSION.
HOPEFULLY FALCON CAN FIND A WAY TO REVERSE IT AND BRING US BACK.
HE MANAGED TO GET AWAY.
WE KNOW--
WE'VE BEEN WATCHING THROUGH THESE PORT-HOLES.
HULK CAN'T SMASH THROUGH THEM.
NOT EVEN MY HAMMER MJOLNIR CAN BREAK THROUGH.
LET'S HOPE THEY'RE NOT AS DUMB AS THEY LOOK. IF THEY GET MY MACHINE WORKING THEY'LL OPEN UP A PORTAL THAT'LL ALLOW US TO PASS FREELY TO THE OTHER SIDE.
BUT WON'T THAT ALLOW THE OTHERS TO PASS THROUGH AS WELL?
THE OTHERS?
YES--
--THEM.

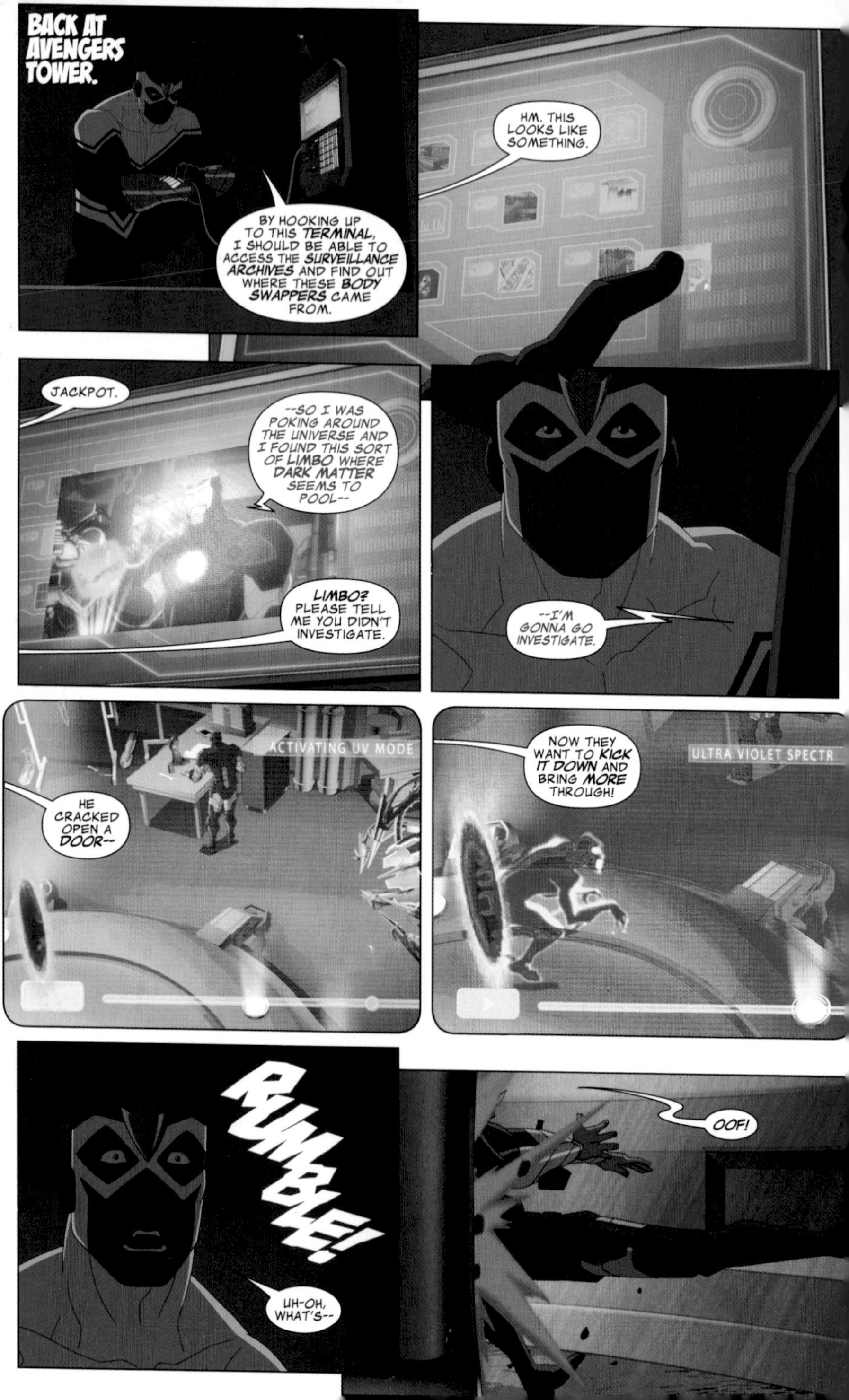
BACK AT AVENGERS TOWER.
BY HOOKING UP TO THIS TERMINAL, I SHOULD BE ABLE TO ACCESS THE SURVEILLANCE ARCHIVES AND FIND OUT WHERE THESE BODY SWAPPERS CAME FROM.
HM. THIS LOOKS LIKE SOMETHING.
JACKPOT.
--SO I WAS POKING AROUND THE UNIVERSE AND I FOUND THIS SORT OF LIMBO WHERE DARK MATTER SEEMS TO POOL--
LIMBO? PLEASE TELL ME YOU DIDN'T INVESTIGATE.
--I'M GONNA GO INVESTIGATE.
ACTIVATING UV MODE
HE CRACKED OPEN A DOOR--
ULTRA VIOLET SPECTR
NOW THEY WANT TO KICK IT DOWN AND BRING MORE THROUGH!
RUMBLE!
UH-OH, WHAT'S--
OOF!

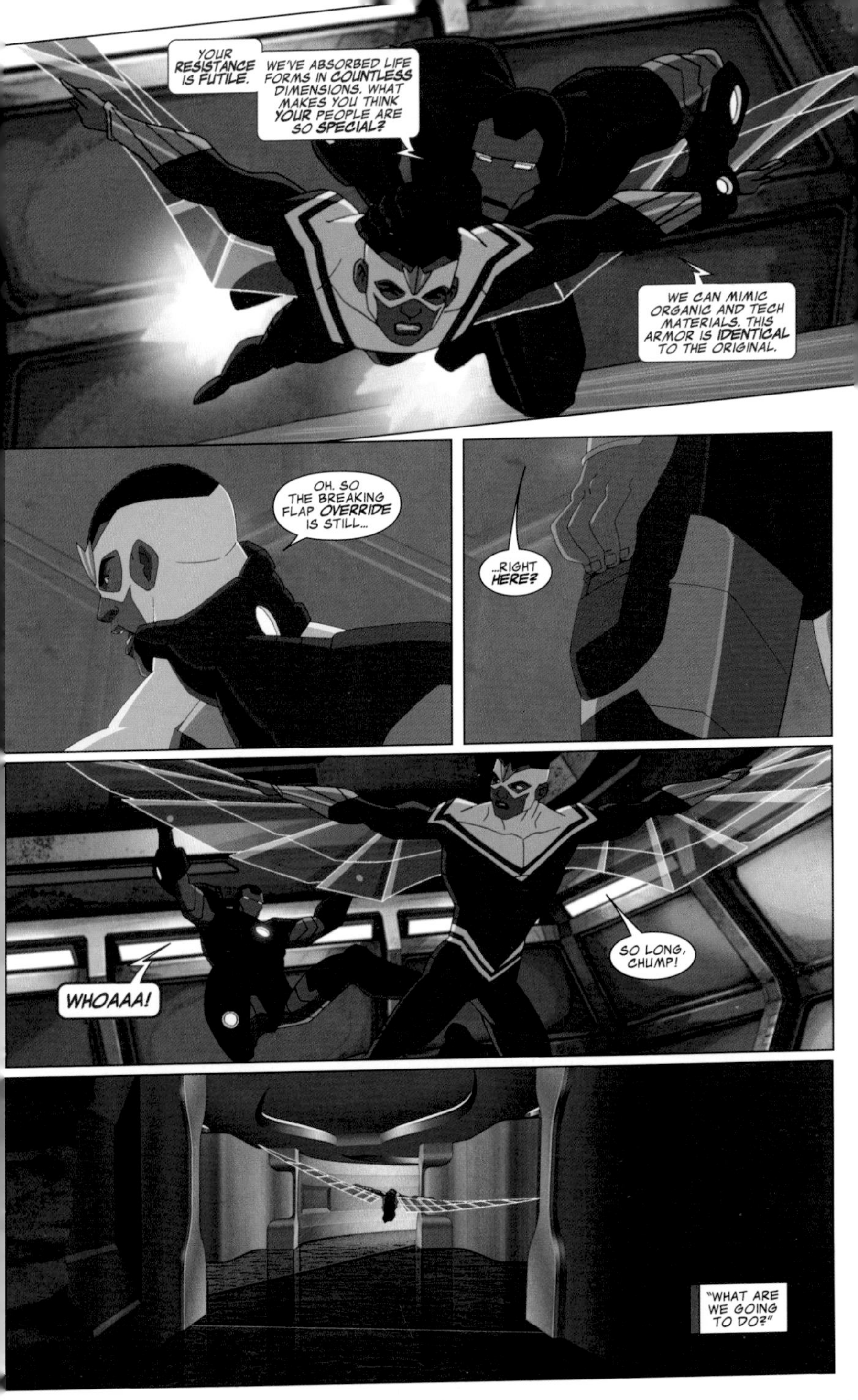
YOUR RESISTANCE IS FUTILE.
WE'VE ABSORBED LIFE FORMS IN COUNTLESS DIMENSIONS. WHAT MAKES YOU THINK YOUR PEOPLE ARE SO SPECIAL?
WE CAN MIMIC ORGANIC AND TECH MATERIALS. THIS ARMOR IS IDENTICAL TO THE ORIGINAL.
OH. SO THE BREAKING FLAP OVERRIDE IS STILL...
...RIGHT HERE?
SO LONG, CHUMP!
WHOAAA!
"WHAT ARE WE GOING TO DO?"

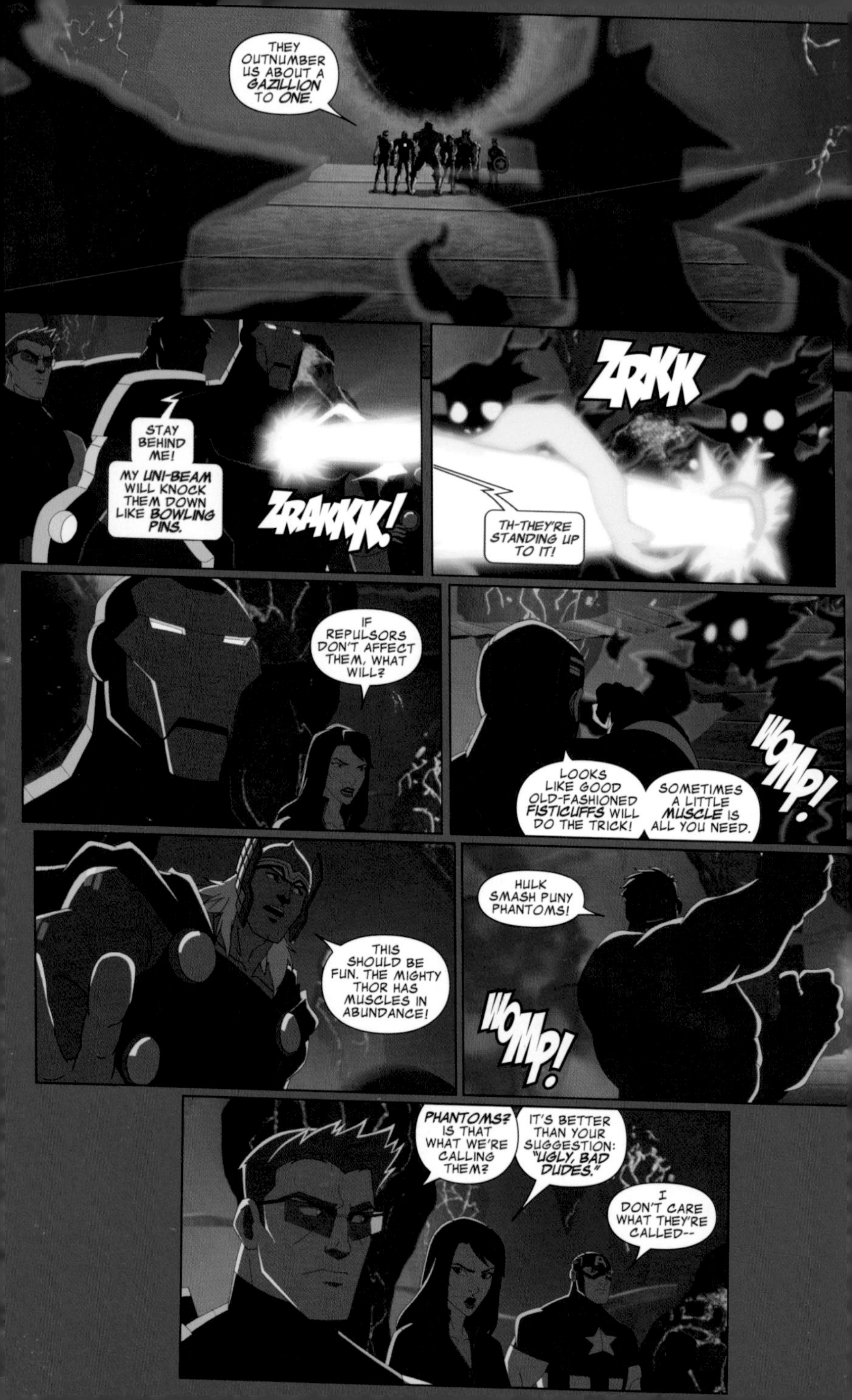
THEY OUTNUMBER US ABOUT A GAZILLION TO ONE.
STAY BEHIND ME!
MY UNI-BEAM WILL KNOCK THEM DOWN LIKE BOWLING PINS.
ZRAKKK!
ZRKK
TH-THEY'RE STANDING UP TO IT!
IF REPULSORS DON'T AFFECT THEM, WHAT WILL?
LOOKS LIKE GOOD OLD-FASHIONED FISTICUFFS WILL DO THE TRICK!
SOMETIMES A LITTLE MUSCLE IS ALL YOU NEED.
WOMP!
THIS SHOULD BE FUN. THE MIGHTY THOR HAS MUSCLES IN ABUNDANCE!
HULK SMASH PUNY PHANTOMS!
WOMP!
PHANTOMS? IS THAT WHAT WE'RE CALLING THEM?
IT'S BETTER THAN YOUR SUGGESTION: "UGLY, BAD DUDES."
I DON'T CARE WHAT THEY'RE CALLED--

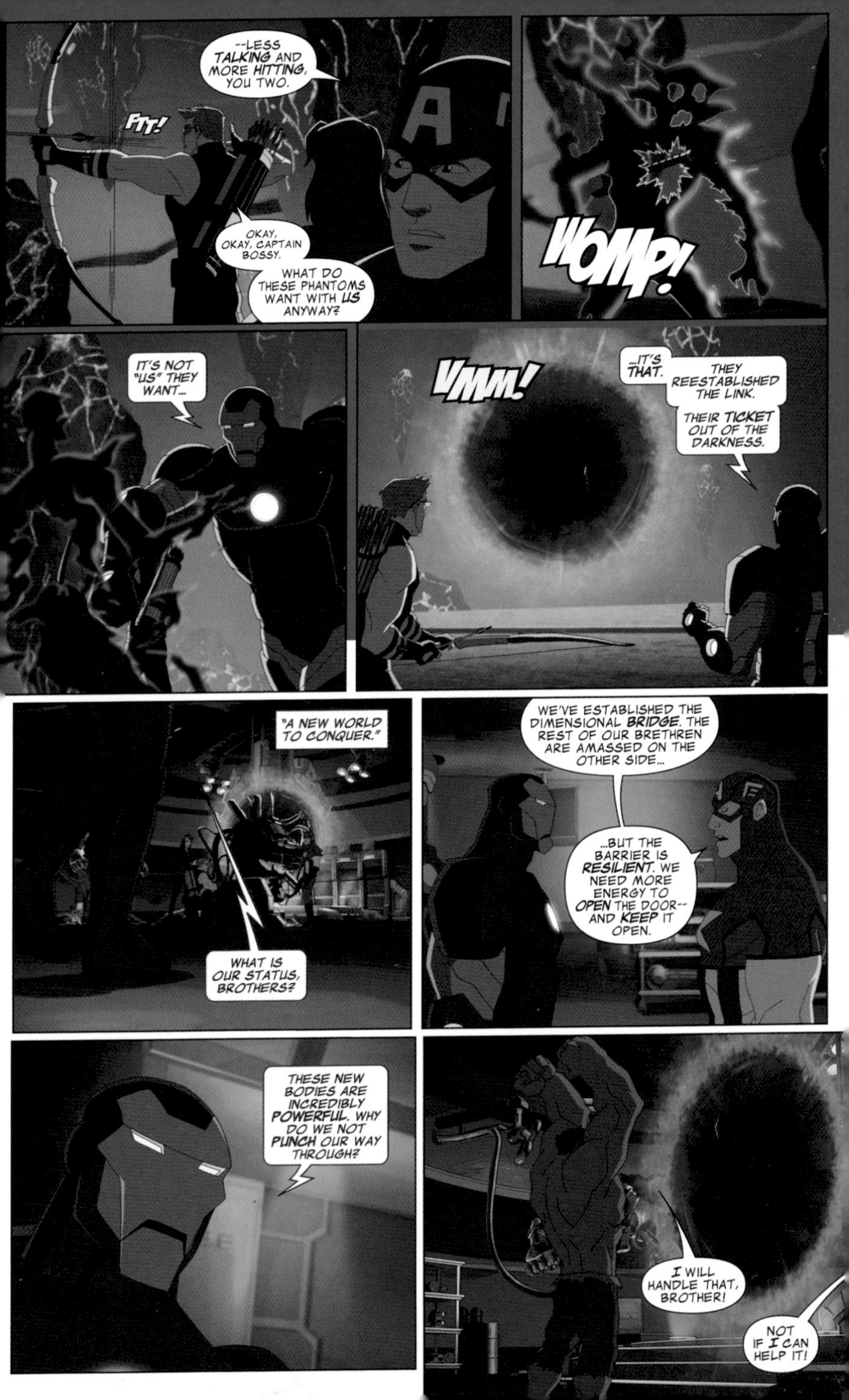

--LESS TALKING AND MORE HITTING, YOU TWO.
FTT!
OKAY, OKAY, CAPTAIN BOSSY.
WHAT DO THESE PHANTOMS WANT WITH US ANYWAY?
WOMP!
IT'S NOT "US" THEY WANT...
VMM!
...IT'S THAT.
THEY REESTABLISHED THE LINK.
THEIR TICKET OUT OF THE DARKNESS.
"A NEW WORLD TO CONQUER."
WHAT IS OUR STATUS, BROTHERS?
WE'VE ESTABLISHED THE DIMENSIONAL BRIDGE. THE REST OF OUR BRETHREN ARE AMASSED ON THE OTHER SIDE...
...BUT THE BARRIER IS RESILIENT. WE NEED MORE ENERGY TO OPEN THE DOOR-- AND KEEP IT OPEN.
THESE NEW BODIES ARE INCREDIBLY POWERFUL. WHY DO WE NOT PUNCH OUR WAY THROUGH?
I WILL HANDLE THAT, BROTHER!
NOT IF I CAN HELP IT!

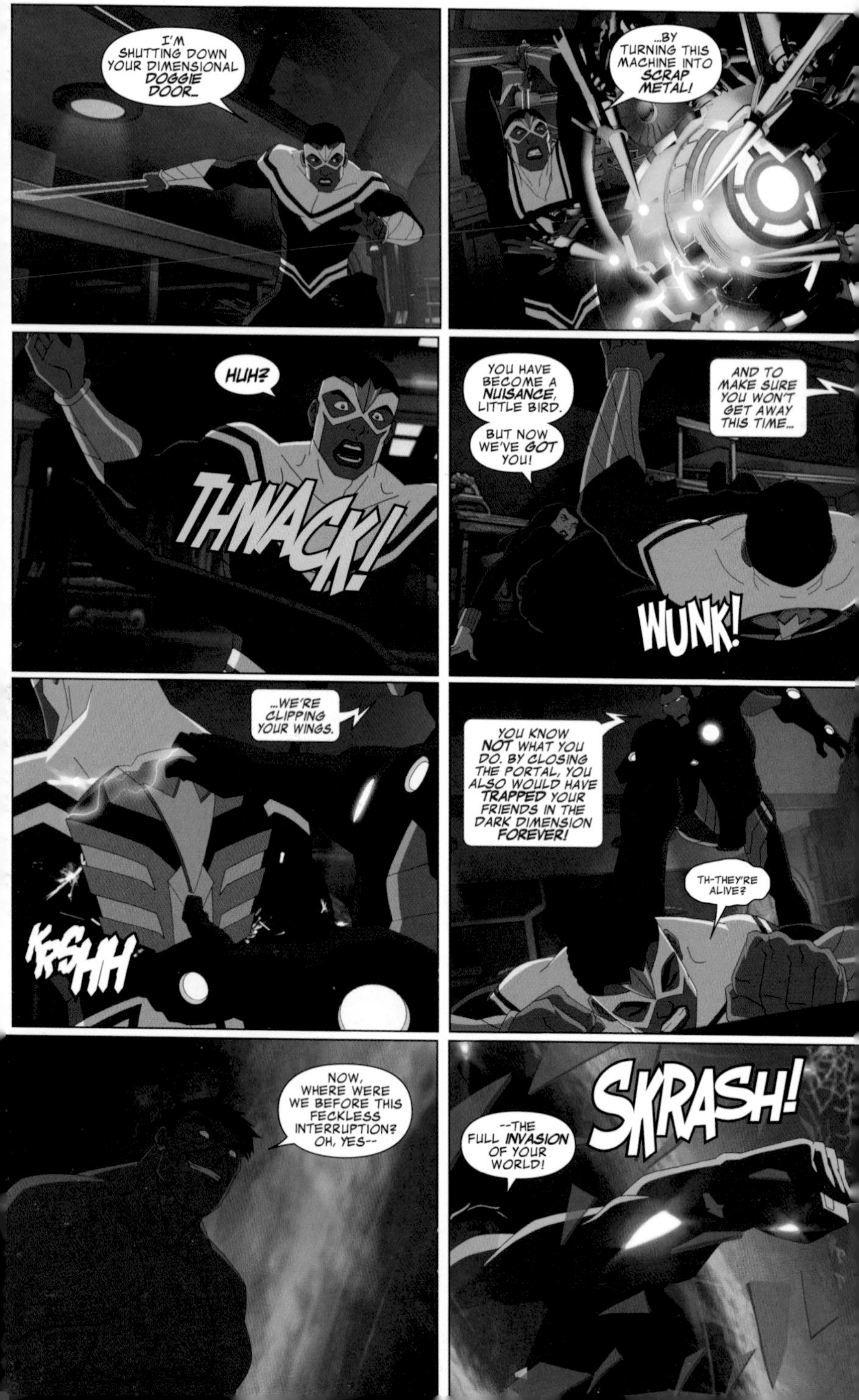
I'M SHUTTING DOWN YOUR DIMENSIONAL DOGGIE DOOR...
...BY TURNING THIS MACHINE INTO SCRAP METAL!
HUH?
THWACK!
YOU HAVE BECOME A NUISANCE, LITTLE BIRD.
BUT NOW WE'VE GOT YOU!
AND TO MAKE SURE YOU WON'T GET AWAY THIS TIME...
WUNK!
...WE'RE CLIPPING YOUR WINGS.
KRSHH
YOU KNOW NOT WHAT YOU DO. BY CLOSING THE PORTAL, YOU ALSO WOULD HAVE TRAPPED YOUR FRIENDS IN THE DARK DIMENSION FOREVER!
TH-THEY'RE ALIVE?
NOW, WHERE WERE WE BEFORE THIS FECKLESS INTERRUPTION? OH, YES--
--THE FULL INVASION OF YOUR WORLD!
SKRASH!

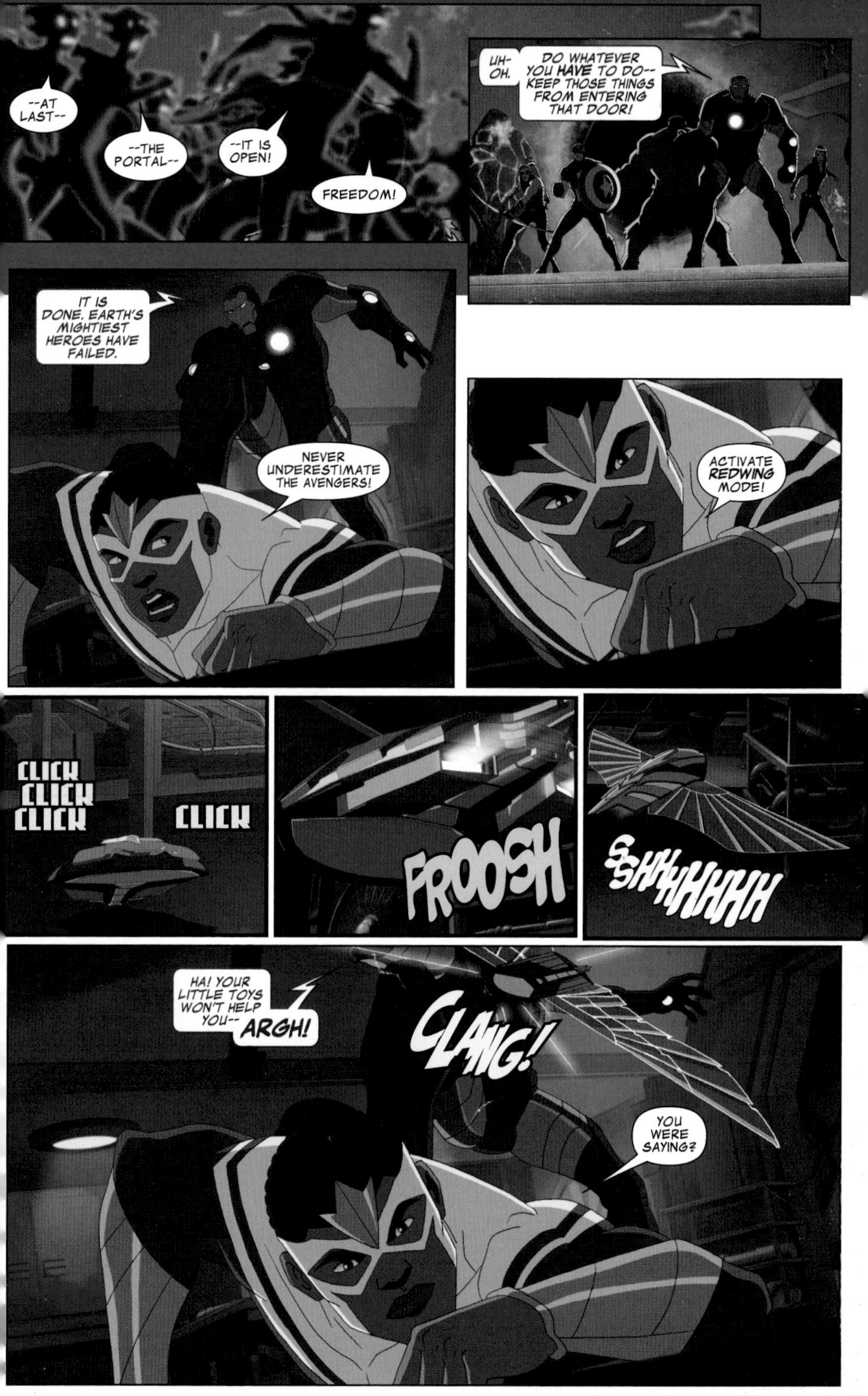
--AT LAST--
--THE PORTAL--
--IT IS OPEN!
FREEDOM!
UH-OH.
DO WHATEVER YOU HAVE TO DO-- KEEP THOSE THINGS FROM ENTERING THAT DOOR!
IT IS DONE. EARTH'S MIGHTIEST HEROES HAVE FAILED.
NEVER UNDERESTIMATE THE AVENGERS!
ACTIVATE REDWING MODE!
CLICK
CLICK
CLICK
CLICK
FROOSH
SSHHHHHHH
HA! YOUR LITTLE TOYS WON'T HELP YOU-- ARGH!
CLANG!
YOU WERE SAYING?

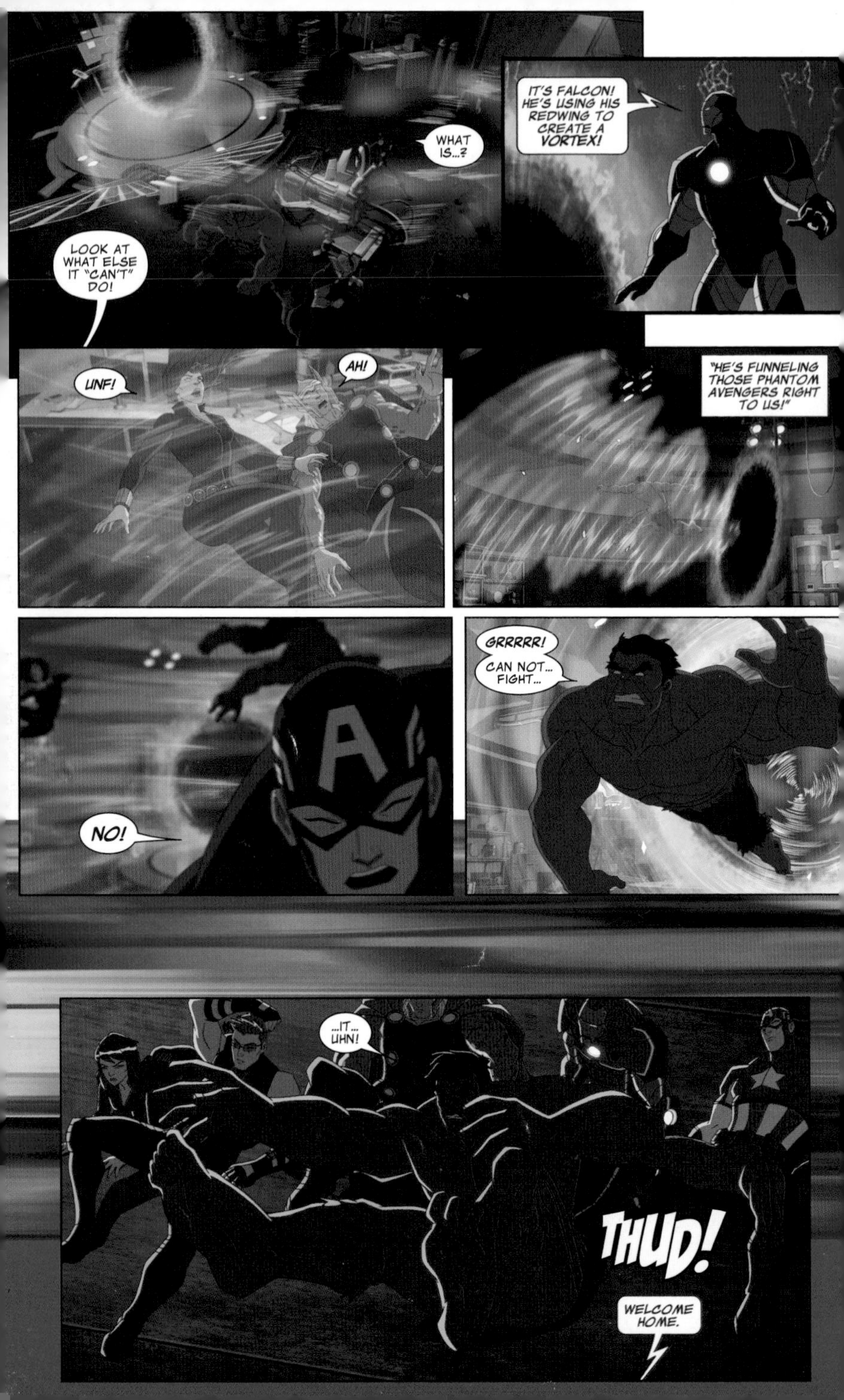
WHAT IS...?
LOOK AT WHAT ELSE IT "CAN'T" DO!
IT'S FALCON! HE'S USING HIS REDWING TO CREATE A VORTEX!
UNF!
AH!
"HE'S FUNNELING THOSE PHANTOM AVENGERS RIGHT TO US!"
NO!
GRRRRR!
CAN NOT... FIGHT...
...IT... UHN!
THUD!
WELCOME HOME.

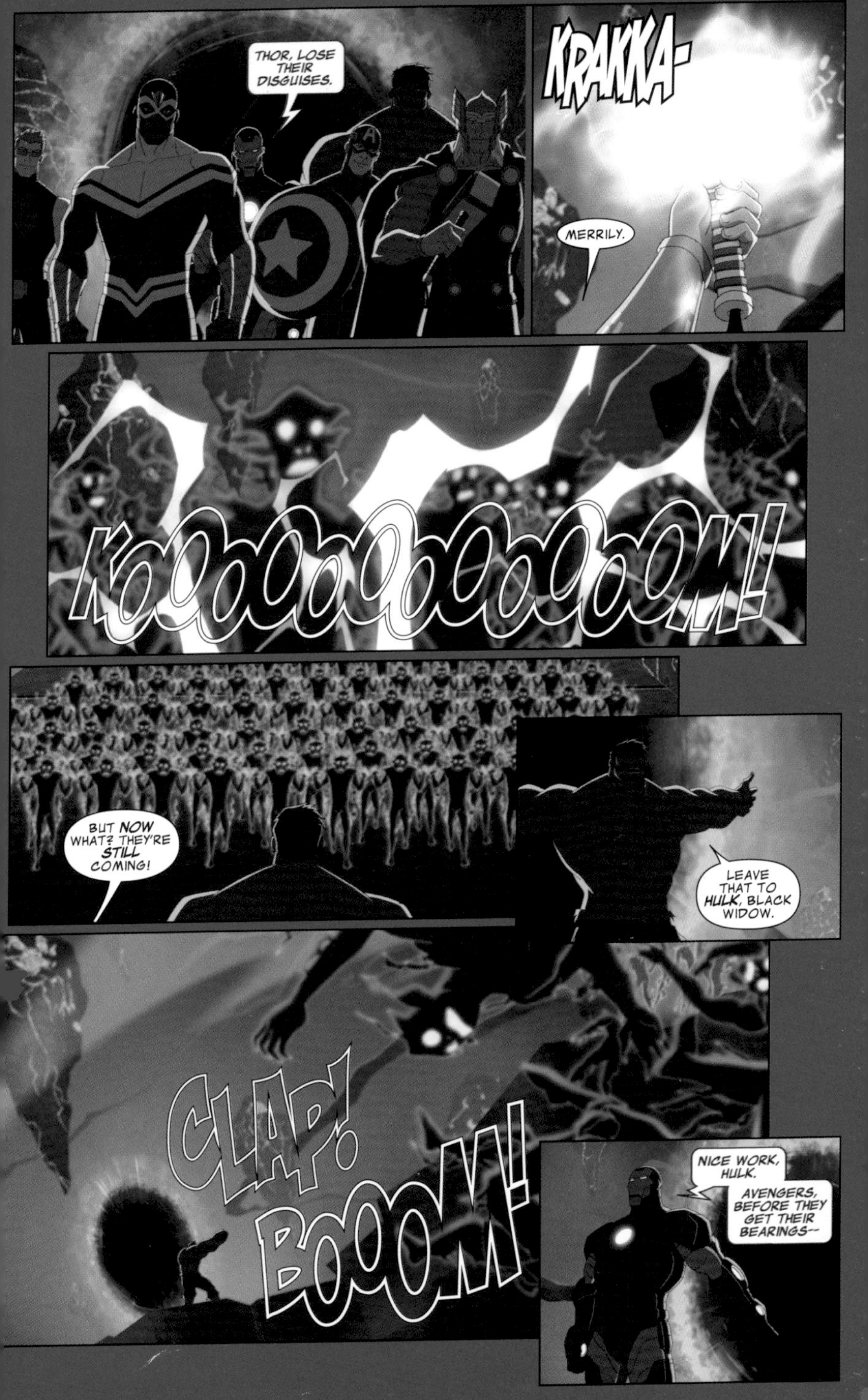
THOR, LOSE THEIR DISGUISES.
KRAKKA-
MERRILY.
KOOOOOOOOOOOOOM!
BUT NOW WHAT? THEY'RE STILL COMING!
LEAVE THAT TO HULK, BLACK WIDOW.
CLAP!
BOOOM!
NICE WORK, HULK.
AVENGERS, BEFORE THEY GET THEIR BEARINGS--

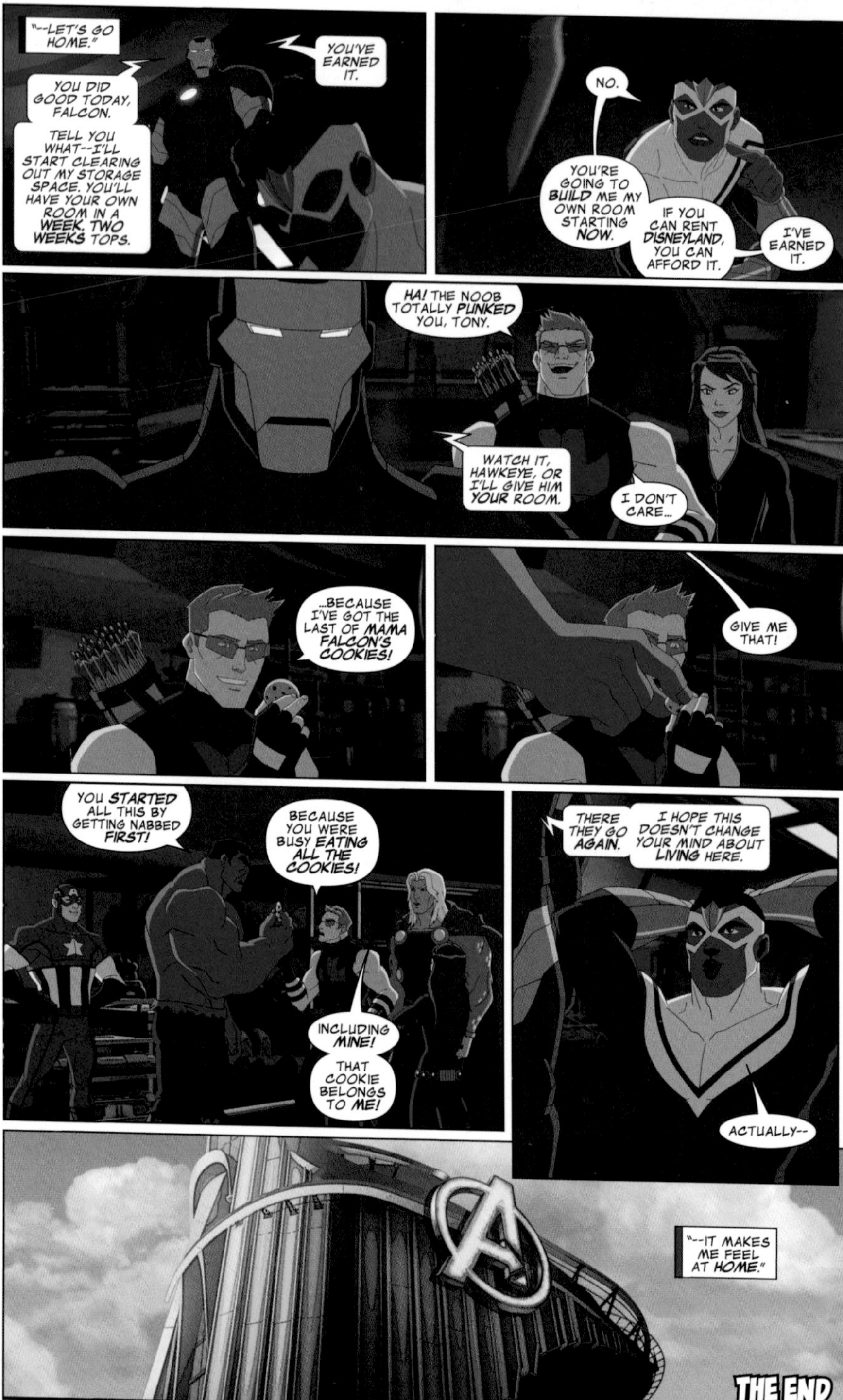
"--LET'S GO HOME."
YOU DID GOOD TODAY, FALCON.
YOU'VE EARNED IT.
TELL YOU WHAT--I'LL START CLEARING OUT MY STORAGE SPACE. YOU'LL HAVE YOUR OWN ROOM IN A WEEK. TWO WEEKS TOPS.
NO.
YOU'RE GOING TO BUILD ME MY OWN ROOM STARTING NOW.
IF YOU CAN RENT DISNEYLAND, YOU CAN AFFORD IT.
I'VE EARNED IT.
HA! THE NOOB TOTALLY PUNKED YOU, TONY.
WATCH IT, HAWKEYE, OR I'LL GIVE HIM YOUR ROOM.
I DON'T CARE...
...BECAUSE I'VE GOT THE LAST OF MAMA FALCON'S COOKIES!
GIVE ME THAT!
YOU STARTED ALL THIS BY GETTING NABBED FIRST!
BECAUSE YOU WERE BUSY EATING ALL THE COOKIES!
INCLUDING MINE!
THAT COOKIE BELONGS TO ME!
THERE THEY GO AGAIN.
I HOPE THIS DOESN'T CHANGE YOUR MIND ABOUT LIVING HERE.
ACTUALLY--
"--IT MAKES ME FEEL AT HOME."
THE END

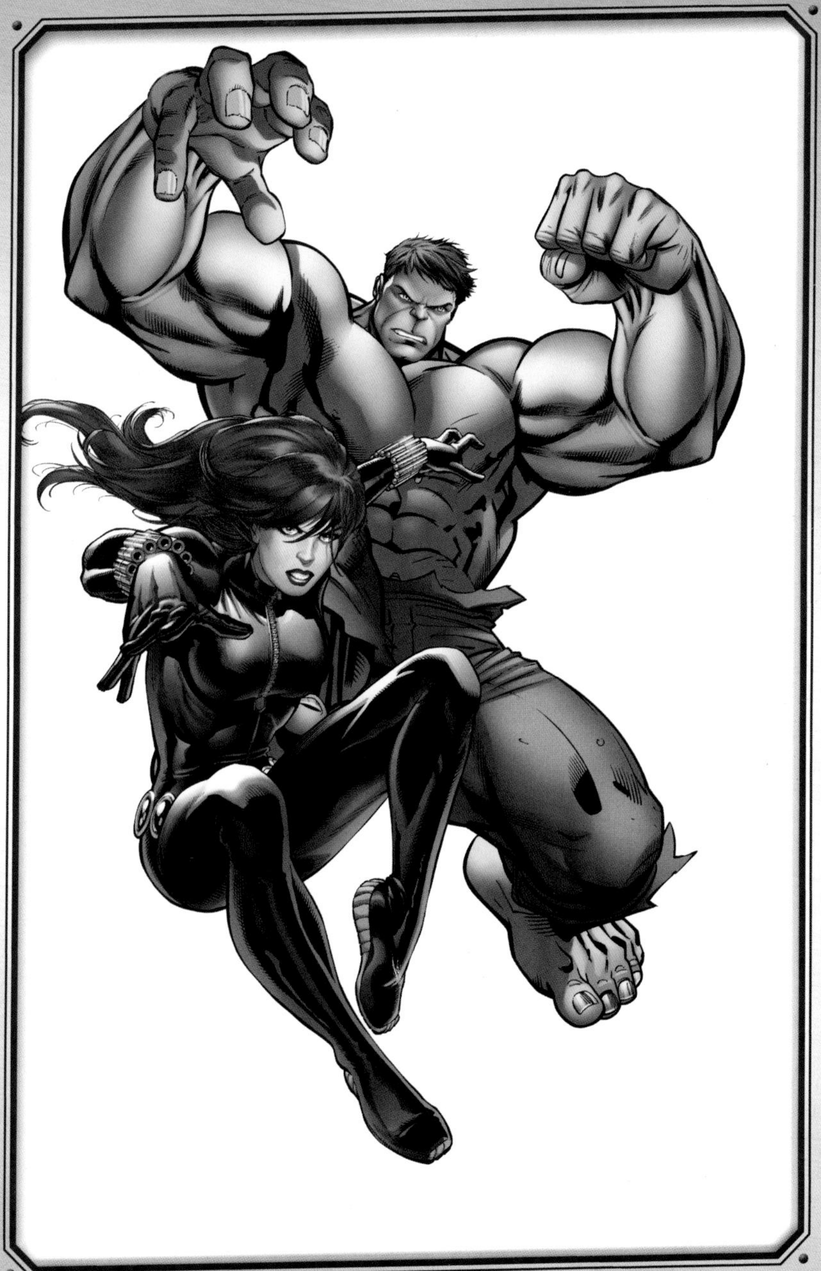

MARVEL UNIVERSE
AVENGERS ASSEMBLE #11

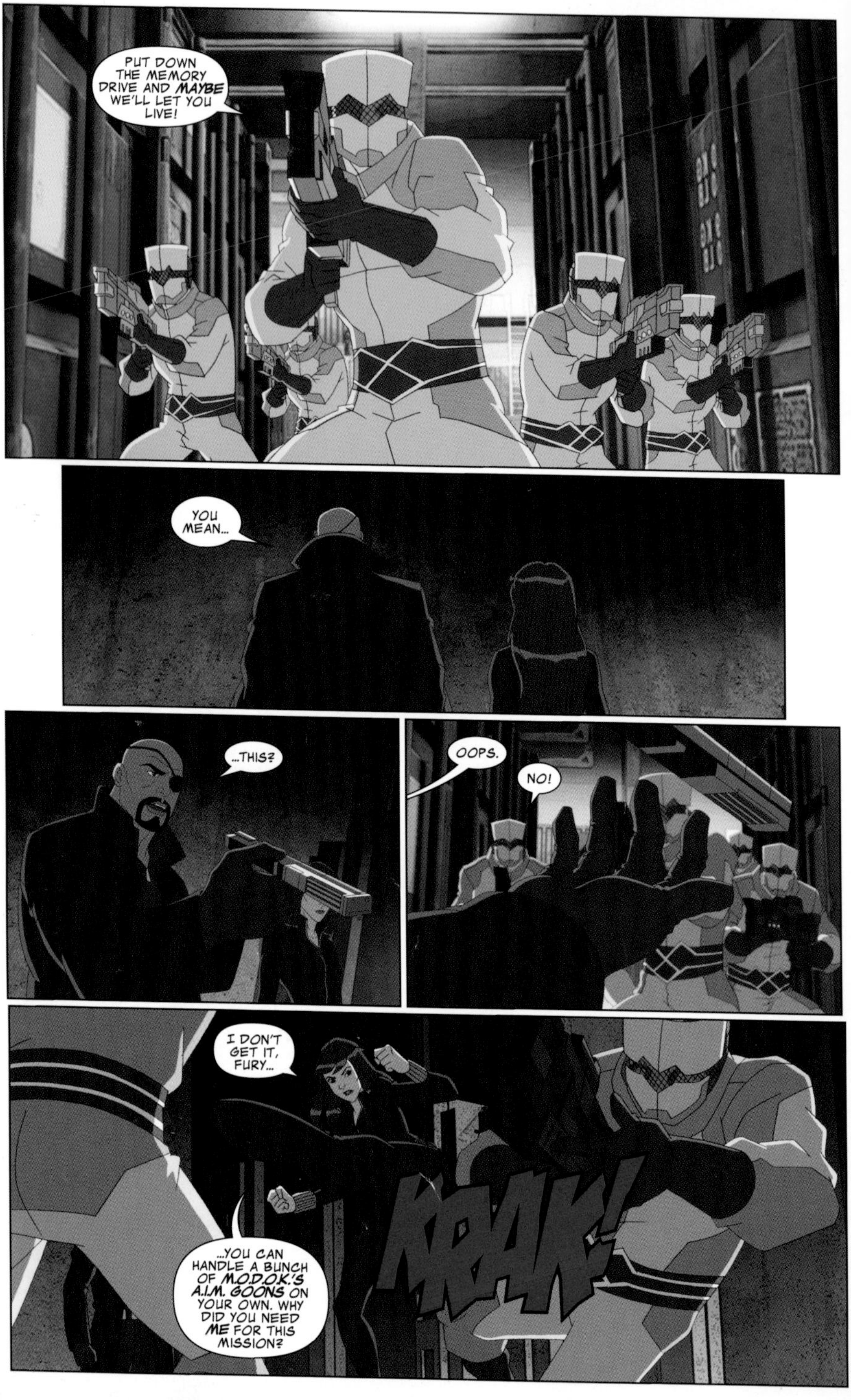
PUT DOWN THE MEMORY DRIVE AND MAYBE WE'LL LET YOU LIVE!
YOU MEAN...
...THIS?
OOPS.
NO!
I DON'T GET IT, FURY...
KRAAK!
...YOU CAN HANDLE A BUNCH OF M.O.D.O.K.'S A.I.M. GOONS ON YOUR OWN. WHY DID YOU NEED ME FOR THIS MISSION?

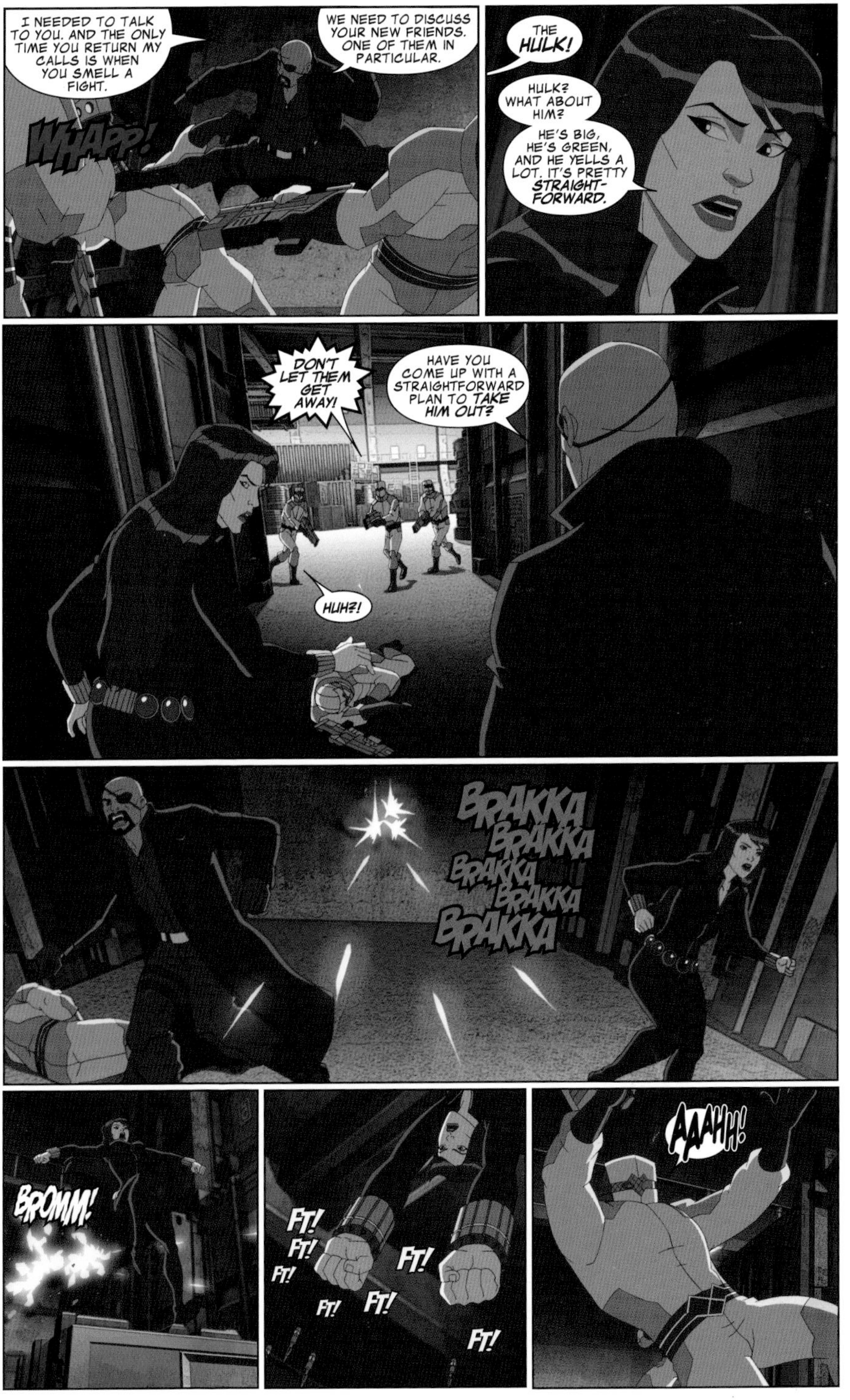

I NEEDED TO TALK TO YOU. AND THE ONLY TIME YOU RETURN MY CALLS IS WHEN YOU SMELL A FIGHT.
WE NEED TO DISCUSS YOUR NEW FRIENDS. ONE OF THEM IN PARTICULAR.
WHAPP!
THE HULK!
HULK? WHAT ABOUT HIM?
HE'S BIG, HE'S GREEN, AND HE YELLS A LOT. IT'S PRETTY STRAIGHT-FORWARD.
DON'T LET THEM GET AWAY!
HAVE YOU COME UP WITH A STRAIGHTFORWARD PLAN TO TAKE HIM OUT?
HUH?!
BRAKKA BRAKKA BRAKKA BRAKKA BRAKKA
BROMM!
FT! FT! FT! FT! FT! FT! FT!
AAAHH!

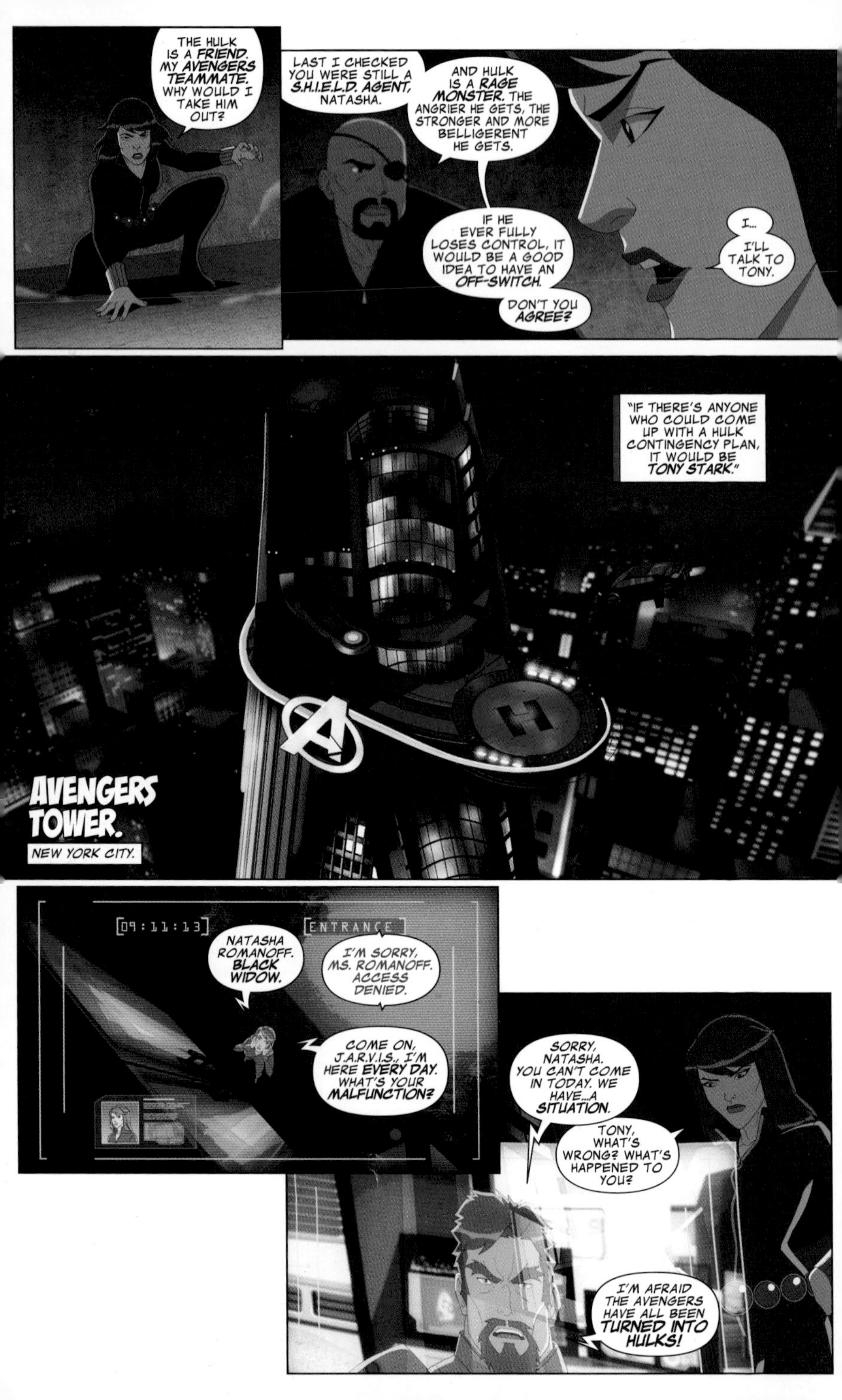
THE HULK IS A FRIEND. MY AVENGERS TEAMMATE. WHY WOULD I TAKE HIM OUT?
LAST I CHECKED YOU WERE STILL A S.H.I.E.L.D. AGENT, NATASHA.
AND HULK IS A RAGE MONSTER. THE ANGRIER HE GETS, THE STRONGER AND MORE BELLIGERENT HE GETS.
IF HE EVER FULLY LOSES CONTROL, IT WOULD BE A GOOD IDEA TO HAVE AN OFF-SWITCH.
DON'T YOU AGREE?
I...
I'LL TALK TO TONY.
"IF THERE'S ANYONE WHO COULD COME UP WITH A HULK CONTINGENCY PLAN, IT WOULD BE TONY STARK."
AVENGERS TOWER.
NEW YORK CITY.
09:11:13
ENTRANCE
NATASHA ROMANOFF. BLACK WIDOW.
I'M SORRY, MS. ROMANOFF. ACCESS DENIED.
COME ON, J.A.R.V.I.S., I'M HERE EVERY DAY. WHAT'S YOUR MALFUNCTION?
SORRY, NATASHA. YOU CAN'T COME IN TODAY. WE HAVE...A SITUATION.
TONY, WHAT'S WRONG? WHAT'S HAPPENED TO YOU?
I'M AFRAID THE AVENGERS HAVE ALL BEEN TURNED INTO HULKS!

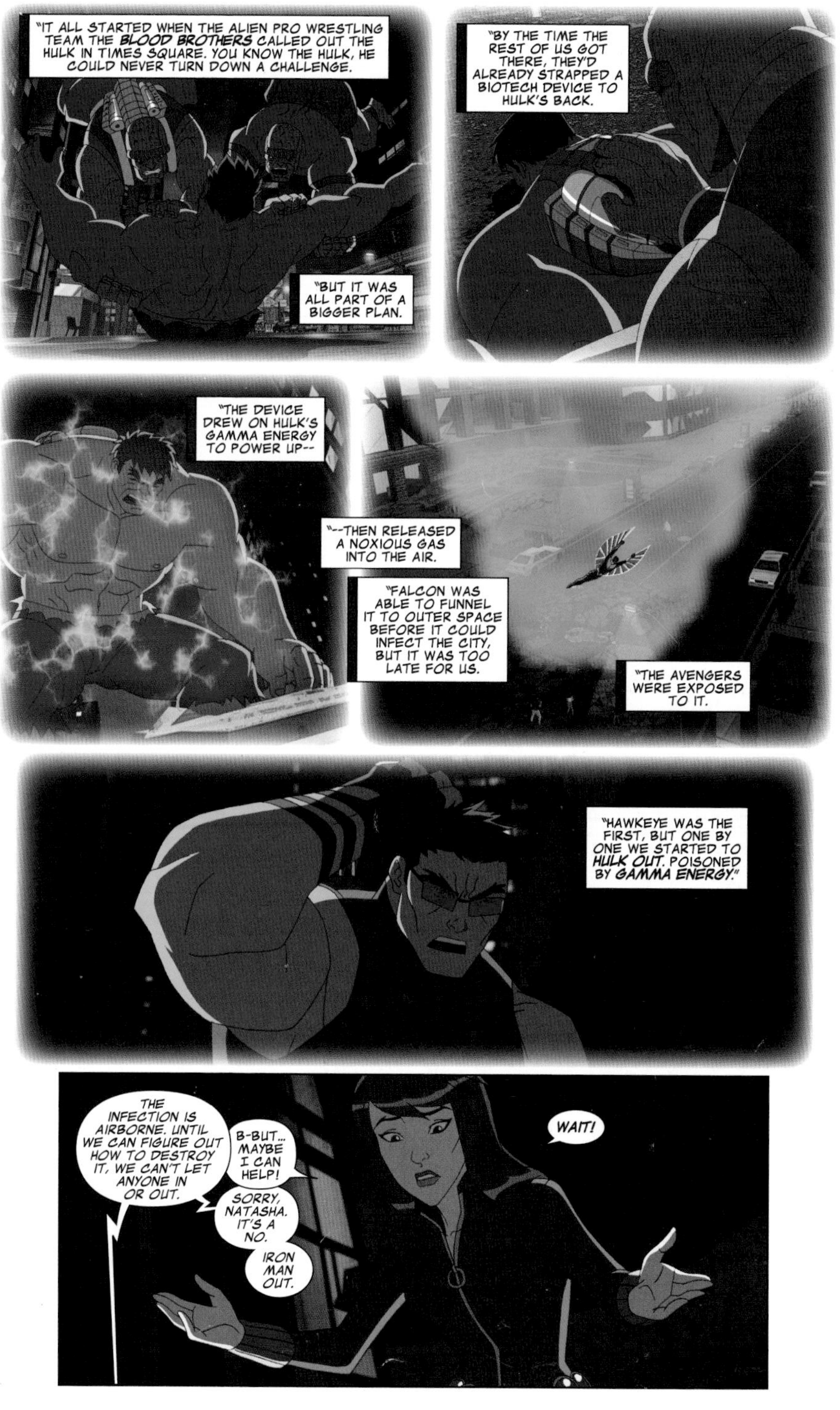
"IT ALL STARTED WHEN THE ALIEN PRO WRESTLING TEAM THE BLOOD BROTHERS CALLED OUT THE HULK IN TIMES SQUARE. YOU KNOW THE HULK, HE COULD NEVER TURN DOWN A CHALLENGE.
"BUT IT WAS ALL PART OF A BIGGER PLAN.
"BY THE TIME THE REST OF US GOT THERE, THEY'D ALREADY STRAPPED A BIOTECH DEVICE TO HULK'S BACK.
"THE DEVICE DREW ON HULK'S GAMMA ENERGY TO POWER UP--
"--THEN RELEASED A NOXIOUS GAS INTO THE AIR.
"FALCON WAS ABLE TO FUNNEL IT TO OUTER SPACE BEFORE IT COULD INFECT THE CITY, BUT IT WAS TOO LATE FOR US.
"THE AVENGERS WERE EXPOSED TO IT.
"HAWKEYE WAS THE FIRST, BUT ONE BY ONE WE STARTED TO HULK OUT. POISONED BY GAMMA ENERGY."
THE INFECTION IS AIRBORNE. UNTIL WE CAN FIGURE OUT HOW TO DESTROY IT, WE CAN'T LET ANYONE IN OR OUT.
B-BUT... MAYBE I CAN HELP!
SORRY, NATASHA. IT'S A NO.
IRON MAN OUT.
WAIT!

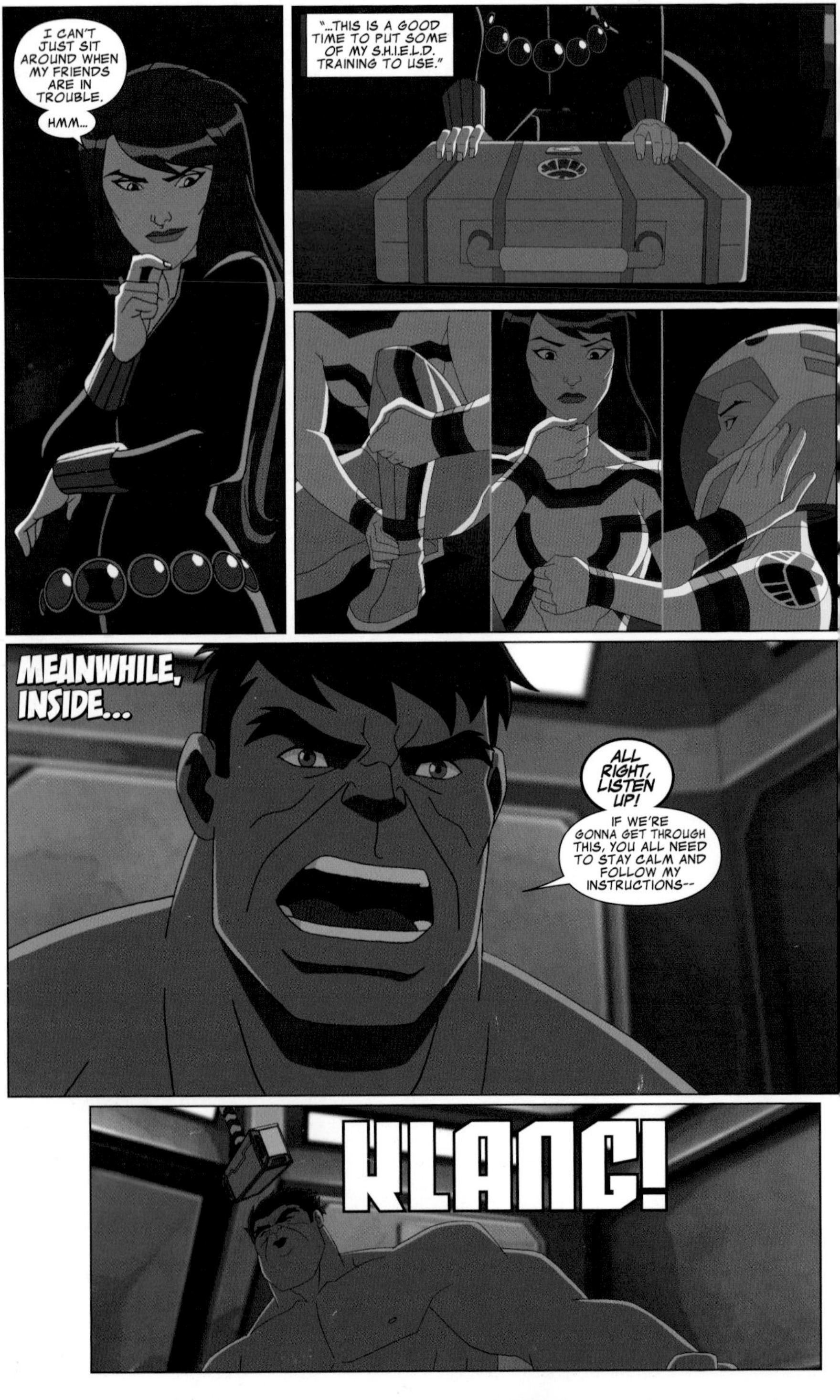
I CAN'T JUST SIT AROUND WHEN MY FRIENDS ARE IN TROUBLE.
HMM...
"...THIS IS A GOOD TIME TO PUT SOME OF MY S.H.I.E.L.D. TRAINING TO USE."
MEANWHILE, INSIDE...
ALL RIGHT, LISTEN UP!
IF WE'RE GONNA GET THROUGH THIS, YOU ALL NEED TO STAY CALM AND FOLLOW MY INSTRUCTIONS--
KLANG!

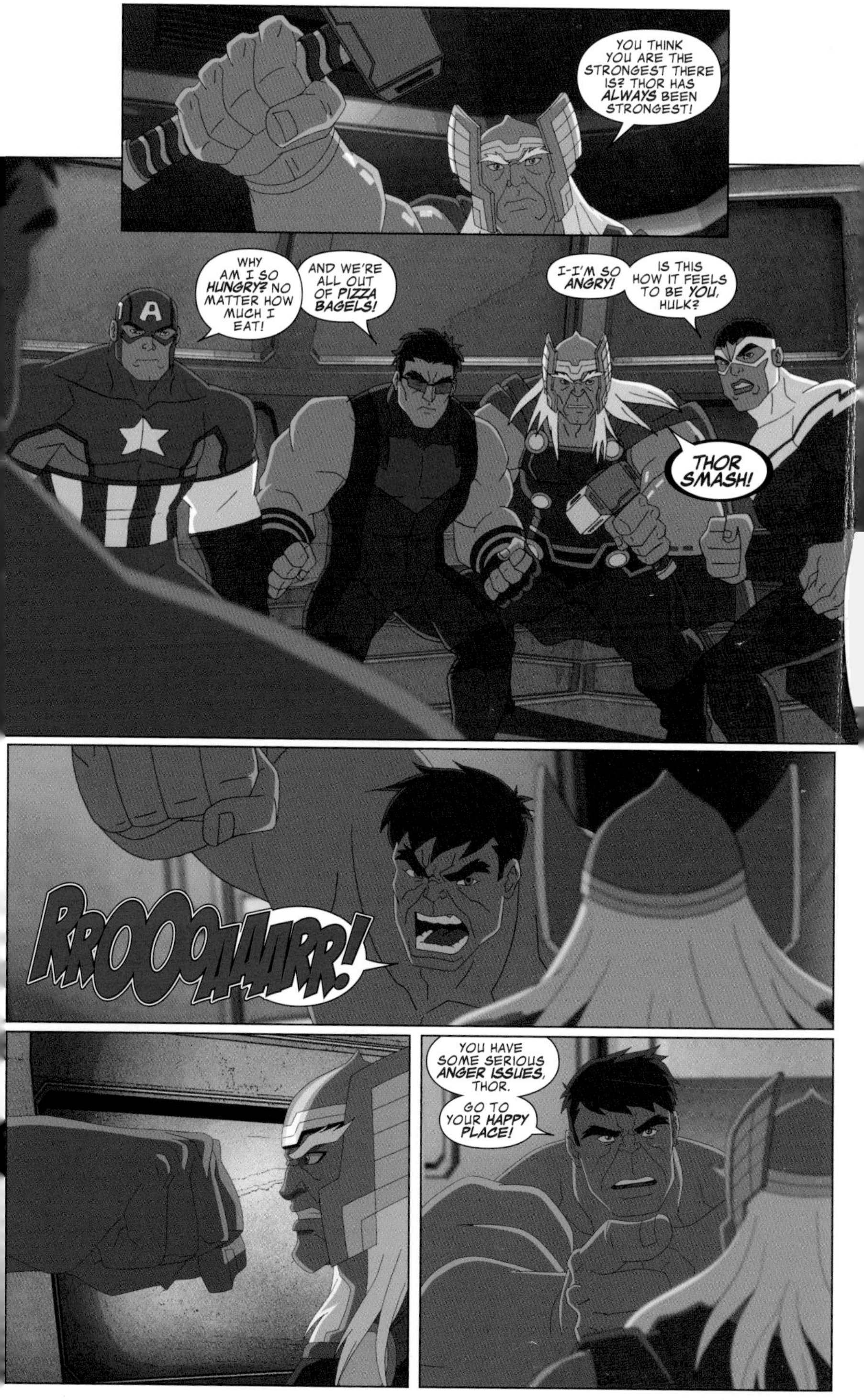
YOU THINK YOU ARE THE STRONGEST THERE IS? THOR HAS ALWAYS BEEN STRONGEST!
WHY AM I SO HUNGRY? NO MATTER HOW MUCH I EAT!
AND WE'RE ALL OUT OF PIZZA BAGELS!
I-I'M SO ANGRY!
IS THIS HOW IT FEELS TO BE YOU, HULK?
THOR SMASH!
RROOOAARR!
YOU HAVE SOME SERIOUS ANGER ISSUES, THOR.
GO TO YOUR HAPPY PLACE!

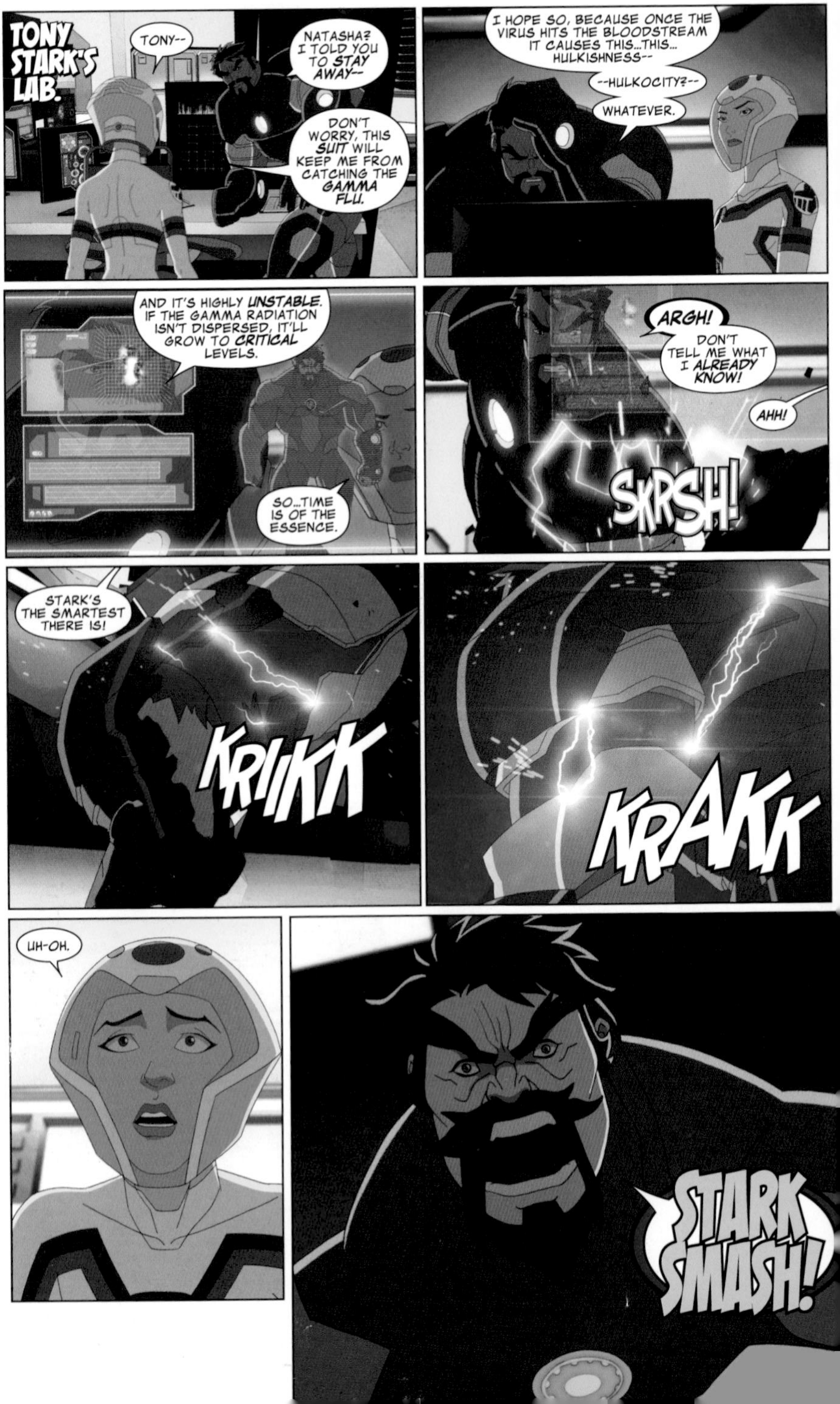
TONY STARK'S LAB.
TONY--
NATASHA? I TOLD YOU TO STAY AWAY--
DON'T WORRY, THIS SUIT WILL KEEP ME FROM CATCHING THE GAMMA FLU.
I HOPE SO, BECAUSE ONCE THE VIRUS HITS THE BLOODSTREAM IT CAUSES THIS...THIS... HULKISHNESS--
--HULKOCITY?--
WHATEVER.
AND IT'S HIGHLY UNSTABLE. IF THE GAMMA RADIATION ISN'T DISPERSED, IT'LL GROW TO CRITICAL LEVELS.
SO...TIME IS OF THE ESSENCE.
ARGH!
DON'T TELL ME WHAT I ALREADY KNOW!
AHH!
SKRSH!
STARK'S THE SMARTEST THERE IS!
KRIIKK
KRAKK
UH-OH.
STARK SMASH!

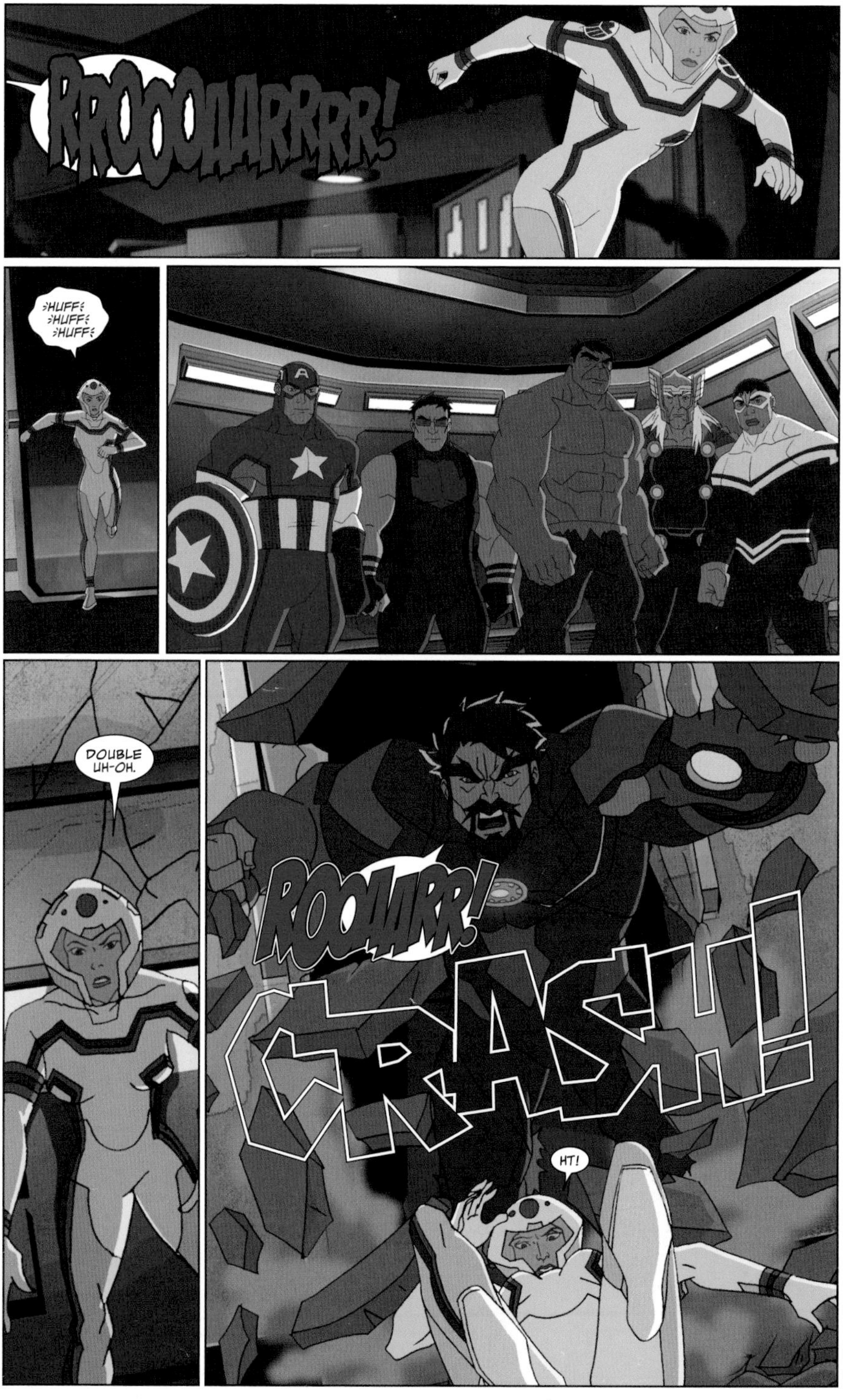
RROOOWARRRR!
HUFF HUFF HUFF
DOUBLE UH-OH.
ROOWRR!
CRASH!
HT!

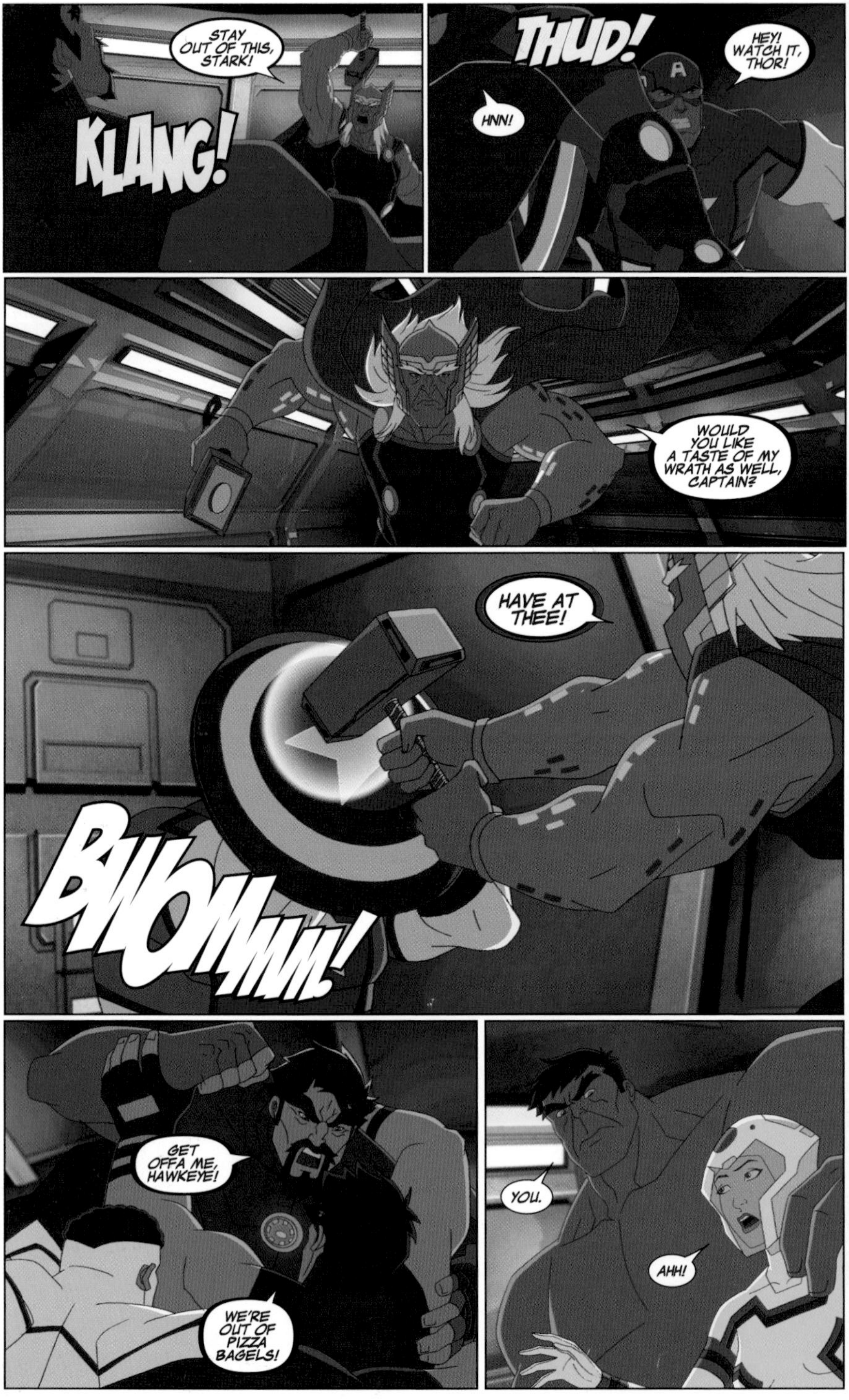
STAY OUT OF THIS, STARK!
KLANG!
THUD!
HEY! WATCH IT, THOR!
HNN!
WOULD YOU LIKE A TASTE OF MY WRATH AS WELL, CAPTAIN?
HAVE AT THEE!
BVOMMM!
GET OFFA ME, HAWKEYE!
WE'RE OUT OF PIZZA BAGELS!
YOU.
AHH!

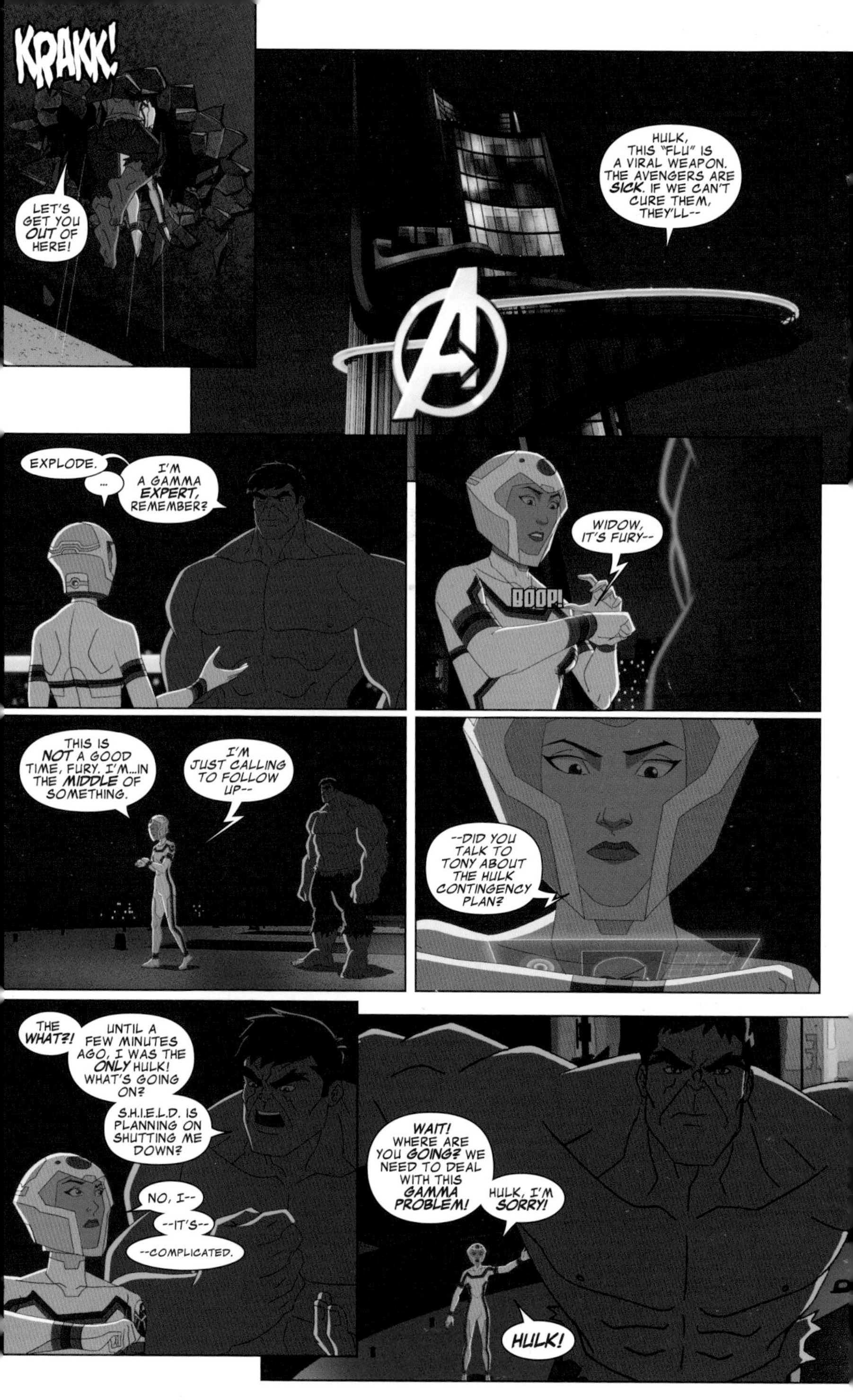
KRAKK!
LET'S GET YOU OUT OF HERE!
HULK, THIS "FLU" IS A VIRAL WEAPON. THE AVENGERS ARE SICK. IF WE CAN'T CURE THEM, THEY'LL--
EXPLODE.
...
I'M A GAMMA EXPERT, REMEMBER?
WIDOW, IT'S FURY--
BOOP!
THIS IS NOT A GOOD TIME, FURY. I'M...IN THE MIDDLE OF SOMETHING.
I'M JUST CALLING TO FOLLOW UP--
--DID YOU TALK TO TONY ABOUT THE HULK CONTINGENCY PLAN?
THE WHAT?!
UNTIL A FEW MINUTES AGO, I WAS THE ONLY HULK! WHAT'S GOING ON?
S.H.I.E.L.D. IS PLANNING ON SHUTTING ME DOWN?
NO, I--
--IT'S--
--COMPLICATED.
WAIT! WHERE ARE YOU GOING? WE NEED TO DEAL WITH THIS GAMMA PROBLEM!
HULK, I'M SORRY!
HULK!

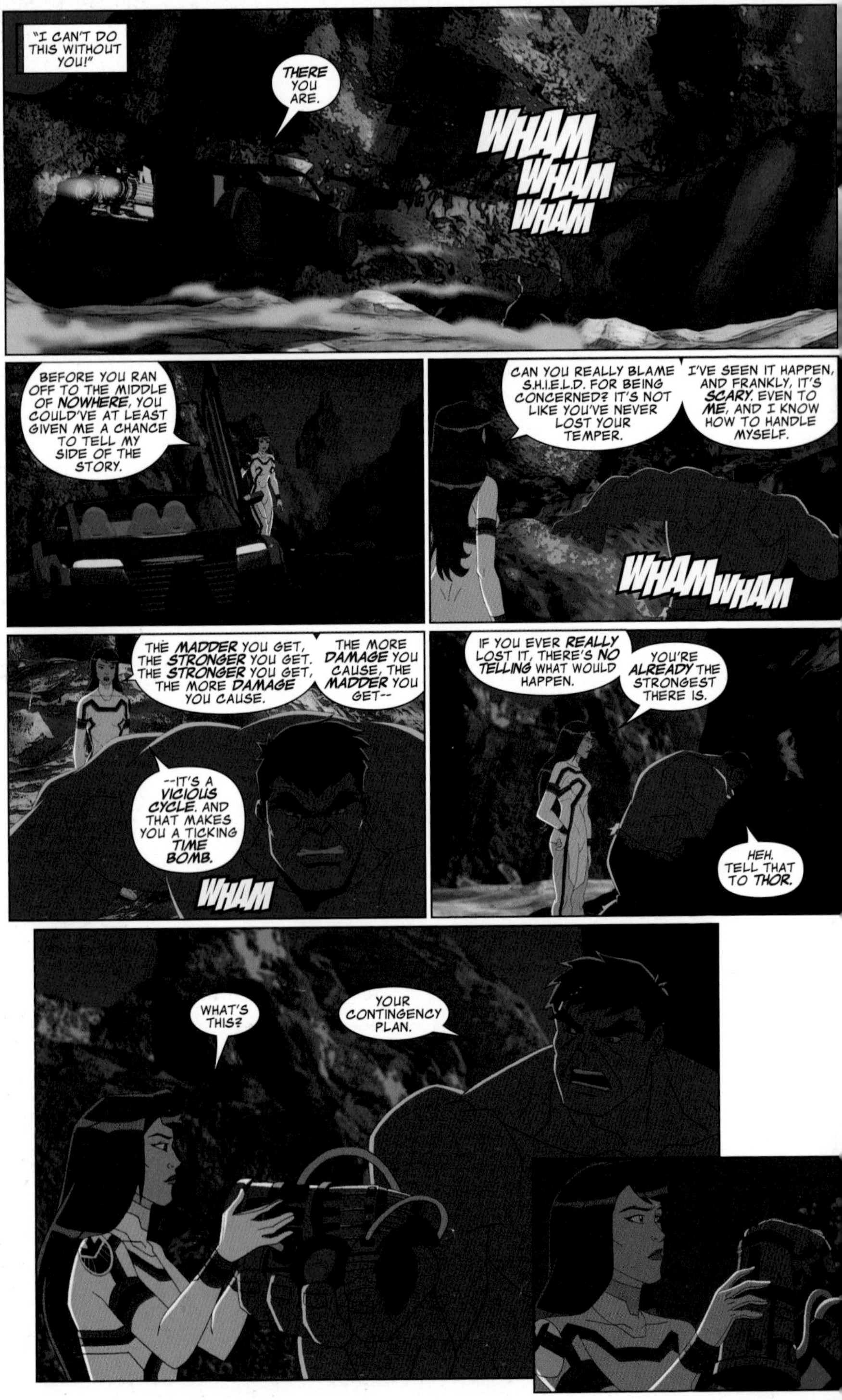
"I CAN'T DO THIS WITHOUT YOU!"
THERE YOU ARE.
WHAM WHAM WHAM
BEFORE YOU RAN OFF TO THE MIDDLE OF NOWHERE, YOU COULD'VE AT LEAST GIVEN ME A CHANCE TO TELL MY SIDE OF THE STORY.
CAN YOU REALLY BLAME S.H.I.E.L.D. FOR BEING CONCERNED? IT'S NOT LIKE YOU'VE NEVER LOST YOUR TEMPER.
I'VE SEEN IT HAPPEN, AND FRANKLY, IT'S SCARY. EVEN TO ME, AND I KNOW HOW TO HANDLE MYSELF.
WHAM WHAM
THE MADDER YOU GET, THE STRONGER YOU GET. THE STRONGER YOU GET, THE MORE DAMAGE YOU CAUSE.
THE MORE DAMAGE YOU CAUSE, THE MADDER YOU GET--
--IT'S A VICIOUS CYCLE. AND THAT MAKES YOU A TICKING TIME BOMB.
WHAM
IF YOU EVER REALLY LOST IT, THERE'S NO TELLING WHAT WOULD HAPPEN.
YOU'RE ALREADY THE STRONGEST THERE IS.
HEH. TELL THAT TO THOR.
WHAT'S THIS?
YOUR CONTINGENCY PLAN.

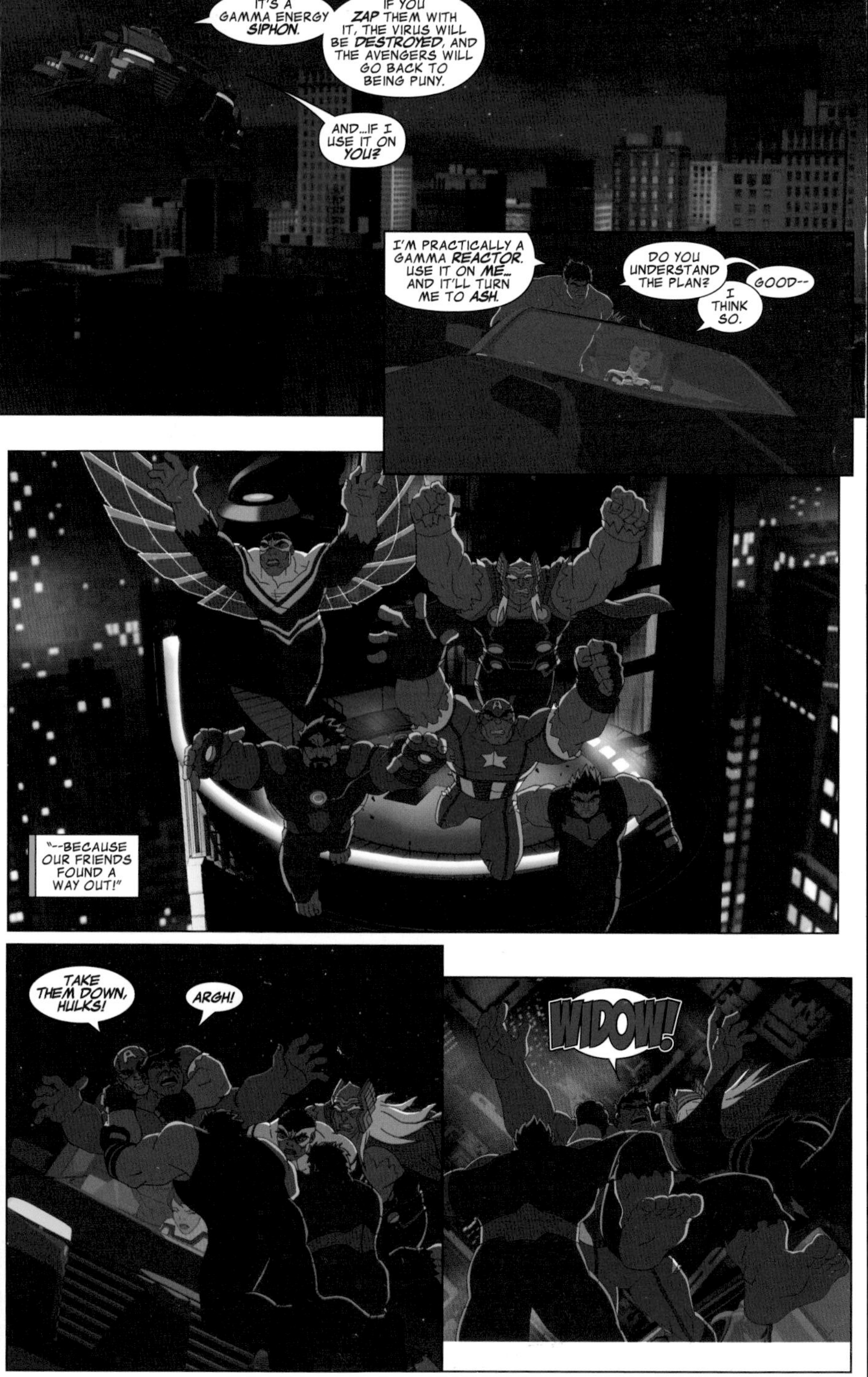
IT'S A GAMMA ENERGY SIPHON.
IF YOU ZAP THEM WITH IT, THE VIRUS WILL BE DESTROYED, AND THE AVENGERS WILL GO BACK TO BEING PUNY.
AND...IF I USE IT ON YOU?
I'M PRACTICALLY A GAMMA REACTOR. USE IT ON ME... AND IT'LL TURN ME TO ASH.
DO YOU UNDERSTAND THE PLAN?
I THINK SO.
GOOD--
"--BECAUSE OUR FRIENDS FOUND A WAY OUT!"
TAKE THEM DOWN, HULKS!
ARGH!
WIDOW!

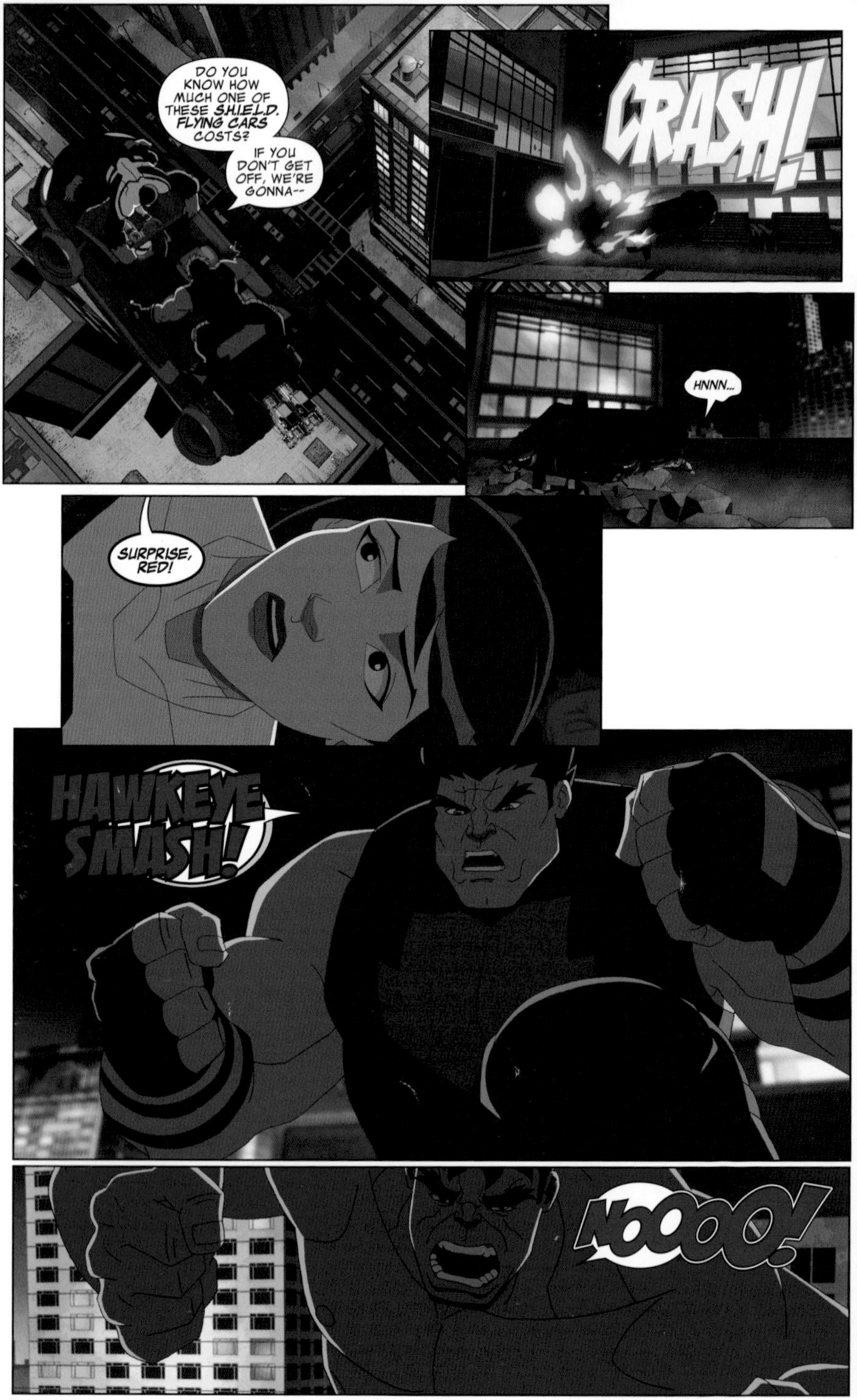

DO YOU KNOW HOW MUCH ONE OF THESE S.H.I.E.L.D. FLYING CARS COSTS?
IF YOU DON'T GET OFF, WE'RE GONNA--
CRASH!
HNNN...
SURPRISE, RED!
HAWKEYE SMASH!
NOOOO!

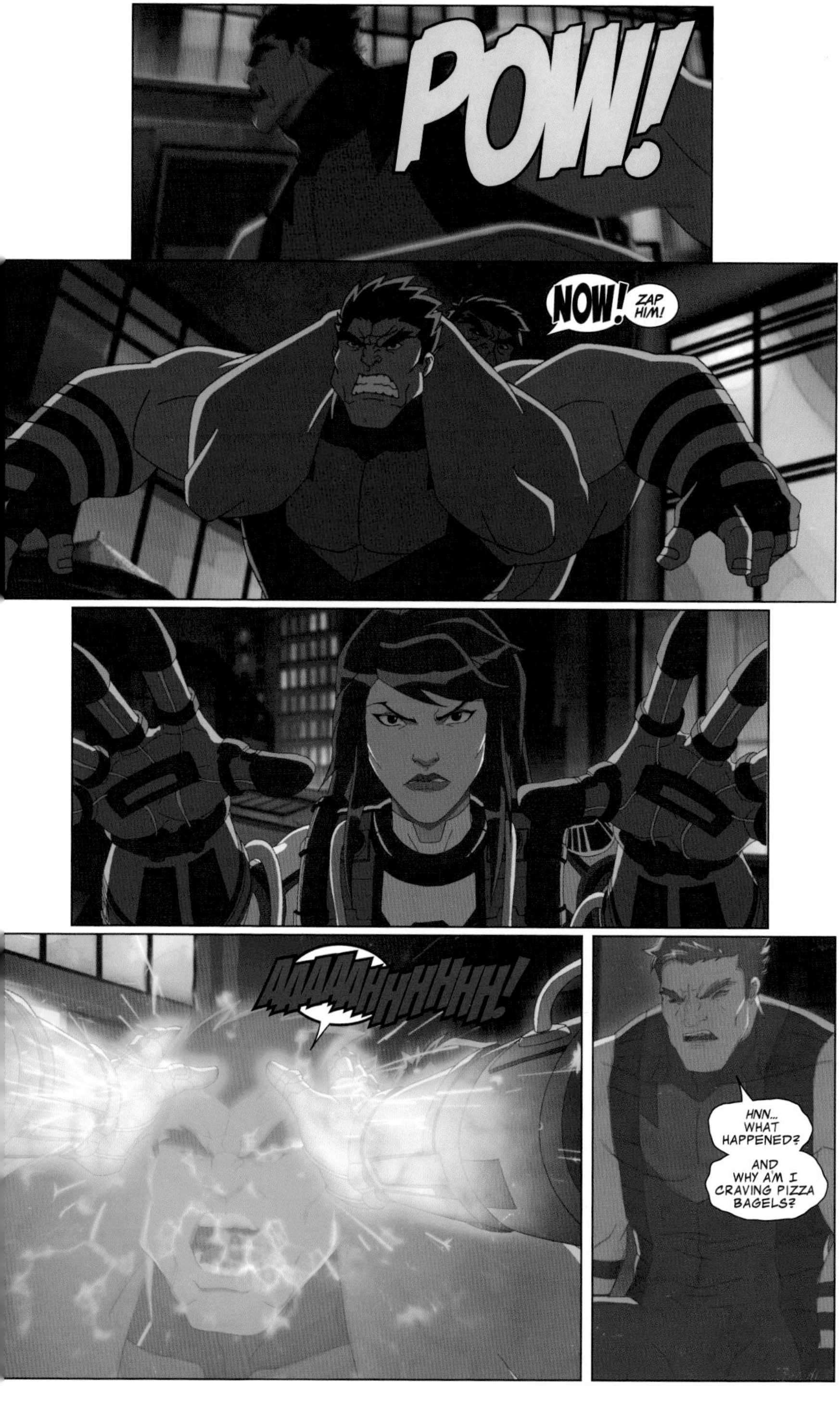
POW!
NOW!
ZAP HIM!
AAAAHHHHH!
HNN... WHAT HAPPENED?
AND WHY A'M I CRAVING PIZZA BAGELS?

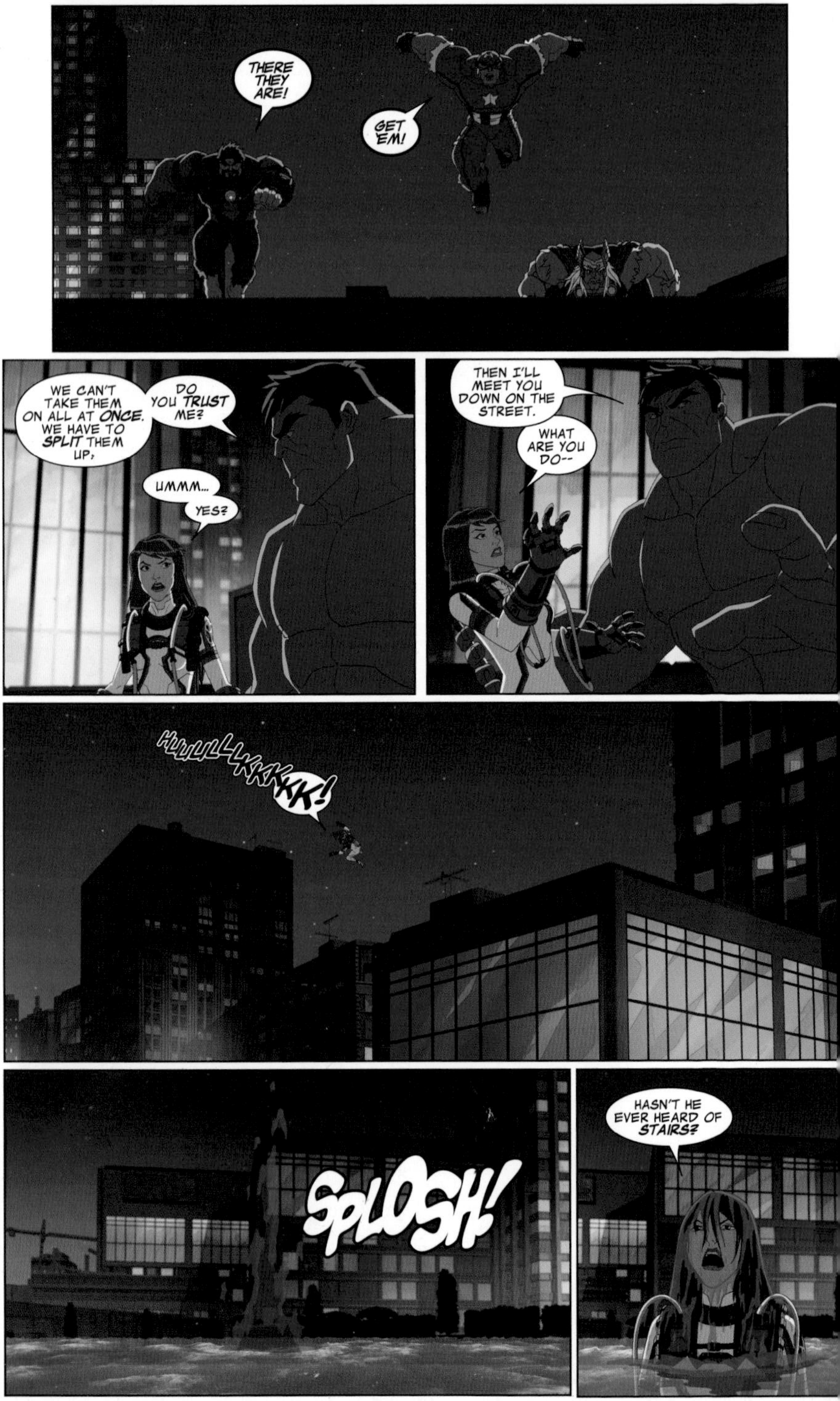
THERE THEY ARE!
GET 'EM!
WE CAN'T TAKE THEM ON ALL AT ONCE. WE HAVE TO SPLIT THEM UP.
DO YOU TRUST ME?
UMMM...
YES?
THEN I'LL MEET YOU DOWN ON THE STREET.
WHAT ARE YOU DO--
HUUULLLKKKKKK!
SPLOSH!
HASN'T HE EVER HEARD OF STAIRS?

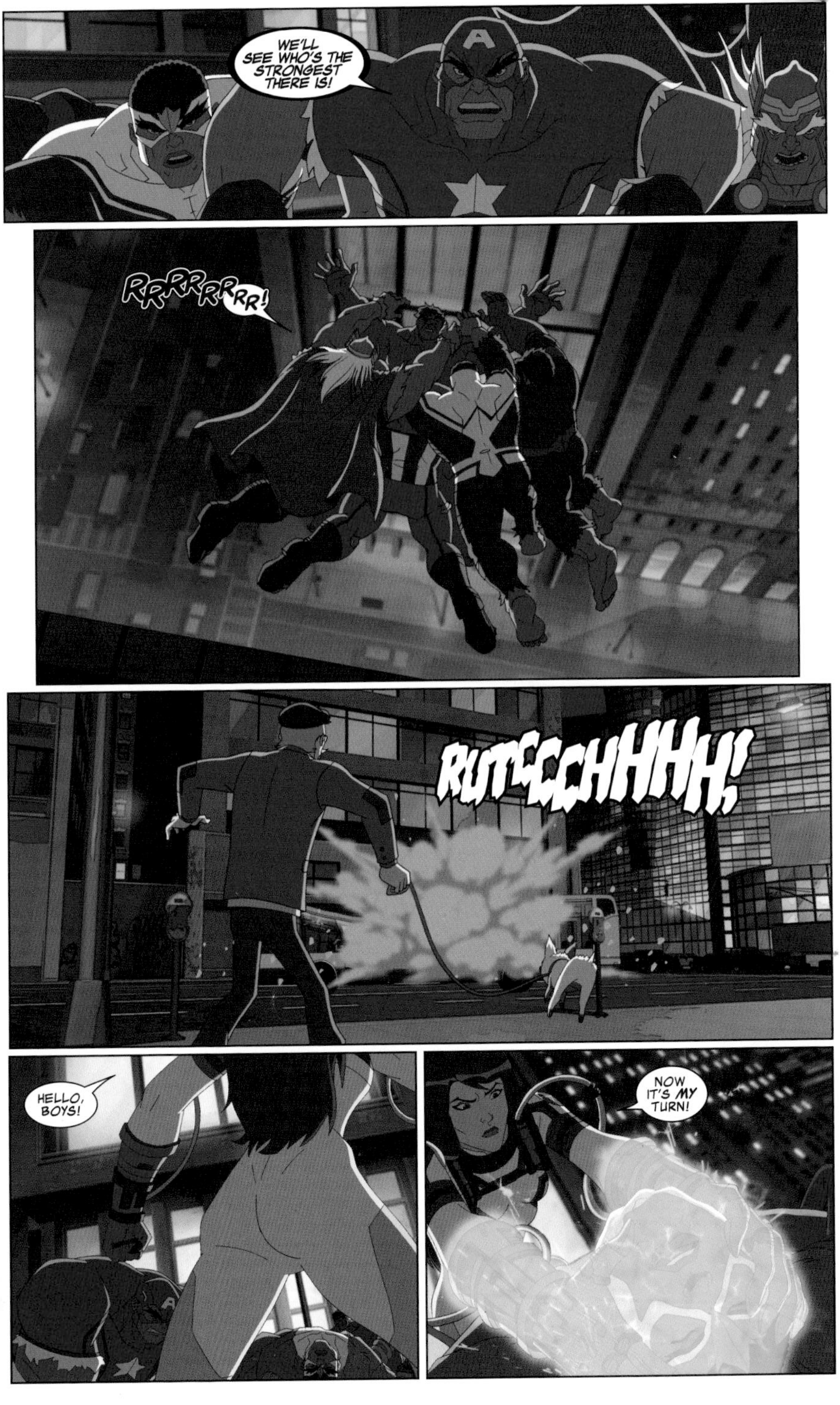
WE'LL SEE WHO'S THE STRONGEST THERE IS!
RRRRRRRR!
RUTSCCHHHH!
HELLO, BOYS!
NOW IT'S MY TURN!

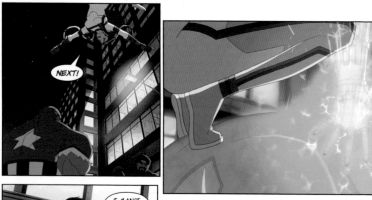

NEXT!

I CAN'T GET THEM ALL! WE'RE OUT OF TIME!

"THOR AND IRON MAN ARE GOING *FULL GAMMA!*"

THEY'RE NOT TOO FAR GONE YET! BUT WE'LL NEED SOME EXTRA SMASH TO TAKE THEM DOWN!

TIME TO GET ANGRY!

RRARRR!

THWOK!

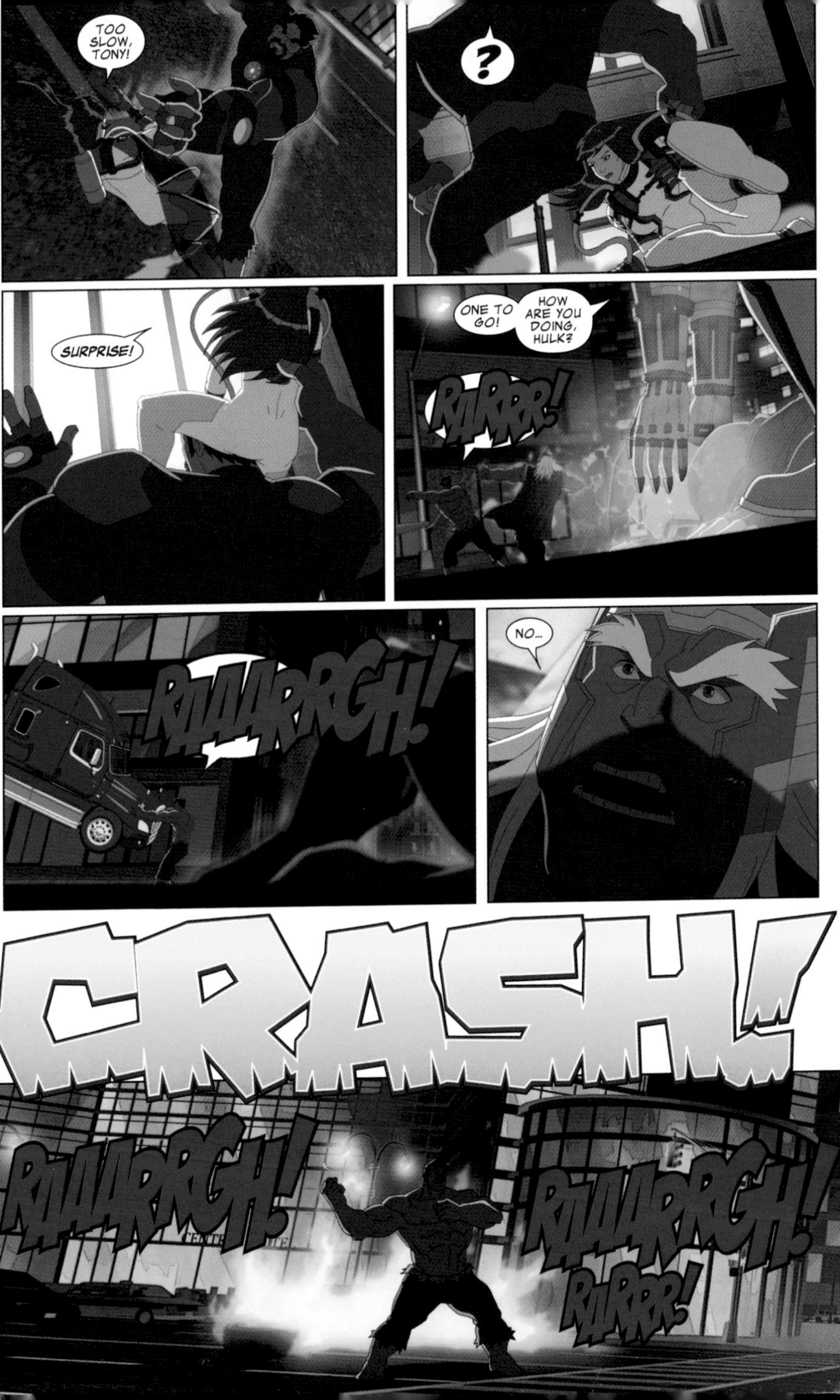
TOO SLOW, TONY!
?
SURPRISE!
ONE TO GO!
HOW ARE YOU DOING, HULK?
RARRR!
RAAARRGH!
NO...
CRASH!
RAAARRGH!
RAAARRGH!
RARRR!

HULK! AM! STRONNGGGESSST!

DO YOUR THING, WIDOW.

YOU SAW!

YOU'RE MY WITNESS!

I TOTALLY BEAT UP THOR!

I AM THE STRONGEST THERE IS!

HE OWES ME FIVE DOLLARS!

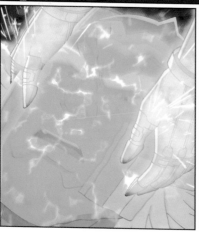

THAT WAS EASY. THANKS TO YOU.

I'M SURE GLAD YOU'RE ON OUR SIDE, HULK.

YOU'RE NOT SO BAD YOURSELF.

"WALK ME THROUGH THIS AGAIN. ONE MORE TIME..."

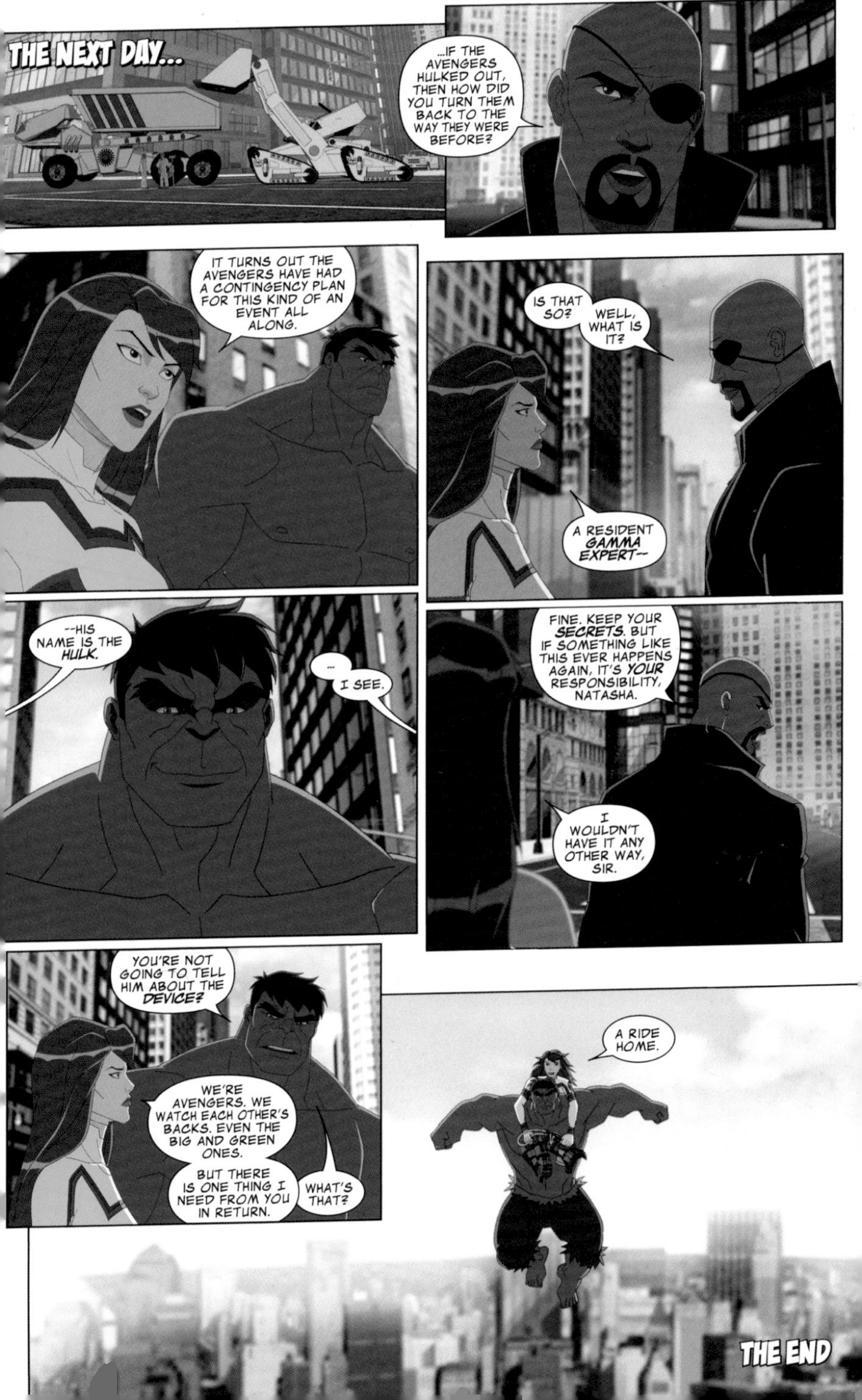
THE NEXT DAY...
...IF THE AVENGERS HULKED OUT, THEN HOW DID YOU TURN THEM BACK TO THE WAY THEY WERE BEFORE?
IT TURNS OUT THE AVENGERS HAVE HAD A CONTINGENCY PLAN FOR THIS KIND OF AN EVENT ALL ALONG.
IS THAT SO?
WELL, WHAT IS IT?
A RESIDENT GAMMA EXPERT--
--HIS NAME IS THE HULK.
... I SEE.
FINE. KEEP YOUR SECRETS. BUT IF SOMETHING LIKE THIS EVER HAPPENS AGAIN, IT'S YOUR RESPONSIBILITY, NATASHA.
I WOULDN'T HAVE IT ANY OTHER WAY, SIR.
YOU'RE NOT GOING TO TELL HIM ABOUT THE DEVICE?
WE'RE AVENGERS. WE WATCH EACH OTHER'S BACKS. EVEN THE BIG AND GREEN ONES.
BUT THERE IS ONE THING I NEED FROM YOU IN RETURN.
WHAT'S THAT?
A RIDE HOME.
THE END

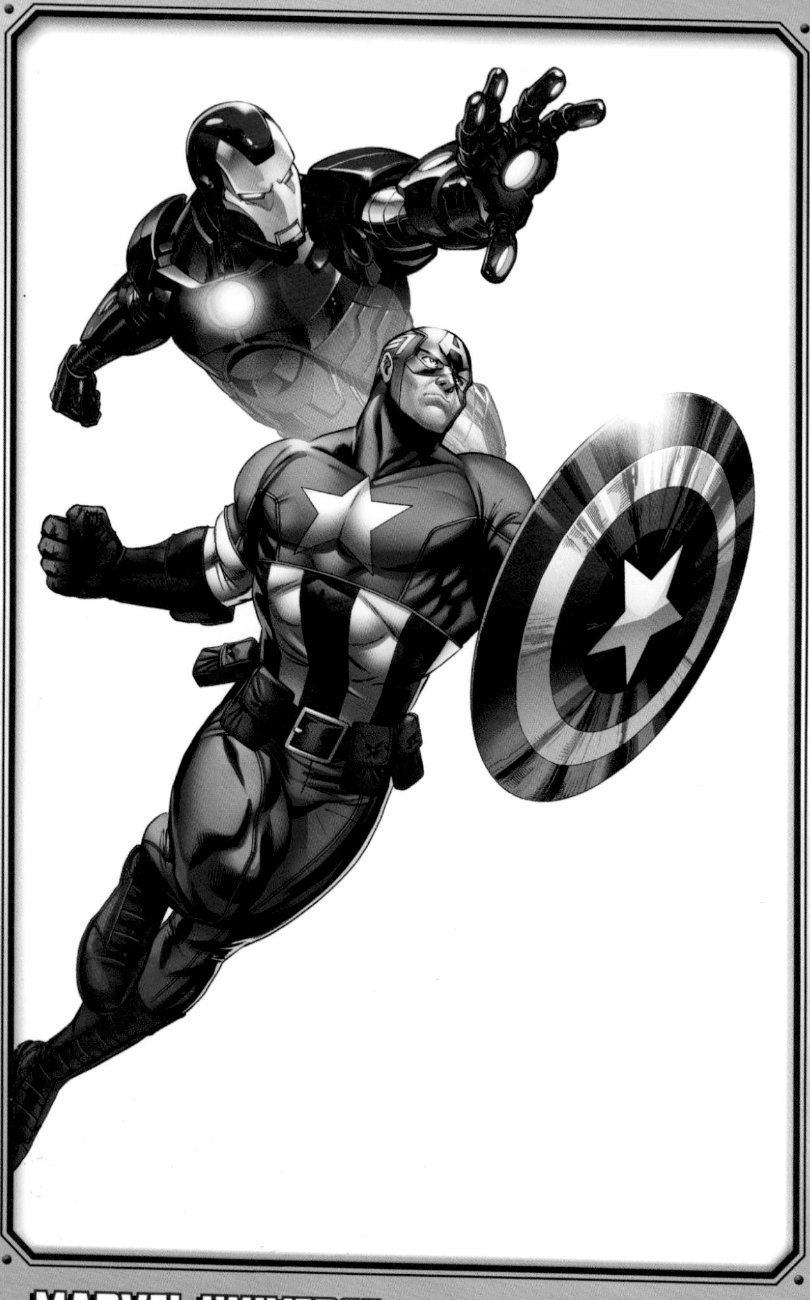

MARVEL UNIVERSE
AVENGERS ASSEMBLE #13

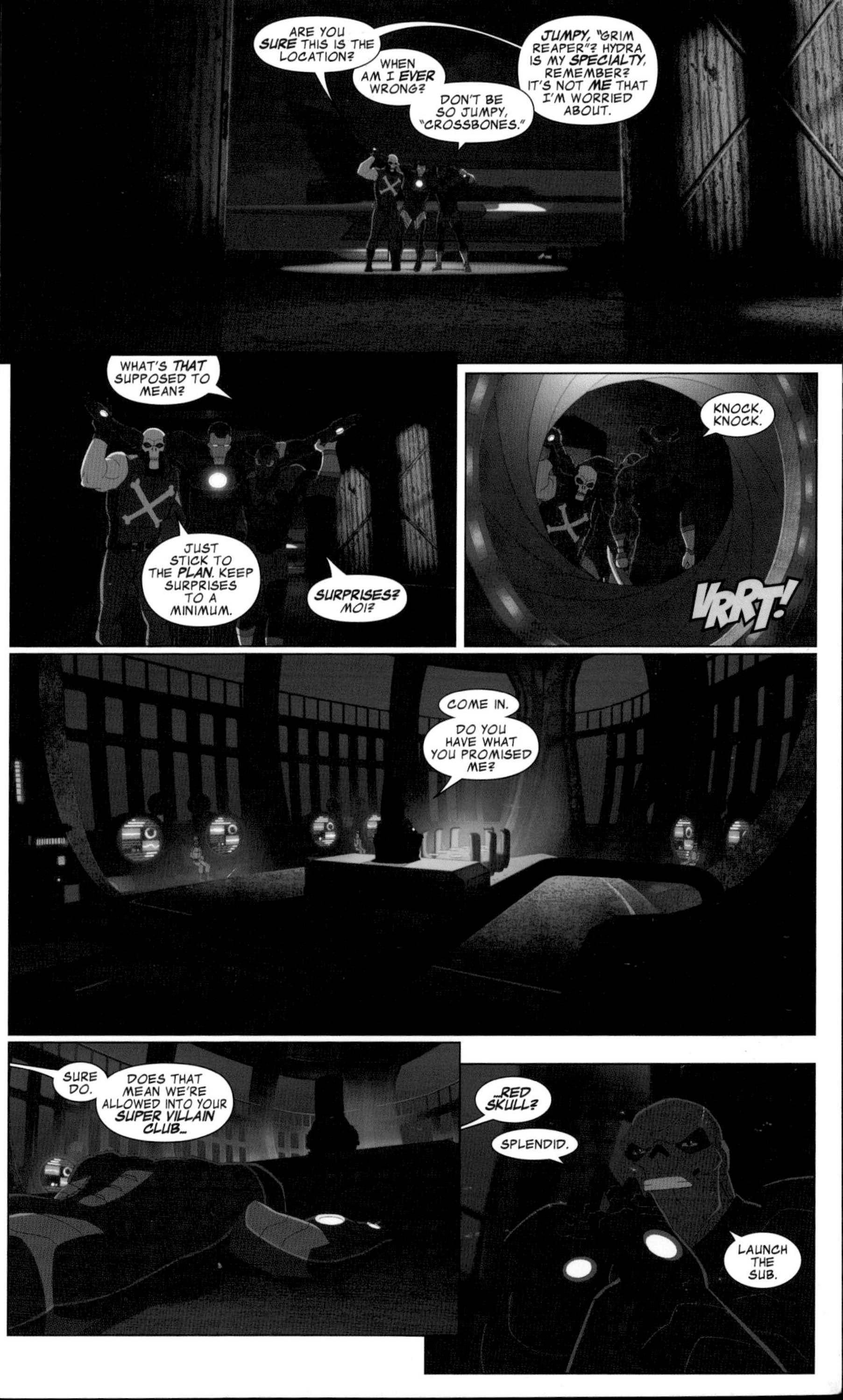

ARE YOU SURE THIS IS THE LOCATION?
WHEN AM I EVER WRONG?
DON'T BE SO JUMPY, "CROSSBONES."
JUMPY, "GRIM REAPER"? HYDRA IS MY SPECIALTY, REMEMBER? IT'S NOT ME THAT I'M WORRIED ABOUT.
WHAT'S THAT SUPPOSED TO MEAN?
JUST STICK TO THE PLAN. KEEP SURPRISES TO A MINIMUM.
SURPRISES? MOI?
KNOCK, KNOCK.
VRRT!
COME IN.
DO YOU HAVE WHAT YOU PROMISED ME?
SURE DO.
DOES THAT MEAN WE'RE ALLOWED INTO YOUR SUPER VILLAIN CLUB...
...RED SKULL?
SPLENDID.
LAUNCH THE SUB.

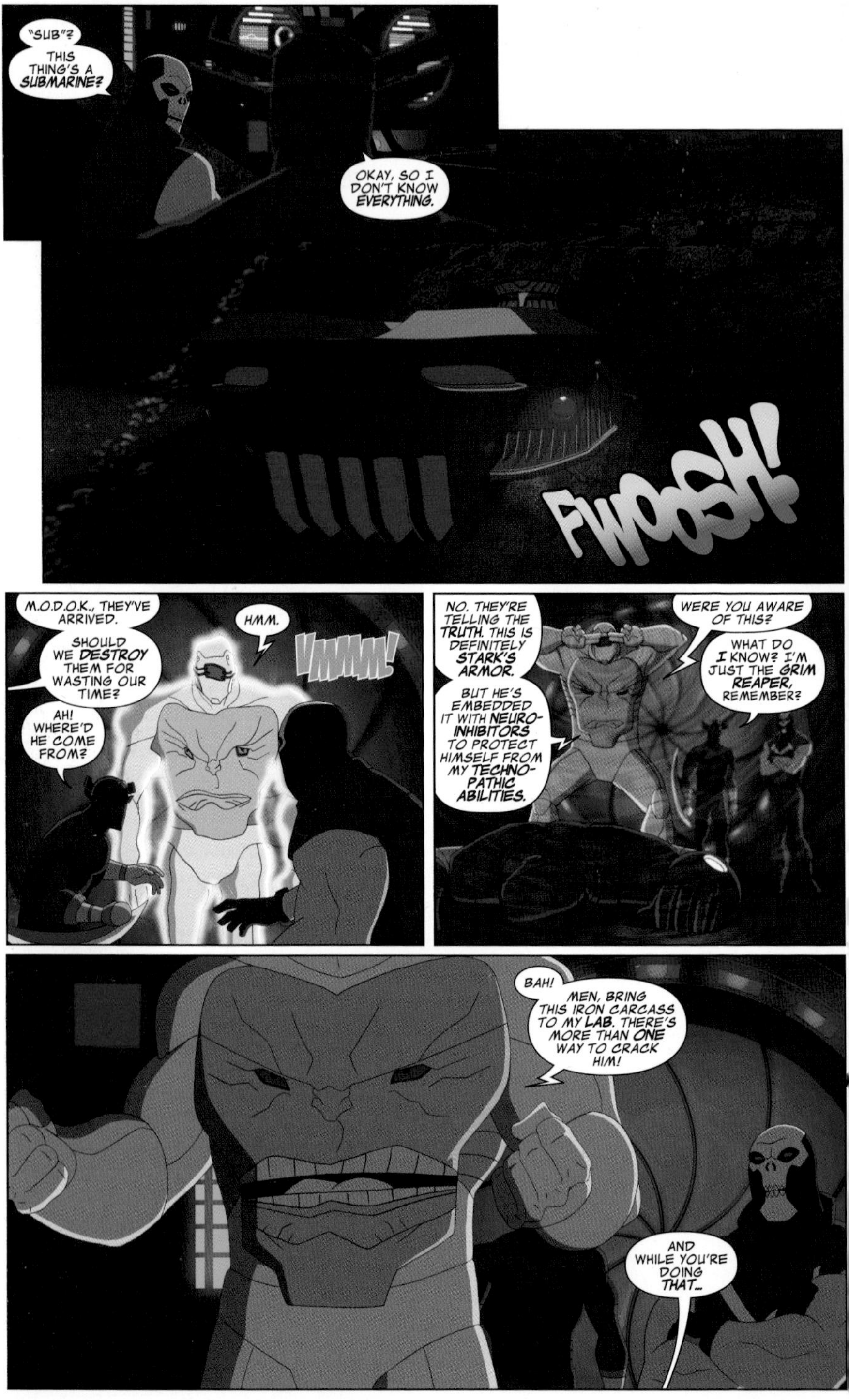
"SUB"? THIS THING'S A SUBMARINE?
OKAY, SO I DON'T KNOW EVERYTHING.
FWOOSH!
M.O.D.O.K., THEY'VE ARRIVED.
SHOULD WE DESTROY THEM FOR WASTING OUR TIME?
HMM.
VMMMM!
AH! WHERE'D HE COME FROM?
NO. THEY'RE TELLING THE TRUTH. THIS IS DEFINITELY STARK'S ARMOR.
BUT HE'S EMBEDDED IT WITH NEURO-INHIBITORS TO PROTECT HIMSELF FROM MY TECHNOPATHIC ABILITIES.
WERE YOU AWARE OF THIS?
WHAT DO I KNOW? I'M JUST THE GRIM REAPER, REMEMBER?
BAH!
MEN, BRING THIS IRON CARCASS TO MY LAB. THERE'S MORE THAN ONE WAY TO CRACK HIM!
AND WHILE YOU'RE DOING THAT...

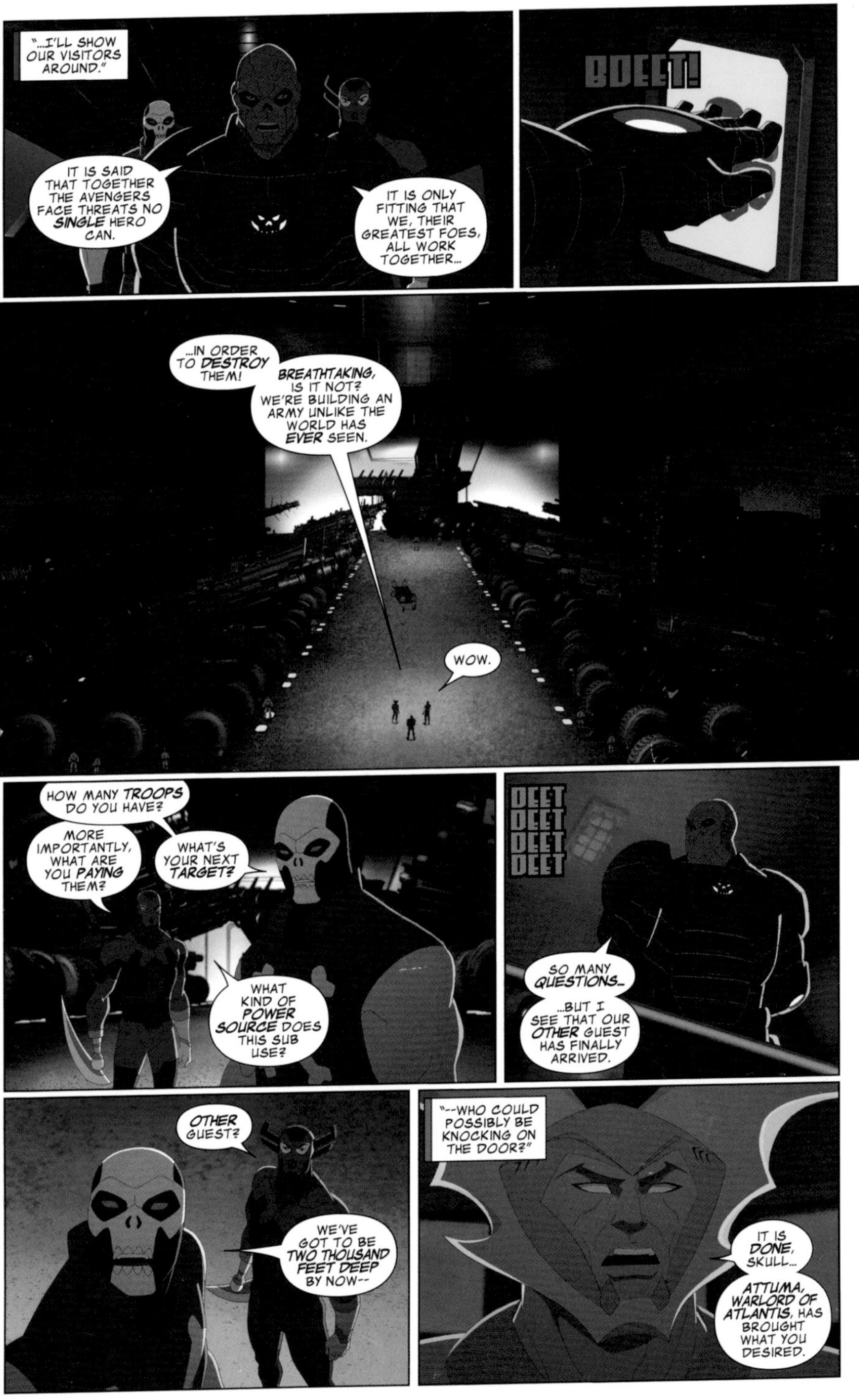
"...I'LL SHOW OUR VISITORS AROUND."
IT IS SAID THAT TOGETHER THE AVENGERS FACE THREATS NO SINGLE HERO CAN.
IT IS ONLY FITTING THAT WE, THEIR GREATEST FOES, ALL WORK TOGETHER...
BDEET!
...IN ORDER TO DESTROY THEM!
BREATHTAKING, IS IT NOT? WE'RE BUILDING AN ARMY UNLIKE THE WORLD HAS EVER SEEN.
WOW.
HOW MANY TROOPS DO YOU HAVE?
MORE IMPORTANTLY, WHAT ARE YOU PAYING THEM?
WHAT'S YOUR NEXT TARGET?
WHAT KIND OF POWER SOURCE DOES THIS SUB USE?
DEET DEET DEET DEET
SO MANY QUESTIONS...
...BUT I SEE THAT OUR OTHER GUEST HAS FINALLY ARRIVED.
OTHER GUEST?
WE'VE GOT TO BE TWO THOUSAND FEET DEEP BY NOW--
"--WHO COULD POSSIBLY BE KNOCKING ON THE DOOR?"
IT IS DONE, SKULL...
ATTUMA, WARLORD OF ATLANTIS, HAS BROUGHT WHAT YOU DESIRED.

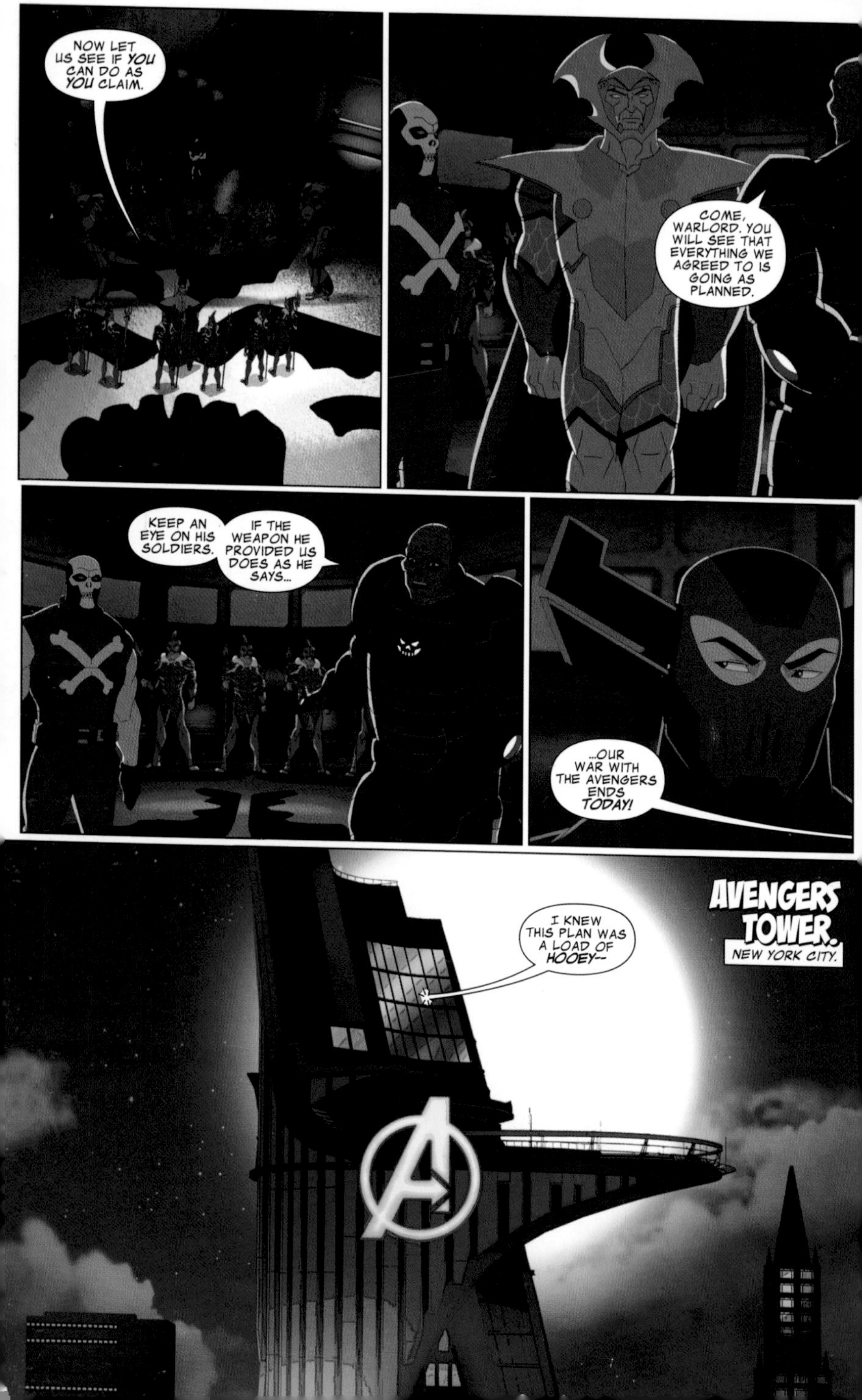
NOW LET US SEE IF YOU CAN DO AS YOU CLAIM.
COME, WARLORD. YOU WILL SEE THAT EVERYTHING WE AGREED TO IS GOING AS PLANNED.
KEEP AN EYE ON HIS SOLDIERS.
IF THE WEAPON HE PROVIDED US DOES AS HE SAYS...
...OUR WAR WITH THE AVENGERS ENDS TODAY!
AVENGERS TOWER.
NEW YORK CITY.
I KNEW THIS PLAN WAS A LOAD OF HOOEY--

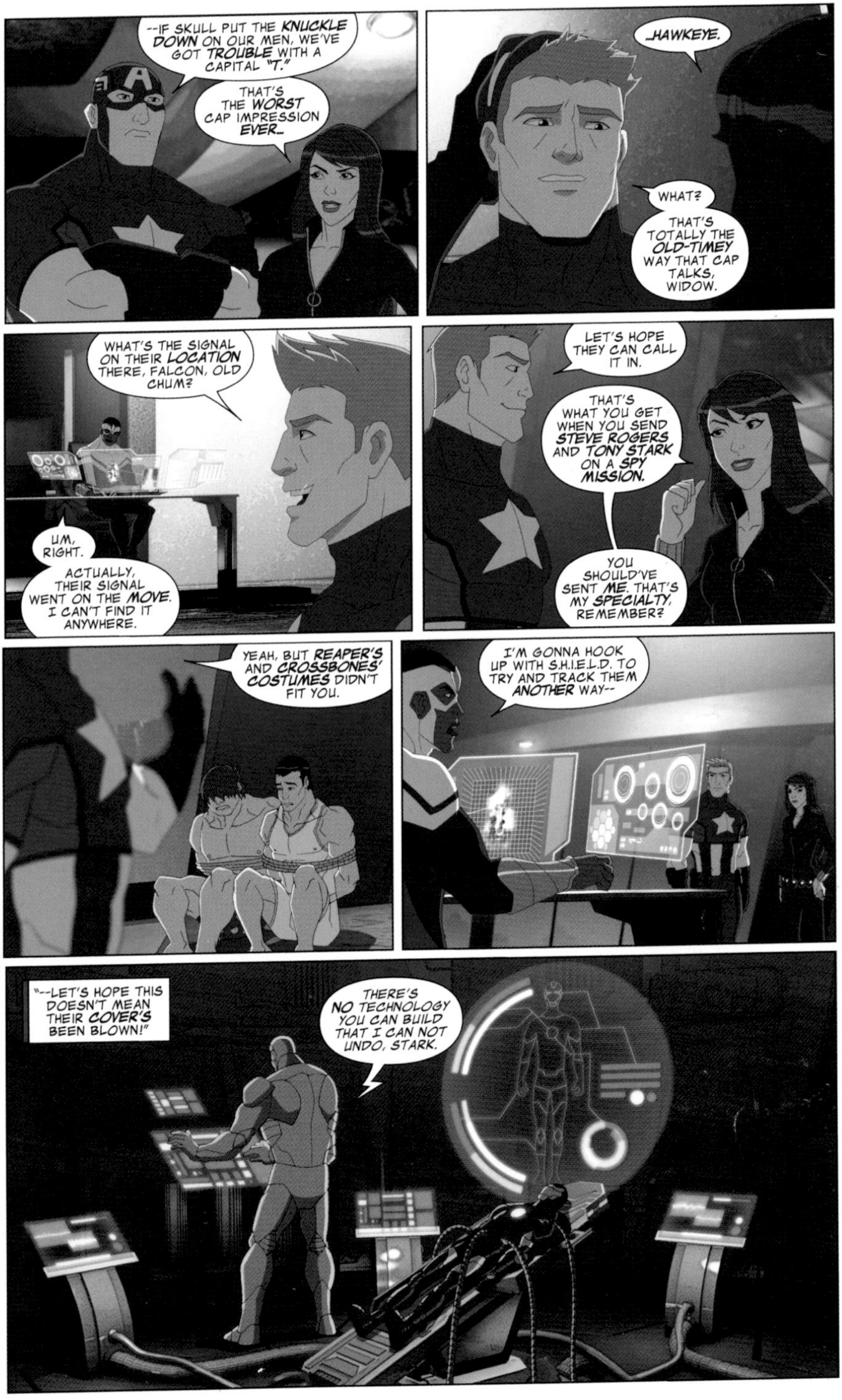
--IF SKULL PUT THE KNUCKLE DOWN ON OUR MEN, WE'VE GOT TROUBLE WITH A CAPITAL "T."
THAT'S THE WORST CAP IMPRESSION EVER...
...HAWKEYE.
WHAT?
THAT'S TOTALLY THE OLD-TIMEY WAY THAT CAP TALKS, WIDOW.
WHAT'S THE SIGNAL ON THEIR LOCATION THERE, FALCON, OLD CHUM?
UM, RIGHT.
ACTUALLY, THEIR SIGNAL WENT ON THE MOVE. I CAN'T FIND IT ANYWHERE.
LET'S HOPE THEY CAN CALL IT IN.
THAT'S WHAT YOU GET WHEN YOU SEND STEVE ROGERS AND TONY STARK ON A SPY MISSION.
YOU SHOULD'VE SENT ME. THAT'S MY SPECIALTY, REMEMBER?
YEAH, BUT REAPER'S AND CROSSBONES' COSTUMES DIDN'T FIT YOU.
I'M GONNA HOOK UP WITH S.H.I.E.L.D. TO TRY AND TRACK THEM ANOTHER WAY--
"--LET'S HOPE THIS DOESN'T MEAN THEIR COVER'S BEEN BLOWN!"
THERE'S NO TECHNOLOGY YOU CAN BUILD THAT I CAN NOT UNDO, STARK.

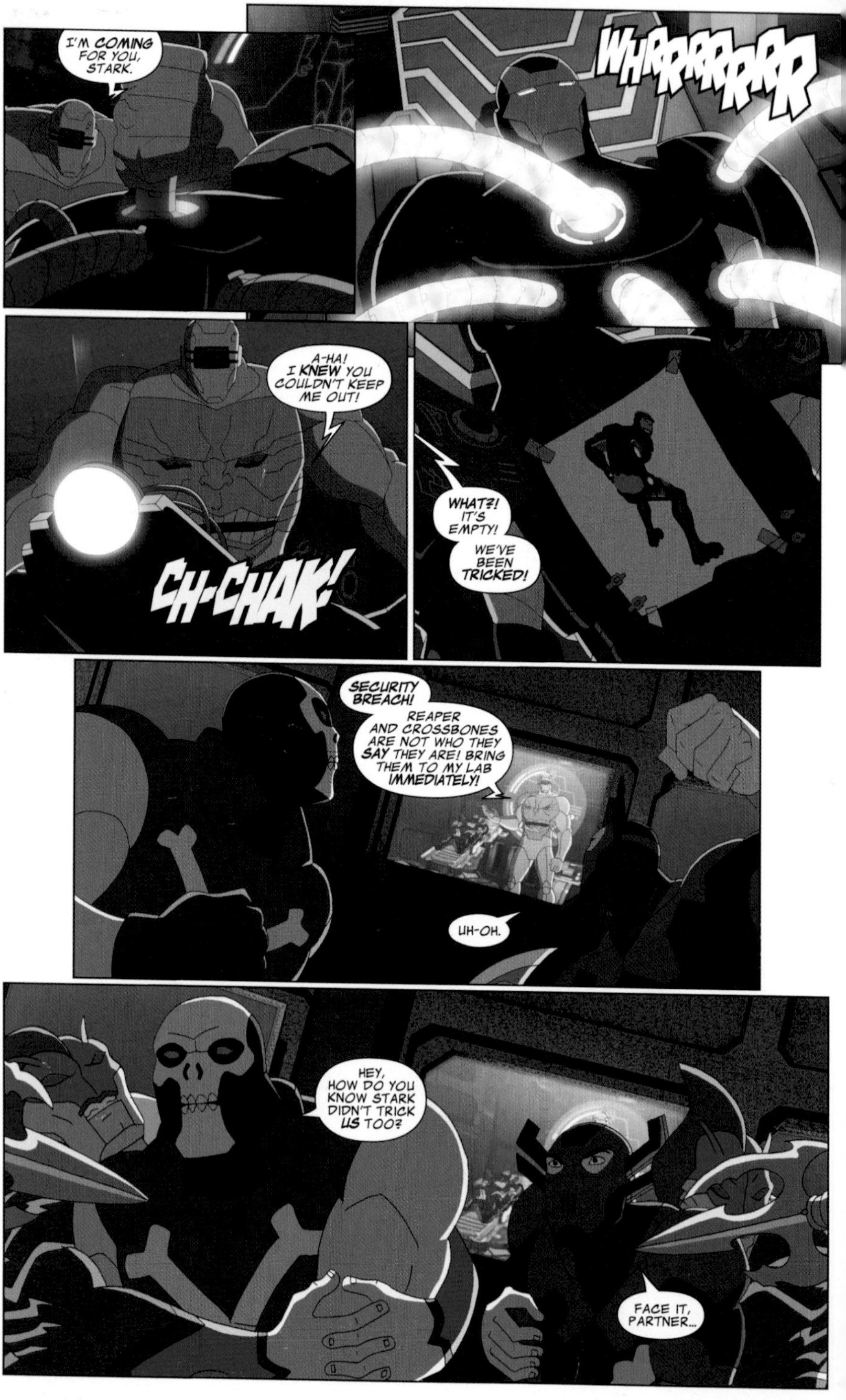
I'M COMING FOR YOU, STARK.
WHRRRRRRRR
A-HA! I KNEW YOU COULDN'T KEEP ME OUT!
CH-CHAK!
WHAT?! IT'S EMPTY!
WE'VE BEEN TRICKED!
SECURITY BREACH! REAPER AND CROSSBONES ARE NOT WHO THEY SAY THEY ARE! BRING THEM TO MY LAB IMMEDIATELY!
UH-OH.
HEY, HOW DO YOU KNOW STARK DIDN'T TRICK US TOO?
FACE IT, PARTNER...

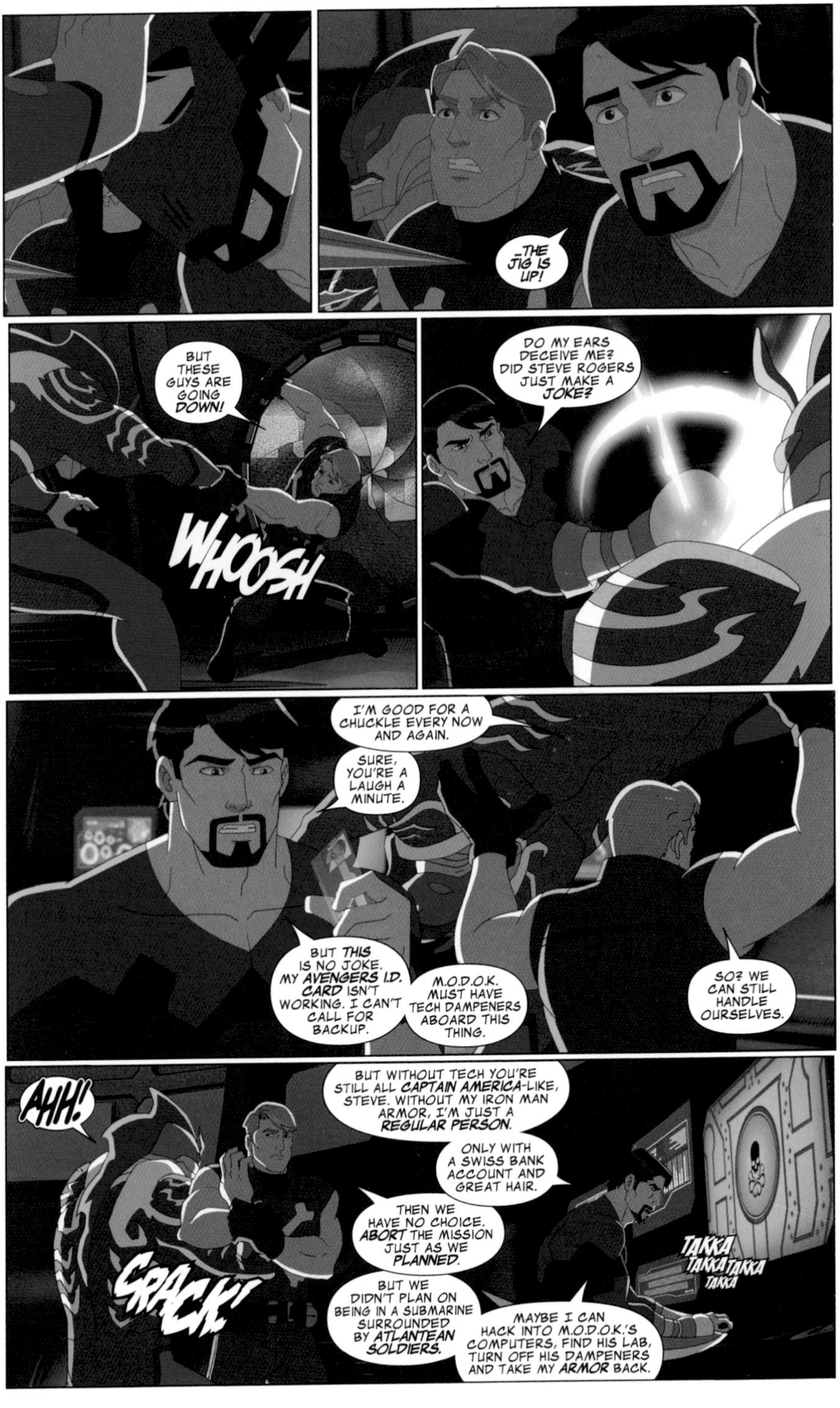
...THE JIG IS UP!
BUT THESE GUYS ARE GOING DOWN!
WHOOSH
DO MY EARS DECEIVE ME? DID STEVE ROGERS JUST MAKE A JOKE?
I'M GOOD FOR A CHUCKLE EVERY NOW AND AGAIN.
SURE, YOU'RE A LAUGH A MINUTE.
BUT THIS IS NO JOKE. MY AVENGERS I.D. CARD ISN'T WORKING. I CAN'T CALL FOR BACKUP.
M.O.D.O.K. MUST HAVE TECH DAMPENERS ABOARD THIS THING.
SO? WE CAN STILL HANDLE OURSELVES.
AHH!
BUT WITHOUT TECH YOU'RE STILL ALL CAPTAIN AMERICA-LIKE, STEVE. WITHOUT MY IRON MAN ARMOR, I'M JUST A REGULAR PERSON.
ONLY WITH A SWISS BANK ACCOUNT AND GREAT HAIR.
THEN WE HAVE NO CHOICE. ABORT THE MISSION JUST AS WE PLANNED.
CRACK!
TAKKA TAKKA TAKKA TAKKA
BUT WE DIDN'T PLAN ON BEING IN A SUBMARINE SURROUNDED BY ATLANTEAN SOLDIERS.
MAYBE I CAN HACK INTO M.O.D.O.K.'S COMPUTERS, FIND HIS LAB, TURN OFF HIS DAMPENERS AND TAKE MY ARMOR BACK.

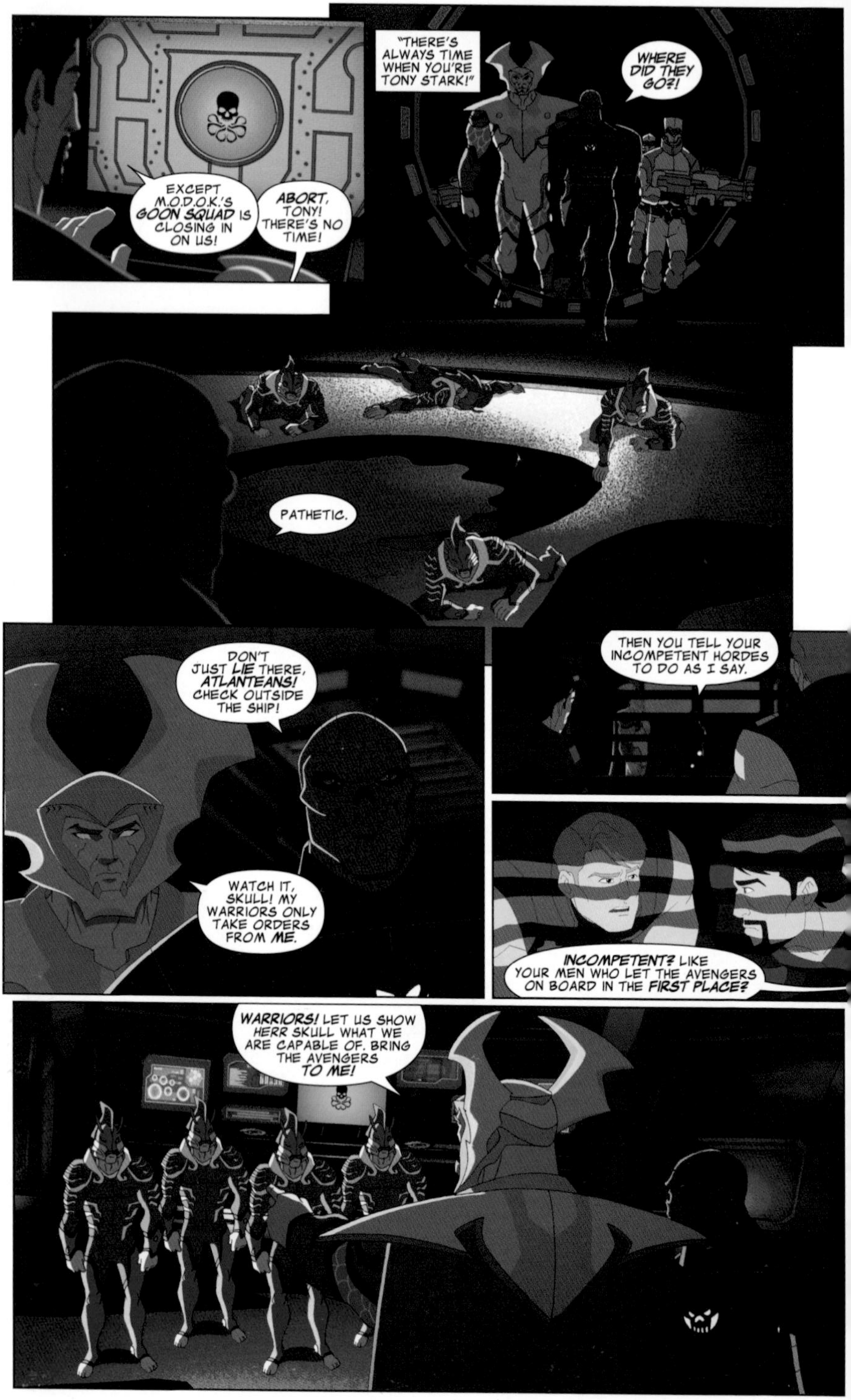
EXCEPT M.O.D.O.K.'S GOON SQUAD IS CLOSING IN ON US!
ABORT, TONY! THERE'S NO TIME!
"THERE'S ALWAYS TIME WHEN YOU'RE TONY STARK!"
WHERE DID THEY GO?!
PATHETIC.
DON'T JUST LIE THERE, ATLANTEANS! CHECK OUTSIDE THE SHIP!
WATCH IT, SKULL! MY WARRIORS ONLY TAKE ORDERS FROM ME.
THEN YOU TELL YOUR INCOMPETENT HORDES TO DO AS I SAY.
INCOMPETENT? LIKE YOUR MEN WHO LET THE AVENGERS ON BOARD IN THE FIRST PLACE?
WARRIORS! LET US SHOW HERR SKULL WHAT WE ARE CAPABLE OF. BRING THE AVENGERS TO ME!

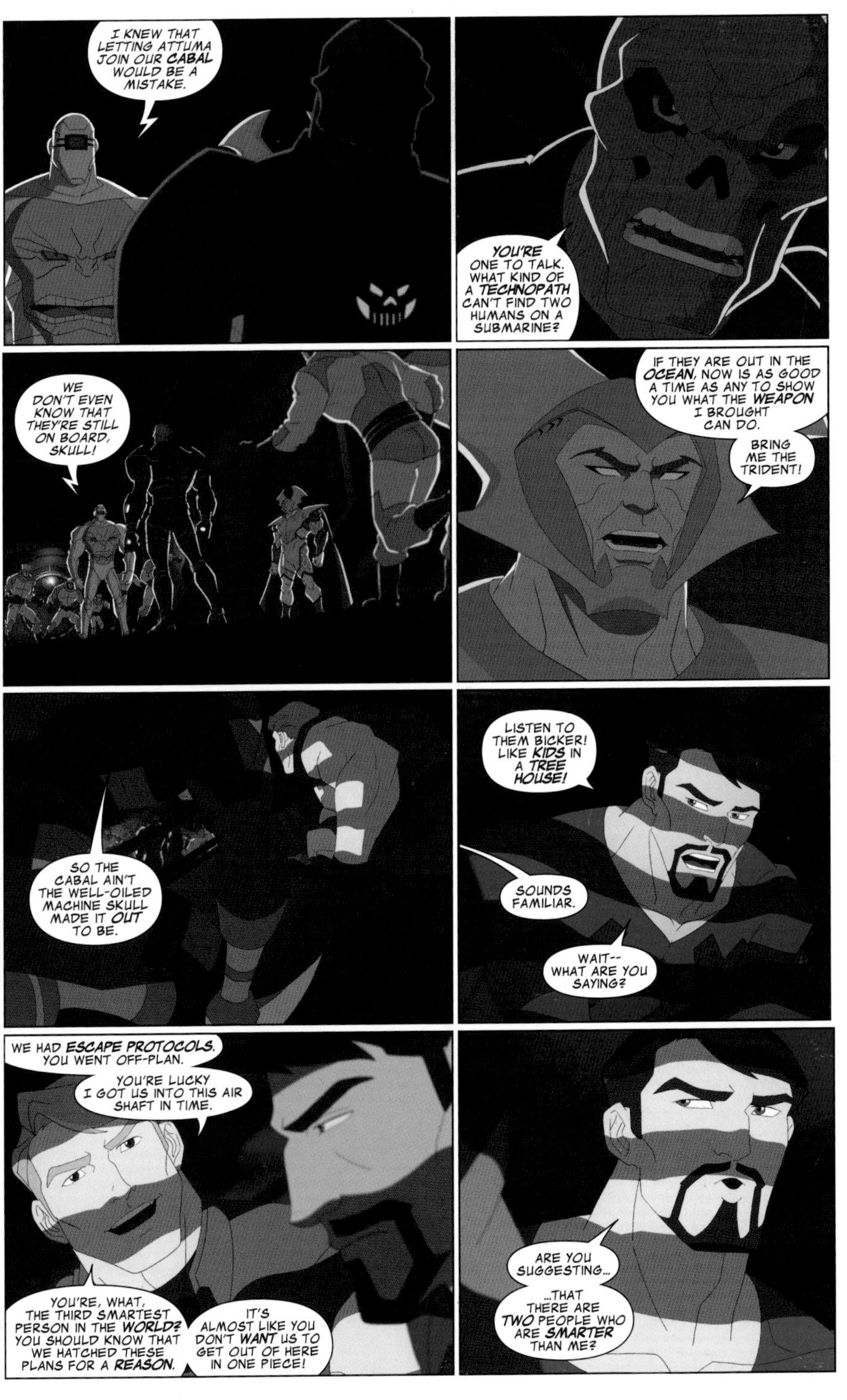
I KNEW THAT LETTING ATTUMA JOIN OUR CABAL WOULD BE A MISTAKE.
YOU'RE ONE TO TALK. WHAT KIND OF A TECHNOPATH CAN'T FIND TWO HUMANS ON A SUBMARINE?
WE DON'T EVEN KNOW THAT THEY'RE STILL ON BOARD, SKULL!
IF THEY ARE OUT IN THE OCEAN, NOW IS AS GOOD A TIME AS ANY TO SHOW YOU WHAT THE WEAPON I BROUGHT CAN DO.
BRING ME THE TRIDENT!
SO THE CABAL AIN'T THE WELL-OILED MACHINE SKULL MADE IT OUT TO BE.
LISTEN TO THEM BICKER! LIKE KIDS IN A TREE HOUSE!
SOUNDS FAMILIAR.
WAIT-- WHAT ARE YOU SAYING?
WE HAD ESCAPE PROTOCOLS. YOU WENT OFF-PLAN.
YOU'RE LUCKY I GOT US INTO THIS AIR SHAFT IN TIME.
YOU'RE, WHAT, THE THIRD SMARTEST PERSON IN THE WORLD? YOU SHOULD KNOW THAT WE HATCHED THESE PLANS FOR A REASON.
IT'S ALMOST LIKE YOU DON'T WANT US TO GET OUT OF HERE IN ONE PIECE!
ARE YOU SUGGESTING...
...THAT THERE ARE TWO PEOPLE WHO ARE SMARTER THAN ME?

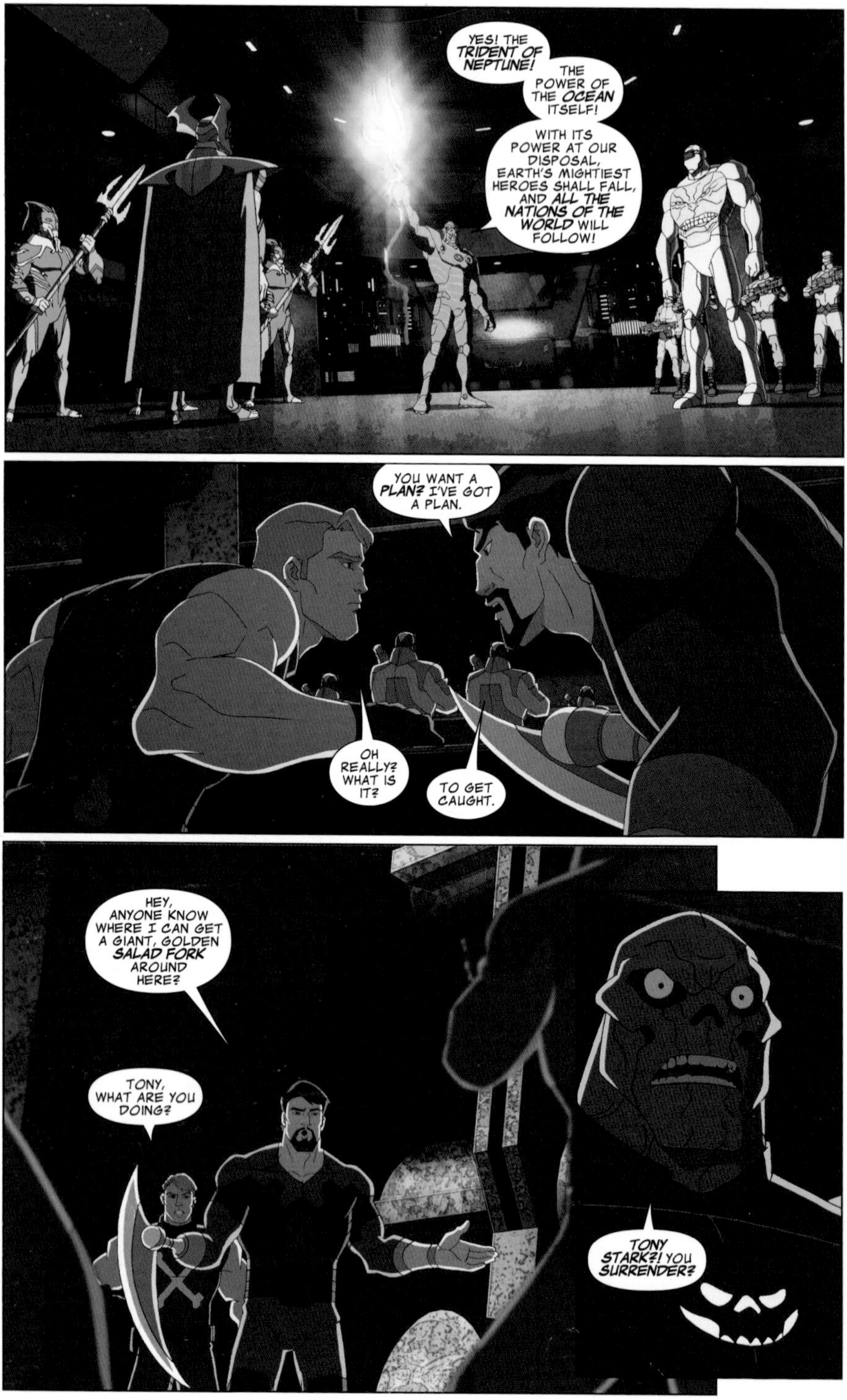
YES! THE TRIDENT OF NEPTUNE!
THE POWER OF THE OCEAN ITSELF!
WITH ITS POWER AT OUR DISPOSAL, EARTH'S MIGHTIEST HEROES SHALL FALL, AND ALL THE NATIONS OF THE WORLD WILL FOLLOW!
YOU WANT A PLAN? I'VE GOT A PLAN.
OH REALLY? WHAT IS IT?
TO GET CAUGHT.
HEY, ANYONE KNOW WHERE I CAN GET A GIANT, GOLDEN SALAD FORK AROUND HERE?
TONY, WHAT ARE YOU DOING?
TONY STARK?! YOU SURRENDER?

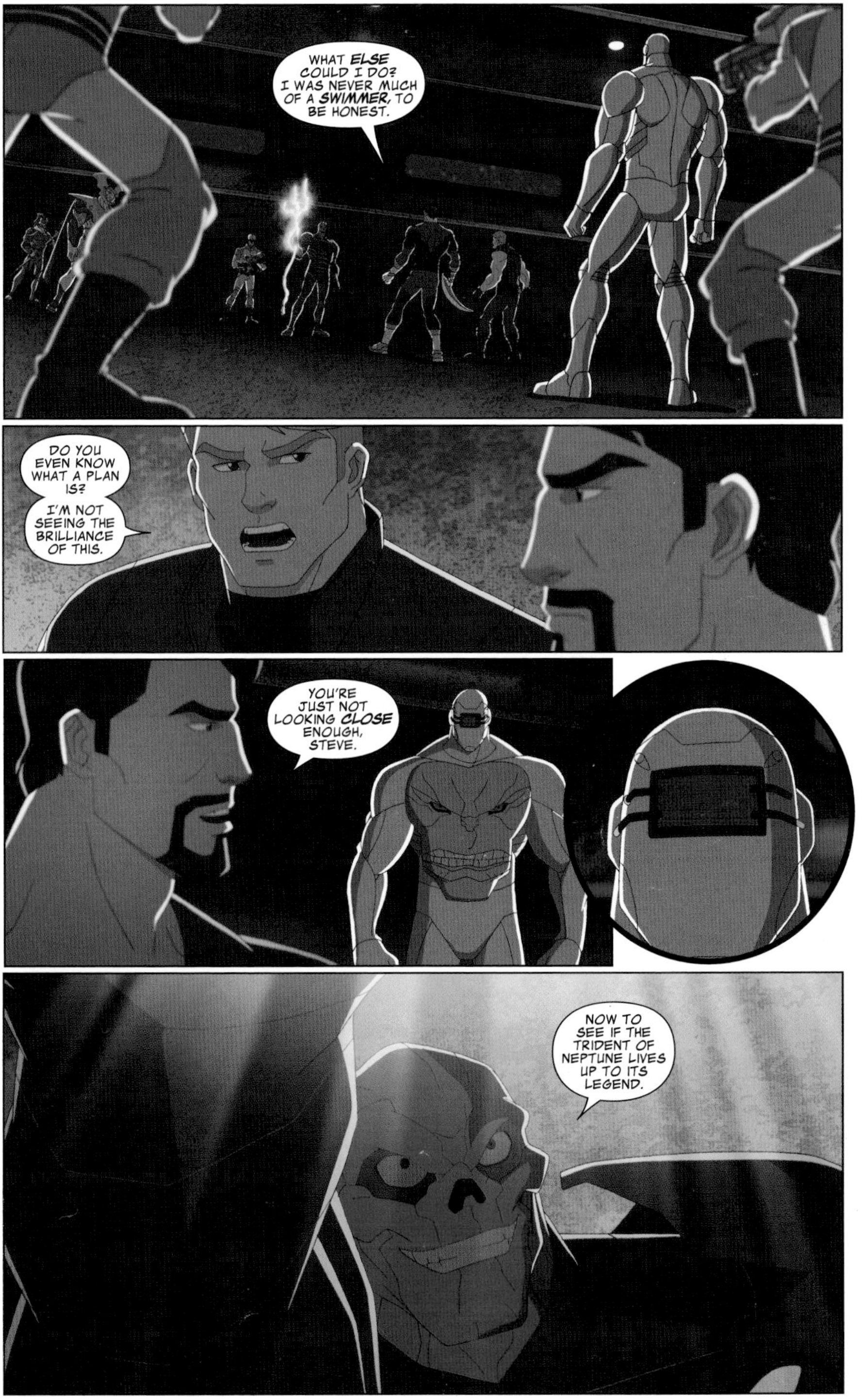
WHAT ELSE COULD I DO? I WAS NEVER MUCH OF A SWIMMER, TO BE HONEST.
DO YOU EVEN KNOW WHAT A PLAN IS?
I'M NOT SEEING THE BRILLIANCE OF THIS.
YOU'RE JUST NOT LOOKING CLOSE ENOUGH, STEVE.
NOW TO SEE IF THE TRIDENT OF NEPTUNE LIVES UP TO ITS LEGEND.

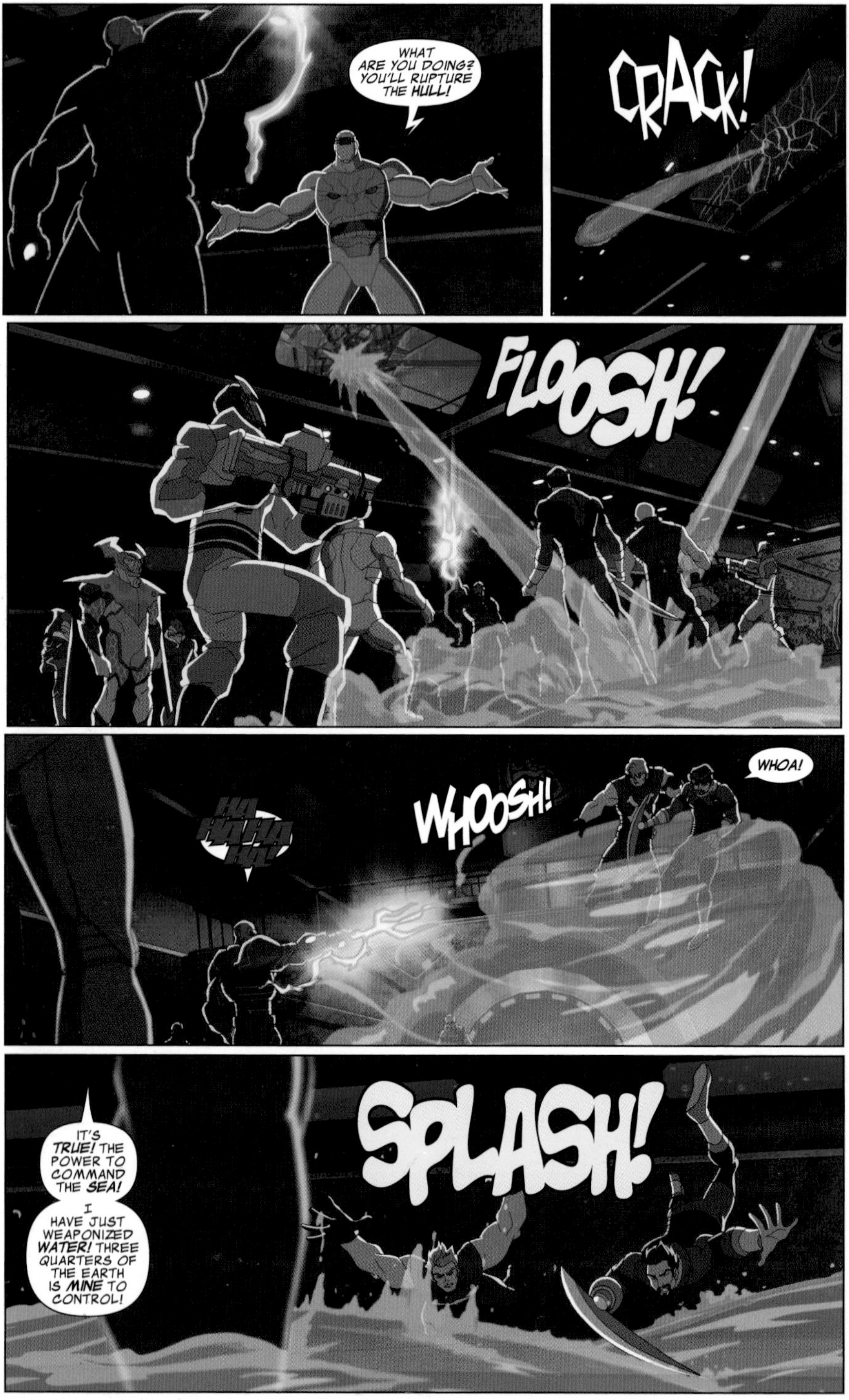

WHAT ARE YOU DOING? YOU'LL RUPTURE THE HULL!
CRACK!
FLOOSH!
HA HAHA HA!
WHOOSH!
WHOA!
SPLASH!
IT'S TRUE! THE POWER TO COMMAND THE SEA!
I HAVE JUST WEAPONIZED WATER! THREE QUARTERS OF THE EARTH IS MINE TO CONTROL!

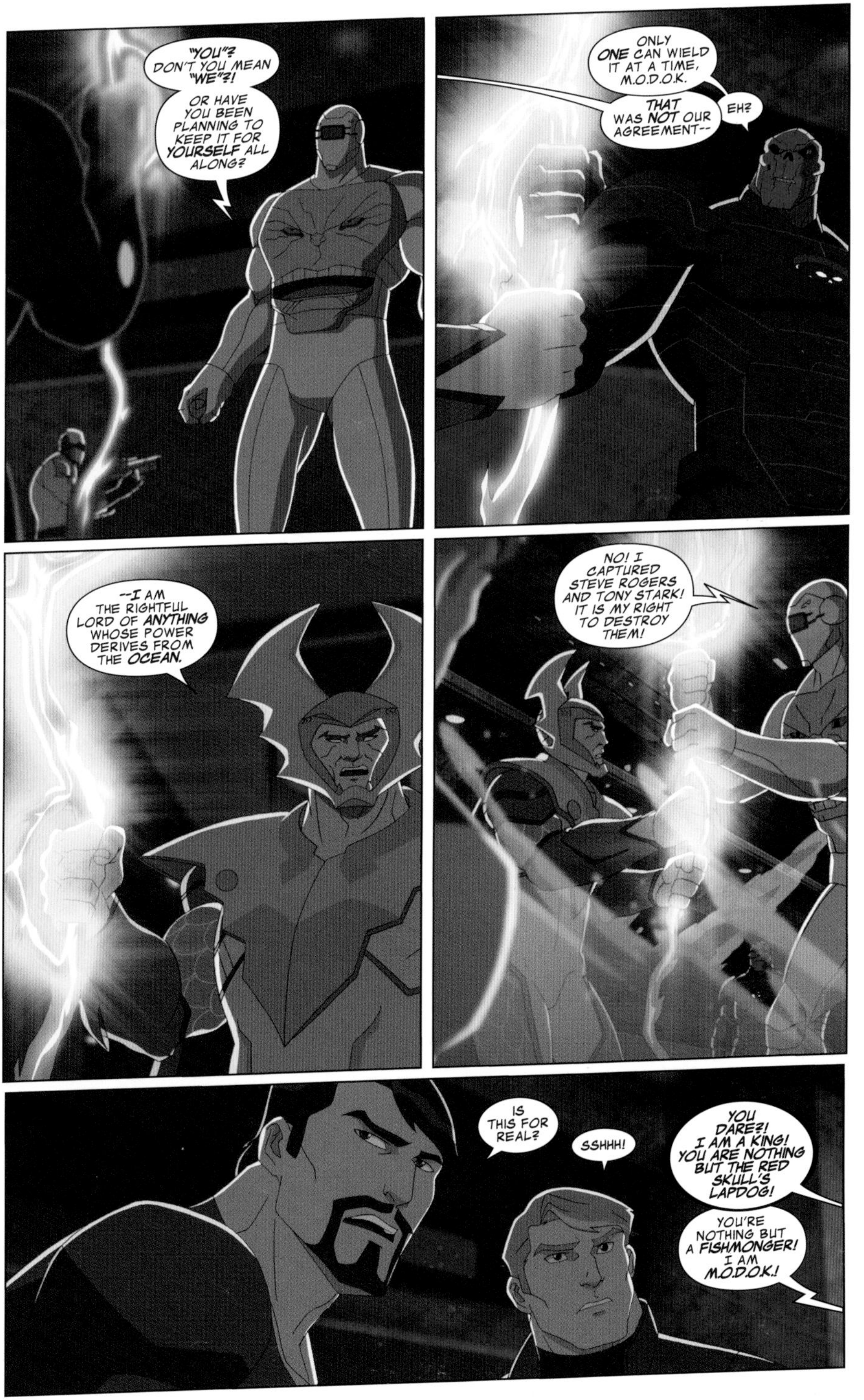
"YOU"? DON'T YOU MEAN "WE"?!
OR HAVE YOU BEEN PLANNING TO KEEP IT FOR YOURSELF ALL ALONG?
ONLY ONE CAN WIELD IT AT A TIME, M.O.D.O.K.
EH?
THAT WAS NOT OUR AGREEMENT--
--I AM THE RIGHTFUL LORD OF ANYTHING WHOSE POWER DERIVES FROM THE OCEAN.
NO! I CAPTURED STEVE ROGERS AND TONY STARK! IT IS MY RIGHT TO DESTROY THEM!
IS THIS FOR REAL?
SSHHH!
YOU DARE?! I AM A KING! YOU ARE NOTHING BUT THE RED SKULL'S LAPDOG!
YOU'RE NOTHING BUT A FISHMONGER! I AM M.O.D.O.K.!

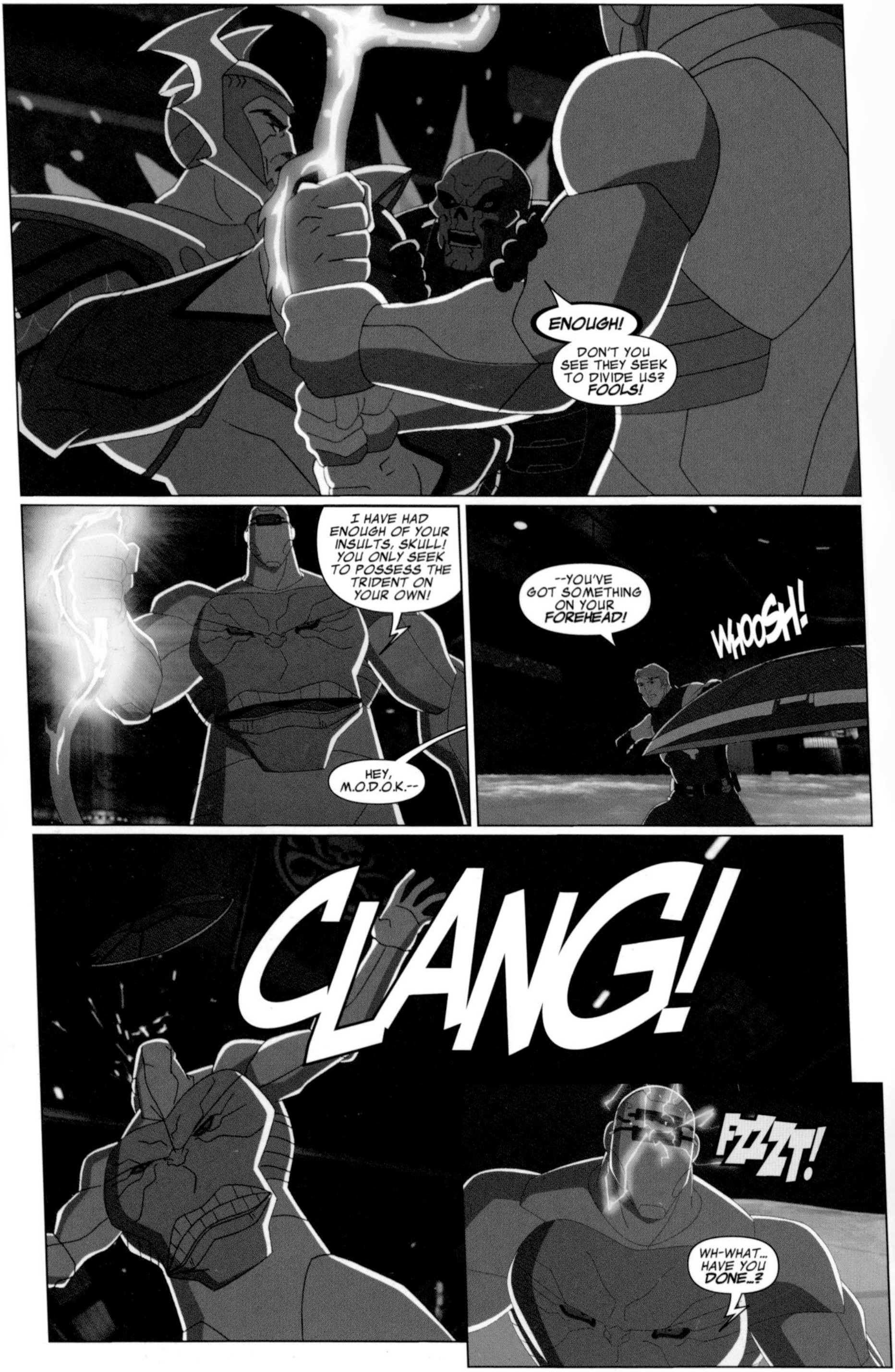
ENOUGH!
DON'T YOU SEE THEY SEEK TO DIVIDE US? FOOLS!
I HAVE HAD ENOUGH OF YOUR INSULTS, SKULL! YOU ONLY SEEK TO POSSESS THE TRIDENT ON YOUR OWN!
HEY, M.O.D.O.K.--
--YOU'VE GOT SOMETHING ON YOUR FOREHEAD!
WHOOSH!
CLANG!
FZZZT!
WH-WHAT... HAVE YOU DONE...?

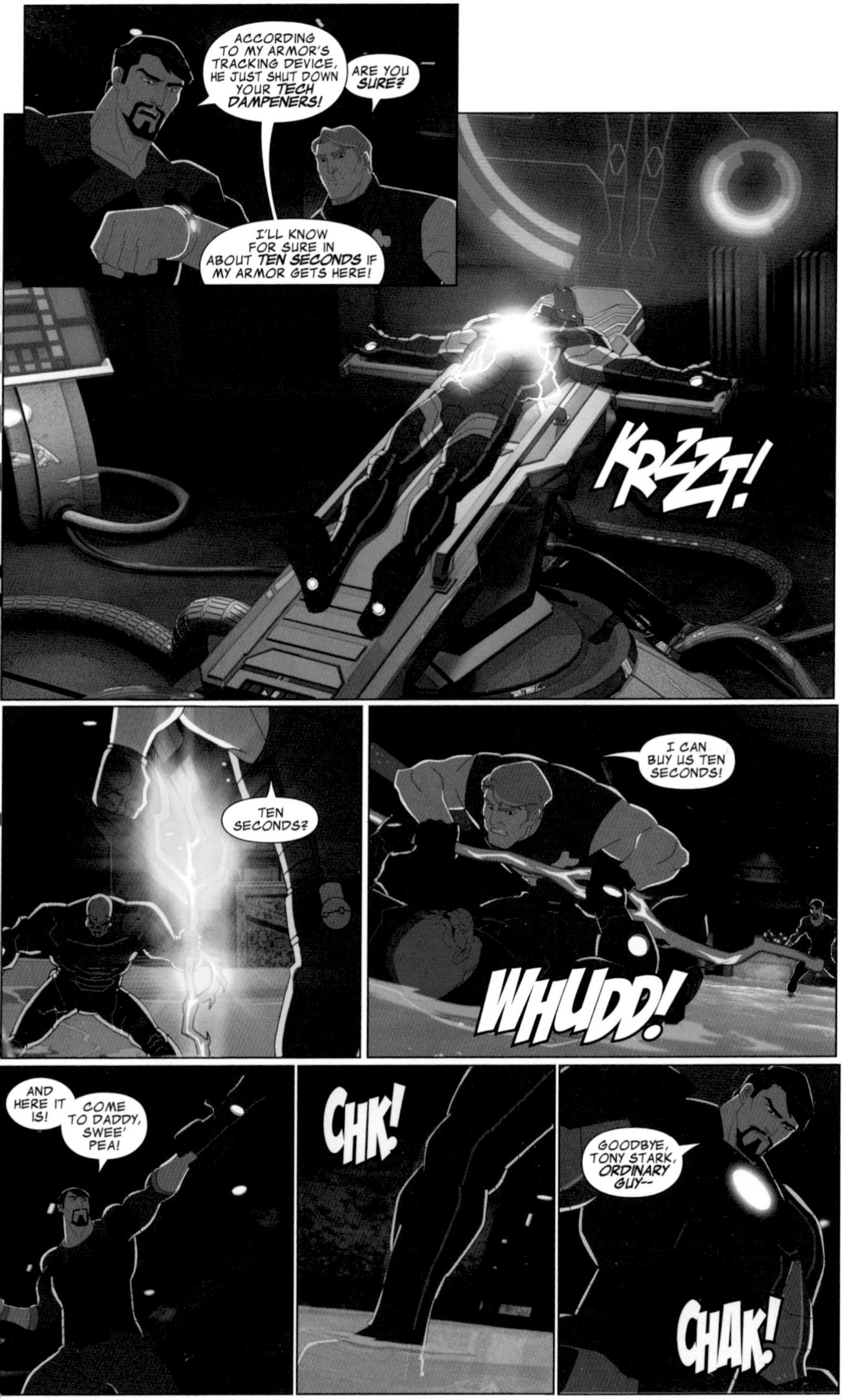
ACCORDING TO MY ARMOR'S TRACKING DEVICE, HE JUST SHUT DOWN YOUR TECH DAMPENERS!
ARE YOU SURE?
I'LL KNOW FOR SURE IN ABOUT TEN SECONDS IF MY ARMOR GETS HERE!
KRZZT!
TEN SECONDS?
I CAN BUY US TEN SECONDS!
WHUDD!
AND HERE IT IS!
COME TO DADDY, SWEE' PEA!
CHK!
GOODBYE, TONY STARK, ORDINARY GUY--
CHAK!

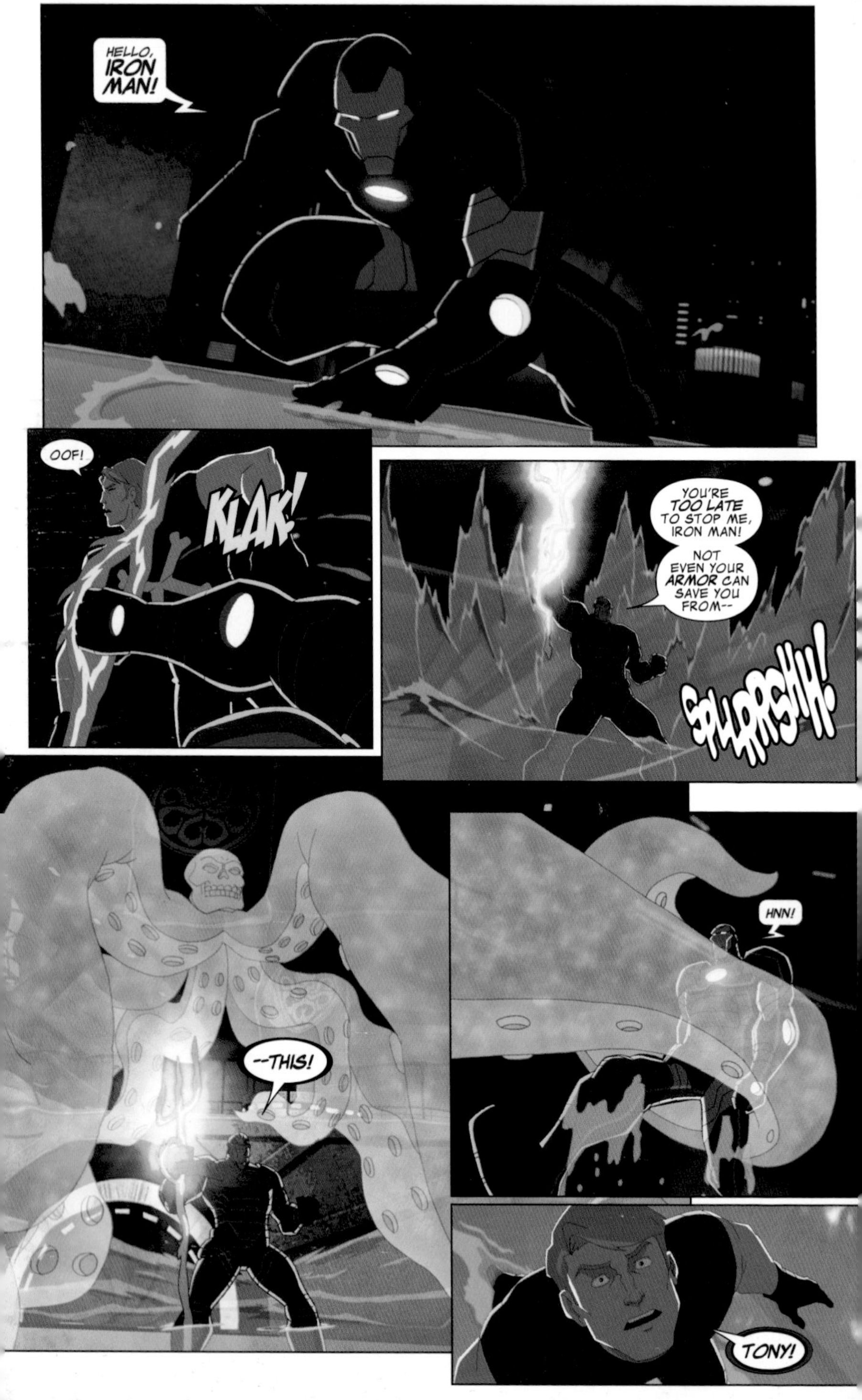
HELLO, IRON MAN!
OOF!
KLAK!
YOU'RE TOO LATE TO STOP ME, IRON MAN!
NOT EVEN YOUR ARMOR CAN SAVE YOU FROM--
SPLURRSHH!
--THIS!
HNN!
TONY!

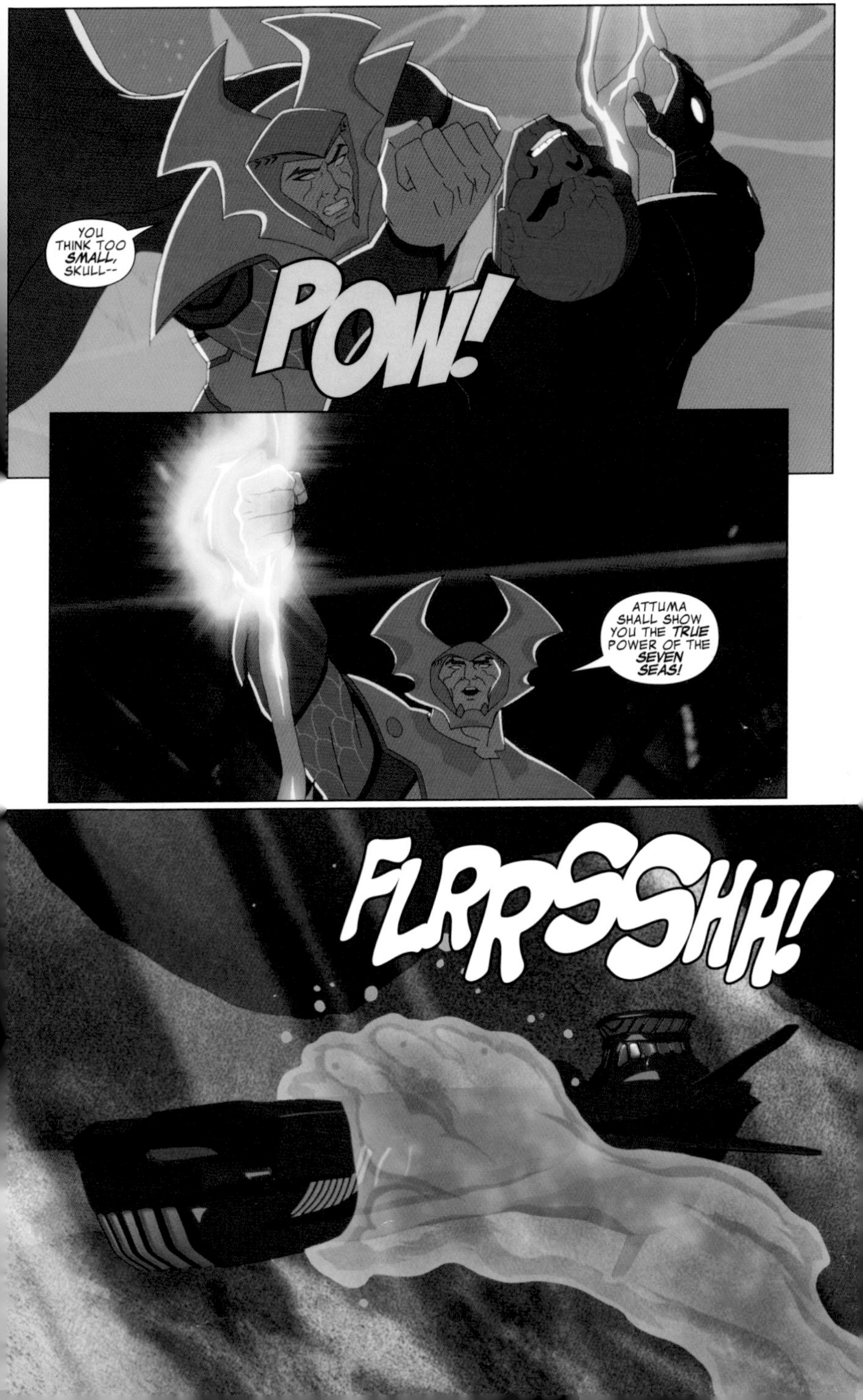
YOU THINK TOO SMALL, SKULL--
POW!
ATTUMA SHALL SHOW YOU THE TRUE POWER OF THE SEVEN SEAS!
FLRRSSHH!

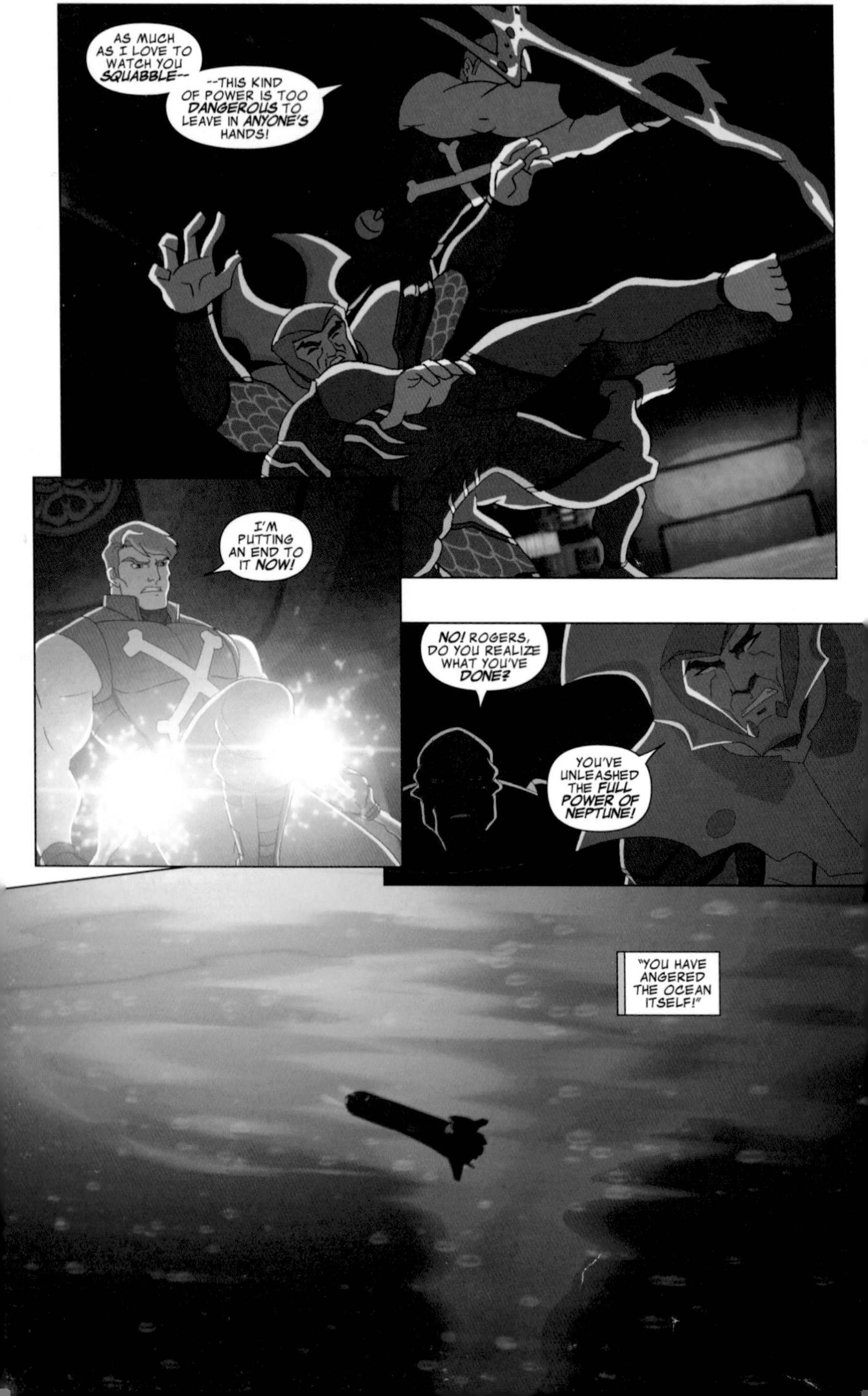

AS MUCH AS I LOVE TO WATCH YOU SQUABBLE--
--THIS KIND OF POWER IS TOO DANGEROUS TO LEAVE IN ANYONE'S HANDS!
I'M PUTTING AN END TO IT NOW!
NO! ROGERS, DO YOU REALIZE WHAT YOU'VE DONE?
YOU'VE UNLEASHED THE FULL POWER OF NEPTUNE!
"YOU HAVE ANGERED THE OCEAN ITSELF!"

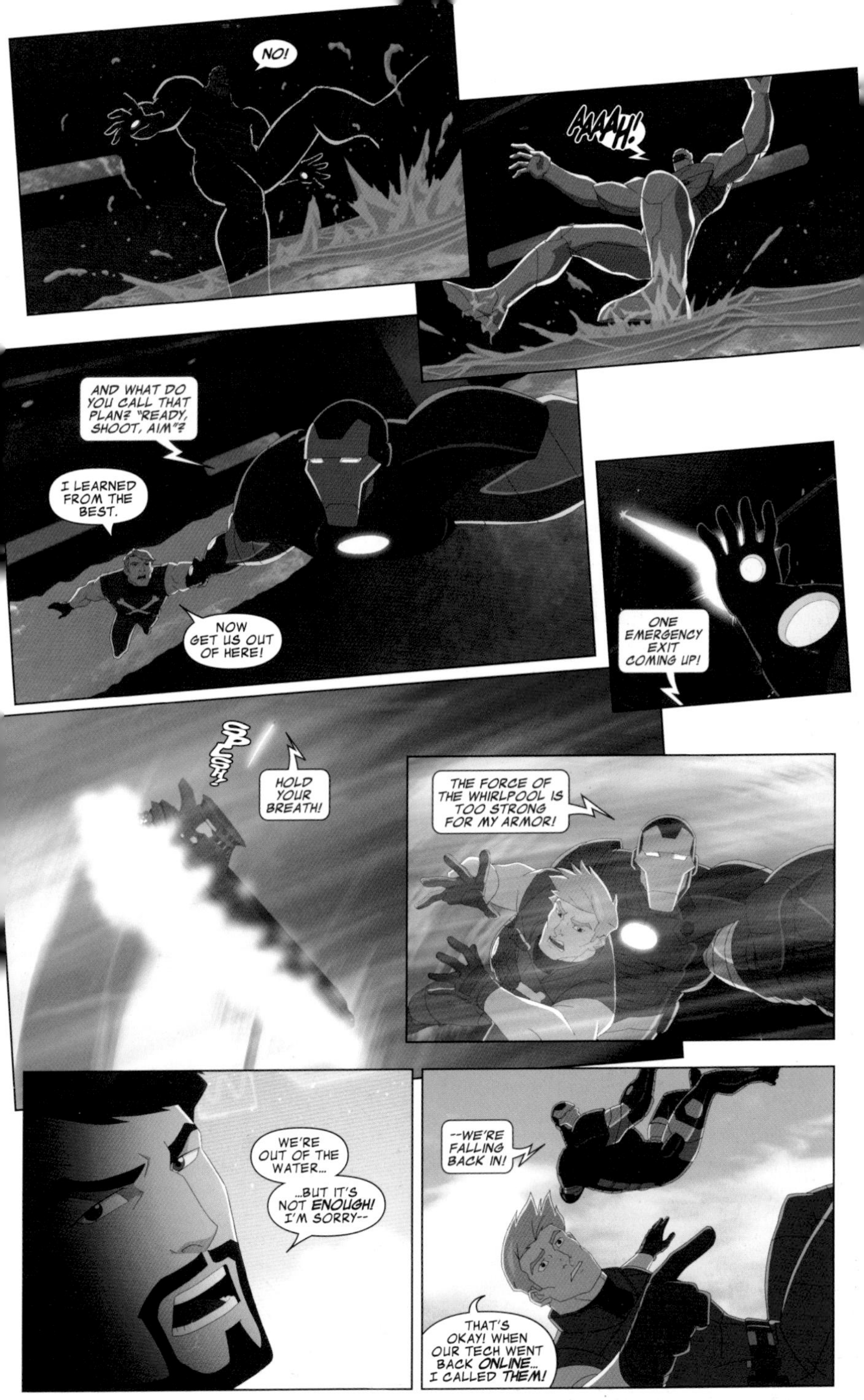
NO!
AAAAH!
AND WHAT DO YOU CALL THAT PLAN? "READY, SHOOT, AIM"?
I LEARNED FROM THE BEST.
NOW GET US OUT OF HERE!
ONE EMERGENCY EXIT COMING UP!
SPLOOSH!
HOLD YOUR BREATH!
THE FORCE OF THE WHIRLPOOL IS TOO STRONG FOR MY ARMOR!
WE'RE OUT OF THE WATER...
...BUT IT'S NOT ENOUGH! I'M SORRY--
--WE'RE FALLING BACK IN!
THAT'S OKAY! WHEN OUR TECH WENT BACK ONLINE... I CALLED THEM!

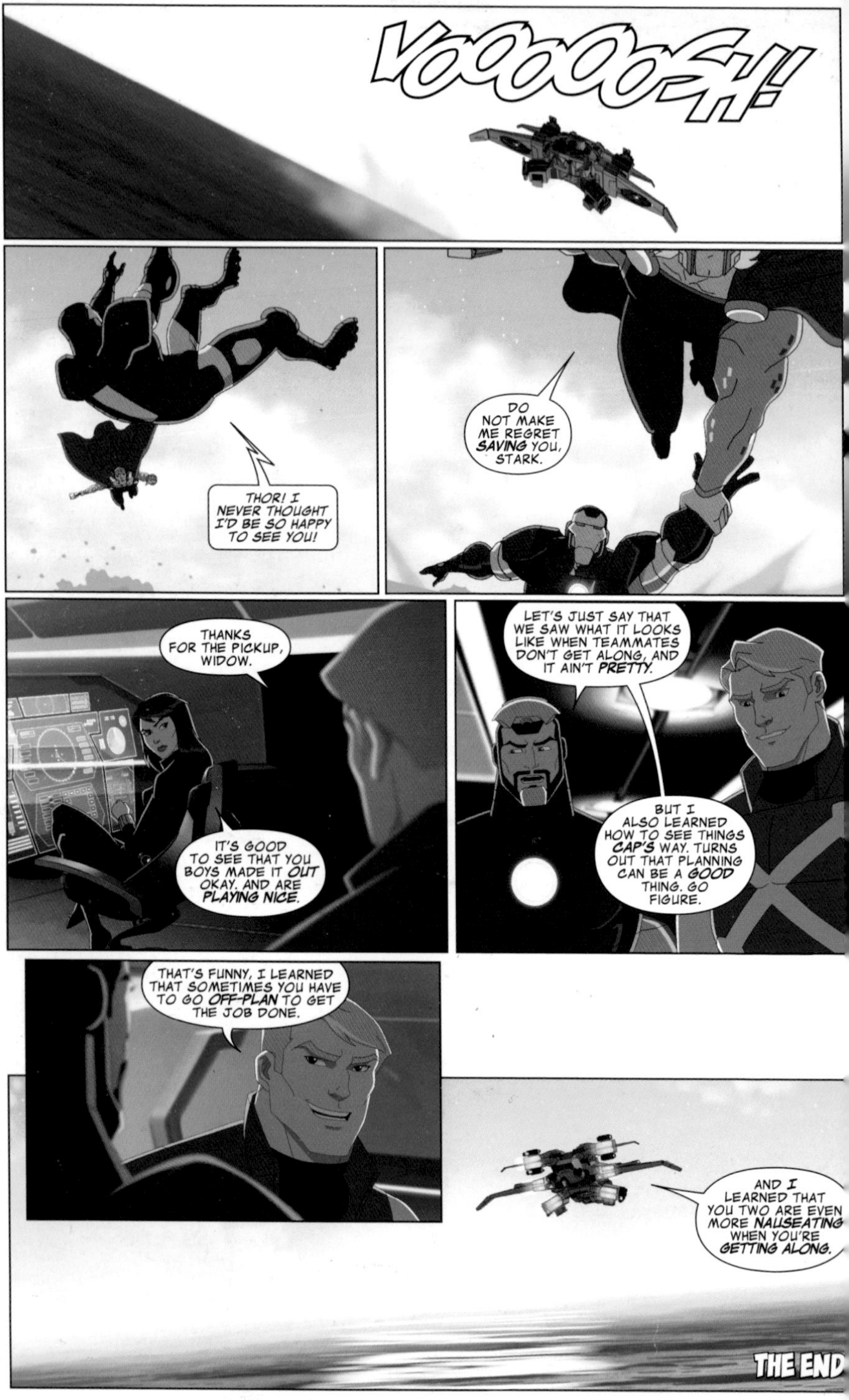
VOOOOOSH!
THOR! I NEVER THOUGHT I'D BE SO HAPPY TO SEE YOU!
DO NOT MAKE ME REGRET SAVING YOU, STARK.
THANKS FOR THE PICKUP, WIDOW.
IT'S GOOD TO SEE THAT YOU BOYS MADE IT OUT OKAY. AND ARE PLAYING NICE.
LET'S JUST SAY THAT WE SAW WHAT IT LOOKS LIKE WHEN TEAMMATES DON'T GET ALONG, AND IT AIN'T PRETTY.
BUT I ALSO LEARNED HOW TO SEE THINGS CAP'S WAY. TURNS OUT THAT PLANNING CAN BE A GOOD THING. GO FIGURE.
THAT'S FUNNY, I LEARNED THAT SOMETIMES YOU HAVE TO GO OFF-PLAN TO GET THE JOB DONE.
AND I LEARNED THAT YOU TWO ARE EVEN MORE NAUSEATING WHEN YOU'RE GETTING ALONG.
THE END

CAPTAIN AMERICA

IN 1940, AS AMERICA PREPARED FOR WAR, a frail young man volunteered for an experiment that transformed him into the ultimate physical specimen. As **CAPTAIN AMERICA, Steve Rogers** fought the good fight until a freak mishap placed him in suspended animation for decades. When he awakened, Rogers was truly a man out of time, though no less committed to fighting the evils of this perilous new era.

IRON MAN

INVENTOR. BUSINESSMAN. LADIES' MAN. SUPER HERO. Gravely injured and kidnapped during what should have been a routine weapons test, billionaire genius **Tony Stark** saved his own life by designing a life-sustaining shell — the high-tech armor that is the invincible **IRON MAN**. A modern-day knight in shining armor, Stark faces corporate intrigue and super-powered menaces — both alone and alongside his fellow Avengers.

BLACK PANTHER

WITH THE SLEEKNESS OF THE JUNGLE CAT whose name he bears, **T'Challa** — king of Wakanda — stalks both the concrete city and the undergrowth of the veldt. So it has been for countless generations of warrior kings, so it is today, and so it shall be — for the law dictates that only the swift, the smart and the strong survive. Noble champion. Vigilant protector. **BLACK PANTHER.**

BLACK WIDOW

NATASHA ROMANOFF IS AN AVENGER, an agent of S.H.I.E.L.D. and an ex-KGB operative. As an enemy agent, the femme fatale tangled with a number of heroes — including Iron Man, Hawkeye, Nick Fury, Spider-Man and Daredevil. Now, the **BLACK WIDOW** uses her amazing acrobatic abilities and fearsome fighting skills for good.

FALCON

TRAINED BY CAPTAIN AMERICA, and serving as his longtime ally and fellow Avenger, **Sam Wilson** is the high-flying hero of the people known as the Falcon. Motivated by a strong sense of community and accompanied by his falcon Redwing, the **FALCON** focuses his efforts on making a positive difference in the world.